ALL INVOLVED

ALSO BY **RYAN GATTIS**

THE BIG DROP: IMPERMANENCE

THE BIG DROP: HOMECOMING

KUNG FU HIGH SCHOOL

ROO KICKKICK & THE BIG BAD BLIMP

ALL INVOLVED

RYAN GATTIS

PICADOR

First published 2015 by HarperCollins Publishers

First published in the UK in paperback 2015 by Picador

This edition first published in 2015 by Picador
an imprint of Pan Macmillan, a division of Macmillan Publishers Limited
Pan Macmillan, 20 New Wharf Road, London N1 9RR
Basingstoke and Oxford
Associated companies throughout the world
www.panmacmillan.com

ISBN 978-1-4472-8316-4

All Involved is a work of fiction. While based on true events,
the characterizations and specific incidents presented are
totally products of the author's imagination.

'All Involved' lettering by Chaz Bojorquez

9 8 7 6 5 4 3 2 1

A CIP catalogue record for this book is available from the British Library.

Printed and bound by CPI Group (UK) Ltd, Croydon, CR0 4YY

Visit **www.picador.com** to read more about all our books
and to buy them. You will also find features, author interviews and
news of any author events, and you can sign up for e-newsletters
so that you're always first to hear about our new releases.

DEDICATED TO THE MEMORY OF
COLONEL ROBERT HOUSTON GATTIS SR.

CONTENTS

THE FACTS

At 3:15 P.M. on April 29, 1992, a jury acquitted Los Angeles Police Department Officers Theodore Briseno and Timothy Wind, as well as Sergeant Stacey Koon, of excessive force used to subdue civilian Rodney King. The jury failed to reach a verdict on the same charge against Officer Laurence Powell.

At roughly 5:00 P.M., riots began. They lasted six days, finally ending on Monday, May 4, after 10,904 arrests had been made, over 2,383 people had been injured, 11,113 fires had burned, and more than one billion dollars' worth of property damage was sustained. In addition, 60 deaths were attributed to rioting, but this number fails to account for murder victims who died outside active rioting sites during those six days of curfews and little to no emergency assistance. As LAPD Chief Daryl Gates himself said on the first night, "There are going to be situations where people are going to be without assistance. That's just the facts of life. There are not enough of us to be everywhere."

It is possible, and even likely, that a number of victims not designated as riot related were actually the targets of a sinister combination of opportunity and circumstance. As it happened, nearly 121 hours of lawlessness in a city of close to 3.6 million people contained within a county of 9.15 million was a long time for scores to be settled.

This is about some of them.

DAY 1

WEDNESDAY

AN EVEN MORE INTERESTING QUESTION IS: WHY IS EVERYBODY
WORRYING ABOUT ANOTHER RIOT—HAVEN'T THINGS IN WATTS
IMPROVED ANY SINCE THE LAST ONE? A LOT OF WHITE FOLKS ARE
WONDERING. UNHAPPILY, THE ANSWER IS NO. THE NEIGHBORHOOD
MAY BE SEETHING WITH SOCIAL WORKERS, DATA COLLECTORS,
VISTA VOLUNTEERS AND OTHER ASSORTED MEMBERS OF THE
HUMANITARIAN ESTABLISHMENT, ALL OF WHOSE INTENTIONS
ARE THE PUREST IN THE WORLD. BUT SOMEHOW NOTHING MUCH
HAS CHANGED. THERE ARE STILL THE POOR, THE DEFEATED, THE
CRIMINAL, THE DESPERATE, ALL HANGING IN THERE WITH WHAT
MUST SEEM A TERRIBLE VITALITY.

—THOMAS PYNCHON,
NEW YORK TIMES,
JUNE 12, 1966

ERNESTO VERA

1

I'm in Lynwood, South Central, somewhere off Atlantic and Olanda, putting tinfoil over trays of uneaten beans at some little kid's birthday party when I get told to go home early and prolly not come back to work tomorrow. Maybe not for a week even. My boss is worried what's happening up the 110 will come down here. He doesn't say trouble or riots or nothing. He just says, "that thing north of here," but he means where people are burning stuff and breaking out storefronts and getting beat down. I think about arguing, because I need the money, but it wouldn't get me anywhere, so I don't waste my breath. I pack the beans away in the truck's fridge, grab my coat, and leave.

Earlier in the afternoon when we got there, me and Termite—this guy I work with—saw smoke, four black towers going up like burning oil wells in Kuwait. Maybe not *that* big, but big. The birthday kid's half-drunk father sees us notice them as we were setting up tables and he said it was because the cops that beat Rodney King aren't going to jail for it, and how did we feel about it? Man, you know we weren't happy, but we don't tell our boss's client that! Besides, it was a raw deal and all, but what did it have to do with us? It was blowing up somewhere else. Here, we shut up and do our jobs.

I been working the Tacos El Unico truck going on three years. Whatever you got, I'll sling. *Al pastor. Asada.* No problem. We do some nice *cabeza* too, if the mood hits you. Otherwise there's *lengua, pollo,* whatever. You know, something for everybody. Usually we park over by our stand on Atlantic and Rosecrans, but sometimes we do birthday parties, anniversaries, anything really. We don't get paid by the hour at these, so I'm happy when they're done sooner. I say bye to Termite, tell him not to show next time without washing his hands good, and head out.

If I walk fast, it's twenty minutes home, fifteen if I take the Board-walk through the houses. It's not a boardwalk like Atlantic City or nothing. It's just a thin little concrete alley between houses that serves as a walkway between the main street and the neighborhood. That's our shortcut. As my sister would say, "fools been running from the cops on it since forever." Go down and it takes you straight to Atlantic. Go up and it leads into the houses, street after street. That's where I go when I get there. Up.

Most people's porch lights are off. Backyard lights too. Nobody's out. No familiar sounds. No Art Laboe Oldies music playing. No people fixing cars. When I'm passing houses, I only hear TVs on, and all the anchors are talking about is looting and fire and Rodney King and black people and anger and that's cool, whatever, because I'm focused on something else.

Don't get me wrong. I'm not being cold or nothing like that, I'm just taking care of what I need to take care of. You grow up in the same neighborhood as me, one with a gun store that sells single bullets for twenty-five cents to anybody with bad thoughts and a quarter, then you might end up the same way. Not jaded or pissed or anything, just focused. And right now, I'm counting months till I can get out.

Two should do it. That's when I'll have money saved up to get some wheels again. Nothing fancy. Just something that gets me to work and back without having to walk these streets. See, I been cooking someone else's recipes forever, but I'm not trying to stay that way. When I get my own car, I'm driving to Downtown and begging for an apprenticeship in the kitchen at R23, this crazy sushi spot smack in the middle of a district that used to make the majority of toys in the world, but now the warehouses are all empty, and the toy stuff is up to China.

I heard about it through Termite, because he loves Japanese too. I mean, he loves everything Oriental, especially women, but that's besides the point. He took me up there last week, and I dropped thirty-eight *pinche* bucks on a meal just for myself, but it was worth it because of what these Japanese chefs did. Stuff I never even dreamed of before. Spinach salad with eel. Tuna seared up so good with a blowtorch that it's cooked on the outside and all buttery and raw in the middle. But what really shook me was this thing called a California roll. Outside it's rice pressed into these little orange fish eggs. Inside it's a green circle of seaweed around crab, cucumber, and avocado. It was that last ingredient that messed me up bad.

Man, you don't understand. I'll do anything to learn from those chefs. I'll wash dishes. I'll sweep floors, clean bathrooms. I'll stay late every night. I don't care! I just want to be near good Japanese food, because in the time it took me to order the roll for its name, stare at it and decide I didn't want it because I'm sick of avocado, only for Termite to call me out and by then I just had to shrug and take a bite. When it hit my tongue, something sparked inside me. My whole brain just lit up and I saw possibilities where I'd never seen any before. All because some chefs took something I was so bored with, something I see every day, and turned it into something else.

Cut, scoop, and mash enough avocados and you'll know. You'll get an ache in your bones quick, the kind that only comes from your hands memorizing movements by doing them over and over till you do it in your dreams sometimes. Make guacamole every day but Sunday for almost four years and see if you don't get sick of those slimy green suckers too.

Something smacks the fence by my head and I jump back with my hands up and ready. I laugh when I see it's just a fat orange cat because damn, that got my heart going.

I keep moving though. Lynwood's no place to be caught standing still, not if you're smart. Downtown's different. It's a better world up there, at least it could be for me, and there's so many things I want to know, so many questions I want to ask those chefs. Like, how does this place affect food anyway? I may not know much, but I'm pretty sure they don't have avocados in Japan. Our roots in this city are in Mexican food, because California used to be Mexico. California's even got a little Baja beard that still *is* Mexico, even though the land north of it is something else now. Like me, kind of. My parents are from Mexico. I was born there, and carried to L.A. when I was one. My little sister and brother were born here. Because of them, we're Americans now.

This's what my walks home are for. Kicking questions around in my head, dreaming, thinking. I get lost in it sometimes. As I'm turning the corner onto my street, I'm back to wondering what the hell a Japanese chef was thinking before inventing the California roll and my mind's ticking over how even avocado can become something new and beautiful when put in different circumstances, and that's when a car with a grumbling engine comes up behind me.

I don't think much of it. Not really. I move to the side but it brakes next to me. So I move all the way over, right? Like, no problem, he'll just go by when he sees I'm not involved. No *cholo* uniform. No tattoos. Nothing. I'm clean.

But the car keeps up with my pace, inching forward, and when the driver's-side window rolls down, Motown-style fast piano pours out. Around here, everybody knows KRLA. 1110 AM on the radio dial. People love their oldies around here. The opening bit of "Run, Run, Run" by the Supremes is going. I recognize the sax and piano.

"Hey," the driver says to me over the music, "you know that homeboy Lil Mosco?"

The second I hear my little brother's street name in this stranger's mouth I start booking it back the way I came. With every step it feels like my stomach's trying to claw its way out of my body. It knows this is some serious fucking trouble.

I hear the driver laugh as he throws the car into reverse and slams on the gas. The car passes me easy, and barrels to a stop. That's when two guys get out of the front and one jumps out of the bed in the back. Three guys all dressed up in black.

My adrenaline's all the way up now. I must be more alert than I ever been in my life and I know if I make it out of this, I need to remember as much as possible, so I turn my head and look while I'm running and try to memorize everything. It's a Ford, this car. Dark blue. I think it's a Ranchero. It has a taillight out. Left side.

I can't make the plate number because I'm turning my head as I take the corner back onto the Boardwalk, and I'm breaking between houses, trying to bust out onto the next street, hop a fence, and disappear into somebody's yard, but they're on me too fast. All three of them. They haven't worked ten hours over a grill, serving tacos to a bunch of damn kids and drunks. They're not tired. They're strong.

I hear them coming up hard behind as blood thumps up in my ears, and I know I'm as good as caught, man. I get one cold second to gulp air and brace myself before they swoop in, kick me off my feet, and smash me in the jaw with something hard as I fall. After that, shit goes black for I-don't-know-how-long.

I been hit in the mouth before but never like that. I come to as they're dragging me back to the car and it feels like my face is going to fall apart in two pieces. Around the ringing in my ears, I hear my boot heels slide-grinding over the asphalt and I figure I couldn't have been out for more than a few seconds.

"Don't do this." I hear myself say the words. It surprises me how calm they are, considering my heart is going a million beats per minute. "Please. I didn't do anything to you. I have money. Whatever you want."

They respond, these three, but not with words. Rough hands jerk me up to my feet, out of the Boardwalk and into the back alley with garages on both sides. But they're just setting me up.

Quick, weak punches hit me in my kidneys, my stomach, my ribs too. I get it from all angles. They don't feel hard but they steal my breath away. At first, I don't understand, but then I see the blood, and I stare at it on my shirt, and as I'm wondering why I didn't feel the stabs, a bat hits me.

I see a flash of black a second before it lands and flinch away. The heavy part only gets me in the shoulder, but I go from being upright and looking at my shirt to flat on my back and staring at the night sky. Damn.

"Yeah," one of them screams in my face, "yeah, motherfucker!"

I crumple up into a ball, my jaw feeling like somebody's frying it up in a pan. I bring my hands up and protect my face but it doesn't help. The bat comes down again and again. I catch one in the neck and my whole body goes numb.

A different voice says, "Tie that shit off while he's flat like that."

I can't hardly breathe.

Another voice, maybe it's the first voice, joins in, "Yeah, do it if you so big, Joker!"

One's named Joker. I need to remember that, I think. This's important information. *Joker*. The word sticks in my brain and I turn it over. I don't know any Jokers except for comic books, and it doesn't make any kind of sense why they're after me and not my brother if he did some stupid shit again.

"Please," I say when my breath comes back, as if a plea ever worked on these monsters in their whole lives. No way. They're too busy yanking my ankles away from me, but I'm so numb I can't even tell which one. Beneath me, my legs just get tight.

"There it is," one of them says.

As I open my eyes, I think, *There* what *is?* All around, I see a neighborhood I recognize. For a second, I think I'm safe when I hear them walk away and I see the brake lights of their car turn the garages around me red. Relief sinks into me. They're leaving, I think. They're leaving! That's when I see a little boy, maybe twelve years old, hiding in the Boardwalk. His face goes red in the brake lights and I see, yeah, he's looking at me. His eyes are all big though. His look messes with me so much that I follow his gaze down my body to my feet and I almost throw up when I see both my ankles tied to the back of the car with heavy wire.

I pull hard, but the wire doesn't loosen, it just cuts into my skin. I kick out with all the strength I got left but nothing happens. Nothing shifts. I struggle to get my fingers down to it, to push it off somehow.

But then the car's engine goes and I get smashed flat and dragged, the speed sending my skull skidding over the asphalt. Air rushes over me fast and every bit of skin on my back feels like it's going up in flames when the car smacks its brakes hard.

Momentum throws me forward. Ten feet? Twenty? I must bounce because I go airborne before something hard and cold like metal smashes me in the face, and this time I feel my cheek break. I actually feel it give from the inside, the way its crack echoes in my ears, the bone giving and blood gushing onto my tongue. I turn my head, open my mouth, and let it go. When I hear it hit the street, when it doesn't stop dripping, I know it's over.

I know I'm done.

Maybe I had a chance before, but not now.

A voice from the car, I don't know which, shouts, "Grab that wire up, fool, and make sure that motherfucker's dead!"

A door opens, but I don't hear it close. I hear footsteps coming close, and then there's a shape looming over me, checking to see if I'm breathing.

I don't even think. I spit as hard as I can.

It must land because I hear a quick scuffle and the shape moves back.

"Jesus," it says. "I got his fucking blood in my mouth! Are you tryna give me AIDS or something?"

Right then I *wish* I had AIDS just so I could give it out! I try opening my eyes wider. Only my right opens. I see the shape put something in its mouth and then I see it sneer at me and show teeth. Then the shape's on top of me, so fast I don't even know what's happening, but he's punching me hard three times in the chest. I don't feel the knife at first but I know he has one from the sounds, from the way it takes my breath out with it. There's this hollow thumping as he pushes it in deep. As deep as a knife can go.

"Tell your brother we coming." He whispers it like my ma whispers when she's mad at you in church. Quiet mad.

The one giving orders from the car yells out, "People are *watching*, fool!"

The shape above me disappears then. The car does too. It kicks up gravel on me as it goes. I'm still breathing but it's wet. Half blood. I'm numbing up all over. I try to roll. I think if I can turn over, the blood will just fall out and not choke me. But I can't. I see a new shape above me. I blink hard and it's a face. It's a lady brushing hair from her eyes as she leans over. She's telling me she's a nurse, to stay still. I want to laugh, want to tell her I can't move, so not to worry, I'll stay still because I can't do anything else. I want to tell her to tell my sister what happened. There's another shape beside her, a smaller one. It looks like the boy I saw, almost, but it's too fuzzy to tell. I hear the kid's voice clear though, "This fool's gonna die, huh?" For a second, I think he's talking about somebody else. Not me. The lady whispers something I can't hear then, and I feel hands on me. Not hands so much as pressure. The pain isn't the biggest deal. The problem is I can't breathe. I try and I can't. My chest won't rise. Feels like a car's parked on it. I try to tell them this. If they could please tell the car to move, I'll be fine. It won't be so heavy and I can breathe and everything will be okay if I can just get air. I try to shout this, any of it. But my mouth won't work and my skin feels big, loose, and the sky feels too close, like it fell on me, on my face, like a sheet, and I have the strangest feeling, like it's coming down to fix me, that it's getting inside me with some dark kind of concrete, trying to patch my holes up and make it so I can breathe and I think how good that'd be if that were true but I know I'm just dying, the kid is right, I know I think I'm just melting into it because my brain's low on oxygen, and I know because that's logic, because brains don't work right without food, and I know I'm not really becoming part of the sky, and I know because, I know because

LUPE VERA,
A.K.A. LUPE RODRIGUEZ,
A.K.A PAYASA

APRIL 29, 1992

8:47 P.M.

1

Clever's studying a textbook while Apache's sketching *Teen Angels* magazine style at the kitchen table, and over on the stovetop Big Fe's slapping chorizo around in a pan with a wooden spoon. He's halfway through shouting his Vikings story at me in the living room, talking about how one night at Ham Park shots pop off and everybody hits the floor, and how bullets whiz, man, how they really *do* make that sound, when a knock hits the front door of my house all hard and fast, like *bam-bam-bam*, like whoever is on the other side doesn't give a fuck about his hand.

We *were* watching a bunch of *mayates* tear the city up after putting a brick through some white trucker's face on Florence and Normandie, but the news got boring quick so we clicked over to the small dial to watch something else. There's a western on TV now with the sound down, but whatever. It's safe to say my eyes aren't on the guns and hats anymore though. I'm looking at Fate (Big Fe pretty much only goes by Big Fate, so you know) and Clever and Apache and they're all looking at me. We're thinking the same thing: this ain't sheriffs.

Sheriffs don't knock. They ram. They come in screaming behind shotgun barrels and flashlights. They don't care if you're a girl like me. They fuck everybody up regardless.

No way this is sheriffs.

Fate's got the juice card around here. Under his wifebeater he's that natural type of big that pro wrestlers wish they could be. His right arm ripples with Aztec tattoos as he pulls his khakis up at the belt and moves the pan off the heat even while the sausage keeps pop-popping.

I nod at him and he keeps talking, to sound normal in case whoever's outside can hear us, and he nods back as he bends down and comes up with a pistol. There's always one in the pan drawer under the oven.

It's a .38. It's real small, but it makes real holes.

"So I'm on my back," Fate says as he moves to the door all slow, "looking up at stars, and, like, little shreds of leaves falling down on me cuz the bullets cut straight through them. They're just *raining* down on me."

I slip to the floor. I eye the windows, but I can't see shadows for shit behind the curtains. Apache's right up on them though. I see the white comb he keeps in his back pocket peeking out. He's not much taller than me but he's solid muscle, and he wears baggy clothes too so nobody can tell how strong he is. He's the kind of guy you need in a situation like this, in any situation, really. I mean, he scalped a fool once. That's how he got his name. He took a knife and peeled the skin off, inch by inch, hair and all. He threw it in a sink when he was done. I wasn't there, but I heard.

"You know me," Fate's still going, "I just army-crawl my ass over to the nearest tree so I can look out to see who's shooting."

I must've heard Fate's story two hundred times. We all have. By now it's like call and response. It's our story, we all own it, and when it gets told, you gotta ask questions at the right times.

As I crawl to my room I say, "Could you see who it was, like faces or whatever?"

The knock comes again, slower and heavier this time. *Bam. Bam. Bam.*

Fate blinks. I'm hunched down by the door to my room, running my hand along the baseboard for the rifle my little brother hides there behind the nightstand. He does that. Hides one in every room, two in the bathroom.

"It was *Vikings*. Leaning all out over the hood of that cop car, headlights off, letting go of shots, man, just squeezing!"

That's Lynwood. We got our very own neo-Nazi sheriff gang. I wish I was lying. I'm not. We heard they even got tattoos. Minnesota Vikings logos on their left ankles. The law don't matter to them. Their idea of fixing gang problems is rolling up in a neighborhood with their lights off like Fate said, then loosing shots at whoever even looks like a gangster before rolling out, hoping to set off a gang war where we kill each other cuz we think another gang shot at us, not sheriffs. That's some criminal police work right there. But to them, if you're brown or black, you're worth nothing. You're not even human. Killing us is like taking out trash. That's how they think.

With nail polish in one hand and one of them application things in the other, Lorraine pokes her head out my room with a curious look on her face, a big, dumb look with her high school *chichis* jiggling at me underneath it. She's not even wearing a bra, and only three toes out of ten are done up in blue glitter. Obviously, she got interrupted.

My glare stops her cold. I mouth the words, *Puta, get back.*

She looks mad at first, but she sinks back into the darkness of the room as I wrap my finger around the butt of the rifle and draw it into my lap. It's a light little thing in my hands, a .22. I only ever shot it twice at targets in my life.

I check it's loaded. You know it is.

Clever's whispering at Fate, looking at the closed-circuit monitor that shows every angle of the house outside, "Got nothing on video. It's the Serrato kid."

"Alberto?"

"Nah, the youngest. I don't know his name."

The knock comes again and it's loud as fuck. Hard to imagine a twelve-year-old kid hitting my door that hard. That's when my stomach drops like I'm riding a Knott's Berry roller coaster. See, that's when I know something's real wrong. Something that maybe can't get fixed.

2

Fate's on the phone, doing the smart thing: calling across the street, calling two houses up, two houses down, to make sure the avenue is clean, carless, nobody lurking. You never know who they might use to get you to open a door. Could be kids, could be anybody. Gotta have eyes everywhere. He nods slow before handing the piece to Apache. Clever backs him up.

Clever's toothpick thin. A real *palillo*. He keeps the chain on the door but turns the knob and cracks it so Apache can slide the snub-nose .38 to the metal grating of the security door, a few inches from the boy's face. "You need something, lil homie?"

The kid is dead out of breath, coughing a little, not even looking at the barrel or even looking up. "Miss Payasa, I . . ."

Lupe Rodriguez. That's been my government name if you need to know. Not that it matters. It's not my real one. I've changed it twice already. But it's Payasa since I been all involved. (That's the polite way of saying I'm into some gangster shit.) Calling me Miss, though? Ha. If my stomach wasn't fighting itself, I might even think that was cute. Even now, even in the heat of whatever, respect is necessary.

Around here, that stuff isn't courtesy. It's currency. Can't ever forget that.

Apache leans in. "Spit it out, lil homie."

The kid raises his eyes from my front stoop and his face is all hard. "It's her brother, he's like—"

Clever undoes the chain then the security door, and Apache snatches the boy inside by his shoulders, slams the door with his heel as the security metal slams behind it, and frisks the kid quick and efficient. The boy has too-long black hair and a chipped tooth. He's got blood on him too.

Fate picks up from there and shakes the kid a little. "*¿Adónde?*"

I can't even lie. See, I'm thinking it's Ray, my younger brother. He goes by Lil Mosco. (Mosco means "mosquito." He caught that name cuz he never stopped buzzing around when we were little. He's got Lil cuz there used to be a Big Mosco until last year. Drive-by. Rest in peace.)

It takes the kid a minute to tell us the body is two blocks away, dead as dead can be. That's when the blood really beats up in my ears cuz that doesn't make any sense.

Lil Mosco's running to Riverside and back, I'm thinking, like, how could he . . . ?

Shit. It hits me in that second, hits me right in the face and tilts the whole house on me. I gotta catch a wall with my hand just to stay upright.

It ain't Ray.

"Oh, fuck," I say.

Fate lets go of the kid and he's got this sad look on his face, the saddest look I ever seen. He knows it too. Clever's already got his mouth open like he forgot what breathing was. Apache has his head in his palms.

It's Ernesto, my big brother. My guts know it, but my brain's disagreeing, saying things like, he's not even a player. He's not involved. He's civilian. He's off-limits, so there's no way. No fucking way.

But then it dawns on me like a math problem my stupid ass finally figured out. There are no rules now. None. Not with people rioting. I shiver when I realize every single cop in the city is somewhere else, and that means it's officially hunting season on every fucking fool who ever got away with anything and damn, does this neighborhood have a long memory. I snort and take a second to appreciate the evil weight of it.

I mean, me, Fate, and Clever joked about something like this happening when we saw the dude getting bricked on the TV before Apache came over, and we were saying how now would be a good time to even up some scores if we felt like it, but I guess some homies were already out there, calling in old debts, blasting.

Behind me somewhere, Lorraine comes out of my room and says, "No, baby, no . . ." like she's trying to comfort me or something, but I'm not even sad right now and I sure as hell don't want her hands on me.

I'm angry.

I mean, I never been so mad at anybody in my life. I see flashes of red dotting my vision as I dig my nails into the rifle butt.

Like, how many times did I tell Ernesto to pay attention how he walked home? The dividing line between our neighborhood and theirs is too close as it is. Lazy-ass motherfucker got what he deserved for not listening to me!

I bite my lip and realize I been holding my breath.

I hear myself say, "Who knows?" It comes out sounding like rage.

The kid looks confused. "Like, who did it?"

"No," I say. "Who knows Ernie's gone?"

The kid gets around to it: just the people in the alley where he got dragged. *Dragged*, the kid says the word and I don't even know what it fucking means in this situation. The word just doesn't click for me. I don't get it. Not right at that moment. Not with the house still spinning, not with me still holding on. I swallow hard and say, "How much time we got?"

Clever gives me a look like he doesn't get what I'm asking at first, but Fate does. I don't even need to say it.

He looks at the wall clock and shrugs. "Hour and a half most likely."

That's how long it'll be before Lil Mosco buzzes back and hears about this. Nobody takes pagers on runs. That eliminates the temptation of using it while you're doing business.

So ninety minutes then, maybe less. That's how long we got to find out who did it, find them, and put bullets in them before wild-ass Lil Mosco gets home and starts shooting up house after house of anybody even halfway connected to this shit. But that's not my style.

I need to look whoever did it in the eyes, because what else is a sister to do?

They need to know I know before they get it. It needs to be justice.

Everybody in the living room can tell I'm on fire. Nobody says shit when I turn off the TV on a posse scene, badges getting handed out to a bunch of white hats. For a second, that feels like us. I hand Fate my rifle and pick up the phone to call *mi mamá*. We moved her out of Lynwood last year to somewhere safe, somewhere I can't even tell you. She still hears things though, like the grapevine still runs right through her kitchen.

Takes me five tries to get through. Phone lines must be jammed everywhere tonight. Guess I'm just lucky. When she comes on the line, I can tell by the tone of her voice she doesn't know yet, but she knows something's wrong cuz of my tone. I tell her not to answer the door, to lock it up good. I tell her not to answer the phone again until I get there cuz I got something important to tell her but it needs to wait, and I need her to hear it from nobody but me.

"*Por favor*," I say. "*Prométeme.*"

She promises.

I hang up the phone and tell the kid to take us there, take us to the place where my brother got fucking dragged to death.

3

The drive over in Apache's Cutlass is the longest two minutes of my life. My left leg shakes like I-don't-know-what and only putting my hands on my knee makes it stop. But that's when the other one starts up and I'm like, fuck it, and just stare out the window at the mailboxes going by fast, at the front doors caged with bars. Everything's locked up good and tight. I don't blame them. It's not so dark that you can't see smoke over the tops of houses and know shit's still burning in the distance.

I remind myself to breathe as Clever parks one street over from the alley and me, Fate, and the lil Serrato homie cut between houses on the Boardwalk and come up into an alley with garages on both sides. The air is still here, like a bunch of people been holding their breath till we came. I'm too hot, so I undo the buttons on my flannel till it's blowing out behind me and I only got my wifebeater left as a shield.

Normally we'd roll in, see what we can see, and roll out quick. But we got time tonight. Even if somebody called the sheriffs, they ain't coming for a while. Not tonight. Tonight the streets are ours.

Clever's right behind us with a flashlight and some of them bags with zippers already open and prepared. Clever's an all-star for shit like this. We sent him to L.A. Southwestern College for Crime Scene Investigation last year. He's almost got his A.A.

I mean, part of you doesn't ever want him to use what he learnt. But that's the crazy life. Soon or late, it's somebody's turn to feel the cut. And you hate it when it happens to others in your *clica*, but you hate it more when it happens to you. I felt it twice already, for a cousin and *mi padre* gone down. Now that spinning wheel landed on me again. It's my turn. Again. And I need Clever and his answers. I need 'em fast.

I tap Fate on the elbow. He knows for what.

He shines his watch's face at me. Still got over an hour and fifteen before Lil Mosco goes Tasmanian Devil. That's if we're lucky.

Homies already locked down the alley on both ends. Ranger, Apache, and Apache's cousin, Oso, are guarding up the way. Like soldiers, you know? I can't see far enough down the other side to know who's down there, but they're there, four long knives of shadows pointing up the alley cuz of the softball field lights a few blocks over, which is weird cuz I can't imagine anyone playing a game with the city burning up like it is, but whatever. It ain't my electricity.

The alley is wide enough for two compact cars maybe, nothing else. The backsides of wooden houses on either side are old as fuck, like 1940s, and rotting at their drainpipes. Some garages are separate from houses and between them there's mattresses, old couches, and all the other shit people don't want in front or on the lawn. It's definitely that depressing kind of place no owner ever thinks you'll see, the backs of houses nobody bothers to paint.

All around us, the streets are watching.

Blank faces tucked up in the shadows of garages. Scared faces acting like they ain't scared. A couple look familiar and I mark them in my head. One's a nurse though, still with hospital blues on. She flinches a little when I look at her. Beside her there's a shuffling black bum I don't recognize from the neighborhood. He's short, with a cane, and he's moving toward the body like he's curious.

When he sees me eye him, he says to me, "Hey, what happened here?"

I don't even break stride.

"Somebody get this eyeballing motherfucker out of here." Feels like I spit it more than I say it.

Fate nods back behind us, and some soldier must've branched off to take care of it cuz I hear a quick scuffle but nothing worth paying attention to. I'm already focused on something else.

As we walk up on my big brother's body, it looks too small to me. Like, his shoulders are too small, and I always remember them being wide enough to carry me around and pretend he was a horse when I was just a little *chavalita*. I don't flinch when I see his face, but I stop. I stop hard.

That's cuz Ernesto's face is busted the fuck up. I mean, it's his face but it's not. Not no more.

Both his eyes are blown out like a boxer took shots on him, all methodical and shit. Grit from the alley floor is pressed into long wounds on his cheeks, into his mouth. Little bits of sand. Tiny pebbles. One of his front teeth is turned all the way around. His cheek's caved in. He's missing an ear.

"That's him," the lil homie says, but he doesn't have to.

Shit. It's fucking obvious.

I don't say that though. I'm all trapped inside my head.

I'm looking down at my big brother who doesn't look so big.

I work my jaw and it pops. Ernesto was taller than that, I think. Stupid, I know, what with everything else I see but you can't help that shit. The thoughts just come, unoriginal shit just bubbling up, and my skin's prickling. That's when I realize I'm sweating hard.

He's still wearing his uniform, my big brother. He's wrapped up in dark and dirt and still-drying blood. On this whole busted-up excuse for an alley, there's only one tree tall enough to put its shadows on him, and it's swaying back and forth, pulling this dark outline up and down his legs like a blanket, like it's trying to tuck him in or something.

Worse than that, he's wearing the cowboy boots I got him for Christmas two years ago. Black leather and an elm-colored heel and sole. Real classy shit. He never wore 'em at work, only to walk to and from. For some reason, that hits me deepest. I remember his crooked smile when he opened that box, how his eyes got wide, and I gotta take a minute.

I walk away with my fists clenched up tighter than double knots. Staring at the field lights till I blink blue copies onto the nearby garages doesn't do much for me, but it's something. When I look back to the asphalt and start walking it, I'm careful not to step on the tire marks that lead away from Ernesto like black railroad tracks. I understand the dragged thing now.

He must've gone fifty, sixty feet on the asphalt after they beat him.

Fuck that *pinche* shit! I understand too good.

First, they beat him. They put their fists through his face, prolly the butts of their guns too, if they had 'em. They did this to a guy that never did nothing to them. They crossed a line when they did that, and only one thing about it made sense. They were trying to get at us instead, at Lil Mosco's stupid ass most obviously and most likely. This was them sending a message. They just didn't think I'd be the first to get it.

I'm so mad I'm shaking. All that anger I had for Ernesto, the same dude that raised me when *mi padre* died, that made sure I always ate up my *chilaquiles* and had a lunch for school every day, changes over.

I actually feel the click. I feel that shit deep inside me, like a light switch flicking on. How all the anger I had for my brother walking home the wrong way just goes away, and how, at the exact same moment, it blazes up at the fools that did this. And I need to know who did it worse than I ever needed anything. Seeing his face like that—shit. Seeing his face like that.

I know I can never go back to who I was before I saw.

These cowards made a new me when they did what they did to my big brother, my Ernesto. I'm standing here all reborn and shit cuz of them. Right now, I'm like starving and thirsting and burning all rolled into one. I look at his face again, and I need to know who I need to do *that* to. I need to know whose hearts need holes to match the ones in mine. And I need that shit like five minutes ago.

Out in public like this, Fate calls shots. I force my hands to unclench. I force myself to walk back to him.

It don't matter how much I'm feeling this. I can't be running my mouth out here, can't ever be undercutting *machismo*. It doesn't work like that. I'm not even really a full foot soldier yet, just related to one. And besides, women got no say-so. I can cry about it or work with it. I do that latter shit.

But Fate already knows what I want. It's like he's reading my mind.

"If you're good to, Payasa, go talk at some people. And keep doing what you're doing, Clever." Fate nods at us both, then turns to the boy. "The fuck were you doing out here, lil homie?"

I don't hear his answer, don't really care.

I'm already ten steps closer to that nurse I seen before. She's standing right in the alley like she's expecting somebody to ask her questions.

4

This nurse, she's maybe five three, still in her hospital blues and whiter-than-white, chunky shoes. She's got a scar on her chin, short hair like black nail polish shining under a streetlamp, and blood on her, all down her front. What I think is, she tried to save him, and my brother's blood looks like purple on her smock, like not even real.

"You Sleepy's sister? Gloria?"

She nods. She knows I mean Sleepy Rubio, not Sleepy Argueta. There's a big difference. Sixty pounds, give or take.

"I'm so sorry," Gloria says.

I put on the calmest voice I can because she looks shaken up. It feels fake as fuck, but I got to. "Tell me what you know."

She hugs herself like she's cold and points at the nearest garage, some box that looks navy in the dark. "I pulled in, was just going through my mail, you know. I don't pick it up enough and . . ."

Gloria sees my got-no-time glare and speeds up.

"This car, it looked like a little truck with a bed and everything, went by fast. In the rearview, I saw it, and I saw something being dragged behind it and I got out and looked and when I saw it was a person, I just couldn't believe it. It was like something out of the movies. They stopped, like, four houses up and two guys get out."

I'm counting in my head. "Out the driver's side too?"

"No. Out the bed and the passenger door."

"So there was a driver who didn't get out?"

"I guess."

My eyes must've flashed at that cuz she backs up a little. I say, "What'd the other two look like?"

"I dunno. One was normal tall."

I roll my eyes at that shit. Seems like the majority of people on earth pay less attention than rocks. For us, though, you gotta pay attention in this crazy life. If you don't, you don't deserve breathing.

"But the other," Gloria says, "he was taller than me. Six foot maybe?"

I say, "Okay, that's good," but it isn't good, not really. It's something though. I try encouraging her cuz it's what Fate would do. He's better at it than I ever was. I nod up at her. "Did you see their faces? Any marks or like anything out of the ordinary?"

"No. It was dark. They wore sunglasses though. I thought that was weird at night."

"What were they built like? What'd they wear?"

"Built like normal, I guess, but the tall one was muscular, like he lifts a lot. They both wore black. Hats and everything. I couldn't see anything."

That figures. When I do some evil shit to get some back for Ernesto, I'll prolly be wearing black too.

"What make of car was it?"

"I dunno. Like, a Cadillac or Ford, one of those long, boxy cars from the seventies or something, but did I say it had a bed to it? One of those half-car, half-truck things."

"It have anything different about it? Bumper stickers or a smashed taillight or whatever?"

Gloria squints her eyes for a second before saying, "No."

I shake my head and give up on that shit. "Tell me what they did when they got out."

She gasps a little, won't look me in the eyes. "They stabbed him, like, a lot. Again and again. I never saw anything like that before. It makes a *sound*."

Gloria shivers and chews her lip. She doesn't need to explain.

It makes a sound all right, and it depends on how loud if you're bouncing off ribs or if somebody's holding their breath when you sink in. Don't even ask about cartilage. Truth: it ain't easy to stab somebody to death. It takes time. Sometimes it takes luck. It's way easier if they don't struggle, and maybe Ernesto was too hurt to do that.

I bite the insides of my cheeks so hard I taste blood like burnt copper in my mouth. I'm shaking again, balling my fists up. "How many times they stab him?"

"I dunno," Gloria says.

I nod and swallow, trying to push my feelings down as low as they'll go. Past my feet even. Down into the ground. "And then they just took off, right?"

It's what I would've done. In and out. Nothing left behind. Clean. I notice I got my fists balled up, so I force my fingers straight. I already know the answer to this question is a yes.

"No," Gloria says.

My ears are ringing when I pounce on that shit. "What do you mean?"

"The tall one, he wiped off his knife and tucked it in the pouch of his sweatshirt and then he took out some gum, put it in his mouth, and threw the wrapper. Or maybe he got the gum first?"

"Wait." Hair on the back of my neck stands up. "Where?"

She doesn't hear my question at first, she's still talking, her eyes far off and remembering. "And then they all got in the car and—"

"Hold up." I put a hand on her shoulder. Maybe it's too hard cuz she whimpers a little. Ask me if I fucking care. "*Where* did he throw it?"

Gloria starts and looks down at me. "What?"

"The gum wrapper."

She points up the alley, to the right of where Fate is standing with the Serrato kid. I start moving that way, fast. She's trailing behind me, still talking. "I tried to save him. I want you to know. But it was just too much."

I shoot a look over my shoulder to see Gloria waving her hand at her nurse smock, at the blood marks. At Ernesto's . . .

I should thank her. I can't.

I'm too busy searching through weed clumps and kicking up

pebbles till I find a white little ball of paper wadded up in a divot. It looks new. Brand new.

My heart pounds up in my chest when I see how clean it is, only a little wet on the bottom, like it was recently chucked. This shit's definitely it.

I turn, about to call for Clever, but he's right beside me, holding out a baggie. Shit, he's good. On top of everything. I drop the thing in there.

He's got a pair of long tweezers he uses to hold an edge and then presses his fingers through the plastic like a makeshift glove and unwraps it. The other side is blue. We both look close.

There's some weird writing on it, like calligraphy or some shit. Fate's beside us too then, pressing his face in.

I say, "Is that Oriental style? Like Korean writing?"

"Nah. Not Korean." Clever holds it up to the light. "Looks Japanese. These letters are all sharp. Korean is the one with circles."

I don't know but I nod anyway. "What's it say?"

Clever unrolls it before tapping his tweezers on a picture of fruit in the middle. He narrows his eyes at it. "Not sure, but doesn't that look like blueberries?"

"Who the fuck chews blueberry Japanese gum around here?"

"Put the word out," Big Fate growls. He takes off toward the soldiers. "We're about to find out. Everybody tell everybody."

I walk back slow to Ernesto and look at the baggies Clever has lined up on the chipped asphalt. Six of 'em. One holds Ernie's wallet. I open it and check if there's still money in it.

There is. This just makes my burning worse. When they didn't even bother faking a robbery, that's when you know that shit was a message. Not like you can fake anything when you beat somebody, drag them, and then stab them all cold-blooded. Shit.

I pull his card and pictures of me, Ray, and Ernie when we were little, a picture of Mamá too. I put the wallet back in his pocket and leave the money so the sheriffs'll know it wasn't a robbery, only twenty-three bucks anyway, but I got to make them work for an ID.

Buys us more time. Just in case.

By now, somebody's called 911. No telling how long it'll take for someone to come pick him up though. My stomach actually convulses at the thought of him lying here for god-knows-how-long. One hour? Two? I take my flannel off and cover his face with it. I lift his head up a little and put the sleeves underneath like a pillow. My hands come back bloody.

After that it's just Clever grabbing baggies and me standing dumb right beside him, working up the courage to say what I got to. I lean down next to Ernesto, close enough to touch him.

I close my eyes and I say, "We'll get you buried good and right, big bro. I promise. But we can't just now, okay? So please forgive me just this one thing."

I blink and close my eyes again, but only after I latch on to the only clean part left of his uniform, a seam on the shoulder, near the collar. I squeeze it hard between my thumb and index finger.

"We need the time a little more right now is all."

5

Back at the house, the place's thick with homies wondering what the fuck we're going to do, how we're going to come back on them for what they did to Ernesto. That's the talk. Soldiers want guns and cars, a caravan even. They want blood and they don't even know whose. And it's good to hear and all that, but Ernesto wasn't theirs, you know? He's mine. His death's on me.

Fate's smart as fuck though. He gives them just enough time to get the steam off before sending everybody but Apache home to wait for orders. Reason why Apache got to stay is cuz he recognizes the gum wrapper, he just can't remember where from, so we're all just hanging on it cuz Clever's still laying his shit out and it's tense as fuck.

The walls feel closer, the ceiling way too low. Even my skin feels all thin and stretched out over my bones. It hurts worse every time

I look at the kitchen clock and feel Ray's guaranteed chaos getting closer and my chance at justice getting farther away.

If anybody feels much about Ernesto, they ain't showing it. Ain't crying or nothing. Even if they wanted to they can't, cuz that's bitch shit. Pure weakness.

"Wait." Apache holds the baggie with the wrapper up and finally says, "The Cork'n Bottle! That's where I seen it!"

It gets real quiet then. We need to know he's sure, like sure-sure.

"For real," Apache says. "They got all that kind of crazy shit there. Even, like, black licorice gum. Shit's nasty."

Fate makes a face like he doesn't doubt that, but he needs to know something else too. "How you know?"

"Well, me and Lil Creeper were out this one time . . ."

Fate is already waving his hand at the name like it's a bad smell. It means it's okay, he gets it, so stop, you don't need to keep talking. All Apache had to say was Lil Creeper and it's done. Dude's name is a conversation ender. It means you don't need to explain cuz we believe you. How that dude hasn't been killed a hundred times or locked up for life I'll never know. It's like he's high all the time. Always in the wrong place. Always guaranteed doing dumb shit. And yet, miraculously, he's always wriggling out of tight spots. He's a real wormy motherfucker, but he's our wormy motherfucker.

One time when we were little, Ray wanted a bike, a Dyno. It was a BMX bike, the hottest shit on the street. This was back when Creeper was first using. Heroin, coke, whatever, it never mattered to him. If it could go in his body, it was going in. So Ray tells him he wants a Dyno, tells him the colors and everything.

That's how it works with junkies, you know. You don't gotta tell them to do shit. You just tell them what you want and drop it. It works better than aiming them. Cuz two days later Creeper comes up to the house with a bike, white and red just like Ray asked, but there's a problem. See, it wasn't a Dyno he stole from J.C. Pennies, it was a *Rhino*—some cheap-ass fucking rip-off bike with that dumb brand name written in the same type of lettering. Man, we laughed so hard at that, and Ray couldn't help but pay anyway. Ernesto laughed harder than anybody, his whole body shaking.

Remembering this hurts my ribs. I say, "Hey, Fate, shouldn't we prolly page him up though?"

"Who? Creeper?"

"For why?" Clever wants to know.

I make a gun with my right hand, index and middle for the barrel, and point at it with my left.

Guns aren't easy to get. Not one that traces to somebody else, or one that's unregistered or filed down. And no disrespect to Ray's arsenal, but a .38 ain't gonna do it. A .22 rifle ain't gonna do it. Biggest piece we got in the house is a .357 revolver that needs cleaning. That's still only six shots though.

I need like seventeen if I'm gonna do what needs to be done.

Fate's way ahead of me, as usual.

"Already did," he says.

I nod at him and head into my room. I cut a look at my Lorraine sitting on the bed. She's done with her toes now. They look blue and small in the dimness, like shiny gumdrops. Her eyes are wide, and I can tell there's a lot of words dammed up behind her mouth but she won't say shit. She'll wait till I do. As she should.

I look at the clock by my bed, and my stomach balls up. It says I got an hour. Sixty fucking minutes. And that's bad. Cuz, see, there's a problem with that Cork'n Bottle Apache knows.

It's over the line.

It's not technically our neighborhood and since we don't own that shit, we can't go there unless we're stealth as fuck. And we don't got time to round up everybody, go over there, get it, come back, and then do something.

I get an idea then, a stupid one. Fast as I can, I'm out of my chucks, my khakis, my undershirt . . .

Lorraine cocks her head at me like she knows I'm about to do something crazy but is way too scared to ask what. I'm pulling one of her dresses out of my closet, grabbing some eyeliner off the dresser and handing it to her.

"Do it good and fast," I say.

She looks at it, then at me, and smiles real wicked. Before I know it, I got cat-eyes, penciled-in eyebrows, and my hair's getting feathered. I look like a bad copy of her in a gold sparkly dress, whoreish as fuck.

When Lorraine checks her finishing touches, somebody finally says it in the next room: "Wait, Cork'n Bottle on Imperial?"

"Yeah, that's the one," Apache replies.

"Shit," Clever says.

Fate's already thinking his way around it. He's been doing it. He knew when I knew that it was over the line. "We roll deep over there. Grab the tapes. See if we can't get a face on the fucker that chews this."

"Or we do something unexpected," I say, stepping out from my room. The wedge heels are a new thing. They feel like stilts.

"Damn," Apache says and leaves his mouth hanging open. He's about to say something about how I look, but Clever nudges him quiet.

"Lemme go over there and grab them tapes," I say. "It'll be in and out. Fast as hell."

I put a please on the end of it so Fate knows it's his call, but he also knows it's prolly the best chance we got right now. At least, it's the best chance I got.

"Could be a trap or something," he says to me.

I just kind of shrug. If it is, it is. I know he's right, though. Cuz Fate's twenty-five. He's seen things every which way. You don't live as long as him, putting in work for a decade, without being paranoid.

"They catch you over there, it ain't gonna be tickling," he says.

That's his way of saying I get a bullet if I'm lucky, a knife if I'm not.

I know it. Everybody in the room knows it.

Clever doesn't like it either. "I still think we just roll deep over there, like five, six cars, grab the tapes, and be out."

Apache's eyes light up, so you know he agrees.

Big Fate glares them both down. Sometimes he's more fam to me than Ray ever was. He knows me so good, knows I can't get talked out of shit like this when I get locked on to it. He stares at me hard, but there's something in those eyes though, a shiny spot like he's proud and he doesn't like it but he knows better than anybody how I gotta go. He wants me to be careful. He wants me to come back safe. He's just not going to say it.

6

I can't walk normal outside, can't really sway like I usually do, so I gotta slap my heels down after my toes kind of. It's enough to get me to the curb without eating shit. I feel eyes on me, but I don't turn around and check the cameras. Could be the last time I see any of them. That occurs to me, but I don't wave or nothing. I just get in the car.

Lorraine's got some sort of Japanese piece of shit riding on three good tires and a spare. Used to be her cousin's. It's got no lighter cap and a Dodger-logo baseball stuck on top of the gearshift. I slide in and turn the key. Smokey Robinson comes on the radio, but I shut him off as I notice the blinking clock on the dash is off by six minutes.

I got fifty left. That's it.

The starter sputters, but the car kicks in gear and I shoot down my street with the sticker of the Virgin Mary staring at me while I scrunch around in my seat cuz Lorraine's dress is twisted around on my hips. Figures. She's two sizes bigger than me but I can't help it now. I fight that shit down at a stop sign, looking at my eyes in the rearview, all Cleopatra'd. I hit the gas.

Times like this, I'm glad I never got no tattoos. You're burnt right away being marked up like that. It was Fate's idea for me not to get any ink. Shit though, he's got his work from this dude's garage that everyone's been talking about. Pint. That's his name. Fate says he'll be a famous dude that came from Lynwood someday, like Kevin Costner is, or Weird Al Yankovic, and now people are saying Suge Knight too. Death Row Records. That guy.

I'm jealous of Fate's tattoos, but fuck it. He said years ago that I gotta keep clean, that I'm scarier that way. I can go anywhere without them, that I can blend in. He says I'm the element of surprise, and I get that, but he knows I'm entitled to two tattooed tears. My next thought hits me hard and blunt, baseball-bat style.

Shit. *Three* tears now. Counting Ernesto.

My breathing gets tangled up in my lungs. It's starting to feel normal almost, like I only got half my breathing space to use, not all of it.

I don't exactly have my license, but Ernesto taught me to drive good, how to drive defensive. And you know it's funny when I think that, cuz some old lady who can't see past her hair curlers puts half her van into my lane and I honk hard, dodge that shit, speed up, and change lanes easy. I swear, fucking people drive around like this is Culiacán, ignoring lanes, never signaling. I freeze a little after thinking that cuz it's something Ernie used to say all the time.

You know, he never complained when he had to sell his truck a year ago to pay Ray's bail after the dumb fucker caught an aggravated assault charge. Ernie volunteered to do it. He knew we couldn't be showing drug money or they'd be finding a way to investigate us, audit or some shit, whatever the fuck they do.

That truck of his was our only family asset besides the house. And Ernesto did it. He sold it and didn't even blink. Walked to work every day after that. He worked longer hours. He wouldn't even take the money Ray offered for a new ride. Instead he just walked and saved for a new one.

Him and Ray never got along. I mean, they loved each other, but they scrapped like crazy growing up. Ernie never lost, not that I ever saw, which of course made Ray raw and competitive, mean as fuck. Made him want to join up too. Made him always want to prove himself and overdo shit, like two weeks ago when he shot up a club.

It's an old story. You prolly heard something like it a million times. That doesn't make it untrue though, just makes it stupid that people keep repeating this shit. See, Ray gets loaded out of his mind, goes to a club, and when some *cholo* claims another set, he heads to the car and gets his piece and decides everybody needs to be talking about how bad Lil Mosco is, then it was just that bang-bang-screech shit: shooting and squealing the tires and boning the fuck out.

He shot somebody in the eye, a girl with parted hair and big shoulders. We know cuz the TV said so. Well, it didn't say she had parted hair and big shoulders. That's just my observation.

Her parents held her picture up on the news when they were pleading *en español* for more information regarding her death. Some white dude on Fox 11 translated their words with all the emotion of a grocery list and not like two people crying. Ray was smoking when he saw it and he laughed at that girl's parents, took another hit, and laughed again.

What the news didn't say and maybe her parents didn't know was that she was all involved, not civilian. That doesn't mean she had it coming, but when you're in, it's always a possibility. You can be involved and still be a wrong place, wrong time kind of girl when you catch one. No gang ties ever protected anybody from a bullet. A click is not a vest—I remember Fate said that at the time—it's a family.

Just thinking of that makes me mad at Ray all over again, about how he's been laying low since then, mostly away, doing errands as amends to Big Fate for being dumb as fuck. Everybody knows he did what he did, and they didn't say shit, but they were waiting for him to pop his head up so they could get one back on him.

But he didn't. Guess they got tired of waiting. Figured one was good as any other, civilian or not. Brother for brother. Same thing, right? That's the only thing that makes sense.

My eyes are wet and itching, so I roll the window down and

get some dry night wind on my face cuz I'm not about to mess up Lorraine's work. I can smell the fires, like everybody in this neighborhood got wood-burning stoves overnight and stuffed them with tires, garbage, whatever.

That girl in the rearview isn't me. I convince myself of that shit. She's a spy. Dangerous. She's got a .38 in her girlfriend's borrowed purse.

Outside, the city's busy making night sounds. *Banda* music from a backyard party fades back when I hit Atlantic, and as I turn out into traffic, there's cars with bad carburetors getting their pedals pushed down before the light goes all the way green. They bump out beats. They compete. Even now. Even when people are rioting and killing each other a couple miles away.

Crazy. But that's priorities, I guess.

Five miles over the limit, I'm good for a few blocks. I hit a left on Imperial. Soon as I'm on it, I feel eyes on me, and you know for sure I'm not looking sideways at lights. My ass is only looking straight.

Last thing I need is windows rolling down and some homeboy fronting me, asking me where I'm from.

My blood feels fuzzy and fast in me when the Cork'n Bottle comes up, and I grip harder on the wheel than I need to as I cut behind a Dodge and slide right on a yellow light. I'm staring at the dash clock as I slip behind the store and park in the back lot they share with the tire store. It's all empty.

Forty-three minutes, that's what I got left.

7

It's brighter than daylight when I roll in through the back door, steady as I can on those wedge shoes. I scan the store and don't see nobody but the clerk. He's half bald, wearing a button-up shirt that's not buttoned or tucked. He's got dark circles under his eyes and a junkie shoulder slant to go with his wifebeater and black beard.

He's not Mexican, or Salvi even. He looks like something else, like Afghanistan or some shit. His arms are crossed on his chest as he's watching dudes dash in and out the front door ripping open the coolers and snagging beer and Cokes while others stuff candy in their pockets. There's three or four of them. Like an assembly line of looting. Or a disassembly line. Whatever it is, the clerk doesn't care. He's not about to get killed on account of this. Smart, I think, a man worth talking at.

The gum's up front. I quick-scan all the types and see it there, blue and shiny right in front of me.

I say to the clerk, "You speak English?"

He says sure, but he looks surprised anybody's talking to him, so I hold a pack of that blueberry gum up in his face so he can't fucking miss it.

I say, "You know who buys this?"

I'm looking up behind him at the camera focused on my side of the counter. It's the perfect angle. Whenever Ernie's killer bought gum, he's on tape for sure. The clerk watches my eyes come back to him and he shrugs.

"Gum is gum," he says. "All the same."

I slip my feet outta them wedges and smirk at that shit. I can't move fast in them. I could hop the fucking counter, put myself between him and the police button, and shove him hard against the cigarette case as I pull my .38 faster than he can see. I could put that shit under his chin, in the soft skin directly beneath the tongue. I could watch his eyes go big. Could muscle him as he tries to squirm away before figuring out I got too much leverage.

I could, but I don't.

Instead, I just say, "Look, man, we know Julius owns this place and you don't, so just give over the tapes and it's all good."

I nod up at the camera and then to the door next to the coolers that leads to the back room, where they keep the tapes. This ain't the first time anybody ever came in wanting tapes. People that own these stores don't live in the neighborhood, but the employees sure as shit do. We know where their *mamá*s live, their girlfriends, their babies too. When we ask, when anyone asks, they drop a dime like a motherfucker. It's how it works.

I rip some plastic bags out of the metal holster at the counter. The clerk blinks at me, but I'm not me. I'm dangerous.

He sees it in my eyes and he gets it. We walk just the two of us to the storage closet. It's full of monitors, cases of beer and toilet paper and chips everywhere, crowding the walls. Cool as hell, he hits eject-eject-eject on three VCRs and throws the tapes in one of them plastic bags.

I point at the shelf of tapes above the machines. I say, "All them motherfuckers too."

He puts the tapes in the bags like he's bagging groceries, stacking 'em right. Must be twenty tapes in both bags when I say, "You should prolly go home. No use standing around while they take everything."

He looks at the tapes and then back at my face.

"And you never saw no girl taking tapes," I say.

He shrugs at that and I figure that's the most I'm likely to get out of him, so I slide out of the closet and past an old man who's half leaning into a cooler, fighting with a case of beer, his pockets stuffed with jerky, fitting to get away with all of it. Wow. You know that shit is none of my fucking business.

I'm too busy snagging Lorraine's wedges from under the front counter, jamming my feet in them, and slapping back out into the night the way I came, my blood buzzing like crazy. But I haven't even taken four steps into the parking lot when I hear a guy's voice behind me.

"Hey, girl"—it's all calm as fuck—"where you from?"

8

I got two fingers snaking down into the bag, touching the pistol handle as I turn. I don't try to hide the bags behind me or nothing. That shit's suspicious. I just pray it's dark enough for whoever not to see the tapes in them and wonder why I got so many, and where that shit come from, and why the hell I need it.

My heart sinks when I see who the voice belongs to.

He's taller than me by a head, wide shoulders, bald *cholo* style, and he's standing a few steps from the doorway.

Fuck.

My stomach hates me for this. It punches up on my ribs to tell me so.

He's looking gee'd up too: khakis pressed, black tattoos you can kind of see through his undershirt that's whiter than teeth in toothpaste commercials—all that. Worse though, he's eyeing me and smiling. I can't tell yet what kind of smile it is, or what he wants me to do about it.

Behind him two of his homeboys are busy holding up both sides of the door frame with their shoulders, posing hard. You know how some people think like they're always in a movie, like the camera never stops rolling on 'em? *That.*

He steps to me and I hold my breath. All my blood vessels and veins decide they're racetracks right then.

When he frowns, there's a twenty-car pileup in my chest somewhere.

"Uh, don't take this the wrong way or nothing." He licks his lips. "But you're walking out like you stole something."

I don't even blink. "Cuz I did."

I breathe though. Shit, I *breathe.* This idiot only thinks I'm fuckable, not a rival. Relief rocks my knees a little, but I keep standing. I also take my fingers off the gun.

He says, "Yeah, I knew right away, you look the robbing type."

"Biggest robber you ever seen," I say.

He shakes a finger in my face, trying to be playful. "You know, you do look kinda familiar."

He turns to his boys. "Don't she?"

They don't move. They're too busy looking tough for their close-ups. That, or they think his shit's as tired as I do.

His look changes though, gets a cutting edge on it, and he nods up. "Serious though, where you from?"

A moment like this is when the unexpected is my friend. Gotta use it to put his brain somewhere else, guide him, so I already know where his next couple questions will be coming from. Put him on a new path, you know. It's what spies do.

I smile my best Lorraine smile. "The Valley."

He leans back at that. "Like, what, Encino or something? All respect, you don't look like no Valley girl."

He means this as a compliment.

I slap at his shoulder. His muscles sure aren't painted on. I say, "It's more like Simi Valley."

He gets a look on his face like he never saw that one coming. Perfect.

"Why didn't you just say that then? Gotta be all misleading."

"Cuz nobody cared about Simi until they moved that Rodney King trial up there, and even less know how to get to it. Try it. Do you know where it is?"

He smiles an embarrassed smile. "Yeah, of course I do."

"Oh yeah," I say and giggle like Lorraine, "where then?"

"Like, north? Right?"

"Yeah"—I say it like how Lorraine would say it—"good job. '*North.*' You're going to have to forgive me but I had this conversation my whole life and next thing is, you'll ask where it's really at and then I'll have to explain how to get there and how big it is and polite shit like that and I'm just not feeling it. So I'd just rather say the Valley and let you think whatever."

He understands this. I see it flash in his eyes and get filed away. He's not stupid, this one. But he still asks the question I was guiding him to. Can't even see my traps before he steps in them.

"So what're you doing down here?" He genuinely wants to know why the fuck I'd drive down from Whitepeopleville to here. He's testing me, wondering if I'm stupid, or slumming, or looking for trouble, or all of the above.

"My cousin lives here. Maria Escalero. You know her?"

Maria ain't my cousin, but her name's safe to use. She was my high school crush, a senior when I was still a little freshman going to class and not dropped out. I used to run behind her in gym class. Ass like you wouldn't believe. She used to live by Lugo Park. Ended up going to college in Colorado somewhere. Damn shame.

"Nah, can't say as I do."

"That's too bad," I say. "You look like the type that knows people."

His eyes bug a little at that, like he wasn't expecting it. It's cute in a sad way, like he's not nearly as smooth as he thought he was, not as practiced. And he spills then, the reason why he called me out in the first place.

"Hey, so, you want to come to a party tonight? It's like a celebration and you got the"—he pauses, drifting his eyes to my chest without bothering to bring them back up—"*profile* we're looking for."

The bag handles are cutting into my palm pretty good by now. My fingers are going numb.

"And you ain't even seen my side yet."

I turn to the side and show him, hiding the bags better.

"That's nice, you know?"

"Oh," I say in my best Lorraine style, "I *know*."

He's turning red now, losing his nerve. "You should come, really."

It's my turn to give him a good long stare, freeze him up.

"I'm good," I finally say. "I promised Maria we'd do the clubs tonight if the whole city don't burn down."

"It won't. And you could come by after."

"No, thanks. You're cute though. You have a nice night."

I step and you know his eyes are glued to my ass and that's okay cuz I got my bags in front of me and then I'm opening the door and I'm in the car smashing the bags onto the floor behind the front seats and turning the key in the ignition before he even knows what hit him.

The clock says I got thirty-five minutes. It ticks over, right in front of my eyes. Thirty-four now.

My stomach sinks down into my seat. I'm thinking there's no fucking way we'll get through these tapes fast enough, that it's just—

Something hits the passenger window so hard, I jump.

It's his fist. He's knocking.

I smile and reach back for the .38 when he opens his hand and presses a piece of paper to the window. Behind it, he smiles.

I let go of the gun. I roll down the window.

"Here's the address just in case you decide," he says, "well, you know. It's got my number on it too. Right there."

He points at it like I actually need help figuring out which one is the phone number, then says, "Hey, how old are you?"

I give him a look as I figure out if I should lie or not. I decide not to. I don't know why.

"Sixteen," I say.

"Nineteen," he says and points to himself.

"What's your name anyway?"

He must've figured I was down for the dark side, cuz he says, "Around here they call me Joker."

"That ain't no name. What's your real one?"

"That *is* my real name."

If I wanted to push it, I'd ask him how he got his name. I don't. I knew a Joker once. He got it cuz every time he put his knife in somebody, he laughed. Didn't matter why, if he was nervous or high or what. He just did. There's some shit in this life that happens and nobody knows why, not even the people that do it, and that was definitely that.

I say, "That's not the one your *mamá* gave you. And that's the only kind I got, so how else we gonna trade?"

Something cold and hard balls up in my chest then. Just a truth: if this motherfucker right here knew he was looking at Payasa, Lil Mosco's sister, he'd prolly shoot me in the face. Wouldn't even hesitate. The spy in me smiles at the power of being someone else. He thinks it's for him. And that's good. Useful.

"Ramiro," he finally says.

"Lorraine," I say. "With two *r*'s."

"Right," he says and nods. "See you later, Lorraine-with-two-*r*'s."

9

Clever's been a busy man since I been gone. He knows how wide the tire tracks were apart, which means he knows the width of the undercarriage and the type of tire and the rough speed and all that. He says we looking for a Ford Ranchero, prolly 1969, but he's not totally sure. I tell him that fits with what the nurse said, since she said it had a bed on it. Clever nods. From the ligature marks they used metal wire to tie up Ernesto's ankles, and he says they tied it to a trailer hitch before they dragged him. That same trailer hitch is prolly what busted my brother's cheek when they hit the brakes and he flew into the back of the car.

I nod at all that, kind of numb to it, but panic hits me when I spill them tapes out on the kitchen table and I don't know which ones came out the three VCRs that recorded the most recent footage. It's stomping in my stomach, hard like body blows, when Clever, Fate, Lorraine, and Apache lean in to look.

"Damn, girl," Apache says, "this is a serious come-up!"

Serious, sure, but overwhelming is what it is. But when you don't know what's what, you just take it all. Better too much than too little, right?

Lorraine bumps me a little like she wants to ask something stupid, like how many tapes there are. I just pop her with a look and she knows better. She's trained.

I tell Clever, "Three of these are the latest, but I'm not sure which."

"Easy," Clever says. He lays them flat now, one after another. "See how none of them are rewound?"

Clever's right. On every one of them, the left side is nothing but a white spool. The right side of each one is lopsided with black tape though.

"And none of them are fucking marked either," I say. "Shit's sloppy."

Sometimes, Apache wonders shit and blurts it. "They don't even bother watching these? Just take them out when they're done and put new ones in? Why?"

"Cuz why bother? Takes work to watch," Fate says. "And if nothing happened, then it's work you don't got to do. But if you caught something, you just turn that shit over to the sheriffs and make them do the work, you know?"

Clever's nodding at that as he dominoes two more tapes, then three. I help. We flip every last one till the table has a solid layer of black on it and we can see the spools.

"But some you pulled before they were full," Clever says.

Clever and me snag out the three that don't match and head to the television. He pops one in and the Cork'n Bottle's in my living room. It's the counter area, and it occurs to me then that the other two tapes are different store angles. Static hits my finger as I poke the screen.

"That blueberry shit is right *there*."

"Any of that moves," Clever says, "we'll see it."

There's a knock at the door and Apache moves to get it. We got homeboys outside so there's no need to take the usual precautions.

He swings it open and Lil Creeper is there, dressed in all-over black: black hoodie, black jeans, black shoes. He sniffs and he's got a shake to him, one that starts in his left leg and works itself up to his shoulder and back down. There's a brown paper bag in his left hand too.

He takes one look at me sitting on the couch and starts laughing.

He says, "Is this shit Halloween or something?" When he doesn't get a reaction, he tries to drag Apache into it. "Why's she all dressed up like that?"

It's no use saying shit or looking scary or anything. Lil Creeper has screws loose. He don't take to no training. We all know this, especially Fate, so he just says, "Gimme the fucking bag."

Creeper takes a little step back. "Okay, but, Fate, it's like this: I only got a Glock and thirteen."

"That makes the price different, don't it?"

"Like, it *could*." Creeper moves the bag from hand to hand for a moment. "I mean, I acknowledge that shit, but there's got to be some kind of honesty bonus in it too, you know? Cuz, like, I coulda just swapped the bag for the money and run, right? But I didn't. I stood up like a man and told you before you found out. So that's worth something, right?"

Fate just has his hand out.

Creeper exhales. "Right?"

Fate's hand doesn't move an inch. He never wanted anything but for Lil Creeper to put the bag in it, so Creeper finally does. Fate rips the bag, pulls the piece, and sees that all down the handle it's wrapped in white athletic tape, which is weird but not a big deal, so long as it works. Fate shrugs at it and makes sure the safety's on, ejects the clip, counts bullets with his thumb tip, then checks the chamber and the firing pin, before counting out from a wad and folding it.

Creeper says, "That's everything there was in the safe, Fate."

"Whose safe?"

Creeper licks his lips and shrugs. "Some fucking guy's. Who cares?"

"You sure that's all there was?"

"Yeah." Creeper bounces up and down a little. "*Yeah*."

Big Fate holds the money out. "Take it."

Glock 17Ls hold seventeen rounds, sixteen in the clip, one in the chamber. Creeper brought us one four bullets short of full. If I end up in a group of people, that's four less chances to make it out.

Clever and me are straining our eyes at the screen on fast-forward so I don't see what happens, but I know what happens. Creeper takes the fucking money, bones out, goes and gets high somewhere. Like always.

Inside the Cork'n Bottle, nobody goes near the gum. We burn twenty minutes of real time and nobody goes near the fucking gum. It's all beer and cigarettes and standing around. It's nothing.

"What if," Apache says all serious, "what if the shooter bought this, like, a week ago and only just now chewed it?"

It kills the energy in the room. I look at Clever and Clever looks at me. We both look at Fate. He's frowning at the Glock on the table. Lorraine's busy digging a hole in the carpet with her shiny toes.

Apache's still going though. "Or, like, what if he didn't even buy this for himself? What if somebody else bought it for him?"

Nobody says a word then.

It hits us all at the same time how futile this shit could be.

"But it's what we got," I say, and I don't mean for it to come out as angry as it does. "It's *all* we got."

I'm mad on the surface, but underneath I'm giving up.

This is inevitable shit.

We're out of time. I know it. Everybody does.

We've got thirteen minutes before Ray gets home and turns this shit into Desert Storm. Thirteen minutes's nothing. Less than nothing.

It's a pit trying to swallow me.

I'm not even looking at the screen anymore. I'm smashing my forehead into the flat of my hand when another knock hits the door, a fast one, like *bam-bam-bam*.

I know it's over then. It's done.

Cuz I know it's Ray. It has to be. He's just early. And I got to tell him about Ernie somehow. I'm the one that's got to make him madder than he's ever been. But something else occurs to me right as Fate moves to answer it.

Joker could've followed me home.

10

I got this pain ripping through my stomach when the door opens. I'm eyeing the Glock on the table like it's too far away. The sound of the VCR whirs behind me as two people step in the house, the Serrato kid from before and a *hina* I recognize from Will Rogers Elementary School, Elena Sanchez.

I sigh some relief at that.

I mean, it was stupid of me to think it'd be Joker. If it'd been him, it wouldn't have been no knock, and we would've heard them coming. Guess that's just my guilt acting up for not telling Fate about what happened outside the Cork'n Bottle. There just wasn't time.

Elena swings a look around the house. She used to have blond hair about seven years ago, badly bleached. It's her natural brown now, nice and light, with just the right kind of wave in it. And that's not all she lost. Her baby fat's nowhere to be seen in cuffed black jeans and white T-shirt with a lace neck on it. She looks real fine now. No doubt about that. Lorraine sees the look on my face and hunches up like she's mad.

Fate talks at the kid, "You need something, lil homie?"

"I asked around about the gum like you said," the Serrato kid says. "Asking everybody, and, uh, she has something to tell you."

Elena says, "I know all about the motherfucker you're looking for who chews that blueberry gum."

You'd think the hair on the back of my neck would get tired of standing straight up but it doesn't. It reaches right for the ceiling. Next to me, Clever scrambles to his feet. Apache even takes a step forward.

We all need to hear this.

Right the fuck now.

"Couple months ago, I was with this dude who always chewed that shit. Met him at a party, and you know I thought he was all that.

Big smile, smooth talk. A good kisser. Kissing him was like kissing candy. I swear he had the worst sweet tooth . . ."

Fate gives her a look like she needs to speed her shit up. Now.

"We go seeing each other a lot more and you know he was always like, 'baby, me and you' and 'love of my life' and all that. And we even talked about getting married. He talked about that shit all the time. But you know that was before I found out he knocked up Elvia, that's my best friend! When I flew at him about that shit, he said he didn't mean to, that he was drunk and she trapped him into it, but when I asked him—"

Jealous bitch that she is, Lorraine interrupts, "You ever think that maybe you deserved it?"

Elena's on it. She takes a hard step at Lorraine and pops off, "Who the fuck are you, bitch?"

I get Lorraine's wrist in my grip and twist. She yelps.

Elena smiles when she sees it.

Apache nods up and says, "This dude have a name?"

"His name's Ramiro," she says. "He trying to make a name for himself, but really he's just a lame-ass *leva*. He's got to *go*."

Ramiro. My cheeks light up like someone set fire to them.

I never felt so stupid as in that moment. As I'm remembering how he stood, how scared I was, what he smelled like, one thought claws its way up to the top: he was an arm's length away from me.

That's it. Maybe three fucking feet.

I had the .38. I could've snapped it out and done him right there.

I could've already avenged Ernesto.

"Joker." I whisper that shit like it hurts.

Cuz it does.

Elena puts a look on me like maybe she's jealous, but definitely like she needs to know how I know.

She narrows her eyes before finally saying, "Yeah, that's him."

Shit. Fate wants to know how I know the dude's name too.

I say, "You know anything about the guys he runs with? Two of them?"

She knows they're into some serious bad shit, but no, she don't know their names. "The both of them think they're models or something. Always wearing sunglasses at night like a couple of *idiotas.*"

"Yeah," I say, thinking how that fits with what Gloria said, but at the Cork'n Bottle they weren't wearing them. "That's them."

Fate looks at me sideways to see if I'm done with her.

When I nod, he says, "We appreciate you coming."

"Like I said, he needs to *go,*" Elena says one more time to Fate. "And before he does, you tell that disloyal motherfucker I told you who it was. You tell him it was me. Elena. I want *my name* on his brain when you put a bullet through that shit."

She used to be so shy in elementary. She had glasses. Liked to read. Wouldn't say shit to teachers. Wouldn't say shit to anybody.

"Damn." Apache tosses a look at Clever. "A woman scorned and all that, right?"

Elena's eyes flash at him with a hard kind of hate.

"Yup," she says.

After she leaves with the kid, I tell Fate how I know what I know.

I tell him about the Cork'n Bottle too. I hand him the piece of paper with the address and the phone number on it.

Apache pops first. "Wait, what? Like, what are the odds of that? I mean you're like the luckiest—"

Fate cuts him off. "Small town, *primo.*"

He says it cuz he's talking to Apache.

But he's looking at me.

He says, "Ready to ride?"

11

Clever's driving Apache's Cutlass, Big Fate's up front, and Apache's next to me in the backseat. We talk it out on the way. We talk up the idea of me calling Joker and being all sexy while asking him to meet me somewhere, but then Clever says if we did that, he might come alone and we miss our chance to get the other two that did Ernesto. And that's not acceptable. Not to anybody.

Somebody says something about it being better just to show up and use my element of surprise. And then Clever says what I been thinking all night, that I'm like a spy or something. It's still true.

I've changed and everything. Lorraine moped around when she was done getting mad at me about Elena, then she just sniffled a lot, trying not to cry as she put me in some sort of chiffon thing that feels like I'm wearing a droopy umbrella around my waist. Only battle I won on was shoes. I got white chucks. Flat soles so I can run. I lost on everything else.

Like, I'm wearing pearls. I'm wearing little white gloves that end in a lace kind of frill around my wrist like I'm some *quincé* princess who wants to be Cinderella or some shit. The gloves are important though. No fingerprints.

Fate's not so sure about sending me in alone. I can tell by how quiet he is. He wants everybody. All in. Special Forces shit.

But I say, "Ain't no safe option, Fate. If it's me, then it's my time. That doesn't mean it's got to be everybody else's too."

I don't have to say that Ernesto wasn't a player, that dude had no juice. That he's mine to get back for. And I definitely don't say me going in is better than Ray scaring up an AK-47 from some big brothers and putting a whole bunch of air holes in somebody's house and then another, and another.

So we put our heads together.

Fate says, "You go in. You mark them. Hang back a bit if they're not together. Blend in with the crowd. See if you can't wait to get them together in a clump so you can get them close. Harder to miss then. And a lot easier to get it done quicker."

We pull up to a house I never seen before and a dude fast-walks off the porch to the car. When Apache puts his hand out the window, the dude drops something in Apache's hand and turns back around.

It's four bullets, all 9 millimeter.

I see them glint up and then Clever pulls out and we're gone, headed to that address Joker gave me, the address where he's supposed to be.

Apache hands the bullets to Fate and I watch him load the Glock full before he hands it to me. I squeeze it and the taped handle feels weird in my hand, grippy. Fate shows me where the safety is and how to click it off with my thumb, so I do.

There's all kinds of rules for how to do this. It's almost a list.

When I pop, I gotta count the rounds.

"Keeps you focused," Fate says. "Keeps you from just squeezing till you're out."

No cowboy shit. Close range is best.

Don't aim for the head first. Aim for the body. It's bigger.

Cluster for the heart. Finish in the head if you got time. If you're close.

When I'm done—when *it's* done—I drop the weapon. No excuses.

Apache will have my back then, and then we run, and then Fate has our backs, like a chain almost, and then we hit the car.

That's the plan cuz Fate says so.

I stare at the thing in my hands. It's the heaviest pistol I ever held, all black and shiny on top and white from its tape on the grip. And right then I think how some poor bastard is going to get his house raided tonight or tomorrow or whenever people quit rioting in the fucking streets and the sheriffs have time to figure out it was his gun used in a shooting. Soon enough anyway. Vikings always come.

If I do like I'm told and drop this shit in the grass or wherever and sheriffs find it and trace the serial number to find out it belongs to some guy legal, they'll go into his house at 4 A.M. behind one of them battering rams and wake him up with a shotgun to his head, wake his kids up, his wife too, and they'll cuff him on the living room rug in front of his family like he's a murderer, but I don't feel bad. Hell no. Fuck that guy and his gun safe.

He'll get exonerated eventually. He'll go home right after. He'll be grateful and happy and free.

Not like Ernesto.

Maybe they haven't even zipped him up into his bag yet. Maybe he's not even at the morgue. Like, maybe he's still in the alley with my flannel on his face. That thought burns the worst.

But then Clever turns on the radio to KRLA and "I Wish It Would Rain" is playing. Fucking Temptations. That shit's not even fair.

Apache nudges me and opens his hands up. He's got a vial of liquid in one and a cigarette in the other.

"You need to get wet, Payasita?"

He's not looking at me. He's uncapping it, dipping just the cig tip, and closing the vial back up after.

He says it makes it easier.

Light stabs in through the window as we speed past streetlamps. I look at the tip, how it's stained and dark.

I say, "Makes what easier?"

He won't even look at me.

He just shrugs and says, "Everything."

12

It's so dark and the party's so loud that nobody notices us take over the street outside: not Clever parking half a block down, not Apache getting out and crossing the street to post up at somebody's mailbox, and not Fate standing on the other side halfway in between.

I'm feeling hotter than if I was sitting on top of a bonfire when I get out the car but, goddamn, a little breeze kicking up on my face feels good. I wipe the back of one of my gloves up over my forehead and find out I'm sweating. Wow. I don't know why but that shit's funny to me all of a sudden.

Doesn't stay funny for long though, cuz it turns out Clever was right. In less than a minute we find the Ford Ranchero, the one with the trailer hitch. It's got a dent in its bumper.

I stare at that for a second wondering if my brother's head made that mark and how I feel about that, but I don't feel much of anything. Apache told me that's the PCP. It numbs you right out, he said.

When I turn to the house, I'm thinking how it's late enough that whoever's gonna be at the party is already there. The street's real quiet except for music. And voices.

I hear people out back so instead of going through the house, I walk around and see if there's a fence or anything between me and it.

There isn't.

It's just a stretch of concrete that extends up from the driveway and guides me into a backyard. It's a good backyard. Half grass, half deck. A little roof of red-looking wood that extends off the house and over the patio. Under that, near the house, is Joker.

He's got a beer in his hand. One of his boys is behind him.

The other leans against the far side of the patio by the back fence, maybe fifteen feet away. He's rolling something in his hands.

I cross the grass toward Joker, ignoring people's looks.

Like, it's crazy how calm I feel when I think, *Oh, I'll just kill two, and walk to the other.* Whatever, you know? No big deal.

Cuz I don't really feel like waiting right now. I feel like shooting. For Ernesto.

Joker sees me and kind of bugs out. He gets a big smile on his face, like he's so happy to see me, like he's so fucking glad I came.

I can tell, and I like it, cuz it makes it so much better that this motherfucker doesn't realize I'm the angel of death.

"Hey, I thought you weren't coming," he says, all enthusiastic. "Where's your cousin at? She here?"

I reach into my purse.

And I bring out Lorraine's lip gloss.

I do my lips up in front of him, all sexy, with my eyes on him. I think of doing it for Elena.

As I'm putting it back in, I wrap my hand around the Glock, around its tape.

I smile the sweetest smile I got at Joker, one of them I-been-thinking-about-you smiles.

And I say, "For Ernesto."

When I whip the gun free, the top sight snags on the zipper. But only a moment. Less than a second.

That's when time slows down. It isn't bullshit.

It does happen.

Joker makes a face where his forehead gets bumpy and he opens his mouth like he's shocked as he tilts his head.

He turns too, looks away, toward the house.

I give it to him in the ear. Right below it.

That shit goes clean through his skull, puts a bunch of him on the people behind.

And that's good. I like that.

It makes sense cuz Ernesto didn't have his ear either when he got it. That's justice right there.

Joker's nearest homeboy starts ducking, reaching inside his jacket. He only gets his hand halfway in before I blast on him too.

The piece booms like a cannon in my palm, shakes my whole body.

Dude's chest opens up as he stumbles backward. He gets one more in the top of the head when I'm close, like, *blau.*

That's what it sounds like. A German word, kinda. That's what I think it sounds like.

I don't see people, not really. I see scrambling.

I see waves of clothes rippling and rolling back. Like I'm Moses. Like the motherfucking Red Sea's parting just for me.

I turn toward the fence as Joker's other boy is making a break.

I shoot and miss.

I shoot and hit a girl.

I shoot and hit him in the leg. He falls off the fence. And I laugh.

That's six, I think. *Is that six?*

I do the add-up, that mental math.

Yeah. That's six spent.

I think he screams, but I can't hear anything. My ears are ringing like crazy.

I'm standing over him saying, "For Ernesto."

Halfway through him saying, "Who?" I blast.

I miss. From four feet away, I miss. The next one doesn't though.

It goes through his eye, out the back of his skull, and makes a hole in the bottom of the fence that's golf ball big and red. Real red.

That's kind of funny too.

But damn, I'm hot. Burning up. I need water bad.

I don't even feel my finger on the trigger, but I shoot him again in the collarbone. At least I think I do.

His chest doesn't explode or nothing, just shows a hole that turns red right away.

That's nine or it's ten.

The backyard is almost empty now. People are smashing through the sliding glass door into the house, and past them I see dudes trying to get out.

Dudes wanting to get at me.

Drop the gun, I think. *Run.*

So I do.

My foot slips in the grass and I go down in somebody's blood puddle. I don't know whose. I think that's funny too.

But I'm up fast and it's bad cuz a dude with a beard and a big fucking pistol is shoving through the door, lowering the thing at me.

I can't feel my feet. But they move. I'm sweating like I've been running for hours.

Out of nowhere, Apache's there, walking toward me, like magic. He's got the .357 and he opens up on the dude. And he must've got him cuz we're not getting followed anymore and he's pulling me, yanking me forward, saving me.

I look back and there's another body on the grass and two more guys coming out the house.

We turn the corner, hit the driveway, the sidewalk.

When Joker's homies turn the corner of the garage, Fate opens up with the shotgun. Shit's so loud it sounds like a plane crash. And I laugh.

It goes like that, like planned, cuz we're in the car and driving. But I don't know which way's which.

I feel thin like Kleenex. I want to laugh again. I want to tell the whole story of what it looked like, what it felt like.

And then I feel like I need to puke maybe.

"You got them motherfuckers?" Fate wants to know and I want to answer.

I can't. I try but my mouth won't work.

I never shot nobody before.

I mean, I shot plenty. Targets and birds and all that.

But I never shot no *body* before.

It's different.

"You got to fix up," Fate says and yanks the rearview so he can see me. He stares at me hard. Nobody argues with that face. Never.

The car feels like it's moving faster than fast, but I know Clever's going the speed limit.

That was part of the plan too.

I nod.

I know I need to fix up.

But my arms don't move. They don't do what he wants. Or what I want.

Fate tells Apache, "Fucking do that shit."

Apache lifts my arms up, smashes a hoodie down over my dress.

He swipes the makeup off my face with a cloth, pinches my earrings out, and mashes a ballcap down on my head before pulling the hood up.

They're looking for a girl shooter.

If they're looking. And even if they were, it wouldn't matter anyways. I don't look like that anymore. Not from outside.

But, shit, sheriffs sure ain't looking. They're all on TV. I laugh at that too.

I laugh at how they're busy in Florence, Watts, putting out Los Angeles's fucking fires tonight. You think they care if some all involved shit got handled in Lynwood? No way. They're prolly glad.

Glad they don't have to investigate. Glad they can just put on body armor and march into crowds instead.

I pick my pager up off the floor. I've got it in my hand. All's I can think about is *mi mamá*. All I can think about is her worried face.

And I feel the sadness fall on me like a blanket, making it so I can't breathe.

"Fate," I say, and my voice's real small.

He's watching the road. "What?"

"How am I gonna tell her what happened?"

Fate doesn't get it at first. He looks at Apache but Apache's looking out the window, so Fate looks back at me.

He gets it then, but I can tell he doesn't have the answer when his mouth drops open in the rearview and stays like that.

We're on Imperial, cruising by the swap meet, when Fate says, "You tell your *madre* you did justice. That's what you fucking tell her."

1

I don't even know what Fate's fucking problem is. I only did what he would've done. Back in the day, he made his name doing what I did and way worse. He's all punishing me now cuz of what happened with me shooting up the front of that club, trying to check me or something by making me do his errands.

I been overseeing distribution for a year or more. I'm past this shit. Serious, pickups are for new booty motherfuckers like Oso. Truth is, he'd *been* doing them before Big Fate decided it was on me. Today he sees them riots going on TV and out of nowhere decides to send me out of town on a run. Sure, he says the right thing, like, "We're sending you cuz the cops are everywhere else," but he knows me too well. He could see in my eyes how bad I wanted to get up in some shit. I mean, who couldn't use a new TV, right?

Only good thing about this trip, and I mean the *only* thing, is I get to drive Fate's car, this big old Chevy from the '70s. Swear to God, the engine on this thing, it just eats up the 10 Freeway. We *fly* east. It's Monterey Park, then El Monte, then West Covina before I even know my foot's on the gas.

Oh, but you know what though? There's all kinds of rules I gotta go by now. Cuz Fate fucking says so. Number one is lay off the sherm. Yeah, right. Number two, I always got to drive the speed limit. To that I'm like, try to make me, motherfucker. Number three, I'm not supposed to bring nobody on my runs cuz I need to be better at being alone and reliable.

But how's he even gonna know what I do, so long as everything gets done? Besides, it ain't like I'm stupid enough to do any of that shit after I pick up. Well, except, I have to break the one about not bringing anybody, but it's not like it's that bad. Fate has at least met my homeboy Baseball, so I don't think he'd be mad if he ever found out. Not that he's going to though. I mean, I'm not telling. And Baseball isn't either.

It's obvious how he got his name. His head looks exactly like a baseball, like with stitching and everything, cuz his dad got in a bad car wreck when he was little and put him through the windshield. He ended up having half his scalp stapled onto the top of his head and his hair grows funny around that scar now. He's sensitive about it too. He wears a Los Doyers cap low, never takes it off.

Baseball's a fiend for stories. He's always wanting to hear about the club again, always wanting another detail or wondering how it felt for me to do what I did or some shit like that.

He says, "Did that dude really call your sister a *manflora*?"

I'm done talking about that shit, and I show him by sinking down into the seat a little more and rocking my wrist on top of the wheel. I don't even look at him, like to show him I'm above it, you know?

Besides, he's heard a thousand times how that dude said he was gonna rape my sister, Payasa, how he was gonna stick a knife up her pussy, and then, when he said my address, like my actual address, even the zip code and everything, I just lost my shit, man. Went out to the car and waited until he came out with his girl and I just let go. She got it. He didn't.

Oh well. Can't be a hundred percent all the time. No regrets in this crazy life. I knew they might come back on me though.

I started stashing guns in the house after that. Every room, man. Can't help but take that shit serious. I even keep *two* in the bath-room. Got one in the medicine cabinet, one under the sink. Something ever happen to Lu, I'll go Rambo on that shit. Everybody knows I'm good for it. Hurt my family and you're done. I'll shoot you in church. I'll shoot your mom in her sleep. I don't give a fuck. The streets know it. Lil Mosco's not to be fucked with. How else you think I got my respect? They don't call you nothing if you sit home playing fucking Neo-Geo all day.

Baseball's trying to start the conversation again. "Hey, did you know the big homies put the word out on Manny Sanchez cuz of what happened way out in Norwalk?"

"Like, Elena's brother, Manny?" I know of him but I don't know him. "I fucking went to elementary with that girl. What's he go by now?"

"Lil Man."

It's not ringing any bells. Swear to God, Baseball won't shut the fuck up about the big dogs. He idolizes them. What's that saying? Can't see the trees for the forest, or whatever? That's him. No idea about the big picture.

So I'm like, "Yeah, well, all them rumbles about a peace treaty is about making money, right?"

"It's about *raza*, man," he says. "Being united. Being a fucking army."

I take my hand off the wheel and steer with my knee for two seconds. That gives me the freedom to smack the back of his baseball-shaped head.

His eyes come up mad and I laugh in his face.

"You even know how stupid you sound right now? Real gangsters don't give a fuck about *raza*. They only care about money. Shit, it's what I would do if I was there. You would too. Say what you say to advance your goals. That's it. Get a dude to focus on something way in the distance and then put your fucking hand in his pocket. It's genius, *vato*."

"I mean, like, maybe." Baseball rubs the back of his head. "But getting a green light on you is fucking real, bro. Sometimes they put whole *varrios* on."

"Why don't you tell me what happened with Manny already? Shit. Talking so much and never getting to a point!"

"Okay, so he did that one drive-by, killed that grandma on her porch by accident. How the fuck didn't you hear about that?"

I smash him with a look. "Shit, man, how did *you* hear about it? You ain't even involved yet and you spout more stories than a *veterano*."

"I got ears." He's kind of pouting and shit. "Everybody knows it."

He gets quiet after that, not saying anything until we hit the outskirts of Riverside. That's when he finally says, "You ever worry they might put a light on you for that girl or what?"

"Never happen, fool." But then I'm thinking about it. I'm wondering if they might. "Wasn't even a drive-by. That shit was a walk-up."

"Raza's *raza*, man. Player or not, she was that. She was our people."

I'm like, "She ain't our fucking people. Don't be stupid."

But then I'm thinking, like, *was she?* I don't feel like talking no more, so I turn on the radio to keep him from responding but Art Laboe's nothing but static this far out. It's a shame too. This drive's perfect for them oldie sounds, but I put that new Kid Frost into the tape deck instead. Shit only came out like last week, so I don't know if it's no *Hispanic Causing Panic* yet, but it's good. I been listening to "Mi Vida Loca" on side 2 like nonstop since it came out.

Man, I never told nobody this, but I love the desert at night. I roll the window down just to see the stars and feel the wind, but a big rig goes by and I have to seal it up. Two exits later, I pull off the freeway, and we zigzag up onto a hill and cut through a giant batch of tract homes all built on a slant. Every one's two or three stories tall. They're houses with attics, you know? Every one with the same colors, like sand or wood or whatever, but nothing else. Pretty much the American dream if it wasn't for the hourlong commute both ways every day.

"Work in L.A.," I say, "live way the fuck away."

"*La neta.*" Baseball agrees with me cuz he knows it's the truth, and like that, we're friends again.

We stay that way through the front door, past the fake plants, and into the living room. There's a kitchen right next to it, separated by a little wall with stools up against it. My connect is standing in there, mixing a drink and looking all sexy and shit.

Through her thin silk robe, I can see a green-and-blue flowery bikini. She's white, forties-ish, all tan and hippied out with a red flower in her hair, but she's got good meat on her. Good thighs. Good ass. Tits to match. She's solid.

I didn't believe when she first told me, but she's actually a social worker. No shit, that's her job. Puts her in touch with the right kind of people, I guess. Her old man's up at Men's Central Jail in L.A., but she runs his business on the outside. I don't know her real name. Behind her back everybody I ever heard calls her Scarlet. I'm sure she knows and doesn't mind it.

The television's on loud and her son's sitting in front of it, leaning kind of hard toward the screen. It's on basketball for a second, then it's on news, and I blink and try to figure out which part is burning now, but then it's back on basketball. He's my age, maybe older. I can't tell. He's white like T-shirts and laundry, like he never goes outside. The skin under his eyes is all blue with veins.

"Hey," I say to him.

"Hey," he says back, not taking eyes off the screen.

I turn back to Scarlet and tell her, "This's my boy Baseball."

She nods up at him after taking a sip. "Why do they call you that?"

I answer for him. "Cuz his *huevos* are bigger than baseballs."

She gives me a you're-so-full-of-shit look, but I just shrug and then she looks curious. Scarlet will fuck anybody. She ain't particular. Which is exactly why I brought Baseball.

I owe him some money and he's never had any from a woman, so I figured it was an easy trade. Cuz, shit, you know I already hit it. It was okay. Would've been better if she wasn't smoking the whole time. Shit was gross, man. Kind of made her pussy taste sour too, if you wanna know the truth.

She comes out of the kitchen pantry with bags and we flow the exchange cuz we've already done it a few times before.

It goes through quick. I give her the envelope. She gives me two big brown grocery bags she packed special. I don't know what all's in there. Definitely sherm, coke, and heroin. Not sure what else. Maybe meth. Whatever Fate wants. I'm just the pickup man tonight.

I see Scarlet eyeing Baseball, so I don't bother thanking her. I know what's coming. Guess her son does too. I can already see him kind of cringing on the red couch. She shoots a look his way before opening her mouth.

"You said you would take out the trash—"

She doesn't even get to finish her sentence before he turns bright red and shouts, "Shut the fuck up, Mom! *God*, I heard you the first thirty-two times."

He's not even looking at her. He's focused on the TV. But me? I'm dying inside, man. All mortified and shit. I'd *never* say that to my mom! Fucking white people are crazy, I swear.

"I haven't given you the tour," Scarlet says to Baseball, but she's staring at her son, all mad. Her robe's already open. One of her bikini straps is down. She's pulling a cigarette out, turning, and guiding Baseball up the stairs. Takes a minute or two before she's moaning, but it's fast. That's just her speed, I guess.

The television's back on basketball. Lakers and Portland, looks like. The volume's getting cranked up too. I don't blame him. If my mom was a whore like that, I couldn't even stand to be in the same state, much less the same house. Shit. You know that's the truth.

I feel bad for him. I do. But when he gets up off the couch all quiet and goes to the door that leads to the garage and presses the garage door button and it raises, I'm thinking, like, *What the fuck? Is he letting in a dog or something?*

I'm still wondering why someone would do that when that same door leading to the garage cracks open and three cops stealth in. Big dudes. Dudes with shotguns. They got vests that say LAPD all big on the front. *Damn.*

Man, there ain't shit I can do! They're on top of me so fast, putting my face in the fucking carpet, handcuffing my wrists too hard, and pulling me up on my knees. But that's when I'm wondering why the hell they didn't identify themselves as cops. Why they didn't shout.

On the television, the crowd's screaming. The clock's ticking down.

Right then, Scarlet's kid walks to the pantry. He opens it and shows the guys where the shit's hid at. He points at my bags too. And he makes damn sure to point upstairs and hold two fingers in the air. It hits me then.

This shit is a motherfucking *robbery*.

Behind me, somebody says, "You're on the *lista*, Little Fly."

My lungs stop working. Hold up. *What?*

When one of the dudes circles in front of me, I see tattoos on his neck, behind his ears too. He's bald and has a mustache, Bronson style. It's a sick feeling I get then, cuz these ain't cops.

These *ain't* cops.

And I feel extra stupid cuz I'm in Riverside and the LAPD vests *still* worked on me. It's not even the same fucking jurisdiction, homes!

"We'll pay you," I say. "Whatever you want. We'll make it right."

That makes them laugh, hands over their mouths, all quiet on purpose.

Above our heads, Scarlet moans and moans.

"All right, who did it then?" I try to wet my lips, but I'm dry and can't get up any spit. "Who set my ass up? I'm begging you, man! Tell me that much."

Sure as shit looks like Scarlet didn't do it, and there's no fucking way this was her son's idea. I mean, if it wasn't, then there's only two choices and one of them is Fate. Fuck. That one hurts too much. But maybe it was Scarlet's old man, I think. There's sense to that one. Maybe he was just tired of her fucking around, and maybe she fucked up his money too. I got no idea how connected he is, how big he might be. I just can't shake the feeling this is some two-birds-one-stone shit.

In the game on TV, somebody takes a shot. It misses, but a team-mate's there for a rebound. The crowd goes fucking crazy when it banks in. The whistle blows right after that as the other team calls time-out.

"You set yourself up, *pequeña mosca*. Nobody to blame but you. You should've been shooting *mayates* if you wanted to shoot some-body."

Right now, Scarlet's getting close, screaming like her pussy's about to explode. Out the corner of my eye, I see one of the shot-gunners creep upstairs. Damn. That's some cold shit. She doesn't even know what's next.

Me, though, at least I see it coming. At least I know it's last words time. At least I get that respect.

"Tell my sister I love her. My brother too. And my mom. Tell them."

"Sure," the voice behind me says, "we'll get right to that."

The shotgun goes off upstairs, just boom. It sounds like a fuck-ing rocket hitting the house. Up there, Baseball screams and calls my name out. But before he says any more, there's another boom and it's all silence.

It's only like that for a second or two before the restart whistle from the basketball game cuts into me and I jolt as the crowd gets to their feet, cheering all loud in anticipation. When the whistle goes again, and the ball gets inbounded and some guy I never heard of chucks the ball up from way behind the three-point line, even the announcers hold their breaths.

Big and round and cold, I feel the shotgun barrel kiss on the back of my neck. I try saying a prayer. I try saying, *Our Father who art in heaven* and all that, I try saying, *hallowed be thy name*, but the right words get stuck down in my chest and I can't find them, so I just breathe out, letting go of all the air inside me as I close my eyes instead.

DAY 2
THURSDAY

YEAH, THEY THINK A LOT ABOUT WHAT HAPPENED TO RODNEY KING.

I MEAN, THAT'S THE *LAST* THING ON THEIR MINDS!

THIS IS JUST—

THIS IS PARTY TIME OUT HERE.

THIS IS ROCK AND ROLL IN L.A.

—JOE MCMAHAN, *7 LIVE EYEWITNESS NEWS*

JOSÉ LAREDO,
A.K.A. BIG FATE,
A.K.A. BIG FE

APRIL 30, 1992

8:14 A.M.

1

Payasa's couch is from the 1970s, lumpy as fuck. I didn't get any kind of sleep from laying there all night, gripping a gun and listening to every car going by, certain each one is Joker's gang coming back on us—until it isn't, until it drives right by and then I worry about the next one.

The fingers on my right hand are all cramped up, so I shake them out as I squint at yellow light coming through the tops of the front windows, up and over old striped curtains. It's morning. I know that.

I couldn't've been down for more than a few hours cuz Payasa had to go see her mama after, just to tell her what happened with Ernesto and how she did justice to the ones that did it, but what came next was ugly. Like, *Exorcist* ugly. Pitching, crying, screaming. Names of saints getting called out. Payasita getting big blame, but Lil Mosco getting more. We only left when her auntie came over— the one who can't talk cuz she bit her tongue clean through as a little girl when a horse kicked her in Mexico—and she started making *pozole* at whatever o'clock in the morning.

On the ride home I drive us back by Ernesto to see if the coroners scooped him up yet and they hadn't. Guess the city was too busy being on fire cuz his body was still there in the alley with his sister's striped black-and-white flannel covering his face like them sad flags that get draped over soldiers' coffins. If that shit doesn't drill a hole in your stomach, then nothing will, homes.

I hear the fridge door open and close, then Clever sliding around the kitchen in his house shoes cuz he's too lazy to pick his feet up. He's hungry, but he'll never get more than juice for himself. He'll wait for me to cook before he eats anything. Eggs, maybe, even though we only got four. *Papas.* We got no bacon left. No tomatoes neither. There's still some *chorizo*, but it's cold. Didn't end up eating any of it on account of last night.

Payasa's door is closed. She's still in there with Lorraine. They've been quiet all night. Cemetery quiet, I call it. I got to know if she's okay, but I don't look forward to her maybe finding out about some shit I did, shit that's been eating at me so much it's bubbling up.

And it burns kind of, and I don't want to think about it right now if I don't have to, so I walk over to the TV and slap it on, dial down the volume, and retreat back to the couch, expecting the same as every other half-wise gangster in L.A., you know? Straight law and order.

Like, cops out in full force with their vests on, locking shit down. Sheriffs throwing shackles on fools, and slamming them into caged backseats so they can haul their asses off to process. Statements. Fingerprints. Photos. Jail. You know, just a bunch of thuggish motherfuckers in uniform running a big-ass net along the streets and scooping up the *idiotas*, the drunk ones, the drugged-up ones— the ones that stayed way too late at the party and now gotta pay for what everybody else did.

But when the screen hums on and the crispy tube static fades, a picture forms from all those blobby colors getting mashed together. A picture forms when they sharpen into shapes. Into city blocks. Into running people. Into running people *carrying* shit. And I don't see what I'm expecting. Not even close. I see the exact fucking opposite.

And I blink to make sure I'm actually seeing it jump off in Compton, where all kinds of shit is laying out in the street. Every-thing looking like a tornado hit it. Clothes, toilet paper, smashed TVs, drink cans, some shit that looks like cotton candy blowing around but can't be. No way. There's busted glass everywhere, on sidewalks, over curbs, and into the street, looking like shiny confetti you never wanna touch.

And fires. Shit. There's fires in garbage cans. Fires in minimarkets. Fires in fucking *gas* stations, man! There's fires on top of fires, and they're spiraling into the sky like they're holding it up. Table legs, I call it. That's what the smoke looks like.

The news switches to a camera on a helicopter, and the sky— man, the sky isn't even blue or that halfway kind of gray we get on the worst smog days. It looks like wet concrete. A gray so dark it's almost black. It looks heavy as fuck.

That's when it hits me I'm staring at a war zone. In South Central.

It's like somebody packed up all the shit I been seeing in Lebanon almost my whole life, put it in a box, shipped it over, and opened up that chaos in my backyard. It's some Gaza Strip shit. *La neta*, homes.

And this whole entire scene says the same to me as it says to every other knucklehead who ever thought bad thoughts across this whole city: now's your fucking day, homie. *Felicidades*, you won the lottery!

Go out there and get wild, it says. Come and take what you can, it says. If you're bad enough, if you're strong enough, come out and take it. Devil's night in broad daylight, I call it.

Cuz the world we live in's completely flipped now. Up's down. Down's up. Bad is fucking *good*. And badges don't mean shit. Cuz cops don't get to own the city today. *We* do.

I feel, like, a jolt of electricity go up and down my neck and I can't pick the phone up fast enough. I page five, six homeboys to get their asses over here as quick as my stiff-ass fingers can dial. I go through numbers from memory until I hit about twelve and then stop cuz I know they'll spread the word how it needs to be spread. We need wheels. We need to roll deep. Already right now it looks like we're behind.

Step one is to jump shit off in Lynwood. You know, get it chaotic like how it's jumping off in Compton cuz that'll spread cops out thinner than they already are. I'm planning shit in my head then.

Places to hit. Shit to gather. Where to hide it. I pick up the phone again and page Lil Creeper.

If ever there was a day made for that fucking *cucaracha*, it's this one. He was put on this earth for ripping and running and stuffing dope in himself and nothing else. Even wasted, even half asleep, *nobody* gets locks off like he gets locks off. Shit might as well be aluminum foil in his hands. Nobody else can look at an iron gate and, in two seconds, figure out how to bust it or get it open like he can.

When the phone beeps for me to key my number in, I do. And I leave my usual code at the end so he knows to call back quick cuz it's serious, and if he doesn't, well, that's when bad shit happens. That's when a homie gets sent to pick his ass up.

Clever scrapes into the living room then, sipping at his juice from one of them Dick Tracy plastic cups you get for eating at McDonald's. He puts his eyes on the screen and stops dead as I hang the phone up in its cradle.

We both watch a pharmacy on Vermont get torn the fuck up while some news dude on the corner just goes on about how this shit doesn't have anything to do with Rodney King, or the verdict, and how it's about poor people with no morals getting an opportunity to do bad and how he can't believe they're taking it. And I'm like, *really?*

But he still goes on about how this isn't his America, the one he knows and loves and believes in. I have to chuckle at that ignorant, been-living-so-long-in-the-burbs-he-doesn't-even-know-what-the-fuck's-real-anymore shit, cuz that's when Clever cracks up and says what I been thinking in my head the whole time.

"Welcome to *my* America, *cabrón*."

2

Fate's not so common a name, not in Spanish. I never heard of anybody else with it. I get asked where it's from sometimes, how'd I get named that, but I never say it's cuz I caught a bullet when I was twenty, and I'm not gonna tell you who shot it or from what click cuz I didn't tell the sheriffs that neither when they asked. It was a big fucking caliber though, and something must've been defective with the bullet or casing cuz even from twenty feet away, it didn't go all the way through me. It stuck.

Didn't go more than an inch deep, but I bled on my neighbor Mrs. Rubio's front walk like you wouldn't believe. All's I remember from that besides the ambulance ride with the fucking sloppy EMT who couldn't find my veins for shit is the *abuela* herself coming up all calm and sitting Indian style next to me, fanning her blue dress out and putting my hand on top of it, on the lace fabric in her lap, as she talked about how I had *una* fate *grande* and I'd live. Right then, I thought she was saying it wasn't my fate to die, but when she said it again, I heard it right. *Una fe grande.* She wasn't talking about fate at all, but a big faith instead. It was too late though, my brain had caught the word *fate* and liked the sound of it, and I promised myself that if I lived, that'd be my name.

I never told Payasa the whole story and I can't think why now. She knows about the bullet, sure, and she knows an *abuela* was there, but not that the granny gave me that name, even by accident. I guess sometimes if you spend enough time with people, you don't question them, not where they come from, not where they got their name, or how. It just is. It's just accepted. But I kind of want to tell her now.

Payasa asked me a long time ago if I'm sorry sometimes for what I done. I told her no then, but it's yes. For sure it's a yes. I don't regret anything though. Me, I'm a soldier. I always went where I was needed and I was always down. *Always.* Even as a lil homie, when circles got called out in the dead end by the park, older homeboys passed me up every time cuz they knew I was down. Nobody's ever had to call my ass out. Not even once.

"You're cool," they'd say, or, "This fucking homeboy's down," and then they'd use my ass as an example to the other lil homies on how to be. That always felt good.

Right now, there's people here in the living room that need

telling what to do. I count 15 out of our 116—and that's not even including the lil homies outside trying to be down and earn their stripes. I look at them, all the faces in this room, and I think, this is why I do what I do. For them. *La Clica. Mi Familia*. All of it for them. They're why I had to give Lil Mosco up.

Yeah, that shit's true. I did it. Payasa won't never hear it from me, cuz what's there to say about it? But the truth's the truth. And I'm sorry, for real, but I don't regret that shit neither.

But right now though, I do wish she could jump inside my head and read my mind, see through my eyes, and understand, like, in an instant, the decision I had to make when the big homies came to me and sat me down and said Lil Mosco's name was in the fucking hat. The green light was on, they said, and I had to choose: either one knucklehead that keeps fucking up, or the whole entire crew. That was that, you know? You can't argue with them, or tell them how they're wrong. He had to go. You take that shit on the chin like a boxer that knows he's got to take a fucking dive.

If I didn't send Lil Mosco to Riverside, it would've been open season on us. All of us. Everywhere. All the time. That shit's a fact. And 1 was not equal to, or greater than, 116 last I checked. Even I know that and I quit school halfway through eighth grade.

But Joker and them getting Ernesto in the same day? That shit tore me *up*.

It was the worst possible timing there ever was, and when that Serrato kid came to the door at first, I almost spilled to Payasa cuz I thought the kid was talking about Lil Mosco and I was tripping on how that could even be possible and it didn't hit me till a few seconds later that it wasn't! It hit me like a sucker punch is what it did, that it was Ernie laying dead for no good reason. And when I knew that, I knew I should've given up Lil Mosco sooner and that burned in me. I also knew I had to do whatever I could to let Payasa do what she had to do. I let her overstep some bounds to do some shit I never would've let no *chola* do cuz that was some vengeance shit and it was righteous.

But Lil Mosco? Shit. I *had* to give him up. Payasa knew better than anyone how he had a bad head on his shoulders. Which was why I gave so many rules, you know? Number one, don't do no fucking drugs. Number two, drive the speed limit, fool. And third, and most especially, don't take nobody with you. Had to make sure it was only him he dragged into it. And I even gave him my car to do the drive in.

Lil Mosco threw himself in that hat. That's just a fact. And I had to make sure we didn't end up in it too. Cuz it wasn't just us. It was our families. The big homies could do it if they wanted to. They've done it before. There's no going against that. It wasn't ever a real choice. It was a no-brainer. Like, think about how it would've gone if a big homie showed up at Payasa's mom's new house, rang the bell, and put a gun to the peephole when he saw the light behind it get blocked by her head? Shit. Makes me sick just thinking about it.

There's another rule I got, one body is not worth everybody. No matter what.

If Payasa would've come out her door before, maybe I could've pulled her aside before the homies came through and made her see the sense to it.

But Ernesto happening? I got no words for that shit. Nobody saw that coming, but that's this crazy life. It comes at you how it wants to, whether you're ready or not, and sometimes it takes what it shouldn't. Sometimes, that's the only thing you can count on it doing—taking.

Her door's still closed. She doesn't even say shit when I knock, so I'm just looking down at every gun in the house sitting in a pile on the coffee table in front of the couch. There's twenty. It's not enough if we're gonna protect ourselves from whatever Joker's big brother ends up coming back with.

So I'm scheming, thinking we could go over and just bash our way into Western Auto cuz they got guns in the back. *Pistolas.* Clips. All that. Why at an auto store? I never wondered that before. I guess just cuz it makes more money than shocks and brake pads. That's that ghetto economy for you. Right when I'm thinking that, the phone rings. I'm expecting it to be Lil Creeper when I pick up. It's not.

It's Sunny from the gun store on Long Beach. As soon as I hear his voice, I know ethicals are out the window. He says they only got two other guys on shift with him, and they've got the lights off. They're supposed to be protecting the guns, but for a price he'll leave the front door open and we can roll in.

I say, "How much?"

"Uh," he says and pauses long enough to pull a random number out of his ass. "Three thousand."

"Sure," I say. Like this motherfucker is ever getting *that*.

"Cash," he says.

"What the fuck else am I gonna pay you with? A check?" I say, "Just make sure the front's open, fool."

Avaro, I call it. Money-grubbing greed.

Sunny's just looking for a come-up. He's selling his job out, selling out the people he works with. I can't respect that shit. See, what Sunny doesn't know is that he can negotiate on any other day but today. When up's down, I don't got to pay him shit. More important, I get to come back on him for being a *culero* and sleeping with my older sister on prom night '86, and for giving her the clap. Fuck whoever he's homies with. Today, he catches one.

I don't tell him that though. I just hang up the phone and cock my gun. It's one of them old army Colts. It says, *Calibre 45* on the barrel. It also says, *Rimless Smokeless*. I think it used to be somebody's grandpa's but that don't matter. It's mine now. It's been mine for almost a year.

I look at the clock. It's quarter to ten and Creeper still hasn't shown.

Hijo de su chingada madre, I think. He must be holed up in some motel, having already spent the money I paid him for that gun and less than a full clip of bullets. He put that shit right into veins. Guaranteed.

I'm deciding if I should give him another minute when Payasa stumbles out of her room, says what's up to Clever while he's finishing up his kit, grabs Apache, whispers some shit to him, and pulls him outside, almost to where the little homies are standing in a circle on the lawn.

I'm not happy to see that, but it's not like I tell her not to. Out the window, I see her and Apache sharing a cigarette. They're getting wet again. Guaranteed.

Every puff of that shit is just running from the real pain. I understand, especially for Ernesto I understand, but I can't recommend it. In my experience, when you do your diligence, and even after, it's best to do it sober. That way, you can face up to that shit you done and own it. That way, it's easier to know the motherfuckers deserved what they got. If Payasa ever asks, I'll tell her. Only then though.

One minute turns into two and still no sign of Creeper. On a day like today I can't spare no homies to go track him down.

So I say, "Fuck it," and walk outside.

3

We make our way to the cars in one big pack. The little ones aren't acting cool. They're hyped up like puppies at a birthday party. Barking. Roughhousing. Only Clever, me, and Payasa get in Apache's Cutlass. It makes me miss my car even more. It's prolly still way out in Riverside. Just sitting. If I ever see it again, I'll be pulling it out of impound, most likely. But I'll have to report it stolen first though. Just so it doesn't get tied in with Lil Mosco. But I can't do that until I hear from the big homies. Sure, Mosco didn't come home last night, but that doesn't mean for sure it's done. So I got to play it cool and walk around with this guilt ripping holes in me.

And I'm thinking that's the biggest of my problems until, as we're loading up the cars with soldiers to go right out and loot and do whatever, my dad pulls up in this busted old Datsun. That thing's rusted and gray and paint's peeling back around the headlights. It's got no hood ornament and only one good headlight. It's just . . . sad, you know?

He's had it since forever, since before my mom died in January of 1985 and my sister went to live with my aunt in '87. And he had it still when he took up with another woman I didn't get along with too good and I guess that was that. I found a place to stay cuz *la clica* wouldn't leave me hanging and that's how I ended up with Toker and Speedy and them first, and then with Payasa, Ernesto, and Lil Mosco later. And all this didn't mean my dad stopped loving me, stopped checking up on me. He was forever worried, forever asking if I was being good and shit like that. When he did, I never lied, but I didn't really tell the truth neither.

And right now, I can see the worry draining off my dad's face through the cracked windshield, like he can't believe what he's seeing. Like, here he was, all concerned about if I'm okay or not, and he gets in this car and drives from Florence to see if I'm still alive and breathing and when he pulls up I'm loading up cars with homeboys— not one of them making any effort to conceal a gun.

My pops, he's not stupid. It clicks for him right then. Me, his son, I'm not the dude to be scared for. I'm the dude to be scared *of.*

His face kind of melts at that, his cheeks droop like he's been holding his breath for miles and he just let his air out, and he looks dead at me with a heavy frown and shakes his head like he's real, real disappointed, and then he throws his shit in reverse, backs up fifteen feet into a T-turn so he can whip around, and when he does, he drives off. Fast. Flashing one good brake light and one bad as he disappears around the corner. That sticks with me. The one busted brake light, shining white around red teeth.

And then he's gone.

First person I share a look with after is Clever. It's a quick nod, but complicated. He knows about my pops and I know about his, the way he jetted out when Clever wasn't even walking yet. I see he gets where I'm coming from, but at the same exact time, he'd do anything for his dad to have cared enough to check on him ever. I see him thinking disappointment's better than disappearing, so I look away, cuz there's nothing I can do about that.

The other older homies know it isn't their business. But the little homies, the ones that don't know better, say shit like, "Who was that *viejo*?"

"Nobody," I say and almost mean that shit.

This satisfies the little homies enough for them to finish loading up, sitting cherry, or with their legs dangling out the back of a hatchback when one of them, all riled up, lets out a high, ay-yi-yi type of *grito*, and it sounds like if he had a horse between his legs right then, he would've kicked it to giddy-the-fuck-up.

4

I didn't believe it until it was real. TV is TV, you never can trust that shit. Except for today. And it's on Atlantic, weaving through light traffic with no cops in sight, that the fever takes hold of us. All of us. It's a sweaty, hot feeling of we-can-do-whatever-the-fuck-we-want. It feels like way too much coffee. It feels like—

I'm sitting shotgun and I roll my window down and put my hand on top of the car. I bang my fist on the roof, like *ba-bop, ba-bop, ba-bop*. Like, a rhythm to how fast we're going. Fifty. Fifty-five. Sixty.

Apache is one lead-footed motherfucker. Normally, I'd tell him to slow the hell down, but not today.

Today, there's no speed limits. There's no *any* kind of limits.

"Hey," Apache says after one too many ba-bops, "that's my *roof*, man."

I shoot him a shut-the-fuck-up look, and real quick he says, "Sorry."

I get in his face and shake him. "I'm fucking with you, homes!"

I punch the radio on. I go up the dial and down. Everywhere, it's news, news, news. Reports. People complaining like it's not the greatest day on earth, but like it's a disaster or something. I flip it to AM. There's no oldies, but there's something. Actual music. Sort of.

It's some fucking cheesy rock. The kind *gabachos* call classic. Electric guitars and clapping sounds. Ba-ba-*bada*-ba, that's what the hook sounds like. This song's called "More Than My Feelings," or some shit.

Apache recognizes it.

"Man, *fuck* Boston," he says, making a big fucking frowny face and moving to shut it off, but I shake my head.

"Let that shit run," I say. I even turn it up just to fuck with him.

Anybody who ever made it out of my neighborhood did it cuz they didn't come out to play. You can't ever explain to those people how good it feels, how *strong* it feels to be with your brothers and do what you want, and a day like today is bigger than you ever dreamed of, a day when you can do anything, but it's all fantasy cuz that kind of shit never happens, until it actually *does* . . .

Fucking electric guitars buzz around me as I reach up as high as I can and try to grab dry air. How it feels cutting around my palm, I try to burn that shit in my memory, how it turns my hand almost cold. I want to remember it forever.

I pull my hand in when we hit Gage though, and the feeling's fading a little cuz it's obvious just by looking around that this is some serious *Mad Max* shit. There's some looting going on, but it's not like on the TV, people running around like crazy, pushing through holes in storefronts like rats. Here, there's no shit that looks like cotton candy in the street, no fires. Smells like smoke though, woody, but also that sharp kind of bitter smell when you burn plastic.

We roll our four-car caravan by Western Auto just to scope it, but they got motherfuckers on the roof with rifles. So I make a decision then and say, fuck *that*.

Apache snaps the wheel around and we're picking up speed again, turning the street into one of them luge courses you see at the fucking Olympics. Albertaville or wherever the fuck it was last. That's us. Except it's four cars together, slipping through traffic, saying *fuck you* to red lights, keeping our heads on swivels to see if any other gang's got their necks out, if they're doing what we're doing too.

As we're passing Mel and Bill's Market we see some white dudes we never seen before looting up some cases of canned beer, loading them in a truck, so Apache aims us right at them and comes in all hard, slamming the brakes at the last possible second, laying down a rubber trail on the street as we squeal to a stop just inches away from these guys. Damn, do they ever look shocked as fuck. Not near as shocked as when I pull my gun though and Apache backs me.

"This ain't your neighborhood." I smile cold when I say it. "You better get the fuck out while you still can."

They do what's good and drop the beer, but I tell them to pick it up and help us load it off their truck and put it into the van we got. So they do. Then we're off and away. Peeling our eyes for the next target.

5

When we hit a *carnicería* for the fuck of it, somebody blasts the security door at its hinges with a sawed-off and it creaks as the stucco front wall spits little bits of gravel and pebbles like it's bleeding. People never think of how brittle stucco is when they put security doors in. They don't think that all you have to do is break *that*, and then rip the metal security door off. It's easy. After it's done, we kick the door's glass out and go whooping in like Indians in a war party, like we're all in some western.

There's no lights on inside, and the smell of meat that's been sitting awhile punches us in our noses cuz the electricity's been off since maybe late last night or early this morning.

"Bags," I say as I point at the registers. "All them motherfuckers."

Little homies grab up plastic bags while me and the older homies jump behind the counter and throw open the clear plastic cases with a *thwack-thwack-thwack*. That's how they sound when they smack the end of their sliders and the sound echoes off glass-doored coolers on the far wall and comes back to me, and for a moment I think of how weird this all is. Nobody around. Nobody to stop us. I try to soak it up, you know?

Now, I had a lot of days in my life wondering where my next meal was coming from, so this's Christmas and Thanksgiving and New Year's and a birthday to me. And I'm not the only one neither. As we're snatching up pounds and pounds of ground beef, homies are yelling and screaming. We rip short ribs off their racks and laugh. We throw lamb shanks over the counter for the little homies to catch. When one gets dropped and the lil dude looks like he doesn't want to pick it up, I yell out, "That's good food, homes! We'll wash it! Pick that shit *up*."

He does, and it takes five of us just to cram everything and anything into those white plastic bags: eight whole chickens, sausages still linked together in a line so long you can swing it around your head like a rope, four fat beef tongues, and on and on. We're in and out, hauling as much as we can carry, filling the trunk of Apache's Cutlass to bursting with meat. Jumping on it. Mashing it down so it'll fit, you know? Apache fights it at first, cuz he sees bags ripping. He sees blood dripping through, blood dragging red lines through the dirt on his spare tire and disappearing into the dark blue carpet the trunk's lined with. I tell him we can clean it later. We'll make the little homies do it with a hose and some soap and sponges while we barbecue like a motherfucker, and he's not happy but it shuts him up.

I slam the trunk shut and already I'm thinking of firing a grill up and how good it's gonna feel to feed every last homeboy till he can't walk no more, and just thinking that makes me happier than I been in a long time—till I look at Payasa anyway.

She's got this look on her face I can't place. It's a coked-out glaze for sure, cuz she's got them PCP glasses on, but there's something else. I don't bring attention to it or anything, but it's tears. Big ones.

She's crying and she must not know why cuz she's swiping at her eyes and then staring at her hands and then swiping again like she can't believe it. Unpredictable shit happens when you sherm. It does. You can cry without knowing why. You can scream, or go numb for hours. But like any type of drug, it can make what you already got inside you worse. And seeing Payasa like this reminds me of what Ernesto's body looked like, all still in that alley.

And it reminds me how she couldn't even look, how she put her hands over her face when we drove by, and I had to lie and tell her they picked him up. That he wasn't there anymore. Even though he *was*. And Clever backed me up, cuz she must not have believed me so she asked him too. He said not to worry, that they picked him up and it was all okay now, as okay as it could be. And then nobody said shit back to the house.

I don't draw attention to Payasa. Instead, I tell everybody to get back in the cars, and just when we're halfway to the gun store and I'm thinking we're cool, she leans out the window and shoots five holes in the side of a station wagon that looks like it's maybe got some Bloods in it. She laughs all hard too when the other car veers to the side of the road, runs up over the curb, and makes a break for it through a strip mall parking lot.

"Mosco would've loved this shit," she says. "Where the fuck *is* he, anyways? Getting stirred up in some shit or what?"

It's that *or what* that hits me. She doesn't really want for anybody to answer her questions though. She just says, "yeah," like she answered them herself and keeps looking out the window.

I look at Clever and Clever looks at me.

He doesn't know about Lil Mosco but he knows. He's too smart. He knew when Mosco didn't come back in the morning that that was prolly it for him.

Nobody says shit till we're parked on the side of the redbrick building that says GUN STORE in big blue letters on the front and we're sneaking around the side in a big long line, guns drawn, and I'm praying all quiet to myself that Sunny really is a piece of shit, and he really did leave this door open so we don't have to shoot it off.

6

The front's open, barely. At first, it looked like it wasn't, but when Apache gave it a shove, it moved. Since I got no idea what to expect, I go in first and we go in crouching. It's a wide-open square of carpet in the middle. On three of its edges—left, right, and dead ahead—are glass counters. Behind these are tall display cases with glass faces and the fancy fucking guns locked up in them. Only the lights of these display cases are on, bright white tubes at the top, shining off metal that's been polished up.

"About time, *raza*. Shit!" Sunny laughs. "I been holding it down for at least a half an hour. You got my money or what, homes?"

I relax and drop my gun down to my side, and as I walk toward the shape I see in the back, my eyes adjust. My homeboys are right behind me, still wary.

Sunny's not my *raza*. He's Lynwood, born and raised, don't get me wrong, but he's white, not no Chicano. Never stopped him from wanting to be one though.

When I get to the back, I finally see what he's talking about when he says he's been holding it down. Behind a big glass case full of snubnoses of every size, color, and handle inlay, I see two dudes sitting next to each other on the floor. There's a white one and a black one. Sunny's pointing a gun at them.

They don't look uncomfortable though, these two. They got a magazine they're sharing. An old *People* issue. It's got that mother-fucker from *Beverly Hills 90210* on the cover, furrowing his brow up under his big hair like his life's real hard to figure out. I can't help but scoff at that shit.

Cuz that's fake L.A. right there, bought and sold. It ain't my L.A. And I bet everybody watching on TV knows different now too.

But why they got that dumb shit in a gun shop I'll never fuck-ing know. I guess it can get real boring selling bullets one at a time. Fucking parasites.

I tuck my lip and cut a whistle at them. This gets their attention.

The black one closes the magazine all slow as they both straighten up, which is good, cuz I need them to see this shit.

"You ain't my fucking *raza*," I say to Sunny as I snap my Colt up to his face, cock the hammer before he has time to think about raising his gun on me, and give him just long enough to realize that this is what happens when you leave the door open and tempt a wolf to come in.

Sooner or later, he fucking eats you, homes.

Pak. That's how a .44 sounds when it pops a bullet that plows through a nose, a skull, and a brain before burying itself in a wooden cabinet. Sunny's dead before he falls, and when he does, he hits the floor funny. He lands arched back on his head and doesn't settle. He just sticks to the carpet like a broken-ass tent.

"Holy fucking shit," the white one says behind me as I step forward to tell Sunny something even though he can't hear and that's cool.

It's not for him. It's for me. And it's for somebody else too.

"That shit's for my sister. This 'hood's got a long memory, *chavala*," I say and then turn to Sunny's hostages. *Ex*-hostages.

"Now I got your attention," I say to their scared-as-fuck faces, "give up them wallets."

The black one's fast. He knows this routine. He's not about to get blasted over something stupid. The white one though, he hesitates. *Cabrón.*

You know I can't be having that. I step to him, and he does a fast crabwalk into the cabinet behind him, smacking his head hard before wincing. The little homies laugh at that shit like a chorus, but Apache steps up quick.

"*Puto*, this is Mister Fate, biggest, baddest motherfucker in Lynwood, *y que*?" Apache scowls. "If he wanted to rob you, he'd have *her* blast you first!"

He points at Payasita. Right on cue, she tilts her head and sneers so good it shoots a shiver down my spine that gets stuck in my knees. Her eyes are fucking dead inside, and anybody with an ounce of sense can see she ain't faking shit. It's a look that makes blood run cold.

White dude knows it too cuz he gets two shades whiter and sets to digging in his back pocket and comes back with a fat calfskin sonofabitch. That's how white people say it, right? Like a drawl?

Sonuvabitch? Man, that's some corny Kurt Russell shit. *Hijo de su chingada madre* rolls off the tongue way better. You can spit it if you want, just adds to the message.

Apache hands me the wallets and I skip the cash, pulling driver's licenses and then dropping their shit on the floor—right in Sunny's blood puddle. I hear the black dude groan. He's smart all right. He knows what fucking time it is.

"See, I'm gonna keep these. Add them to my collection."

I nod at the white one. "We know where you live now, *Gary*."

I nod at the black one. "You too, *Lawrence*."

I bend my knees and crouch down at their level. "Normally now, we don't leave witnesses." I nod toward Sunny all casual but keep my eyes on them. They get it, so I look their licenses over. Both are California. One lives in Gardena, the other in Wilmington. "We know where you live. And the cops, well, they're kind of busy, so I think you'll take it as a favor that the man who put a gun on you ran into some bad luck."

Bad is good, I think.

I turn my head to look at Sunny one more time, at how his eyes are still open. Well, the one I can see, anyway. Blood's running thick from the hole where his nose used to be and dripping over that eye, down his forehead and onto the floor like backward tears.

I flip through Lawrence's wallet and see two little kids that look just like him. Two girls in pretty purple dresses.

"So if you get the urge to tell anybody how you got freed today, well, somebody might have to visit your kids' school." I look at Lawrence, but he's not looking up, he's in a permanent kind of wince. I notice Gary's wedding ring and put my eyes on him. "Or catch up with your wife in the grocery store parking lot or something."

His face crinkles up at that, so I let that sink in. I let it all sink in.

"It won't be us," I say. "But it'll be somebody."

Like Lil Creeper coked out of his damn mind, I think. I let them close their eyes and breathe on their new circumstances for a bit.

When I know the threat is sunk so deep they'll never forget it, I tell them to get the fuck out, and they look at each other for a second before they up and bolt. The little homies crack up at that shit, mimicking it—the looks on their faces, even running mock races in slow motion, but after the back door slams and I hear engines revving up and fading, I motion for everybody to fan out.

All over the store, we bust up cases. We stack guns like nothing I ever seen in my whole life. Pump shotguns. Desert Eagles. Two semiauto AK-47s. Long-range rifles too, real sniper shit. It's something straight out of a heist movie.

A bonanza, I call it. Not that fucking fake western TV show though. A real one.

And as I pick up an AK and feel its weight in my hand, I tell Clever to reach up to one of them fluorescent tubes and rig a real good electrical fire to take care of Sunny's body. A nice slow one, cuz see, where so many fools tip off the arson teams is a fast burn, Clever always says, that's when it's obvious something was used to speed up the process, like lighter fluid, or a Molotov cocktail.

An *accelerant*, he calls it.

And as I watch Clever put on thick-ass rubber gloves and climb up on a case so he can get to work on some ceiling wires, all's I can think about is Lil Creeper, about how sad that fuckup is gonna be that he missed the score of a lifetime.

ANTONIO DELGADO,
A.K.A. LIL CREEPER,
A.K.A. DEVIL'S BUSINESS

APRIL 30, 1992

10:12 A.M.

1

I'm standing in my motel parking lot, trying to figure out which car to jack and being disappointed, mostly thinking like, I may be a junkie, but I got taste, *esé*. I may be a fucking cheap Mexican, man, but I got taste. I come a long way from stealing the wrong bikes at J.C. Pennies. Ask any motherfucker. I know what's good.

Directly after that thought, it hits me that I don't know how I got here.

Like, I was in my motel room that I got with the gun money Fate hit me off with. I woke up alone and the clock said 10:05 in the A.M. The TV was going so I must've left it on, I remember that. I remember feeling like a scrunched-up paper bag, too. No lie.

And like everybody else, I was sure the cops woulda stomped the fucking *mayates* after what happened yesterday. You know, gone all police state 1984 on some Florence and Normandie fools or wherever. But then those *culeros* on the TV (black people, brown people, even *white* people, even *kids*, man!) are looting this fucking pharmacy for beer and popcorn, and my first thought is *You dumb motherfuckers are thinking too small.* Way *too small.*

Like, I get it. You're poor and you haven't had shit for so long that it feels good to get your hands on something. But how long's the shit you're taking actually gonna last? A week? Not even. That's officially a waste of time, people. Wake up. If you're gonna do some shit, *do* some shit. Don't small-time it.

Like, if you could do anything you want, what would it be?

I stop looking at parked cars and trip on that for a second.

I mean, for me, it'd be to fuck Payasa and another girl at the same time. Seeing as how *that* shit's never gonna happen though, I guess I can have a second dream.

But damn, she looked so fine last night, all like a normal girl and shit! Who knew she'd look that good in a dress and heels? Apache didn't say nothing, but he knew. Every dude in there knew, and we were just saving that mental image for later.

So for that *other* dream, my second dream, there's only one other answer: clean Momo the fuck out. Rob him blind.

On any other day, that wouldn't be such a good dream cuz that motherfucker's laced up tight with the click that did Ernesto. Like, he's not quite in there, he's kind of above it. In between them and the big homies, almost. Which seems about right for a Salvi *cerote* that nobody knew was Salvi until he was bigger and older cuz he wouldn't own where his family came from when he was young. That's how fucking shady he is.

He's not a big homie now or nothing, but still, he helps that other click out. Guns. Drugs. Whatever they need, he supplies. And he knows I'm sort of laced up with Fate and them. It's always been a little—what's the word?

Tricky.

Yeah, it's been tricky between us two. But the thing about peacetime and the thing about drugs is that people go where the best shit is, and that was mostly Momo. Dumb-fuck, no-taste-having Momo.

But then Ernesto gets killed and it's not peace no more. It's war.

So I might as well burn that motherfucker. Rape and fucking pillage like a Viking. Not like the Lynwood sheriff kind though. A real one. One out of history.

I got other reasons, but the biggest two are:

1.   I don't even know how many days I got left, and
2.   Few fuckers deserve it as bad as Momo.

Hold up though. Where was I? Lemme back up.

I was talking about taste.

Like, there's a difference between *cocaína* from El Salvador and good shit from Colombia. One makes me jumpy. One makes me slick like a knife. If you got taste, you know that. Taste is really just being able to tell the difference between trash and treasures, that's all.

And I think I bumped Salvadorian off some Cadillac early this morning, and that's *gotta* be why I feel like my heart's gonna pop.

Cuz it's that or it's Big Fate.

I had three pages on my beeper from that scary motherfucker when I finally woke up to the city going fucking batshit *loco*. And let me tell you, that right there is not normal. Man, *one* page from Fate will fuck your head up. It'll rearrange your whole day. Even one gets me breathing different.

But he *never* paged three times before.

Three! When I first saw, I turned away from the TV, picked up my pager, and his number's tagged on the first one and I was like, okay. By the second at 8:54, my stomach's rumbling like a mother-fucker. But the third at 9:12? Fuck off! I had to throw up in the sink when I saw it.

Cuz, see, at first I thought, *Fuck it, I'm dead*. But then I took a big long drink on the faucet and washed my mouth out and spit and then I thought, *Nah. If a dude like Fate wants you dead, that's it*.

There's no pages. No warnings.

You just catch it. In your sleep. In the shower. Whatever.

So then I get to thinking that maybe he knows where I got that mummy-wrapped Glock with all the white tape on it from and he don't like that it came from Momo cuz that makes things complicated. Or he knows I lied about that Glock being the only gun in the safe. I mean, there was one more thing in there. I put my hand in my pocket just to feel it, and once I do that, I gotta look at it again.

I pull out this slick fucking snub revolver, all silver with a pearl-handle grip that shines from white to blue when I twist it in the daylight.

Shit. Fate *has* to know all that.

No other explanation for him wanting to get ahold of me.

So I deal with it by not dealing with it, you know? I deal with it by walking my ass away from the parking lot to the street cuz nothing's catching my interest. It's nothing but Hondas and beat-up trucks, and none of them are good enough. I mean, I need a special kind of car for this shit.

See, if I really am about to be dead, if Fate's just trying to drag my ass out into the open, I think, like, I got to live like this is my last fucking day on earth.

Cuz maybe it is.

It's a stupid fucking plan. But that's my specialty. Maybe if I really burn Momo good, Fate will forgive me lying to him. Even still, there's no way burning Momo will make Payasa drop them *chonies* like I'm her hero.

But I don't give a fuck. It might as well be time for Mister Creeper's Wild Ride, you know? Strap in and go.

Cuz, right now, that's the best idea I got.

Yeah, I think.

Yeah.

I pull my hood up and step off the curb, straight into traffic on Imperial.

I ain't scared when a big fucking Taurus swerves and misses me. A station wagon with fake wood on its doors does the same. The third one?

The third one I aim my shiny new gun at.

The other gun I already stole from Momo.

2

The third one's a big black Chevy Astro van with a bash in the fender. From far away, the old dude driving looks like my old parish priest and boxing coach, Padre Garza, and that shit makes my stomach jerk when the van brakes hard to a stop right in front of me and I hear them tires squeal as I run around to the driver's side and—oh shit!

It fucking *is* Garza.

Small town, I think. *Always* running into fools.

I smile at that shit.

Garza's looking stunned and shaky till he recognizes me too. I even pull my hood down and wait for it.

When he does, I smile and say a prayer to the sky.

To every single fucking saint there ever was and ever will be.

Cuz I didn't even know this was my dream, until he was right in front of me, this dude that told me poise was all you ever needed in the ring, this dude that told me I didn't have no discipline and that he'd never take me pro cuz I didn't listen, this dude that trained me from ten years old to seventeen and every week he said the only way to be a smart boxer was to do exactly what he said, even gross shit that didn't have anything to do with boxing, shit that was just wrong, especially for a kid.

So to this piece of shit that doesn't deserve breathing, I say, "*¿Qué pasa*, you filthy-ass motherfucker?"

If it's anybody else, he lives. But it's Garza.

So you *know* what time it is.

Now, don't get me wrong, I'm no animal.

I don't shoot him in the van cuz I need that shit.

I throw him in the street first.

I kick him so hard in the jaw that I hear his lower teeth crack his upper teeth a solid one. Then I let him spit blood and beg a little before I pop a bullet in his fucking mouth.

It feels good pulling that trigger too, almost like I been waiting my whole life to do it. And I sigh like I never sighed before after that. Peaceful. Like, complete. And then I put one in his chest too.

Just for good measures.

Traffic might've been stopped before, but that's when fools throw their cars in reverse and get the fuck out.

And that's cool. Except I'm looking at the body and thinking, did Garza have a birthmark on his neck like that? Huh. I don't remember that shit.

And then I'm thinking, was Garza really that tall?

But then I'm like, "Fuck it," and I'm up in the van and I'm driving, thanking *Christo* it don't have any windows in the back, but then I figure that figures cuz of the child-molesting piece of shit who owns it.

Well, *used* to own it. Cuz it must've been Garza.

It was *Garza*, I tell myself directly. *Don't even sweat it. Fucker had it coming.*

I point my brand-new van in the direction of Momo's house and slap the last of the Salvadorian shit onto my gums cuz only dumb fucks sniff and drive. All it takes is a pothole and you lose your shit on the floor like a dummy.

I did that once. I had to sniff half a fucking car mat when we stopped. Now I know better.

Well, maybe I don't exactly know better. Not on everything.

Cuz people who know better don't go back to the scene of the crime. That's what the TV says anyways.

Which is why it's stupid as fuck for me to go back to Momo's, seeing as how it was his gun safe I cracked and stole them two pieces out of.

The Glock that Fate probably gave Payasa so she could do business.

And the snub I got in my pocket right now.

So, fuck it. That's my saying today. *Fuck it.*

I'm going back. Might as well.

I push that pedal down.

I blast off.

3

I zone the *fuck out* sometimes. Like, for example, I remember doing the city of Los Angeles a very public service by feeding Garza a *bala*. I'll always treasure that shit.

And I remember getting in the van.

And I remember checking that the gas was above half and it was, and then I'm flooring my foot down like my shit was pulling a caper on *Miami Device*.

And I remember the van smelling like old tortilla chips and like the ceiling would never let go of a million dead menthols.

And I remember thinking that smoking has got to be the *worst* habit there ever was, and then—nothing.

I rack my brain on that. I ask again.

Like, and then?

But I got no memory.

I don't remember how I got parked halfway up the curb in front of Momo's house, stopped a foot from his fucking mailbox, which has a little canary bird painted on it, and who the fuck thought *that* was a good idea? It definitely doesn't look like a drug dealer's house, but that's the point, I guess. Camouflage.

4

My head hurts right above my ears. But the good-hurt kind. The kind that tells me I'm still here. The alive kind. The ready-to-fuck-shit-up kind. So I hit the gas directly, and the van snaps forward. It's got some power to it the way it bends the mailbox back, but it don't crack it or nothing. The thing just comes completely out of the ground like some fucking golfer pushing the pin over at the hole and bringing up a divot with it.

Fuck you, of course I watch golf on TV! What of it? Nothing

better getting stoned to. It's all quiet and green and shit. That's one mellow high.

So, anyways, I back the van up and run over the mailbox again, and again, until I hear the metal box of it crumple under the tires. Shit, yeah.

By the way, I know it's really called *Miami Vice*. I just like it way better as *Device*. Besides, I use it to fuck with people all the time. *All* the time.

I run the mailbox over once more for good measures, stop the van, and get out.

Life goes way better when people think you're *estupido*. That's a fact.

It's like a thousand times easier to get over on motherfuckers when they think you don't know simple shit.

I want you thinking I'm garbage. Disposable. Invisible. Cuz when I'm *that* in your mind, I can pull any fucking caper and get away with that shit clean.

But I'm fucking rambling now. Where was I?

Oh yeah, standing in Momo's front yard with this high grass tickling my ankles and that's when I learn I didn't put any socks on before I left. My feet are naked in my black Vans, man. And I squish my toes around a little, and I'm like, huh. That's weird.

Why the fuck didn't I put socks on?

This shit is not normal for me on *cocaína*.

Normally, she's my best friend. My push. My up-shift to the smooth-talking, fast-hustling, uncatchable me. The fly me. Not like a fucking crazy *mosco*, not like Ray, but like birds. Like liftoff. Like my whole body is a bomb, and *cocaína* lights my fuse just the right way. Not too much. Not that I burn too hot. But just right.

Yeah, I think. *I'm a fucking bomb.*

That thought sticks to me as I cross the grass, get up on the porch, and ring the doorbell like a fucking gee. See, I lean on the bell and I don't let it go. It dings once and holds. It promises that dong sound, but that shit isn't coming until I lean off and that's not happening until somebody opens the door.

Right then I realize I'm standing in front of the peephole and I sidestep cuz you know I need somebody having to open it to find out what's outside.

And that's like some Red Riding Hood shit.

That gets me, but I got to hold my laugh in. *'Hood,* for sure.

I put my ear to the door. I hear the TV on. I hear little shuffly feet, and I got a feeling—no, I *know*—Momo isn't here. He's sitting on his stash house just like he was last night. More product to protect over there. That's when I know I gambled right in coming back.

Those little feet stop at the door. That's when I know they're thinking.

They're thinking about whether or not they should say something, cuz maybe somebody's got a shotgun or something on the other side.

I hear a voice.

"You know you need to come back later cuz Momo's not here, and I ain't opening the door for nobody."

It's Cecilia, the fat whore. I love it.

It's perfect, this setup!

The same bitch that let me in last night when she shouldn't've. The same bitch that passed out on me after taking what I told her was a speedball but was really just crushed-up sleeping pills. The same bitch that doesn't know I knocked over Momo's gun safe cuz I locked it back up and everything looks the fucking same in there still. Now I got in last night by playing to her thirst—cuz you know Momo wasn't stupid enough to leave her with too much to use, she got left with just enough, and you know the second he left she used all of what he gave her and was itching for more when I showed up. Junkies are fucking predictable. And see, that's exactly how I know I can't pull the same shit on her twice cuz she'll get fucking—what's the word?

Suspicious.

Yeah, *that*.

So I switch it up. That's easy though, cuz I'm like a actor some-times. Pure improv. That means you make shit up in the moment, and go, and go. Basically, I *flow*.

"Cecilita, it's me," I say. "Antonio."

See, she don't know me as Creeper. Only as Antonio.

"Toño?" She says it like she don't believe it's me at first. She may be a fat whore, but she's not *estupida*.

I cough a little. And when I talk, it's, like, Oscar-worthy. It's role-of-a-lifetime shit. To the door, I say, "Are you okay, *mi angelita*? Are you safe?"

That means my angel. Girls *love* hearing that shit. Especially big whores cuz nobody loves them. Nobody treats them all tender. I use that to my advantages. I don't got to respect them. I mean, shit, I *shouldn't*. But sometimes, I got to be tender. It's a card to be played, and I play it like a motherfucker—laying it down just right, and I know it's just right when she says . . .

"Why're you asking?" And her voice is soft and kind of like maybe she don't believe me.

I *know* her eye's to the peephole. I know she's waiting to see me and I can't waste this moment, so I rifle my pockets and by God's good luck there's a razor blade in my left hip one. It only clips my pinkie nail as I snatch it up quick.

This kid on my block growing up, his dad used to be a *luchador*—you know, one of them masked wrestling types—down in Sonora or some shit. The Praying Mantis, he was. *Mantis religiosa*. Had those weird bug eyes on his mask too. (I *hated* that shit as a kid. Freaked me the fuck out. I see it in my dreams sometimes, but don't tell nobody. It don't pay for fools to know your weaknesses. Not ever.) But anyways, this kid taught me that his dad said nothing bleeds like the forehead. It tricks a crowd into thinking you're hurt every time. It's practically a fountain of fucking drama, and it *always* looks real.

So you know I cut quick on my hairline and a chunk of black hair comes away in my hand when I pull. Shit. Didn't mean to do *that*.

I stare at it for a second, and then I drop it in the flower bed beside the door, the one with no fucking flowers in it, just dirt. It must help that I'm sweating cuz that blood is in my eyes and burning in a second.

I know she's still looking, so I give it one more second and then step out so she can see me. I hang my head. And then I look up with the best puppy-dog eyes anybody ever did in the history of the fucking world.

That shit's an instant classic, guaranteed. That's what Fate would say. *Guaranteed.* I take it one step further though. I lift my finger off the bell right then too, just to put an exclamation point on that shit.

Dong!

I open my mouth as the sound fades and say, "It's just that I was so worried about—"

I don't even have to finish talking before the locks go—one, two, three, and a slider beam goes *kssssss* as it slides and *bang*, it hits the blue tile floor I know too good—and then the door opens so fucking fast that a little gust of wind ripples up my clothes.

It's like Fort Knox opening its gates for me. No, it's more like, what do they call it in that one story from them condoms?

Troy. Yeah. The wooden horse one.

The real me is hiding inside the fake me as I feel the living room open up. Stale air hits, and I see the same old familiar green couch, the TV on in the corner, Hungry Man TV dinners posting up on the floor. And there's no windows open, no air-conditioning even, but it doesn't smell like a fire in here, not like outside, and that's good.

I hold my head right then and stumble against the door frame. Cecilia squeals and reaches for me.

Oh, Momo, I'm in. That's all I can think. *You stupid motherfucker, what were you thinking trusting this good-for-*nada *to hold your shit down?!*

I'm fucking *in*.

5

Cecilia wants to know what happened to me as she pulls me inside. Damn, she's demanding. She says to me, "Tell me what the fuck happened, Toño!"

She's not my girlfriend or nothing. She's just a chick my dealer fucks with, a chick I sometimes fuck with too. The kind nobody knows where she came from, she's just *there* one day, and fucked up, and why not, you know?

She presses her face into my chest when she hugs me and it feels good.

She's got Betty Boop black hair, all short like the tuft on the tail end of a whip, and bangs. Sharp-ass bangs, man. The kind that sits right over her light green eyes. Those eyes kill me.

Sure, she's got a belly to her, all round like half a good watermelon, but fuck off, man, she's had, like, two kids! She's got construction worker shoulders too, but that means she just hugs better and shit—besides, all I can think about is them eyes anyway. They're green like Gatorade.

I slump into her arms, not busting out of character yet, but wanting to.

Wanting to say, *Bitch, nothing's wrong. Shut the fuck up!* just so I can see the look on her face that she knows she did wrong, that oh-shit-Momo's-gonna-cut-me-up-when-he-finds-out look, and maybe I wouldn't be able to help laughing at that, cuz knowing Momo, he would cut her too. That motherfucker loves a knife, and seeing blood on it. Loves it almost as much as breathing. But I keep it together.

I don't say that. I don't say anything. Not yet.

Cuz, see, she breaks away from me and runs to the kitchen. I see her ass as she goes. I see it flexing and fighting under some dark blue sweatpants and I'm almost sad when she comes back with a fucking fast-food napkin, pressing it to my forehead all sweet like I guess a mama would, cuz I forgot how good that ass was. If there were Olympic ass competitions, she'd qualify. I'm not saying she'd win a medal (fuck, it ain't *bronze* good), but she'd qualify and she'd compete. She'd at least get through a heat or two. *Definitely*.

And right then, I know I don't so much care about gloating.

I care about one thing and one thing only.

I kiss her hard, and I'm fast at the back-clasping thing of her bra, scissoring that shit open through her T-shirt with a fumbly snap, and she's backing away, throwing stop signs with both hands (but not worrying about snapping her bra back up and that detail's important), but she's saying, "What the fuck, Toño? I thought you were *hurt*!"

I look at her for a long second. Not the puppy eyes this time.

Different eyes. Eyes that say, *yes, I'm hurt but I won't ever tell you how much, baby.* There's a art to pausing just right. Nailing them in your talk is like nailing rests in music. Without some good fucking pauses, it's just noise.

When I've held quiet long enough, I blink the blood away, what's left of it cuz I already feel it drying, and I look at the TV, at two dudes on Channel 7 running down a street carrying a fucking giant TV between them, before bringing my eyes back to her and say, "I feel like the world's ending, like we don't got much time left. And I got here as fast I could cuz . . ."

I pause on that shit (yes, *again*, cuz the first one was just buildup, *this's* the crucial one), and I let my words hang as I look deep in her bright green *ojos* and purse my lips a little and say it all deep, "Only thing I could think about was getting to *you*."

Damn, I'm good.

Lies are tools. Shit, *words* are tools, not all that different from guns. I use them to get what I want. Everybody does.

And you *know* that shit worked cuz her face looks like a bomb went off behind her eyes, blew her all up inside.

I'm admiring my work as she tries to catch her breath. I'm like that Warren Beatty motherfucker. I went *Bugsy* on her shit. Just give me that fucking Oscar right now cuz that fat whore's on me so fast that we're already falling, already down on the carpet and getting burns on our elbows before I even knew what hit me.

Her shirt practically takes itself off, the sweats too. Like magic.

With the TV going in the background, with people lifting stolen lawn chairs over their heads and going crazy in front of cameras and shit, I fuck her *so* good, man.

It's the best kind of coke fuck. Like birds fighting, loud and wild and you can feel everything, except the slaps and the scratches don't quite touch you.

Only the good gets through.

Only the good.

And she's yelling at me to stick her from behind, going crazy, grabbing my balls and shit, telling me to bite her earlobe, to dig my fingers deep into her hips like I mean it, to slap her face—slap her *hard*. And you know I do. Shit. I aim to please.

We only have to stop once for a *cocaína* break. I sniff that shit off her right nipple and it's like a minipancake it's so wide and dark. I tongue it clean before she bumps her hit off my dick in one long line.

Where it goes from there, just imagine the craziest shit you got in your head. Shit you always wanted to do with a black-haired bitch with a big ass, a bitch that gets down and flexes all the way. Like, picture her doing some splits on you and sucking your index finger like it's something else, all moaning, eyes rolling so far back in her skull you're scared she's having a seizure.

Yeah, like *that*.

Shit so good even *panocha*-licking Payasa would get off on it.

6

After's when the questions start. Cecilia's sitting on top of me like a cowgirl or something and, man, does she ever look *pissed*. I don't hear her words at first. I don't hear nothing, really. But as I lean forward and try to pick my head up off the carpet, words kick in and sync up with her mouth like somebody just turned my sound on.

It rushes at me.

"What the fuck, Toño? You passed out on me?! What, you got a concussion or something? And who hit you anyway? Some looters or some shit? Are they the ones that cut you?" And that's not the end of it. It goes another minute.

I don't remember passing out. Shit must've been better than I thought!

Nothing like a mad Latin woman though, man.

Nothing.

I finally find my tongue and turn it over. It's dry as fuck and thick in my mouth, but I manage to say, "Bitch, nothing's wrong. Shut the fuck up."

Her eyes go big when she hears that. And yeah, that right there is when she knows she made the biggest mistake she ever made opening up that door.

Cuz I'm already inside the house. Isn't there something people say about not letting wolfs in or something? Cuz that's me right now.

And Cecilia would run, but my hands are in her hair, slamming her back down, and she'd get up, but I flip her too fast. I'm on top, smashing my knees into her armpits and pinning her arms underneath her as I grab my jeans next to me on the carpet and dig for the spy-pockets only I know are sewn on the inside, the kind where you can only get what's in them by reaching down behind the zipper. It's in one of them pockets that I find the syringe, already loaded up with heroin I don't know how old.

But it's still liquid when I tap one of my nails against its plastic, *splik-splik-splik*, and I shake it and I see the smallest swirl and that's good, I think.

Good for Cecilia anyway.

But she doesn't seem to think so. She's shaking her head as I dig my knees harder into her armpits. Veins jump up on her neck as she struggles, and I'm thinking, *That's good. That's just fine. Cuz that'll save me finding one in your arm, baby. Keep struggling. That's* good.

The needle's still good too, not busted off or anything, but dull maybe. A little anyway. And shit, maybe only used once? I tease the tip of it into the biggest, meanest-looking neck vein she's got just to test it, but it goes in pretty easy so I just push the plunger down.

Even she's too smart to fight when I do that.

She knows what happens when you pull veins up. That shit's serious.

She's crying when she takes it, cries quiet tears when I get the plunger down to the bottom and already I'm starting to think about it better, like, how big was that fucking hit anyway?

I give it a second, but I get nothing.

Cuz I got no clue.

I don't even know if I loaded it last night or this morning.

I can't help laughing at that, cuz, man, do I feel bad. I almost blurt too. Almost say, *Oops!* Almost say it all loud too, but I don't.

Cuz I'm already shaking my head. *I need to focus*, I think. *Sharpen up good. I'm here for two reasons, and two reasons only.*

1. I'm here to find the money I know Momo's got hid.
2. I'm here to steal all the fucking drugs I can get my hands on.

That I fucked Cecilita is just icing on the cake. Good icing. Cream cheese and *dulce de leche*, all swirled together. But just icing.

See, Momo's been living off me, and motherfuckers like me, for years. Overcharging. Putting me on the bad shit when he's got perfectly good shit one room away. Sending me out on runs for whatever (like, last week it was a Pampers truck, I shit you not, cuz this *perezoso* can't even buy them himself) and you know he never hits me off for what's fair.

Big Fe, he always pays out on what you deliver. And I think about them pages again and shiver before catching some new adrenaline.

There's no way he could find me right now anyway, I tell myself. He's prolly into some shit of his own. But do I wish I hadn't told that Aztec-looking motherfucker how many bullets were in it when I brought that big boy Glock last night, all taped up like it was? Shit.

Did I wish he just paid me for the whole thing? You bet your fucking *culo*! But he didn't, and that's what I get. That's this life. That's how it works.

See, if I can get over on you, if I can cheat you, if I can lie and you buy that lie, then it's your fucking fault for being *estupido*.

If I rob you, well, then you shoulda *stopped* me, man!

That shit's on *you*.

And Fate, that motherfucker's tried and true. He's like a general or something. All strategic and shit. You can't outthink him. Me and him, we're different breeds. I can't *ever* get over on Fate. Not even once.

More important, he'd never say one price for such and such, and then when you risk your ass to bring it, never does he turn around and give you a lower price, all the while acting like you misheard him the first fucking time.

With Fate, the price is the price. That dude has *honor*.

But that shit's never the case with Momo.

Momo's on his own in a whole other category specifically dedicated to motherfuckers who live for the scheme.

And now's the time for Momo to get fucking schemed.

It's his fault for not stopping me right now.

Where I'm from, they call this shit payback. And sometimes it's the only reason to keep living. For days like today.

Days when you finally get to fuck the fuckers.

I get up off Cecilia real slow and head for the bedroom with a grin as big as the Hollywood sign.

7

I clear the place top to bottom in less than a hour. I can tell by the time on the TV, cuz there's a little clock in the corner. I guess when bad shit happens they want you to know what time it is always.

Took me ten minutes to find the other safe. It was under the waterbed, built into the frame. Smart. Not smart enough though.

I cracked that shit in thirty seconds. Guess you shouldn't've left homeowner's insurance statements and passports and shit in your bedside table, Momo. That shit tells people a lot about you. But then, I guess I didn't really need it cuz you left the combination—your birthday, the exact same combination as your fucking gun safe, *puto*—and I already knew that one.

When I pulled the little safe open, it popped its catch like a grown-up's piñata. Like I hit it just right and I get all the fucking candy.

Inside was $6,000 in six rubber-banded stacks of $1,000 each, and another $522 loose. I instantly decided that's how much Momo owes me.

The rest was just Christmas.

Half a pound, marijuana. One pound, *cocaína*. One pound, H. No doubt about it. This shit was his backup, his oh-shit stash. It stinks of it. Total street value, as they say on them cop shows?

That's a good question. I don't even fucking know.

A lot though!

It's so much that I do a fuck-you-Momo dance on what's left of his waterbed that I cut up with his knife I found in the bookcase.

I put it all in a black garbage bag I snagged from the kitchen, and I throw Momo's little scale in too.

When I come back through the living room, I see Cecilia hasn't moved a inch the whole time. Her bangs look like a broken fan the way they're all spread flat over the carpet. She's so still that I get worried and shoot two fingers under her nose, fingers that still smell like her, to see if she's still breathing and she is, so I'm like, *whew.*

I sit up and cut the world's tiniest eyelid into the wrapping of the *cocaína* using Momo's knife, and then, like a fucking scientist working on hazardous chemicals, I put just my long pinkie nail in, turn it, and pull it out full with a tiny mound of white shaped like a half moon.

This's why I kick everybody's fucking asses at that one game, *Operation.* Just gimme them pliers, and watch me pull out all the white shit!

This one I bump straight into my *nariz* and it stings me up before I go numb all over my face (nose, cheeks, eyes even), but that's when I know it's the shit.

Colombiano. Pura.

I cough a few times hard, but it fuels me up. It pushes me out the door in a hurry. Next thing I know I'm ripping open the van's side door and tossing the black bag on top of the four boxes of every kind of liquor you can imagine, but mostly Puerto Rican *ron*. Forty-four fucking bottles. I counted.

Oh shit, did I already mention I snatched all that?

Well, I did. Every last one.

That Momo, he's a drinker. But I need it for something else.

I grab the nearest bottle from the nearest box, whip its cap off, roll a rag I grabbed from the linen closet (yeah, motherfucking drug dealers have motherfucking linen closets, and they're stocked too, cuz the serious ones always keep shit clean), so anyways I'm rolling a rag in my other hand like I'm rolling a big cloth joint and I push it so deep into the bottle that it touches the tea-colored rum and sucks it up like a sponge.

After that, I light the top of the rag. It goes black as it takes the fire and springs up low and orange.

This's just a simple rule.

When you burn somebody, you got to *burn* them.

The bottle's heavy in my hand as I feel the heat travel up my arm to my face. When the flame gets near the bottle mouth, I look at it for a minute, all yellow and red and orange, with little bits of burning black. I almost don't want to let it go.

Cuz this shit right here is for me, but it isn't too.

It's for Ernesto cuz I owe that motherfucker more than I can ever pay.

You know who went into that boxing gym all them years ago and told that motherfucking Garza if he ever messed with another kid again, the last sight he ever saw would be the wrong end of a shotgun?

Not my parents. Fuck no. Old-school junkies, the pair of them. Junkies before anybody knew what a junkie was, or how a junkie was.

It was Payasa's big brother who went in heavy, that's who.

Never touched a gun in his whole life, but he was mad enough to say he would and mean it too. That fool, not even involved or nothing, he went in there and fucked shit up. He broke a trophy case with a baseball bat before he pulled his little brother, Ray, out (I think he was like thirteen at the time), pulled me out, and two other kids too.

I ended up staying with him and Ray and Payasa and their *madre* for a minute. Good people too. They wanted to believe in me so bad. I mean, they really tried until my tastes got too big. And then Fate came in, and their *madre* moved out, and I was fucking up anyways, so, you know. I was just like them French people when I had to say, "La Vi," and be out cuz this life can get crazy. Whatev—

Shit! The glass bottle's burning my fucking hand up so I just up and chuck it through Momo's open front door. It spins through the air like the perfect chip shot, some Fuzzy Zoeller laying-up-onto-the-green shit, and when it hits the carpet in the living room, the whole thing goes *up*!

Oh man, I love that sound when it catches too. *Wa-fwoom!*

I could listen to that for days. Or . . .

Hold up.

Wait.

Did I just—?

Fuck.

Cecilia's still *in* there!

But I'm already backing away. I can't even help it.

I'm telling myself, she'll be okay. She'll wake up, no problem. The heat, yeah, the heat will wake her up and she'll run out.

I mean, sure, I *think* about running in and grabbing her, about playing hero, but some dude rolls up on some kind of motorized bike blasting punk rock or something from a ghetto blaster he's got bungeed down to the back of it, and I feel like I seen him around before but I can't place where, and besides, he don't look like much (cuz who the fuck wears red suspenders?!). But he's staring at me good, so I bone the fuck out.

I get in the van, man, and I go.

8

So I got a confession to make. Sometimes, I don't *always* know what I'm doing. Sometimes, I just fucking do it.

Impulsive, that's what Clever says. Like, I live on urges, on shit popping up in my brain and then my muscles are moving and I'm acting on it before I even know it.

And as a result of that, sometimes good shit happens, and sometimes bad shit happens. It depends.

Do I have regrets? Sort of.

But not really though.

Like I said, if I can get over on you, it's your fault for letting it go that way.

If she don't wake up and walk her ass out of there, Cecilia's on Momo. Plain and simple. See, if he doesn't leave her in charge, that shit never happens.

Man, *fuck* Momo for making me do that shit.

I scream that out the window to everybody and nobody, and I'm hitting that curve in the streets around Ham Park, where Josephine turns into Virginia, eyeing that dumb fucking handball wall made out of wood and I just think of how many splinters it gave me when it sticks some shit in the ball when you bang it good but then it comes back hard and you hit it again but the only thing you really do is mash some splinters deep into your palm (or worse, in the webs between your fingers) if you're not wearing no gloves, and that's when I know that fucking wall has to go!

I cut the wheel hard, bunny hop the fucking curb, and roll up fast to the wall. Too fast, actually, cuz you can't stop on grass like you can stop on concrete and I find that out when I whip the van all the way around trying not to hit the fucking thing and that's when I go into a skid, ripping up divots in two big lines like skaters leave marks on ice by cutting it up. Shit. I almost tip my shit over.

Almost.

When I'm good and stopped, I grab a bottle up, unscrew its cap, and douse another rag in rum before stuffing it in the neck. I rummage in the van for a lighter then and come up empty before I realize I still got one in my pocket.

I light it and the cloth takes it quick! A little *fwoom* right there in my hand.

I don't even think. I pitch my best fucking fastball at the wall.

It hits the bottom and catches real quick.

It goes orange and starts smoking.

I'm proud of it cuz I know they'll have to build us a good handball wall now. A concrete one or some shit. Something that'll actually last.

It's a good feeling. What would you call it?

Pride.

Yeah. That's what it is. *Pride.*

9

I wake up in the grass and fuck, do I ever have a headache *bad*. Like, pressure everywhere. It's like when I get a really bad cold and it feels like my whole face's gonna cave in. And at first I'm like, how'd I get here?

But then I remember the van and the grass and doing Momo's place up, and I look over and the van's still there, still sitting on top of some big fucking tire marks of torn-up grass.

The fire's extra loud now. It sounds like a wild animal eating the wall, just chomping on it and breathing hard, tearing it up in big chunks, and it's gone black in one big patch.

I back up to the van like it's gonna eat me too and I pick myself up slow.

This shit's starting to be a pattern now.

I'm losing time somehow, like a cut in a movie.

A time jump, you know?

That's my life right now. And it makes me wonder, like, should I slow down or what?

At first that sounds like a really good idea, to just chill out, you know? Find a hotel with a pool somewheres and just fall asleep on one of them chairs that fold down halfway.

But then I think, *nah*.

I got to keep fucking going.

Cuz I'm a bomb.

And if I don't keep moving, I'll explode.

10

I'm fixing to get up on the 105 Freeway, and this thing isn't even done being built yet, cuz fuck it, why not? I'm laughing as I fly past them UNDER CONSTRUCTION signs and up on a ramp that ends in the sky with a bunch of girders sticking out and no asphalt. It's a good parking spot, man. Up here, it feels like my road, like it's been built just for me. I got my eyes north on fire dots and a smoke smudge so fucking big that it goes all the way across the sky. It's black everywhere, like it got dark early. I can't see no San Gabriel Mountains. I can't see Downtown. I can't see shit.

But I can see more than I seen all day. And it kind of feels like I been in a submarine for hours, looking through one of them Paris scopes, but now I'm up on the surface and I open the hatch and look out.

It's quiet too. Quieter than you'd think. I don't even hear any sirens.

Traffic's way good though. I can see the 710 from here and nothing's on it. Every fool's either at home waiting it out or getting into some shit. They ain't out driving. Which means the best time to drive in L.A. is when it's burning to the ground. I think that shit's funny as hell! Even funnier, days like this come once every couple decades around here.

See, when it comes to Mexican people in this city, we know all about the zoot suiters getting beat the fuck down by white marines and navy dudes and shit. Everybody's *abuelo* has got a good story about that. What was that, like 1944 or something? Close enough.

So *that* shit was about race. It was simple, like: see a brown dude looking slick, smack the shine straight out of his shoes with all your white brothers. Unleash on that fool for dressing prettier than you, you know?

After that happens, everybody looks back and is like (in my best white-newscaster-dude voice), "Wow, that was terrible, just awful, no way should that ever happen again."

But then they forget about it, and they forget they even thought it was bad, and for a while nothing happens, but nothing got fixed either, it's just getting drier, ready for another burn, and that's when Watts happens, which I guess blew up in the '60s, cuz nobody's old-as-fuck uncle will shut up about that shit either. (I don't know much about families—shit, I don't know *anything* about families, but it seems like the kids never listen. Me, I always listen to the older people. I might not *look* like I'm listening, but I always am. I might not actually do what they say, but I hear it. I hear them. My ears never turn off, man.)

And then after Watts, the same thing happens as before, right? Everybody looks back and is, like, "Wow, that was terrible, no way should that happen again," and the fucked-up thing is they *mean* it this time, but they sure as shit don't remember last time, and still nothing changes.

And shit hasn't changed since. So that's, what? Twenty years apart for race riots? Enough time for everybody to forget again, right? Cuz it's nineteen-ninety-fucking-two, and this's what? Like, thirty? Probably a little less? Doesn't matter. The way it's blowing up, this one's overdue.

This shit is like a bank loan. *With interest.*

And I might never say much that makes sense to anybody but me, but make sure you write this shit down. Or underline it. Whatever.

If L.A. ever dies, if the people all give up and leave, carve this on its fucking tombstone . . .

L.A. has a short fucking memory. It never learns *nothing.*

And that's what's gonna kill this city. Watch. There'll be another race riot in 2022. Or before, I dunno.

Shit.

Hold up.

It occurs to me right now I really shouldn't be driving around up here too much cuz it could collapse or something. I turn around in my seat and look at the moneybag before busting out in a huge smile. I think about the heroin and weed in there while I dip another fingernail in the *cocaína* and rub it in like a gum treatment, then I turn this van around and ease down the ramp.

Shit is scary sometimes, sounding all crumbly! Was definitely easier going up than coming down. But when I'm back on the ground, I know that what I need is to go back to the hotel. I need to hide this shit good. The money and everything.

But here's another thing about L.A. It's big as fuck but people keep to their corners. There's whole blocks where people only speak Spanish or Ethiopian or whatever.

It's like every race's their own fucking boxer, and when that happens, when you get that mentality, it's easy to look at everybody else as an opponent, somebody to beat, cuz if you don't, you don't get what's yours. You don't get the prizes, you know?

And maybe that's it right there, in nutshells, like they say.

You plunk a bunch of people down from all over everywhere, keep them in their corners and don't let them mix and figure shit out, and they all got minds to compete, cuz shit, everybody in L.A.'s hustling all the time for everything.

Wait, where was I?

Shit.

Man, this headache's fucking *killing* me.

Like, it's so bad I can feel my heartbeat in my head.

Boom-boom. Boom-boom.

I dip into my white stash again and put it under my tongue this time. It tastes like when I had to swallow aspirins without water, except worse. More bitter. I take a big breath through my nose right about then, trying to fill my lungs all the way up before I let it go and push the taste out.

So, uh, like I said, there'll be more of this same shit in 2022. Just watch.

If it were up to me though, that one'd be robots versus people.

Cuz at least then we'd have to get together and shit. Damn. I'd love to be here for that too. You know it'd be some straight-up *Terminator 2* shit. We could bomb down the L.A. River in a semitruck and motorbikes for real then!

Yeah.

That shit sounds tight, but maybe that's cuz my headache's fading and my teeth are buzzing in my fucking head right now, man.

11

I rent another hotel room with the loose cash, one directly across from the room I already got for four more days. Well, now it's ten. When that's up, I'll move to another hotel where no one's ever seen me before in their lives. Maybe out in Hawthorne or some shit. You know, *far*.

For now though, the new room's on the same floor as my old one (the second), across the way, but nobody knows it's mine. I paid that fucker at the desk not to say shit to nobody. And I think I'm good cuz he barely speaks English and he's got no Spanish, which means if Fate or Momo ever know to ask him questions, he won't be any kind of help. I don't know if he's Chinese or what. Korean, maybe?

Fuck it. One's as good as the other to me. The less English the better.

None of the rooms are in my name. One's for Shane, just Shane, and the other's under Alfredo Garcia. You know, like them old western-type movies?

I make sure nobody sees me go in the new room. When the door shuts behind me, I lock it and pull the curtains closed. I drag the fucked-up chair over to the air vent above the TV and use the tip of Momo's knife to undo the screws on it.

It's fucking dusty as shit in there when I open it up! I cough for like two minutes straight before I grab two hand towels and scoop dust bunnies out of there straight into the trash, saying, "Fuck you, dust bunnies! You're never any good to nobody."

Directly after that, I put the H in, the weed, and the rest of the cash. I stack it up neat in there.

In the bathroom, I grab as much coke as will fit into one of them clear plastic Kodak film-holder canisters that I keep around for whatever I'm holding. I tip it in, careful not to spill, but that shit's slippery. Some hits the sink but I'm on it. The rest I wrap up tight in the plastic bag from the ice bucket and put that in the vent too. Then I screw it back up, hang the Do Not Disturb sign on the knob, and bone the fuck out.

Down in the parking lot, I hear somebody call out to me and I almost have a fucking heart attack as I reach for the gun in my pocket.

"D.B.," he says, "hey, Devil's Business! What the fuck, fool?"

I turn and it's Puppet. Poo-Butt Puppet.

I can tell I got to play this hard. "What'd you say? I ain't your fucking fool!"

When I first met this fucker, he didn't think I had a nickname, and he always knew I was up to no good, so he came up with that Devil's Business shit like it was fucking smart or something. Like it had class. Now even though he knows I go by Creeper, he still keeps up with it. I don't know why. Ego, I guess? Who knows why people do the fucked-up shit they do?

"Oh, I'm sorry," he says without sounding sorry. "You holding?"

Puppet wants to know if I got drugs on me. Now, what do you think, I'm gonna tell this fucker the truth?

"No," I say, "not since like a hour ago."

"Oh man, you're fucked up right now, aren't you, homes? You should've fucking *shared* that shit."

Like I'd ever share my shit with Puppet on purpose.

When Puppet gets close and I can tell he doesn't exactly need more cuz he's looking glazed as fuck, but he doesn't just want to know if I got shit, he's also got something on his mind and he's right about to tell me about it.

When this happens, I make sure to fucking listen hard, to listen like I'm not listening at all cuz the streets hear everything and know everything. If you think they don't, think again.

"You hear Fate's crew got Joker and them? Some chick went in last night late and opened up on a party." Puppet turns his hand into a gun by pointing his finger at imaginary targets across the parking lot. Then he thinks better of it and turns it sideways. "Like, *blam, blam, blam*. All kinds of cold-blooded, homes!"

Some chick, huh? He must mean Payasa. Couldn't be anybody else. For some reason, that kind of hits me too, cuz I know she hasn't rolled that hard before. It's like she popped her cherry capping those fools. It's like she's a new woman now. Not a virgin no more.

"Yeah, I heard that," I say, even though you know I hadn't heard that shit.

Still, it's better if he thinks I did but that's only cuz this is the only fucker on earth I want thinking I'm smarter than he is so he doesn't get it into his head that he can get over on me.

After one of them long awkward silences, Puppet finally says, "I bet you I can light more fires than you. We could have, like, a contest or something. What do you think? You man enough?"

He's got a lighter out and he's playing with it like it's something big. I almost laugh in this motherfucker's face. I keep it inside though. Like he has any clue he's already one behind, two if you count the handball wall, which I definitely do. He also doesn't know I got a ton of shit just burning a hole in Garza's van. I mean, not literally, but it could, you know. But then I think, you know, that isn't such a bad idea.

Like, I could burn a hole in this city so big that nobody ever did anything like it in the history of America. In the history of the world. Not since, like, a war or some shit. And, fire? Fire's like a cleaner. It transforms all the dirty stuff and makes room for the new. Cuz bleach burns too, right? It's like the same thing.

I pause and stare at Puppet before moving my eyes to this home-less dude shuffling through the parking lot, hobbling on a little metal cane with feathers tied to it but keeping his head up like he's the shaman of Los Angeles or something. He don't even look at me, but even from far away I can tell he's got a nasty scar on the side of his nose I can see. For a second I think about giving Puppet one just like it.

Then I turn back to him and talk like I'm Charles Bronson. "You're fucking *estupido*, Puppet. Why would I do that juvenile shit?"

Juvenile means childish, like something a dumb fucking kid would do, immature. And Puppet's still trying to explain to me why it's not stupid, why it's not like that at all, but it's too late cuz I'm already in the van and revving the engine and counting the bottles out the corner of my eye. Forty-four, still. No, forty-two.

Did I tell you I rolled up more rags and stuffed them in the bottles? No?

Well, I did.

And when I pop the shift to drive all I think about is how I'm gonna be the biggest fire starter in the history of the world.

The biggest one nobody ever knew about.

A hero, kind of.

A legend.

12

I got my two best lighters in my lap now (black BICs, motherfucker), and I don't even give a fuck what neighborhood I'm in. Lynwood, Compton, whatever. South Gate? HP? Who fucking cares? All I know is I bang a right on Western from Imperial and decide I'm gonna drive north till I run out of gas, hucking cocktails all the way.

I'm gonna light this city on fire all by myself. Burn it to the ground so we can rebuild with better shit. So we can start over. Someday somebody's gonna thank me for this shit.

First thing, I get a routine going.

I pull up to a place that looks like it'll catch good—maybe it's got an awning, or the door's open, or a window, and when I see that, I grab a bottle, light that shit, and chuck it out the driver's window like the world's best paper delivery boy. Except it isn't papers. This shit smashes and goes *fwoom* like a motherfucker!

I think I'm edging up into Inglewood or something when I start seeing the words *black owned* and *black owners* spray-painted on the sides of liquor stores, pawnshops, all that. Big black letters. All caps. At first I got no fucking idea what that's about.

But after a couple blocks it occurs to me that *mayates* need help figuring out which shit to fuck up. I gotta laugh at that. And when I'm done laughing:

1. I throw at those too.
2. And I throw at everything else.

I only stop once when I look east on one of them main cross streets (shit, I don't remember, was it Manchester?) and see what looks like a tank or some shit, all beige and camo'd out with dudes sitting on top with rifles and vests. That shit makes my stomach drop for a second, but they don't even look my direction. They just keep sitting there in the intersection.

So I cool it for a few blocks, you know, to be safe, and it's a good thing too, cuz at a red light a bus pulls up to me on my driver's side and I kind of look up and to the side and I see the whole thing packed with soldiers and one of them looks brown or whatever and he's scoping me, so I smile and wave, and he nods and waves back, and when the green light goes, I just cool it and go below the speed limit until that bus ups and turns. I keep it low-pro for like seven more blocks, until I see people ripping up stores again. Swear to God, in one Vons parking lot, I even see cops parked there and watching! Like, what the fuck? Not trying to arrest anybody. Just standing there. Doing nothing. Only watching.

After that's when I decide to bomb it back up. I don't give a fuck. I light and throw, light and throw.

I hit more than I miss. Pioneer Chicken, boom. Tong's Tropical Fish & Pets, boom. (I kind of regret that one though.) Tina's Wigs, boom. A shack with a sign out front that says SHOE REPAIR in red letters—forget it, that shit went up like a firework.

When I'm done with the second box and halfway into the third, I punch the radio on with my fist and it doesn't even hurt. It pops on, catching on some white boy music, you know the kind, all guitars and screaming, and I ain't exactly in the mood for that, so I slap the AM button in and pray for some Art Laboe shit. Some smooth oldies. Something with a beat to it.

And I must catch the end of what Art's saying cuz he's laying his voice down on the airwaves, telling everybody to be safe and stay indoors, and he says, *This right here's a little something to take your mind off what's going on out there.*

I can't help laughing cuz I am "out there" and *ba-bap-bap*, that's the drums coming in. Snares, I think. And the singer jumps on right after.

I know this song, I think. It's "Rock Around the Clock," and what the fuck is a glad rag anyways?

I'll tell you what it is. It's these wicks, that's what.

All these rags I tore up and stuffed down the throats of these bottles. They sure do make *me* glad. And when that fucking guitar solo comes in, it's like the song's playing just for me, only me, all fast and shit as I'm holding the steering wheel straight with my knees, grabbing a bottle out of the box next to me with my right hand, lighting the cloth with my left, then grabbing the neck as I switch it back to my left hand and throw it underhanded, and as it comes to the end of the song, I get sad and just keep driving.

I wish I could rewind it, and play it again and again and again.

13

My shit is running on fumes when I hit Sixth and Western, and I wouldn't've been if I didn't have to go around a bunch more army-looking dudes, go east on Seventy-Sixth for a bit before riding it to Hoover, then creeping onto Gage until I could sneak onto Western again and head back north. What a detour.

I didn't really plan for that, and I only got a box left when I see a strip mall on Sixth and I think, *Fuck it. Why not? It's as good a place as any for my masterpiece, cuz I'm gonna burn this whole fucking thing.*

All two fucking stories of it.

But it's weird cuz I can't focus so good. See, tastes have been pinging back and forth in my mouth for blocks.

Like, one second it's peanut butter, and I'm thinking when the fuck did I eat peanut butter last? I don't even *like* that shit.

I must've been, like, what? Fifteen?

And then when I'm sure I haven't eaten that shit since I was fourteen, I taste tomatoes. Raw tomatoes. And I can smell them too.

Fuck. I've done *way* too much coke, man.

I try to put tomatoes out of my head by taking the tire iron that's been sliding around in the back since I first started driving this fucker and get out and start banging in some store windows. Once they're popped, I light a rum bottle and toss it in. I've done two doors before I realize there's a crew of fools across the street.

I can't tell from so far away but maybe they're black. Either way, these fuckers are going crazy trying to rip bars off a convenience store window. They're even going so far as to tie some kind of rope to a rusted-out truck's tow hitch and try to yank it out the whole window cage, and then I see why.

There's still someone in there that they're trying to get at. A shopkeeper with a gun or something cuz there's screaming and people jumping back and forth in the opening and popping off shots like it's Beirut or some shit.

That makes me hurry it up.

I bust in a third window, a fourth. I'm only doing the dark storefronts.

Fuck the lit ones. I don't need somebody to be in there with a gun.

I'm onto my fifth, a video store with posters in it I can't fucking read cuz it's got a different alphabet, when I hear screeching behind me, like a car burning rubber and coming to a hard stop, and I'm sure it's the truck, but then somebody's yelling something like, "We will shoot, we will shoot!" But I don't turn around. I bash out another window, figuring it's for the fuckers on the other side of the street. But when I'm hucking a flaming *ron* in the window, I hear, "Stop or I'll shoot," all loud in English and maybe this one's meant for me.

If it is, I think, *fuck it*.

I pick the tire iron back up and go to smash in another window out . . .

But I hear a pop before I can bring the thing forward and smash the glass and my ears start ringing, like instantly. And there's a hole in the window now, a real little one, like someone threw a pebble through it just now.

I cough and blood hits the glass in front of me.

Like, a spatter.

I know right then that that shit is mine. I'm like, "fuck." I whisper that shit as I reach out and touch it on the window.

It looks way darker than I thought blood was supposed to look.

And I try to put it back. I actually try.

Estupido, right?

I try to swipe my blood up off the glass and put it back inside me, but when I touch my cheek, I find out I got a hole in it.

A hole as big as my fingertip. I know cuz I feel it.

And I try to plug it.

But when I try, my finger goes all the way through to the other side and I feel whiskers on my cheek . . .

On the *outside* of my cheek.

That's when it hits me that I'm almost touching my ear.

When half my hand's *inside* my mouth.

Fuck.

That's not good.

The numbness is starting.

In my head. Like, in my skull, I don't feel anything.

Not no more.

And that's weird. Cuz I got no headache.

There's . . .

Nothing.

Just blackness coming up from the floor.

Grabbing at me like hands.

KIM BYUNG-HUN,
A.K.A. JOHN KIM

APRIL 30, 1992

6:33 P.M.

1

It would be a school night—and I would be at home—if the riot hadn't spread. Looting has been reported in Hollywood, at some locations in the San Fernando Valley, and even in Beverly Hills, the radio says. It's everywhere, but it feels like it's here the most: Koreatown, my family's home, my home. I bet nobody in those other places is sitting in the backseat of a car with the radio up loud though, scrunched between his dad and his old neighbor who smells like *bonjuk*, trying to keep a gun gripped tightly between his feet while another gun digs into his hip.

Both actually hurt. I feel rigid metal bruising the arches of my feet, pressing through the leather of my Jordans, but my father's gun is worse: he wears it like a gunslinger, in a holster at his side. Every time he shifts, its weight grinds into my hip and a hot little pain shoots down my leg.

With what's going on, my dad is a different person, not the guy who lets my mom talk over him at the dinner table, or the one who watches the Dodgers in arms-crossed silence. My father leans into me as the car banks left and another stinging bolt goes up and down my leg. I hold in my wince. The last thing I need is him accusing me of being soft, not in front of these people.

Mr. Park is driving. He lives in our building too, but I only met him an hour ago in our lobby. It's his car. He has a big mole on his left cheek and he wears the collar up on his polo shirt to try to cover it, I think. His brother sits shotgun, wearing a Lakers cap. He's got glasses like me. On my left, Mr. hair, and a grayer sweatshirt with checkered pants pulled Because I am the youngest and smallest, I have to sit in the midd It's embarrassing and uncomfortable. I can't even see out the windows. I know there's smoke, though, lots of it. I can't smell anything else now. I might as well have charcoal stuffed up my nose. I also know Mr. Park uses the horn a lot as he drives and curses people in Korean—people in the streets, I guess.

When I did my Modern California History paper on Los Angeles, I found out that there are 146 nations represented within its confines, and 90 different languages spoken. I'll have to check the library encyclopedia for how many countries there are in the world now. I used to know how many there were, but then the Soviet Union broke up last year, and this year Yugoslavia did too, so that could be as many as twenty more with Croatia and others now independent.

"*Ya*." My father elbows me. "*Jib-joong hae*."

He wants me to pay attention to Korean Radio USA, 1580 AM. He knows I'm trying not to because it's depressing. Each story is exactly the same. Everywhere in L.A., Korean businesses have been ignored by police and firefighters. In fact, that's why we're here, in the back of Mr. Park's Toyota hatchback driving up Wilshire, patrolling our neighborhood because no one else will. That's why I have a gun.

"I *am*," I reply in English, but he looks at me like I'm lying.

"Man protect what is his," he says in English without any shame for how incorrect it sounds. "This *America*."

I nod. Mr. Tuttle, my A.P. History teacher, says nothing happens in a vacuum. Everything has context. If you understand the context, you understand the cause, and the effects that come out of it. So if the riot is an effect, what caused it? Rodney King and the video, of course, but there's something else: a girl named Latasha Harlins. She was the subject of my social justice assignment last semester. I had to play devil's advocate and put myself in an African American's shoes.

Less than two weeks after the beating of Rodney King, fifteen-year-old Latasha Harlins was shot and killed in March of 1991 by a Korean store owner named Soon Ja Du. There was video of that one too. Soon, a woman who looked like the old ladies in my building but was only fifty-one, shot Latasha in the back, and was convicted of voluntary manslaughter, fined, and given five years' probation even though the crime she was found guilty of carried a maximum sentence of sixteen years in prison. Understandably, this was viewed as a miscarriage of justice in the black community and people were very angry. Nothing happened after that verdict though.

Mr. Rhee derails my train of thought by pulling out a gun with a long silver barrel. He checks once more that it's loaded. It is. The gold-bottomed bullets are huge in their chambers, thick like my pinkies. In their middles, they have black dots rimmed with little silver circles. They look eerily like eyes: six eyes staring at me from inside the cylindrical cartridge before he snaps it shut. I cannot imagine what they would do to a human body; maybe it would blow somebody's whole head off.

That's when it occurs to me that we are technically vigilantes, and I don't know how I feel about that. The term has a negative connotation, but really, it is just self-appointed citizens who fill the void when there is no law enforcement. The police told us to evacuate, to leave our homes and our businesses. At first, the radio told us to do that too, but then a lawyer called the station and said we shouldn't. He said we have the Second Amendment. He said we have the right to protect our property and ourselves. When my father heard that, he asked me to explain. I said it was from the Constitution; it was our right to keep and bear arms. After I said that, everything changed. My father's face reddened and he nodded. It seemed like whatever was about to happen was my fault when he opened his closet and took the guns out. Some I'd seen from when he took me to the firing range for practice and gun safety a year ago. Most I hadn't. It was scary seeing them lined up on the floor. They looked like toys but heavier, shinier, and I just stood looking at them as my father picked up the phone and called Mr. Rhee.

Mr. Park slams on the brakes and I jolt forward, hitting my chin on the shoulder of the shotgun seat. He curses at someone in front of the car as his brother rolls down the window and aims a gun outside. Whoever got in the way must have scurried off, because soon enough we're moving again.

At this point, I wonder if I'm a vigilante too. The thought scares me at first, but then it feels warm in my chest because I wonder what Susie Cvitanich would think. She probably wouldn't believe me. Susie goes to my high school. Her family's Croatian. She thinks I'm a straight arrow. *Señor Aburrido Amarillo*, she calls me when we're studying A.P. Spanish in the library. That means Mister Boring Yellow. It sounds racist, but it's not like that. It's just that the Spanish words sound funny together.

I pick the gun up from between my feet. It's still in a scuffed brown leather holster that my dad must have gotten in the 1970s. Nobody ever tells you how heavy guns are. I guess it's something you have to find out for yourself. As I weigh it with my hand and figure that it must be at least a pound and a half, maybe two, I'm sure Susie wouldn't call me boring if she knew I was a vigilante.

The more I think about that term though, the less I like it. I would like to think of us more as a posse. Truly, we are just a group of concerned citizens who live in the town and contribute to its daily life and commerce. Mr. Park and his brother run a dry-cleaning store. Mr. Rhee is retired, but he owned a liquor store before he sold it. My dad is the only one who doesn't work in the neighborhood. He's an engineer. He works for TRW. They might seem common, but what people might not know—the people who want to rob us, hurt us, and burn our homes—is that all the men in this car but me have at least three years of military experience. That is because military service is compulsory in South Korea. They all know how to use guns. If Koreatown is saved, it will be because men like my father are trained.

Historically, posses were made up of law-abiding ranchers and shop owners. They were civilians, not sheriffs, but when the time came, they put on badges because they were asked to. They enforced the law when they had to, like when the sheriff needed help, but what happens when the police abandon you?

The sheriffs never abandon the town in western movies. It'd be un-American. But it's happening here. The National Guard is in South Central, but they aren't up here. We don't have badges, but we should. Mr. Tuttle says there is nothing more American than standing up for yourself when people are trying to bully you. It was practically the founding ethic of this country. Britain was a bully, so we beat them. There is nothing more American than defending yourself and others.

Mr. Park takes one hand off the wheel to turn the radio up.

"We have heard from a woman in trouble." The disc jockey's voice sounds panicked. "This is the address: Five Six Five South Western Avenue. Please help!"

"Where is that?" Mr. Park, the driver, wants to know.

His brother, the other Mr. Park, has a Thomas Guide in his lap and a flashlight in his hand that he smacks to get it to turn on. He flips pages before saying, "Sixth and Western. Left up here."

"When you hold a gun, do not think too much," my dad says in Korean. He has his gun out. He pulls the top of it so far back that I can see the small round barrel at the front, but he's only checking the chamber. I only see a fraction of the casing before the slide jumps forward with a heavy click. With a half wave, he motions for me to remove the holster on mine. "I would remind you of Ecclesiastes."

He means Ecclesiastes 3:3, I think—the bad times, not the good times: a time to kill, a time to break down. I take a very deep breath, the deepest one I can with my shoulders squished. Mr. Rhee pats my knee.

"*Gwen chan ah*," he tells me. *It's okay.* "These are animals, not men."

My parents always told me school would prepare me for anything, that school was the most important thing in the whole wide world, but school never prepared me for anything like this. It couldn't. My stomach drops as Mr. Park takes a wide turn on Western and accelerates up the block. For at least the sixtieth time, my father shows me where the safety is on the gun I'm holding, with one major difference: this time, he clicks it off.

2

Everything happens too fast. I've heard that in stories before, and I always thought it was so stupid, a trick almost, but now I know it's true. When it's chaotic, when there are too many things to pay attention to and your heart beats a hundred miles per minute, everything *does* happen too fast. There's just no way to pay attention to everything. You can only do the best you can under the circumstances.

Through the windshield, I see us coming close to a truck. It looks like four people are gathered around it. Two of them have handguns. My mouth goes dry when I see that. All of them are black.

Mr. Park screeches to a stop at the curb—trying to scare them, I think. Whether or not he means to hardly matters, it works. All four of them jump back.

Both Mr. Parks roll their windows down and open their doors like TV show cops and lean out, extending their pistols through the space where glass used to be, but still using the doors as cover. They're both screaming. "Go or we will shoot!"

They scream it at least twice, maybe three times as my dad and Mr. Rhee open their doors too and they get out and point their guns, but they steady their arms on the tops of the doors, which leaves me to scramble out from the middle with the radio blaring behind me.

"I am speaking with the woman," the DJ says in Korean. "She says the shooting has stopped, and it sounds as though help has arrived. Whoever you are, thank you!"

The truck with the looters in it reverses, trying to pull out, but it's still attached to the building by a rope. The Park brothers scream at the looters to unhook it, and oddly enough, one of the guys flopped in the back of the truck bounces up and starts tearing at the knot, trying to free the rope.

Blocks away, I hear a siren. As I stand in the street for a moment, I wonder, is it coming or going? My lungs feel heavy just breathing the smoky air. In front of us, the looters are well and truly spooked. They obviously didn't expect us to fight back.

I hear a crash and look behind and across the street, to a two-story mini-mall where a black figure raises his arm and drops it by a dark window. Several of the ground-floor windows are orange. At first, I don't know why that is, and then it hits me: fire! *Oh heavenly God*, I think, *this guy is setting fires!*

There's no time to think and I need that. I need time to think. One second passes, and two, but I'm no better than when I started. I need to stop him somehow.

"Stop or I'll shoot" is the only thing I can think to shout at him. I feel stupid saying it, but I pray it's enough.

It isn't. He doesn't stop. As I run closer I see he has a crowbar in his hand now and he's leaning back to smash another window when I stop and raise my gun. My dad told me to only fire warning shots, to shoot into the air. Scare them, he told me. Just scare them. I aim, certain I'll miss. I think, *If I can get close, I can scare him more.*

I line the black figure up with the metal sight on the end of my pistol, and then I aim to the right of his head, at a Korean movie poster I recognize in the video shop window: *Death Song.* On it is a cameo with a woman's picture, almost round, surrounded by a field of white. It makes a perfect target in the dark. I squeeze the trigger slowly, like I've been taught, and the .22 pistol pops, jumping in my hands.

This figure, maybe twenty yards away, stops, then sways. He drops the crowbar and it clangs to the concrete. I hear it from across the street. That's when it occurs to me: I hit him. I *hit* him!

Behind me, I hear the truck speed off and both Mr. Parks shouting to the store owner inside the convenience store, telling her she's safe. It doesn't occur to me to run over to the man I shot until Mr. Rhee does.

It doesn't even feel like I'm running. One moment I'm across the street, the next I'm in the parking lot, looking down on him and breathing hard, staring at blood leaking from his face into concrete cracks, as Mr. Rhee takes off his gray sweatshirt and presses it to the man's cheek. There's so much blood, more than I've ever seen.

The siren I heard before sounds closer now. It's coming toward us! Mr. Rhee tells me to run into the street, to flag it down if I can, so I do. From five blocks away, I can tell it's a fire truck. *Praise God*, I think as I raise my hands and wave frantically.

The driver has to see me, I think. *He* has *to.* When five blocks becomes four and three, and then two, he *does* see me, but he's not slowing. He actually speeds up! When he hits our block, I have to run out of the street so I don't get hit!

When I tell Mr. Rhee what happened, my father manages to strike a deal with the Park brothers.

"They will take him to the hospital," he tells me in Korean. "They do not want you involved."

There is no further discussion. Both Mr. Parks pick up the body and waddle over to the open hatchback and tip him in; this guy, who looked so scary from far away, looks so thin and fragile up close, and there's something else. He looks young—maybe a little older than me. The hatch slams down, cutting off my view, and then the tires spin as the Toyota speeds up Sixth toward Downtown, the same way as the fire engine.

I'm sweating as I watch it go. I ask my dad if he's dead, this man I shot.

"Not yet," my father says in Korean. He puts a hand on my shoulder and I can see a new look on his face, not anger, but pride. I think it is, anyway. I've never really seen it before, but I only have a moment with it, because then he's dashing to the nearest fire hydrant and shouting for help to open it.

I don't know how long it takes. Two minutes? More? But the wrenched fireplug finally opens with a gush into the street, filling the gutter in seconds before taking over the asphalt street.

With the truck gone, people appear out of nowhere. Koreans with handkerchiefs tied around their faces to manage the smoke. They're trying to put the fire out. People bail from anything and everything: metal watering cans, red children's toy buckets—anything. Old people and mothers bail from the gutter, and the water there reflects their hurried movements in front of bright orange flames and thick black smoke pouring from the strip mall's windows. I don't know why this trivia occurs to me, but it does: the average house fire burns at an average of 1,100 degrees Fahrenheit, and that gives me the most horrible sinking feeling. This bailing isn't enough to save anything.

That's when I hear another siren, faint at first, but then louder. These are coming right for us, turning from Fifth and racing down Western to pull up at the curb.

When I see the black-and-white police cars with their lights going, I say, "Praise be to God!"

I run to them, filled with relief, but when I get there, one of them is repeating himself loudly to my father as if he's deaf: "You cannot defend these businesses when the owners are not present."

I barely hear it over the sound of the fire. It's groaning almost, and then a roof beam collapses behind us with a thunderous crash. My dad ducks and when he comes up, he has a look on his face like he can't believe what the officer is saying. He points to the fire. Mr. Rhee steps forward too, and that's when I notice another policeman is next to me. He's pointing at my hand.

"Do you have a permit for that weapon?" he wants to know.

No, I want to say, *I'm only seventeen*, but I don't. Instead, I stammer some sort of response in the negative, barely getting my tongue to work because my eyes are glued to windows blackening at their tops. In the hierarchy of emergencies, surely a large-scale building fire, with people possibly inside, must rank above borrowing a weapon to protect one's neighbors, especially when it is utter chaos—

The policeman yanks my arm behind me, disarms me, and throws me over the trunk of his car. My glasses go flying, clattering over the asphalt as handcuffs clamp down on my wrists and I yelp. My world is blurry when my father shouts and I hear people protest behind me in Korean but it's halfhearted. They're torn between helping me and fighting the fire.

"Sir," the officer says to me, "you're under arrest for unlawful possession of a firearm."

"But—the fire!" Even though I'm maybe fifteen yards away from it, I'm sure I could roast marshmallows right where I am. It's that hot. I try to rise. I try to do something—anything!—to help the sad little grandmothers and grandfathers. "Officer, we have to put out the fire!"

An elbow pins me to the trunk by the back of my sweaty neck. As I twist to look to my left, it feels like the weight on my right eye orbit is going to crush it. Through the squad car's back windshield I see the distorted outline of my father getting pushed in by his head, and in the reflection, a flame spouts so big it looks like a flamethrower from a movie. I see now that the hazy second floor is on fire too. Disgust rolls around inside me, mixing with something else: rage.

It's then that I have the first calm thought I've had since Mr. Park turned on Western: this building will burn to the ground, and worse, they're going to *let* it. These public servants we pay who are paid to protect us, to serve us, they're going to let—

A realization hits me like lightning. I think, *This is what injustice feels like*. This disgusted-raging-helpless feeling, this waiting for someone else's better judgment to kick in, this *praying* for this officer, this cop, to realize how insanely stupid he is being and uncuff me so we can *all* fight this fire, so we can actually help people, so we can actually *save* something.

Without warning the elbow leaves my neck and I'm pulled off

the trunk, toward the door of the cop car. I stumble but he forces me up. The cop has to turn me to get me into the car beside my dad, and when he does, I double over and cough.

It's not acting, not really. My lungs really are dry. They really do feel like they're going to crumble to dust inside me. When I'm coughing though, I'm summoning up every last bit of phlegm I have. When I'm done, I know I won't have the words to convince him that what he's doing is wrong, will *always* be wrong, so instead I go from bent over to standing straight up in less than a second, and this cop steps back reflexively, maybe to see if he needs to hit me to get me to obey, but his moment of apprehension is all I need because it gives me the opportunity to look him in his fuzzy peach face and *aim*.

When I spit, every terrible thing I have inside me hits him full in the face.

DAY 3
FRIDAY

CAN WE ALL GET ALONG? CAN WE STOP MAKING IT HORRIBLE FOR
THE OLDER PEOPLE AND THE KIDS?

—RODNEY KING

GLORIA RUBIO, R.N.

MAY 1, 1992

3:17 A.M.

1

I haven't slept since the riot began. I can't get Ernesto Vera's body out of my head. It's like it's burned in me, permanently, on my brain. His name, the look on his face—I can't shake them, and I've seen more death than most people ever should. Part of that I asked for, I know. It's my job. But part of it is my neighborhood too.

Ernesto's, though, it was different. It was personal. He didn't even recognize me when I was there trying to help him, but even beat-up as he was, I recognized him. I knew we went to Lynwood High together, that we even hung out a little freshman year and he was kind. We kissed some in the band room, but it never became anything. He never knew it because I never told him, but he was the first boy I ever did that with.

Years later, I saw him sometimes at the Tacos Al Unico truck or the stand on Atlantic and Rosecrans, and he'd always give my *abuela* one more taco than we ordered, extra onion because that's how my grandma liked it and he always remembered. That was Ernesto, I guess. He remembered the small things. A while later I heard from my cousin Termite that Ernesto had to pay for those extra tacos out of his wages. He never said anything to us about that. He never complained. I guess that was Ernesto too.

Then I come home one night and Ernesto's lying flat in my alley and all this nursing school I had can't save him. He gives up right under my fingers, and then he stays there all night, into the next day. He stays there blocking the way I normally go to work, and insects and birds were getting too interested in him, so I called 911 five times and only got through once, but then got put on hold and they never picked back up. So then I called my aunt's boyfriend that works at the county coroner's and he said he was sympathetic and all, but no way was he coming down, not with how dangerous things were, and besides, he said, he had zero resources. His guys were spread out all over the city, already hours behind on pickups, even in safe areas.

That set me off. I was screaming before I knew it, asking him how he thought it made me feel having to live in the middle of it, having to have the dead body of the first boy I ever kissed outside my garage for more than a day? Did he know that I've had the windows closed in my house this whole time but now I'm starting to smell it, and did he have any idea how awful that was when you can't get away?

After that, I didn't wait for him to say anything, I hung up and called a private ambulance company I know of through the hospital and I begged them to come, but it wasn't until I told them I'd pay the drivers extra that they started listening. I had to lie, too. I told them I was his sister and, please, we just needed him treated right. The guy on the phone I didn't know, but he said he knew of a place to take the body, and then he started building a lie of his own, saying how he'd have to tell the cops there was no crime scene, that it was a body dump, and they were just out doing a run and stumbled across it and the family begged us, and, *Ah, I don't know*, I remember him saying, *I'll think of something. Just make it cash.*

I watched two guys take Ernesto up and put him in the back for $228. That's eleven 20s, a 5, and three 1s. All the banks have been closed since the riots started, so I could only give what I had in the house, every last little thing I'd saved for rainy days. I was going to buy a new TV with that money, but now that seems stupid. I don't even want to look at everything going on in the city anymore. I don't want to see the news. I just want quiet.

The thing that sticks with me about how they took him is that they didn't remove his sister's flannel from his face, the black-and-white one I watched her put on him specially. They just put a white sheet over everything, from head to toe, and tried not to disturb anything about the body. On the chance it had evidence on it, they said. After that, I watched them close the doors up, and I watched Ernesto get driven away. Somebody had to. I've been nursing long enough to know that not everybody can be helped. Sometimes, you just have to be there, be a witness, so they don't pass on alone. I hope I was that for him, but I don't know. I still feel I failed. I stood in the alley for a long time after he was gone, and when I finally left for work, I didn't come home.

So I'm still at the hospital, Harbor-UCLA. I can't bring myself to go home, so I just stay on and think about Ernesto and worry about my brother. He's out there with everybody else banging and looting, I just know it. Him and what he calls his party crew. I didn't even know what that was so I asked him to explain it to me, and he didn't even do that. He just told me a story about how this one time, a bunch of them ditched school and had a ditching party. It was the kind of thing where everyone was taking drugs and having sex in the backyard during the day. He wouldn't shut up about how great it was. Gangster Woodstock, that's what he called it. I *wish* he was kidding. Aurelio is a lot of things, but not a liar.

Stacy must see me just standing there in the hallway so she comes over from the nursing station. "You okay, lady?"

"Long day," I say automatically.

That usually means, *don't ask*, or, *it's not over yet*. For me and the other nurses, it's like a code. We had curfew tonight all over the city. It started at dusk, the news said, but the only thing it did for us in the hospital was slow the flow from nonstop to an occasional flash flood because when people come in, they come in waves. We're in a lull now, but it'll pick up soon.

"*Long* day," Stacy says back, smiles, and walks away, but as she's going she kind of winks at me and points behind her clipboard at a man coming up the hall.

I follow her finger to the man known as Mister So-and-So, and that's when my heart decides to palpitate like it was jumping rope and all of a sudden got tangled up in it.

That's not his real name, by the way. Only me and the other nurses call him that. At first, it was because Filipina Maria—there's two Marias, Abulog and Zaragoza—well, Maria Abulog saw him first sixteen months ago and liked what she saw even though she's married and has three kids, but I guess she felt it was important to tell all the single nurses about him because that's how nurses are: they either wanna set you up, or knock you down. In my experience, there's not really much in between.

Anyways, when Filipina Maria looked at Mr. So-and-So's name tag, she saw a last name that started with *S* that she couldn't even hope to pronounce, so she just called him Mr. So-and-So, and then we all did. Pretty soon everybody got real good at being on the lookout for the tall firefighter, over six foot, with a black mustache and a chin with a dent in it, brown eyes, and good-looking eyebrows like he gets them plucked or something, but I know he doesn't. Lots of girls have made plays for him, but he doesn't seem interested. At least he wasn't into Stacy and she's all blond and an ex-volleyball player, so I don't know what his type is. All the older nurses on the ward say he likes me, but I don't believe them. Maybe I'm too short for him. Maybe I'm too brown.

Here's what I know about Mr. So-and-So: his first name is Anthony, he's thirty-six years old but I don't know when his birthday is and that's a shame because it would be helpful for horoscopes, he has a scar on his left cheek that looks like a lowercase letter *v* but I don't know how he got it, under that scar is a dimple when he smiles but there isn't one on the right side, he lives in San Pedro and he grew up there, his family is Croatian and I know because Teresa over in Billing is from Pedro too and she knows his family because there's only one public high school and one tiny Catholic high school so everybody knows everybody, this is good too because Teresa also knows his family is Catholic, which is great news for my

mother, if, you know, she ever met him or anything. I should probably say I'm not obsessed at all. I just like him a little.

Okay, maybe a lot. And it's weird too, because normally I'm not
so good at paying close attention to anything but my job, but with
him, I can't help it. Like, when he's done talking to me, right before
he has to go, he always bows his head a little, like he's acknowledg-
ing me, like our talks mean something to him, too. And his hands,
they're not like normal size. They're so big, the kind that could
swoop you up, the kind that hold women tight on the covers of the
silly romance books Tia Luz reads, and best of all, his left hand has
got no ring on it. I asked Teresa and she says he's never been married, just engaged once but it didn't work out. I try not to stare when
he sees me and walks toward me.

When I was just a girl, I took ballet because my mother said I
needed culture, and now the only thing I remember about it is how
the pirouetting made me feel all dizzy and twisted up inside after.
That's how I feel when Mr. So-and-So gets close.

I've seen him in a few times, always with other firemen. He's the
driver. I guess they call him an engineer though, like on a train. He
gets them to the fires, and if anybody's hurt, he drives them here.
His look tells me that's why he's here, and my heart sinks.

"Good morning, Nurse Gloria." He says it all quiet.

He does that, calls me Nurse and my first name. I can't think
why or how it started. I like it though. It's become our thing, the
way we greet each other, so I always respond with "Good morning,
Fireman Anthony."

But he doesn't smile at me today, and I don't get to see his dimple,
not like normal. His head is down. I know it's because of everything
going on, but even when things are bad—and when you work where
we work and meet how we meet, there's always *something* bad—he
has a smile for me, even a little one, or a dark joke about something
he saw or something he heard. He usually tries to make me smile,
but not today. Today, he puts his hands in his pockets.

So that's when I know I have to be the one to start the conversation, so I say, "From what's coming in, it doesn't look good out there. What's going on?"

I touch his triceps softly and drop my hand quick. I want him to know I care, but at the same time, I don't want him to know I care. My heart's kind of fluttery, like it remembers tripping over the jump rope and it's a little wary. I look him over to make sure he isn't hurt or anything, not even a little bit.

"Uh" is what he says. Nothing else.

I know not to push it. You hear things in the hospital. You see things. We treated eleven firemen last night that I know of—and trust me, I checked every single name when they came in. One of them had been shot, but he made it through surgery and could pull through. There might've been more. It seems like firemen got it the worst that first day. Everything was so disorganized and there were no cops to protect them, so they got shot at. It seems better now, but still not great. I even heard there were sniper attacks on Fire Stations 9, 16, and 41. As soon as the engines left the stations, people started shooting.

So if I'm acting weird at all, or jumpy, just forgive me because I didn't know if Mr. So-and-So would be safe or if I'd see him again, and women sometimes do strange things when they don't know if they'll see somebody-that-might-end-up-being-really-special-to-them again. That's what my *abuela* said anyways, and she was an expert on all kinds of things, especially on being a woman.

"You be sure to take care of him," Mr. So-and-So finally says.

I don't know who he's talking about exactly, but I know we got one more firefighter to take care of now. I'll ask Stacy about it later, after he's gone. Mr. So-and-So bows his head a little right then, and before he looks back down the hall the way he came—because he always does that right after bowing his head—I say, "You have to go."

He gives me a look like he's not sure how I know that, but I just give him a little smile, hoping he'll give me one in return. He doesn't.

"Be safe out there," I say.

He nods and goes. He doesn't look back at me. I try not to take it personal but it burns a little in my chest. When he's a few steps away, I see dried blood on the back of his neck and immediately I want to reach out and hold him, inspect him, make sure he's okay and it's not his blood, but I know I can't—that'd just be weird of me—so I let out a frustrated-and-flustered-and-worried sigh and start walking.

2

To distract me from how I'm feeling, I go where I was supposed to go before, a patient's room in Neuro ICU for a postsurgical vitals check. This one came in with a bullet hole in his left cheek and his toxicology test off the chart. Get this, he got shot from behind at an angle, so the bullet went in through his cheek and out through his open mouth so there was no exit wound, but he wasn't responding when he came in and no one could figure out why. That is, until we did an MRI and found a brain tumor.

"A miracle." That's what the attending called it at the time. "This sonofabitch has a tumor the size of a golf ball in his frontal lobe and enough cocaine in him to kill a horse, but still he's up and walking around? If he's not shot in the head, maybe we never find it. More things in heaven and earth, Nurse Rubio."

I don't know what that last part means, but I know his surgery went perfect. The tumor was superficial to the surface and came out with an area of normal tissue entirely around it, and now he's on my ward taking up a bed, so my mission is to be the bad guy and clear him as soon as I can, because we have admitted patients taking up lobby chairs around here. Under normal circumstances, he'd be here two to three days, but a riot and martial law isn't normal circumstances.

When I pull the sliding screen, he's awake. He's got gauze and tape on his face, covering his whole cheek, and new stitches scabbing dark red on his cranium. His chart used to say John Doe, but someone before me scratched that out and wrote Antonio Delgado.

He looks cute in a broken kind of way, at least so long as he doesn't open his mouth. Some girls go for that type. Not me, though. Not anymore.

"Nurse, hi," he says, ruining it. "Hi, Nurse. My name's Antonio. *Annnnn-to-ni-o*. But people that know me call me Lil Creeper."

He giggles at that. He really cracks himself up. This is good news, I guess, because it means his morphine drip is working.

Pathology came back and said it was a low-grade astrocytoma, malignant as hell. But we caught it early, which is good, because if we hadn't, he could have been dead in twelve months or less. So, in a way, getting shot saved his life. Incredible. How is it the cockroaches of the world have all the luck but the good ones like Ernesto never seem to? I'll never understand that.

I check his intracranial pressure first, which is normal considering, and then his blood pressure. It's 139/90, a little on the high side, but that's perfect, because it means it'll still push nutrients to the brain through the swelling.

"My heart might be getting fast cuz you're close. Maybe you should check again?"

Yeah, right. I deflate the cuff, pull it off, and shine my light in his eyes. His pupils are reactive, constricting perfectly and symmetrically. More or less on one or the other might mean a problem, but for now, he's good enough for me to discharge to Skilled Nursing as soon as he's stable for twenty-four hours, and, according to me, that will be ten hours from now. I'm noting this when a sick feeling hits me. I *know* this patient.

This is the little junkie that Mrs. Nantakarn is sure stole every one of her good china plates last year for no reason, because it's not like you can sell them for anything much, and she had to buy them back at the swap meet a week later. Him and my brother were the same year in school. I'm sure they know each other. Of course, I don't need to draw attention to that.

"Look at you," Antonio says. He squints like he's thinking. "I know you."

Great, just great. Already I feel the side of me I'm so good at hiding at work about to come out. Just being near this fool brings the neighborhood out in me. Rather than wait for him to put together how he knows me, I decide to go on the offensive. "Yeah? Well, I know you, too. Why'd you steal all them pretty plates last year?"

He smiles like I caught him, but he's smooth too. He slides right out of it.

"I'd never steal nothing, Sleepy's number one big sister. Never in my life. You're insulting me saying that."

I give him a look that says I-can-see-through-you, so-sell-your-bullshit-to-some-other-chick-that-don't-know-no-better.

He sees that and his face changes, almost looks more sad and vulnerable and that stops me for a second before he says, "Okay, but maybe I'd steal one thing."

It's a setup. I see his shit coming a mile away. Grow up in my neighborhood and make enough mistakes with terrible guys, you can too. It wasn't easy, but I had to learn somehow. What ties all the guys that treated me bad together is how good they were at lying to me, and how stupid I was and ate it all up. So with this little one, I put my hand on my hip, like, come-on-I-don't-got-all-day. Cuz for his type, I don't, and I never will again.

He pauses way too long because he thinks he's smooth and I'm already turning to leave when he says, "I'd steal your heart."

My laugh comes out so high and fast it surprises me a little. It's like a bark almost. This little boy couldn't have my heart if he cut it out of me. It's already kind of set on someone else, a good guy for once, except maybe that guy doesn't know it yet, or if he did know, maybe he wouldn't care, but I hope he would. I hope.

I guess I pause there, just a touch, and this kid, because that's what he is, all of nineteen, completely misreads it. He thinks it's for him!

"Come on," Antonio says, all confident. "I'll take you to Sam's and everything! I'm good for it. I'll let you order steak and shrimp cuz that's what type of guy I am. I'll treat you *right*."

Like this fool ever knew what it meant to treat a girl right. If I'd never left the block, that might sound pretty good, but I have, so it doesn't. Besides, no self-respecting girl in her right mind wants to go to Sam's Hofbrau. That place calls itself an adult cabaret, but it's just a dirty-ass strip club with pizza and fried food and ghetto girls shaking their soon-to-be-diabetic asses. It's where the gangsters and wannabe-gangsters throw money around like they're some-body, that's what my brother says.

"No thanks," I say.

"Fine," he says, "but you're missing out!"

I drop his chart in the slot at the foot of his bed and he knows I'm lost to him, so he starts serenading me with "Rock Around the Clock," except he's not saying clock, he's saying something else that my *abuela* raised me not to repeat, but it's slang for penis.

When you've known as many bad guys as I have, you appreciate the good ones, like how rare they are. Like, how sometimes there's so few you get to thinking that there's only ever four or five you actually get to meet, and maybe two you got a decent shot at being with. I had my chance with Ernesto, and he was good—not just good, but good *to me*—even at an age when everyone is an idiot. Maybe Mr. So-and-So can be my next good one. I hope so, because that's a long time between good men, too long.

I puff at some hair stuck to the side of my face, but it's no good. It stays stuck. I look at my watch. I been up for twenty-two, no, twenty-three hours now and I'm getting that tired sweat you get from being up and around in one place too long, so I comb hair off my forehead with my index fingers and tie it back with a little black hairband I always keep on my wrist if I need it. I ponytail it and then flip the end of it back through so I got like a loop on top of my head.

When I'm a few steps up the hall, I decide to pray a little prayer. I shoot a glance behind me to make sure no one's coming up quick with a gurney or a wheelchair before I stop short, and I bow my head. I take my silver cross necklace between my fingers. It feels weird saying "my" about that. My *abuela* gave it to me before she passed. I only have a few things from her, some dresses because they only fit me—all of them lacy and traditionally long and blue, because she wouldn't wear any other color ever—but this is the only piece of jewelry I have. My little sisters and cousins got the turquoises, the rings and necklaces. But this cross was my grandma's favorite, and that's why it's so special. I don't pray on it all the time, only when I really need to.

I hear the fluorescents buzzing above me and shoes squeaking far off, when I say my little silent prayer for my brother to not end up like Ernesto Vera in the alley behind our house, and then I pray for Ernesto's soul because he laid out there so long, longer than anybody should ever have to. Because I'm on a roll I say another little one for Fireman Anthony So-and-So to not be hurt and to come back safe so he can be kind to me one more time, so I can make him smile and show me his one dimple again. I don't want this to be the last time we ever see each other, and if I see him again, maybe then I'll have the courage to make it clear that if he wants to ask me to coffee, I wouldn't mind drinking some with him sometime, you know, whenever.

I put the cross back under my uniform collar then, and I feel kind of sheepish so I check both ways to make sure nobody saw.

ENGINEER ANTHONY SMILJANIC,
LAFD

MAY 1, 1992

2:41 A.M.

1

I have a bad feeling as we enter the cul-de-sac and see our destination lit up like a Roman candle at the end of it. This fire turns adjacent bungalows orange with its light. Right then, I think if ever a place were suited for an ambush, this'd be it. My head's on a swivel as we roll up the street to the blaze. It has been ever since I came on shift, and I don't like what I'm seeing either. Around here, lookie-loos dot lawns in twos and threes—young black ones with hoods up and dumb-ass rags on their heads.

Suzuki and Gutierrez are behind me in the jump seats. My captain is sitting next to me, Captain Wilts. He's black too, but that doesn't mean he likes the look of this crowd either. I tell him I don't like what I'm seeing, and he radios the Strike Team Leader that there are just too many people lurking, trying to look like they're not paying attention to us as we go by. Yelling, I've gotten used to, being pelted by rocks too, but not this kind of quiet. There's about thirty people looking at us like we're dinner on wheels, but the STL says to trust our escort, and Cap nods so I take us in. I follow orders—that's my job, I drive the rig and pump—but I don't have to like them, I just have to keep the hoses charged.

California Highway Patrol has two cars on with us, both from Ventura County down here on Mutual-Aid. Good guys. Not used to what we do, but good guys. They weren't happy hearing we take civilian gunfire even during the best of times, that our rigs get bullet holes and broken windows something regular. Now, in a run-of-the-mill emergency situation, we send a fireman to the hydrant, he opens it, and we squirt. But in the thirty or so hours since this riot kicked off, we've been learning this all over the Southland: you send one to the hydrant, he gets hassled, so you send two to the hydrant, and they get hassled too, so it's gotten to the point where you don't even bother opening a hydrant without two escort cars, each one blocking both ends of the block. It's good then, but everything's better when CHP has their guns out.

But this is a cul-de-sac in a neighborhood of run-down bungalows built too close together. It's an old block, something out of the '50s that was probably built to house aircraft plant workers like those down at Lockheed, the ones who came after World War II. Now it's all falling to pieces: peeling paint, fallen-down carports, and cars on cinder blocks. It's north of my district, which is 57s, so I don't know if this is Blood or Crip territory, but it's something. People are paying too much attention for it not to be, and worse, they're moving toward the fire—and us—like slow moths. None of that is my issue right now, though.

Right now, my issue is the cul-de-sac. If I wanted to lure firemen into a difficult situation to get out of, I'd do my arson here. Operationally, the only thing to do with cul-de-sacs is to lock off the opening. Only problem in this case is that's also our lone out. It's my job to know our outs, to park the rig head out, so we can pull up and leave with no wasted effort. No three-point turns. In and out clean. Here, we can't do that, and it makes me nervous when our only out is back the way we came, but the STL said knock these fires down, so I hook up and lay two lines before setting the pressure relief valve. I have the supply two-and-a-half and an inch-and-a-half down. I'm out of three-and-a-half because we had to cut and run due to a potential mob situation off Slauson a couple hours ago. Once we're going here, though, it goes fast and fine.

We have five engines so we knock it down fast. When it's still smoking, we start pulling back. In a standard situation, we stay on it until there's nothing but ash, because if there's a rekindle, it's your ass and the asses of everyone on your company. That's not the case with martial law. Here it's just pulling lines out, squirting, knocking a fire down, picking up, and heading out because there's always five or ten more to put out. Once you get into a rhythm, it's kind of fun.

For one thing, there's no EMS calls for us tonight and there haven't been since it started. That's almost like a reward. There's no search and rescue going on tonight, only hosing. That's why all the trucks are back at the stations and the knuckle-dragging, holier-than-thou AO's actually have to do some real work for once.

I keep eyes on the crowd when the STL orders us to pull out. They've mashed into one mass near the mouth of the cul-de-sac and that's not good. Quick as I can, I check my water tank's full from the hydrant before disconnecting the supply line and grabbing Gutierrez. We both load the inch-and-a-half back in the transverse bed. Normally, we'd load it up nice and tight and pretty, but there's no time to be in inspection mode. Right now it's all about getting the job done and then doing another two blocks over, or three, or whatever. Speed is the priority, not orderliness. It goes against everything we've been taught, and it's beautiful. It's freedom, is what it is. I'd feel better about it if the crowd was further back though. Every time I turn my head it seems like they're bigger somehow, closer.

I nod to Gutierrez, and he knows to hurry the hell up. He sees them too. We quick-load the two-and-a-half and lift it up between us. We rest it on the tailboard for a moment before the final heft into the hose bed as CHP gets back in their cars and opens our exit up so all the engines can come out, but that's when I know something's wrong. The second CHP shuts their doors, a barrage of debris comes our way, and right behind it, bodies fly straight at us through the dark.

Who knows why? Some race shit? Some authority shit? Excuse me if I never stopped to consider the motive of fucking gangbangers because I'm too busy dropping hose and ducking a chucked rock the size of a softball. The thing dents the back of my rig before hitting asphalt. By the time I pull my head up, somebody's on top of Gutierrez and one of his legs is trapped under the hose and he's struggling to get out of it. I lunge forward to tackle the cocksucker but I'm not fast enough. This big black sonuvabitch built like an offensive lineman slams half a jagged cinder block down on Gutierrez's face point-first.

I see the look on this kid's face then, the seriousness and the sickening glee, and I see the thing drop in slow motion, feeling the sound of it in my stomach when it makes contact with chin and pushes through it, the awful crunch of jawbone snapping under the weight. Gutierrez screams a sputtering scream as I smash into the smiling black bastard on top of him and send him half upright and tripping over the curb to fall on his face in the grass. I'm not the biggest guy in the world but I did put all my weight into it. What I'd do beyond that, I don't have to know because CHP's behind me with guns drawn and they pop off a warning shot that sends the kid scrambling away like a greyhound. As he goes, I see a shiny scar gleam on his shoulder, like he had surgery or something.

"Shoot him," I say. "He got Gutes! *Shoot* him!"

But they don't. They let him get away, over a fence. That burns me up but I can't waste energy on it now.

I look down and assess the injury before me. It's bad—ugly bad. Cap's beside me. He sees it. Suzuki does too.

"Shit," Suzuki says. "Hang in, Gutes!"

Through a new rip in his face, I see Gutierrez's tongue flailing like it's trying to get up and run away. The rest is worse, because I also see his jaw just hanging off, completely out of its left socket, so far out that I can see the flat whites of his molars.

My heart drops when I see that. I'm out of my jacket and ripping my uniform shirt off—because nothing in the first aid box seems big enough for this—balling it up as best as I can before putting it between his shoulder and his jaw, and I'm turning his cheek into it so it'll keep his jaw in one place for the moment.

"Keep the pressure there if you can," I say to Suzuki. "Just for a sec."

Cap runs to the radio as we lift Gutierrez and throw his arms over our shoulders to drag him to the cab. We don't have time for C-Spine. Best we can do is have Suzuki's hands on his neck, supporting it while we get the fuck out of here. I'm breathing thick and fast, and I'm babbling, apologizing with every word I can manage, I'm telling Gutes how fucking sorry I am, sorry that CHP dumbass didn't grease that kid right there, sorry I didn't trust my gut and leave the two-and-a-half behind, that if we hadn't left my three-and-a-half on the last run, I would've told him to leave it where it was on the grass, to not load it, but I didn't want to be without my last supply hose for the next one, and how stupid that all sounds now, how none of it was worth it. None of it.

Suzuki and I get Gutierrez into the shotgun seat of my rig. We lean him against the seat back as gingerly as we can before I'm jumping down and running around the front to my door. Suzuki does the same, scrambling into his jump seat behind and opening the window partition wider so he can support Gutierrez's neck. Cap's in the back now too, and he's strung the radio cord through.

To the mic, he says, "Firefighter Gutierrez has been injured."

"Say again," the STL's staff assistant says.

I'm shouting before I realize I'm shouting, "Some gangbanger hit Gutierrez in the face with a brick!"

Cap ignores me and repeats what he said before. CHP has the crowd all run off now. The four of them comb lawns and sidewalks, looking for strays, but I don't have time for that. I throw it in gear.

"How serious?" It's the STL now. He wants to know.

I'm front engine now and I should wait for a CHP cruiser to get in front of me, but I don't. I'm holding what's left of Gutierrez's jaw in its socket with my right hand because he's managed to twist away from the shirt while Suzuki keeps his neck supported, and I'm flipping my lights and sirens with my left as I put my foot down on the accelerator and speed out of the cul-de-sac.

"Extremely serious," Cap says.

What he doesn't say is that Gutes has got a new hole in his face, some teeth turned around, and, I can't go into the rest.

Gutierrez is 57s—one of ours, and the worst cook you could ever imagine—and he's shaking as I try to hold his face together, shivering more like. It's shock. He's murmuring something about me needing to call his wife and tell her he's okay, telling me not to worry, telling me it's his fault for getting his leg stuck. Through the hole in his face, I feel the side of his tongue shuddering against my palm as he speaks.

"Stop talking," I say to him. "Just stop."

"Harbor-UCLA," the STL finally says.

All over the city, engine convoys have been reporting civilians trying to slow them down or stop them so they can pelt rigs with bottles, rocks, cans—anything. They string themselves across intersections by holding hands Red Rover style, banking on you slowing down.

When Gutierrez whimpers, I feel a vibration in my wrist bone. Right then, I take a breath as deep as I can manage.

"So you know, Captain," I say behind me to Wilts, "if anybody gets in my way, I'm running them right the fuck over."

There's no response right away, only the directional wails of the sirens coming on behind me as the engines fall in. They're with me. All of them.

"You do what you got to do," Cap says.

2

Nobody gets in my way, lucky for them. I'm happy about that, as happy as I can be under the circumstances, because I really don't need anything else on my conscience. Right now, Suzuki's still supporting Gutierrez's neck, but Gutes is moaning a little between breaths. I've managed to press the shirt so his jaw stays marginally in the socket. That freed up my right hand to drive, but it also made the steering wheel sticky with blood, and the feel of it makes me hate myself. That feeling multiplies when I hear Cap relating details of the injury over the radio to the STL.

Vermont's the first major street I come to, so I bang a left but I'm going a little too fast and my right rear tire kicks up as I turn and it lands with a screechy thump that shakes the whole rig. Suzuki grunts and Gutierrez doesn't react, but all the same, I resolve never to do that again.

"Slow down, we're in a hurry."

That's what I tell myself. I actually say it out loud. It's something my ex used to say to me. It was the one good thing she ever left me with, something to remind me to stay calm during storms.

"You're doing just fine," Cap says behind me.

We roll by some National Guards building a sandbag fort on a street corner, on the edge of a supermarket parking lot, and I can't help thinking they'd do more good where we just were, but hell, I know a big part of their job is deterrent, not engagement. Still, it would've been nice to protect someone's neighborhood from burning to the ground without getting attacked by its residents, the very same people we're trying to help. That'd be too much to ask though, right? Fucking animals.

The CHP cruiser pushes up alongside me now. My guess is he's thinking this is my city, and I know where the hell I'm going, which is good, because I do. It's also his way of letting me know he's following my lead and the good news is, the streets are clear enough to allow that, which surprises me because I thought for sure curfew wouldn't work, not with how this city's going up.

I take a left on Gage but this time I'm going slow enough that my rig stays flat. I'm up the on-ramp and on the Harbor Freeway in a big goddamn hurry. My exit's Carson and I'm going over 60 now, but not much over. It's not advisable to push it much past that when you're carrying almost a full 500-gallon water tank and a 50-gallon fuel tank, no matter how full it is. We'll be there in five minutes.

We'll pull up, and everything will be fine. They'll swarm over like wasps wearing scrubs, take him away, and fix him.

Slow down, I think, *you're in a hurry.*

That doesn't make me actually slow down, but it helps me stay atop my feelings. I want to hurt the kid who did this. I want to find him, the one with the shoulder scar, and put a bullet in both his kneecaps. I try to remember what the gangbanger looked like, but I'm eyeing Gutierrez every few seconds to make sure he keeps the pressure on. I can't imagine how much it must hurt to put any amount of weight there. He's one tough sonuvabitch. I'm going to tell everyone that when he heals up. Everyone. *Someday, this is just going to be a story*, I think. *A war story.*

And it might not have been as bad if our EMT trainee wasn't out with 46s instead. I could've used the help. SEAL medics have done their unofficial internships with us for years because the navy believes it to be the most effective way to learn about combat injuries: blunt force, gunshot and stab wounds, explosion trauma— there's more of that in L.A. than anywhere else in America, I guess. It's our own private war zone, and this one just claimed the wrong damn casualty.

Right now, blood loss is getting to Gutierrez. He closes his eyes intermittently, like slow windshield wipers. I don't know if he can hear me, but I talk to him anyway.

"Hell of a way to end your shift, hero." I say it loud enough so he can hear me over the siren. "You'll sure have some stories to tell when you get back to Hawaii."

My cheeks flare up just from saying it, and I feel about a foot tall then, because what's heroic about trying to do your job and getting jumped by a gangbanger the size of a refrigerator? What could possibly be heroic about trying to protect yourself and failing? Nothing, that's what.

I shake my head and check his pulse. It's slow but there.

We'll be there in three minutes, I think.

The freeway's mostly empty. There's nothing to do but stare at new red, blue, or black graffiti that says, "Fuck the Police," and "Fuck the National Guard," and "Kill Whitey," and try not to take it personal while I aim the engine straight and go fast. We pass two LAPD cruisers with their lights on going back the other direction but that's it. I've never seen anything like it.

Gutierrez is one of our commuters. During your probationary period, you have to live inside the city limits, but after that, you can move wherever you want. If you can work shift trades and if it's okay with your captain, you can work whatever schedule fits your needs. The lone thing to worry about is company morale because people being far away all the time can affect continuity and teamwork, but as I said, that's up to Captain Wilts. He's one of the good ones. We have firemen living in San Francisco, San Diego, and Vegas that I know of, but the farthest flung is Gutierrez. He lives on Maui, a little house in Napili with his wife and second-grader, and he flies in for his shifts.

Goddamn. You know how sometimes in the heat of the moment you forget things, and later you remember them and it makes everything worse? That's what it feels like to remember Gutierrez's wife and kid. Kehaulani and Junior, their names are. Well, Junior's just a nickname. He's got his daddy's name. He's next in the line. Cute kid too, wide brown eyes like his mother. Earlier this year I met them before they did a Disneyland trip, the kid's first. In the station house, Junior asked me if I wanted to see what he was planning to give the tooth fairy and when I said yes, he pointed inside his mouth and showed me where a tiny white tooth was loose. He flicked it back and forth like a light switch just for me. After that, he giggled and asked me if I thought Mickey might want to see it too.

I check Junior's daddy's pulse again. It's the same.

"You better be okay," I say to him.

I'm royally pissed at that jury right now. I'm pissed at everything, but I might as well be pissed at them specifically. They come back with even one guilty, this doesn't happen. The least they could've given us was a scapegoat—but no. The whole city's paying for it now, and Gutes is paying more than his share.

Junior's dad works trades so he's on one month, and off one month. April, he was on, so May he's scheduled off. If this riot doesn't happen, if the city doesn't blow up, he doesn't stay out on emergency duty and he's sleeping at the station house and then catching a flight first thing. I know because I've driven him to LAX a bunch of times. Every firefighter has a second job, comes with the territory of so many off days. On his off months Gutierrez does real estate. From what I understand, he does pretty well at it. The part that messes with me the most is that technically, he should have been off-duty when he got cinder-blocked.

Goddamn. That one gets to me, that thought. It spirals into guilt and I let it. I'm the king of beating myself up. Nobody else is better. Except perhaps my mother with the way she self-inflicts. As Croatian Catholics, it's practically our birthright. This particular one starts up like a stabbing pain in my stomach. It ripples out hot from the middle of me, to my fingers and toes and back. It's telling me this is all my fault, how we shouldn't even have executed a quick pickup, how I should've trusted my gut, because if I had, Gutierrez would be okay. He'd have gotten home to his family in one piece. Not now though. Not now.

3

The STL radioed ahead for them to meet us at the entrance to the ER, so when I pull up, there's already four whitecoats out there rolling a gurney. I slide over and hold my shirt tighter to his face as they open the passenger-side door real slow and three pairs of hands come through the opening and cushion him before they open it all the way and lower him down.

"We got him," they say to me.

I don't want to let go, but they say it again. So I have to let go.

For a second I just sit there and watch them settle him on the cot and put a c-collar on him before trying to put an oxygen mask over his mouth and realizing that isn't as easy an undertaking as maybe they thought it'd be. When they get him going and pass through the doors, it feels like a small part of me gets ripped away as he goes.

I grab my heavy jacket out of the cab because it doesn't seem appropriate for me to walk around in my sweaty, bloody undershirt, and I'm already through the doors by the time it seems ridiculous to me to wear my coat indoors, but it's too late, it's on.

Before I can blink, Captain Wilts is next to me.

"They'll take good care of him," he says. "There's nothing we can do now. Listen, the STL wants us back in service, so seventy-nines are sending us a firefighter. They're running him down here in the plug buggy."

We can't run an engine with just three people, so they're replacing Gutierrez so we can keep going. I know that's how it works, but it still hurts.

"I need the pisser," I say and excuse myself.

"Sure," Cap says. His voice is worn out. It sounds about how I feel right now.

In the washroom, I scrub my hands twice. I wash them too hot and only use the mirror to make sure I don't have any blood on me. But I do. There's a sticky dry drop matted in the hair of my left eyebrow like old red honey, a few more flecks over my ear, and even one inside it. How they got there, I'll never know. I scrub them all. After I've used about twelve paper towels to dry my hands, I button my coat up all the way so if I see her, she can't see the blood on my undershirt.

The ICU's not far away. I know where it is and how to get there. I figure I've got about ten minutes before the new guy gets here, and I need to see her, to see just one good thing today. It's not that it would make everything better but maybe it would keep me from sinking. I don't know. That sounds stupid. But maybe it's true. I pass a bald Asian janitor pushing a mop with his Walkman up too loud and treble-y. I recognize the song, "To Be with You," and I shake

my head because it's way too cheesy and I'm actually a little embarrassed, because when I heard it last week on the radio, I thought
about Gloria and had to stop myself getting used to the idea because
maybe she doesn't feel the same.

When I turn the corner and see her standing right in front of
her station, I get a hitch in my step and then have to act like it's
natural. There's something different about this woman. It's hard
to explain, but the way she walks, the ways she carries herself, you
can tell she loves her job and she's steady, someone you can count
on. I like that. She's different from the girls I grew up with, none of
them interested in college, all of them now married for years. The
ones that seem to be left for dating are either working a longshoreman gig or they're driftwood Pedro girls ten years younger than
me, the ones who grow up wanting nothing more out of life after
high school than to hostess at the Grinder until they land a guy
with an ILWU card so they can quit, sit at home, have kids, watch
soap operas, and take two vacations a year on Catalina Island—Slav
Hawaii, as my mother calls it.

It's the Hawaii thought that ambushes me, and once again I'm
thinking about Gutierrez and what happened and how I could have
prevented it. I swallow it down. I think about finding the gangbanger who did it, surprising him, making him pay.

I try to bury that inside me too, because right now, Nurse Gloria's talking to the tall blond nurse—what's her name? I forget, but
she's like a fast-forward button on a VCR, that girl. Second time I
ever met her, she asked me out, and it's not that I wasn't flattered or
that she wasn't attractive, but it put me off a bit. I guess I'm a little
more traditional. I like to do the asking. It's how I was raised.

Anyway, the blond one sees me coming and does some kind of
secret code nod to Nurse Gloria, who turns to look at me and—
sometimes, the way she looks at me, I can't tell if she thinks I'm just
right or not enough. It's this in-between kind of look I can't place.
I try to muster up a smile or something, but I can't stop thinking
about how sticky the steering wheel felt in my hands.

"Good morning, Nurse Gloria," I say, and it comes out quieter than I want.

Maybe it's stupid, using her title like that when I greet her, but I can't help it. In my line, everybody goes by last names, and I guess it's somewhat true here too, because I've only ever seen last names on people's name tags. So the one time I happen to meet her and look at her tag and call her Nurse Rubio, she immediately tells me to call her Gloria, and before I can think, I blurt out Nurse Gloria and she laughs and calls me Fireman Anthony and that was that.

"Good morning, Fireman Anthony," she says.

It feels good to hear her say that, familiar. Since she doesn't smile, I don't smile either. Now, she doesn't look unhappy to see me, but she doesn't look happy, either. I can tell something's going on behind those eyes, though, and I don't know what it is, but I want to find out. She's got a poker face so good that I sometimes wonder where she grew up, and if it was rough there, because I get the feeling that she could turn her toughness on and off like a tap.

I look at my hands, and I see I didn't get all the blood off around my fingernails, so I dig them into my pockets as she says, "From what's coming in, it doesn't look good out there. What's going on?"

She touches my arm with the tips of her fingers and drops her hand fast. It's so slight that I figure it could have been a mistake, but I hope it wasn't. For this moment, I want to try to tell her what happened with the cul-de-sac and Gutierrez as succinctly as I can, but no sentences come out, no actual words even, so all I end up saying is "Uh."

It's like I'm stuck in neutral somehow, and the worst part is, I'm trying to get to drive, trying to shift down but my brain just won't go. What a dumb-ass.

She's probably thinking exactly the same thing because she's looking at me now, not sizing me up exactly, but like she's looking for what's wrong with me and she's not quite sure what it is. It's almost like she's diagnosing me. We pass an awkward moment that way, me looking at her white nurse's shoes and how they're only scuffed on the insides, like maybe she rubs them together without really thinking about it, and I'm not saying anything and she isn't either. She's just looking at me, and that's when I know I need to break the silence somehow, to say anything, right now.

"You be sure to take care of him," I finally say.

I half wince as soon as it's out of my mouth. Idiot! That makes no sense because I didn't tell her about Gutierrez at all, or where he is, and that reminds me that already I've stayed too long, but I can't get words together for how good it's been just to see her, so I don't say anything. Everybody's waiting on me.

I've got to go, I think.

"You have to go," she says, like she's reading my thoughts.

That settles it. I will never play cards against this woman ever, but I admit that the thought of having her on my team is a different story. I must tilt my head as I think that because she gives me a little smile that takes away any comeback I could possibly come up with.

"Be safe out there," she says.

The tone is so polite, but it's almost like an order—a polite order—that I don't know what to say, so I just kind of nod automatically and go. I'm so frustrated and embarrassed with how our exchange went that I don't even look back. I just pull my hands out of my pockets and look at my nails again, how there's still blood underneath my index and ring, and I think about Gutierrez again, and Junior and the phone call he and his mommy will be getting real soon to tell them what's going on, and I walk faster.

4

I compartmentalize. I admit it. I put everything that just happened in a box inside me and try not to open it. Sirens are off as we head back out and I'm not out front this time. The STL's vehicle is back up where it belongs, which is good because I'm not exactly at one hundred percent just now. I'm in the middle of the pack, cushioned in front and back. We've got a new guy in the place of Gutes, McPherson, and we're heading back north, just a little column of lights as we go up the freeway. The STL's already calling out an address on the radio, the newest winner of our little portion of the LAFD lottery, but I'm not really paying attention. I'm trying awfully hard not to pick at the box full of thoughts about Gutierrez and his family or how badly it went with Nurse Gloria or what I would do to that gangbanger's face with a hammer, so I just stay in formation. I try to distract myself. I wonder how many structures are going to burn to the ground because there aren't enough engines to go around.

You know what's hilarious though? What the news thinks of all this burning. The guys on television go on and on about how they can't believe people are torching their own neighborhoods. They think it's sad, some kind of thoughtless, primal rage thing. It's not. It's mostly planned and it's one of three things—grudge, mayhem, or insurance. By the way, this isn't an official definition or anything. It's just what I think. It's grudge if one guy doesn't like the other guy for whatever reason, so he takes advantage of the chaos to do something about it, so even the race stuff, like what the blacks are doing to the Koreans, goes here. It's mayhem if you're deliberately setting it for the heck of it, or if you're trying to cover a crime, or using it as a distraction to draw emergency assistance elsewhere so you can commit a crime somewhere else, which the gangs definitely do. They did it before the riots, they're doing it during, and they'll do it after. In fact, I can tell you right now that I really don't look forward to this summer. All the shit going down now is going to require retribution, if not in the next few days then later, into the summer even. The last and likeliest, it's insurance if you've got a business in a run-down part of the city and it's not making as much money as you want but you do have fire insurance and you've been paying hefty premiums on that policy for damn near too long and then one day the racist cops get acquitted and all of a sudden up pops the opportunity to torch your own premises and get away with it—all you have to do is blame gangs or looters, so why not?

When I first heard the verdict, I was sitting next to Charlie Carrillo on the bleachers at Peck Park in Pedro. Carrillo's 53s, but we went to high school together and now we play on a local baseball team. I'm a catcher. It's the most important position on the field so far as I'm concerned. You could play a pickup game without a shortstop if you really, really had to—you know, eight on eight—but without a catcher? No chance. The catcher is the constant. He calls every pitch, and he's there through every pitching change. Without him, there is no game. Anyway, we'd just finished practice and we had a little radio between us that was going.

So I was sitting next to Carrillo as the newscaster reads out the particulars about the jury acquitting Briseno, Wind, and Koon—which reminds me, what kind of unfortunate name is that for a cop in a race case anyway? There's also mention of failure to reach a verdict on Powell, but something else bugs me.

As I'm unbuckling my leg pads, I turn to Carrillo and say, "How come the news makes such a big deal about all the white cops? Briseno isn't white, is he?"

"I'm pretty sure it's Briseño," Carrillo says, "which is Hispanic."

Carrillo's Hispanic too, so he would know.

"It's not exactly fair saying he's white if he isn't," I say.

"It suits a story, I guess. White versus black."

"Yeah," I say, "but it's shading the facts."

"Big deal," Carrillo says, "they do it all the time. No accountability in that line of work, you know that. The day someone on TV has to write an incident report on a fuckup and admit responsibility for it like we do, that's the day no one wants to be a newscaster anymore."

"True," I say, "but I'm not sure it matters now. All hell's going to break loose."

I called in right after that and asked if they needed me at the station, but I got told that since I was scheduled for the next day, I should just come in then.

So I did, after all hell really had broken loose, more than anybody thought. Of course, I didn't know then that our esteemed black mayor, Mr. Tom Bradley, was going to go on television and say it was time to take it to the streets or something to that effect. The guys at the station wouldn't shut up about that. They couldn't believe it. They felt betrayed, like he threw us under the bus when he said that—put us at greater risk—and I get that, I feel betrayed too, but I'm a realist. It would have exploded regardless. Do you really think people were sitting at home, waiting to see what the mayor said before they decided to riot? Me neither. Crips were out and around Florence and Normandie before Bradley even went on television.

I'm looking at the aftermath spread out before me as I try to prepare myself to get back in the thick of it. From my seat, it looks like Los Angeles has been air-raided. It looks like bombs went off. Pockets of orange blaze on either side of the 110, some in pits of black, here and there, because the fire knocked out the electricity on the block, and not for the first time I think this is what hell must look like. There are no stars tonight and there haven't been any for two nights straight. The canopy of black smoke hanging in the basin is too thick to see through.

I status-check and inform Cap that I'm under a quarter tank of fuel, and if I am, the unspoken truth goes, everybody else is too. Cap relays this. It's the crucial time when the Strike Team Leader will either decide to fuel us all the way up wherever we can and maybe stay out another six hours, or head to R&R to do that and take on some new hoses in the meantime. All he says to Cap over the radio is thanks though, which doesn't help tell me which way he's leaning. This has an implied meaning too—shut up and do your job.

5

We don't have as far to go as we thought because we get called off a Slauson fire and told to exit sooner because we're closer to another one. There's a structure fire on Manchester and Vermont, half a block south. I do my job and get us there. CHP do theirs, too, locking down the block at both ends, giving us the whole street to work with and more important, two exits. I face out on Vermont, my nose pointing toward Manchester because it's the most viable escape route.

We're in the 8600 block, Vermont Knolls. This has all the makings of a grudge burn, but it could be insurance too. Somebody set a Korean-owned furniture store on fire next door and it spread to the adjacent building with a sandwich shop—VERMONT SANDWICH SHOP, FOOD TO GO, the sign says, and then a phone number that's blackening—but next to it is the Universal College of Beauty. Neither looks retrievable. They were already pretty far gone when we get there. No genuine possibilities of recovery, but we can put it out.

I never turn my engine off. A 50-gallon tank will last you six hours or thereabouts if it's full when you start. McPherson lays an inch-and-a-half and I watch the pump pressure, but I don't need to stay right on top of it. Hoses pump at 125 gallons per minute, which would give me about four minutes for one line if we were tank only, but we're not. I do only have one coming off, and Suzuki's jockeying it, arching a stream onto the roof while two other lines from another engine douse what's left of the front window. I throttle up the pressure to 150 pounds per square inch, and the fire's getting pretty well knocked down now, as gray smoke and steam shoot out of every available opening. I run a supply line from the hydrant to mine to top off the water tanks before we pull out.

Part of my job is to see the big picture, to react before there's a need. I failed Gutierrez, which is why I'm extravigilant with the civilian bystanders here. I scan faces twice, but none look like gang members. They look like parents, families. In fact, there's a loose group of older folks across the street, watching us. They're taking pictures, video too, like we're entertainment.

One guy wearing shorts, slippers, and no shirt has a big camcorder propped on his left shoulder and his eye to the eyepiece. He's sweating, and his skin is shiny, almost blue-black at this distance. What's more, he's holding a sandwich in his free hand and eating it. Now, I'm no cop, but if I was looking to make an arson arrest related to a sandwich shop currently ablaze, I'd start with asking some questions of the smart guy eating a ham-and-cheese on the same street at whatever-o'clock-in-the-morning—I check my watch—at 04:02 in the morning.

Before it's 04:08, CHP stretches the perimeter one more block down, near to where there's a National Guard unit, and the STL sends two engines down to put out another fire that's starting up, but we stay on what's left of the furniture store, even though you can see the skeleton of the ceiling peeking through smoke now. It tells the tale. This building's gone.

There's a helicopter overhead—looks like Channel 7—shining a light down on us like we're at the bottom of a deep, dark hole. The people who live around here, they know what that actually feels like. They know how ugly life can get. Everybody else, the people sitting at home, watching this unfold on television, they have no idea. Those are the people shocked by the riots. They can't comprehend them because they don't understand the other side. They don't understand what happens to people with no money who live in a neighborhood where crime is actually a viable career path when there are no other opportunities, and I'm not excusing it or condoning it or saying it can't be avoided, but I'm saying that's how it is.

And let me tell you something else, those people don't have any idea what it's like to roll as a rookie EMT in my district, one of the heaviest gang-involved areas in the gang capital of the world. You can never explain to them what it's like to come on a scene as a first responder and see someone with multiple stab wounds—nine in the upper chest and five in the stomach, including one long rip that cut the outtie belly button in half, like somebody actually tried to gut this little ten-year-old gangbanger like a fish—and here he is, this child, crying, leaking snot down his cheeks and bleeding to death right in front of you, unable to do much else but gulp because he's got a punctured lung. Of course, you don't even think, you do your job. Sure, if he makes it, he'll have to live the rest of his life with a colostomy bag but you don't think about that then, you do what you were trained to do. You provide that vital quick fix and get him sent to County Hospital, and later when you call to check in, you hear you managed to save his life and for a little bit, it feels like your job is worth it—valuable, even—hell, you can even point to it with pride and say, *Look, I'm making a difference.*

But a month and some weeks later, you're out on those same streets having to assist the coroner with a body pickup—because God forbid they ever have the budget to do that on their own—and as you approach the decedent designated for transport at the bottom of a drainage ditch, you find that they haven't sheeted him yet, and it's with a slow-creeping horror that you realize you recognize the wounds—the scars, the placement on the ribs and the stomach, the long one on the gut where there's not much of a belly button anymore, only a purple scar that looks shiny in the dark—and you recognize those before you actually recognize the face. He's still ten. He'll never be older because they didn't bother stabbing him this time. This time, they just executed him, shot him in the back of the head. So you picked him up all those lifetimes ago and you fixed him for what? To alter the course of his life, to change it for the better? No. You bought him a few more days in hell is all you did. That's it. All you did was prolong his death. How does that feel?

There's a truth in that somewhere and maybe it's this—there's a hidden America inside the one we portray to the world, and only a small group of people ever actually see it. Some of us are locked into it by birth or geography, but the rest of us just work here. Doctors, nurses, firemen, cops—we know it. We see it. We negotiate with death where we work because that's just part of the job. We see its layers, its unfairness, its unavoidability. Still, we fight that losing battle. We try to maneuver around it, occasionally even steal from it. And when you come across somebody else who seems to know it like you do, well, you can't help but stop and wonder what it'd be like to be with someone who can empathize.

Nurse Gloria draws me in so much because it's obvious she understands this whole world, not just half of it. I don't need to explain everything to her, because maybe I don't even need to explain me. She's seen this hidden side just like I have. She knows what death looks like, and what futility feels like. She carries it with her, this weight. I can see it in how she moves, how she talks—

"Hey, Yanic," Suzuki says, "check this out."

He's next to me, holding his hand out, gesturing for me to open mine too, so I do. I look up and notice McPherson's on Suzuki's hose as Suzuki puts an iron-gray bullet in my palm, one with a smashed tip and no jacket, still a little warm. I must give him a look—how in the hell?—because he mimes shooting a gun straight up at the sky, makes a bang with his mouth and then traces the trajectory with his finger, scoring it with a little whistle, as it goes all the way up and all the way down before plunking him on the helmet with a flick of the fingernail. I turn it over in my palm, but it's not like I've never seen ordnance before.

We sweep the station roof after every New Year's and Fourth of July, finding more small-caliber stuff than you'd ever believe, but it's just that right now there's so goddamn much of it. Feels like I've seen more buckshot on the street tonight than painted lines. It's the volume that staggers me. How many firearms are there in L.A. city anyway, conservatively speaking? 360,000? That's roughly 1 percent, less than one gun for every hundred residents. Trust me, there's no way gun ownership, both legal and illegal, is anywhere near that low but we're being conservative here. Let's also just say that an outrageously high 10 percent of them have been fired once in the last forty-eight hours. Now that's presuming 36,000 guns were fired only once during the worst conflagration L.A. has ever seen, worse than Watts. Sure. You think a gangbanger is ever going to shoot a gun just once? Even still, that'd be 36,000 bullets. *Thirty-six. Thousand.* You'd get the same number if 5 percent of those guns shot twice, or only 2 percent shot five times. Part of me wants to dismiss it, call it completely crazy, but I actually can't. If anything, the total is too low, but what's more chilling is that we're not out of the woods yet.

"Let me have it back," Suzuki says. "I'm gonna give it to my kid."

I say, "Why do you want your kid having a bullet?"

"I don't know. Drill a hole through it, put it on a chain so he can wear it. Tell him it hit his old man once and he stopped it like Superman."

It's still warm when I give it back to him. I don't know if that's because of his hand or that it was so recently fired. Then again, I don't know that I want to know.

6

When the flare-up down the block is overhauled, the STL tells us we're going to an RTD bus depot in Chinatown for some R&R because the forward command post at Fifty-Fourth and Arlington was too impacted with other emergency personnel vehicles, so we do a quick pickup and go up Vermont to Manchester, then Manchester to the Harbor Freeway and head north. We convoy to Downtown and instead of taking the 101, we exit at Fourth Street, take it to Alameda, and turn left. It doesn't seem the best route, all things considered, but I figure whoever is routing us knows something I don't, so I don't carp.

"Downtown isn't so bad," Suzuki says from the back.

Cap smirks. He's riding shotgun again. To his credit, he hasn't said anything about the blood.

"Yeah," I say, "I thought it'd be worse, but I guess there isn't much worth looting around here."

Downtown has been bombed out since the '70s when building owners gave up, sold cheap, and took their money to the Westside or the Valley. At the same time, slumlords got to work making it the least habitable place in Los Angeles. Skid Row wasn't great to begin with, but it went from gutter to holding cell. The era of the seasonal worker and the hobo died when the city started knocking down cheap housing, the produce markets were slowing down or moving elsewhere as regional supermarkets took over, and Skid Row ceased to be a place for migrant farmworkers and more a pit stop for the mentally ill, the drug inclined, or both. By the time the '80s rolled around, crack made all that permanent. Now there's not a whole lot left around but the courthouse, silent-film-era hotels that need more than a coat of paint to get their glamour back, abandoned burlesque houses on Main, and a bunch of empty warehouses.

As we cross over Third Street, I see two women pushing strollers with no kids in them but plenty of toys, boxes and boxes of them, just like they were out shopping at Macy's or something. One has a scar on her face, from her ear down her cheek. It's keloided and looks like a tusk almost. It's not the same, but it reminds me of the gangbanger's shoulder scar, and that starts the dominoes inside me. I hate him all over again. I want to drop a brick on *his* face and see how he likes it. The thought makes me smile a sick smile, but then I'm thinking of Gutes. The bloody aftermath. The way his tongue looked when it moved. And it's all I can do just to stare at buildings as they pass.

The slow motion is stuck in my head again. The cinder block dropping—the *sound* of it landing—I remember how it made two, a crunch first when it hit the jaw and then a thud when it hit the ground, and I shiver. That gangbanger's face was the worst part. I never thought it was possible to sneer and smile at the same time until I saw it, and I've seen the aftermath of a lot of desperate things done by a lot of desperate people, but this was something else. I make the promise to myself, he will pay for what he did. I will find him. A gangbanger like that? He has a record, guaranteed. You don't just roll out of bed one day and decide to brick a fireman. You work up to it.

McPherson interrupts my train of thought by saying, "Wonder what happened there?"

As we cross over the 101, I see what he's talking about and it suddenly makes sense why we didn't take it to get where we're going. Beneath us, a vehicle is on fire. There doesn't seem to be any reason for it being there, just a Jeep shooting up smoke. It's under control though. I read the number of the engine hitting it with a hose. It's 4s.

Suzuki points out how there's no one parked at Union Station, and no one at the Olvera Street marketplace either. When we pass Ord and Philippe's on the corner, my stomach tells me I'm hungry. The French dip sandwich was invented in L.A. Not many people know that. It was invented at Cole's, supposedly for a customer with dentures who couldn't eat a hard roll so a bartender gave him a little bowl of meat drippings to soak the bread in and soften it up, which eventually became known as *au jus*. Around here, you pick a side. Personally, I like to dip it in the *jus* myself, so I'm a Cole's guy, but it seems like everybody in 57s prefers Philippe's, where they prep the *jus* in the kitchen and slather it on the meat themselves, almost like gravy.

Our destination is a bus depot on North Spring Street between Mesnagers and Wilhardt. It's one of the only safe places to fill up in the city. Outside of emergency protocol, it's an RTD depot, but now, it serves as a temporary FCP for the LAPD, and for us, a place to do R&R—resupply, use the bathroom, call home, and get some food. Since it's a safe zone, it makes sense that it'd be relatively well protected, but it's almost like something out of *Mad Max*, that movie where everybody needs gas for their cars and they'll kill to get it. There's something about that premise that makes too much sense about a city as car-crazy as Los Angeles, so I mention it and Cap nods, but neither Suzuki nor McPherson have seen it, so I don't bother explaining and instead I tell the guys in the jump seats they'll just have to see it for themselves. When the sliding gate with razor wire on its top opens, I pull in, right around a group of green-uniformed men with M-16s.

7

It's later, while we're saying good-bye to our CHP escort before they head back to their main command post on Vermont and the 101, that somebody—Taurino's his name—calls the guys at the front gate ninja turtles.

This makes sense because they're decked out in army green from head to toe. They've got thigh pads and funny-looking military helmets with the same green fabric stretched over them and dark visors hiding their eyes. They really do look like man-size turtles from a distance. Taurino doesn't know if they're FBI or ATF, but he thinks they're federal because he saw them fly in to the National Guard base at Los Alamitos when they arrived from out of town.

"It looks like they're getting ready to deploy, who knows to where," Taurino says. "All I know is I'm glad they won't be paying me a visit."

I look across the lot to where he's looking and see the ninja turtles boarding a black vehicle that looks like a cross between a tank and a giant Jeep with a flat front. It doesn't have any identifying acronym on it. It's just black, like a metal shadow. There must be at least twelve of them and they are kitted out like Special Forces. One guy even has a bandolier of shotgun shells like a Mexican bandit in a western. They look scary. There's no denying it.

I bid Taurino good-bye and I turn away, but he says, "Hey, hang on a second."

I turn back and he whispers to me that I've got dried blood on the back of my neck. He doesn't need to say any more. I know it's Gutierrez's.

I force a smile for Taurino, say thanks, and move to my rig.

I don't blame CHP for what happened to Gutierrez, but I don't not blame them either. It's complicated. When I've had a few days to process and replay it all in my head again, I can try to figure out who gets what blame and how much, because I'll need to when it comes time to write up the report.

I give my rig a once-over with some surface cleaner set aside for anybody who needs it, paying special attention to the dash, steering wheel, and the captain's seat where Gutierrez was. I'm okay through it. I keep everything in the right boxes and nothing spills out.

It's not even dawn yet and Cap's already off doing paperwork, but I head over to the chow station, grab some food, and have an early breakfast with Suzuki, McPherson, some 57s, and a couple more from our light force, as well as a few guys on R&R who trickle in from other crews. The food's bearable. You can tell a fireman didn't cook it, because if he had, it'd be better. There's oatmeal, bacon, eggs, sausage, tortillas, salsa, and some potatoes that have been sitting for a bit. I pick oatmeal and load it with raisins and two packets of sugar.

With this many firemen in one place, taking up five picnic tables on the depot tarmac with nothing to do but eat and stare at each other, it's inevitable that we'll wind up trading war stories. Sure enough, some guy from 58s—I don't know him—starts it.

"You guys run into any trouble with human roadblocks?"

Most of us are chewing, but I nod yes and the other engineers do too, because of course we've encountered people walking into the road in front of us, trying to stop us from doing our duty at best, and at worst, turn us into sitting ducks for projectiles. One engineer tells a quick story about his rig getting pelted with rocks and how the two guys sitting in the back jump seats were basically exposed, but they just kept their helmets on and ducked down and nobody got hurt. Suzuki looks at me. McPherson doesn't. But it's obvious they're both thinking about Gutierrez. I'm not ready to talk about that though, so I nod back at the guy who started all this because I want him to continue.

"Well, last night I'm in K-town, right? We just knock the shit out of a department store fire in Beverly Hills and we're tracking back because we get told to handle something big on West Adams and Crenshaw." He stops and checks to see if everybody's listening, and we are, so he continues. "So I'm chugging east on Sixth and right after the Western intersection this kid runs into the street waving a gun."

I say, "Pointing it at you?"

"No, more like pointing it in the air because he's waving his hands frantically and trying to get me to stop for him. Now that I think about it, I'm not even sure he knew he was holding it."

Someone asks him what kind of kid.

"Korean kid. Glasses. Wearing a prep school blazer."

This creates a thoughtful pause in our crowd because it's unexpected. It's not the image any of us had in our heads when someone brings up a gun-toting teenager.

I say, "What'd you end up doing?"

"What could I do? I aimed right at him, sped up, and prayed he'd get out of the damn way."

"No other option there," I say.

"Did he?" Suzuki wants to know. "Get out of the way?"

"Sure did," the guy says and smiles.

Right after that, another guy from 58s says they've had reports of a Mexican gangbanger committing various acts of arson all over the city and claiming each one by shouting out the number and then his name like he was keeping score and he wanted everybody to know.

"Number twenty-one," the guy says in an exaggerated Hispanic accent, "Puppet did it! Number twenty-six! Puppet did it!"

The name on his uniform is Rodriguez, so he's allowed to.

After a few sighs of disbelief, Suzuki says, "Man, every single *cholo* gang has at least two Puppets! Don't you just wish his name was easier to track down? Like, what if it were Spaghetti? How many gangbangers on earth could possibly be named Spaghetti?"

Most everybody laughs because we know it's true.

After that, the mood gets somber because this engineer from 94s asks us if we heard about Miller. 94s, by the way, couldn't even get out of their station because they took heavy fire from the surrounding neighborhood, and they might have stayed there all night if SWAT hadn't come and shot the street up.

"I heard Miller got hit, but I don't know much more," McPherson says.

Even now, the details are sketchy but we get what's currently known. On Wednesday night, Miller was driving a truck and he got shot in the neck and had a stroke. The shooter drove up alongside and popped him for no reason other than he was wearing a uniform and sitting in a truck, I guess. Miller's been through surgery and he's stable, but that's all we know.

I've met Miller a couple times and like him. He's not like your typical AO, all bluster and swagger—basically the same as an LAPD motorcycle cop, except they ride ladders instead. Not Miller though, he's mild-mannered. The worst part of it is, he just left 58s a couple months before for something on the Westside, something less wild, and then this happens.

"Sorry to hear that," Suzuki says.

It's unanimous. Every one of us is sorry to hear it, but we're quiet about it. We don't say we all hope he pulls through, but it's obvious we do. It just goes unspoken. As I finish my oatmeal, conversation turns to bullets falling out of the sky.

This is Suzuki's cue to pass his bullet around, so I let it skip me and get up. I drop my bowl and spoon off in the mess tray set aside for dirty dishes, hit the pisser to wash the blood off my neck something thorough, and when I'm done, I wander over to the LAPD field command post on the other side of the depot, the back of my collar sitting wet and flush on my skin.

8

Over at the command post, I ask if I can borrow their cellular phone and a young police officer hands it to me. It's got an extendable black antenna, a little readout screen, a gray body, white number buttons with a little green light on underneath that lights them, a few other buttons that I'm only partially sure of, and a square mouthpiece that would cover all the buttons if it wasn't flipped down on a hinge. It's a remarkable thing, completely cordless. I key in the number to the station house and press the green button that says "SND," which I guess means send, and it must be, because it's ringing.

When Rogowski answers, I say, "You heard anything about Gutierrez?"

"Surgery," he says. "Just got out. His spine and neck are fine, but his jaw's wired shut and they put a plate in it. Turns out it was dislocated and busted in two places."

"But he'll be okay?" I catch a breath and hold it.

"Yeah," Rogowski says. "He'll be eating through a straw for however many months, but he'll be okay. You did good, I hear. Didn't take any shit. The story goes you tore out of there so fast that the STL had no choice but to order everyone to follow *you* to the hospital."

"I don't know about that," I say, but when I exhale, something shifts inside me, because just now gravity is a little less heavy. I wonder where Rogowski got that information until it occurs to me the captain must've already called in first, probably while I was cleaning.

"So, listen, his family has been told and they're en route." Rogowski is just trying to reassure me now. "It's not fine, but it's as fine as it's going to get under the circumstances. You did good."

I don't know that I need to hear anything else after that, but Rogowski laughs and changes the subject to something I've been secretly dreading. My mother has called every hour on the hour to see if I'm okay. I thank Rogowski, hang up, and call her. She picks up on one ring like she's been waiting by the phone. She probably has been.

She says, "Vhat are you doing, *dušo*?"

Where anyone else would have *w*'s in English, my mother has *v*'s instead. She can't help it. It's the only way her tongue works. *Dušo* is just an expression of affection, like how someone might tack "sweetheart" on the end of something said to a loved one. By the way, this is the first question she asks me, anytime, for anything. Always, it's this. To her, it means lots of things all at the same time, like where are you, how are you, and have you eaten?

"I'm fine, Mama. I'm at a dispatch center in Chinatown. I just ate."

"Vhat did you eat?"

"Oatmeal."

"This is not a meal," she says.

To my mother, only something with two courses, one of them

pasta, is a meal. In her world, if I have not eaten pasta, I have not eaten enough. It is not a battle worth fighting, so I change the subject. I ask her how she's doing.

"I stay in house. I do laundry."

My mother lies about many things—how much *kruškovac* she's snuck, how many knives are hidden in her house, or how much she doesn't hate her very dear friends—but she never lies about housework. She is doing the things she says she is, but she's watching television while she does them, which means she's watching news coverage, which means she's worrying about me, and when she worries about me, she calls the station to check on me.

Just to be clear, I say, "Which house?"

I live three houses up the block from my mother and the house I grew up in, on West Twenty-First, between Cabrillo and Alma—the north side of the street, where you can see down into the port. Even so, my mother feels we are too far away from each other. My father passed this winter, heart attack. It was sudden. So any distance for my mother right now is too much distance.

She says, "Yours. Is nicer."

She doesn't mean that. She doesn't think mine is nicer. I frequently regret giving my mother a key. She knows I don't like her there alone when I'm away—reading my mail, poking through medicine cabinets, opening drawers, all of which she does—but it can't be helped now. I'll just have to yell at her later. I think she does it because it helps her feel closer to me, and it helps her be out of the house she shared with my father for thirty-seven-odd years. Once again, this is a battle not yet worth fighting. There is, however, one thing that still needs to be said.

"Mama," I say, "don't call the station anymore."

"If I think of you, I call."

"Mama," I say, trying to keep my voice calm even though she drives me completely crazy, "during an emergency situation, we need those lines open so people with actual emergencies can call."

"Vhen I don't know vhere you are," she says, "is emergency for me."

"Good-bye, Mama," I say through gritted teeth.

"*Dušo*. Go eat. Eat real food this time. For me. Please. And also—"

I press the red End button on the phone and hand it back to the officer. He doesn't say anything but he's got a look on his face like, *mothers—can't live with them, can't kill them*. Najarian, his name is, which I think is probably Armenian, and if that's the case, I figure he might understand. He's wearing his blues the way LAPD do, with a triangle of their silly white undershirts visible between the collar ears. He's young, early twenties maybe, and eager with his slicked black hair. I wonder what kind of work he does over there to draw this kind of detail during the riots.

I notice a barrel of shotguns beside Najarian, butts up, like a flower display made only of stems, no blooms. There must be thirty in there. I think about all the bullets again, and I guess it's just morbid curiosity, but I ask him how many people have been killed during the riots, if he has any idea.

"Oh," he says, "you got to see this. Come on."

I follow him away from the building, to a big tractor-trailer away from the line of ambulances, away from anything, really. It's sitting on its own without a rig, which I guess in a bus depot isn't anything out of the ordinary, but I notice this one's a refrigerated trailer, and there's something odd about it. It's humming.

"Open it up," Najarian says.

I'm starting to get the feeling like I'm walking into something I don't want to be walking into.

"That's okay," I say.

"No, seriously," Najarian says with a smile on his face, "open it up."

Najarian points to the metal ladder with three grated steps, indicating that it's the best way to get up and pull the doors.

It's getting to be dawn behind the peaked roof of the depot—well, dawnish. Faint orange light filters through the black mass of smoke and clouds above us, gleaming off the side of the trailer.

"You just have to pull that first," Najarian says, and his pointing finger indicates a metal pole I need to tug out of its catch so I can pull the doors open.

I step up and pull the catch and when I do, the right door opens with a puff of fog, and a blast of cold air hits me. It's not until I jump back down and stare in that I realize I'm looking at a portable morgue. There's nine—no, ten—bodies arranged on stainless steel shelves built into the walls of the trailer like bunk beds, each one sheeted in white.

Najarian climbs up and in. He pushes open the left door.

"Check this out," he says and moves to the nearest body.

A thought occurs to me. *The cops are just greasing people.* And if they are, I don't blame them one bit, not with what I've seen tonight. For a second I wish the gangbanger who got Gutes was in there too. But only for a second.

"This one," Najarian says as he pulls the sheet back on the corpse, "was a body dump yesterday afternoon, right there on Spring, right over there." He points at the fence between the street and us. "It was suspicious too, because it wasn't there before shift-change, but it was there after, so they must've done it during or real close to it, which means somehow they knew about it or got lucky. Either way, it was slick."

He's pulled the sheet all the way back now, but I don't see what I'm expecting to see. Instead of a face, there's a flannel there, black and white striped.

Najarian nods at it. "Eerie, right? Why would they cover his face like that unless it was shot off or something, right? But I checked. It's still there, except the cheek's smashed in a bit and an ear's gone, but he didn't die of that. He was stabbed."

But this one, it doesn't look so eerie to me. To me it just means whoever hurt him didn't put the flannel on. Because whoever did that cared about him. They did it almost like they didn't want him to be cold. And there's something else too. The way the sleeves are wrapped down and around—it hits me and I don't know why—the flannel sleeves, they're nearly frozen in place underneath his head but they've been folded that way, almost like a pillow, almost like what I did for Gutierrez except different, because I know, and I don't know how I know, but it was done for him after he passed. To me, it just looks like a good-bye, like the way people put things in coffins for the journey.

No, I think, *not eerie. Somebody cared for him an awful lot, whoever he was.*

When Najarian sheets him back up, I can't help it, I touch my necklace where my St. Anthony medal is, the saint I was named for, and I say a little prayer in my head for the man in the flannel, for whoever he was, for however he got here, and for his body to get home safe so his family can find whatever solace they can.

ABEJUNDIO ORELLANA,
A.K.A. MOMO

MAY 1, 1992

4:22 P.M.

1

¡Puchica! I should've never trusted Cecilia. Staring at the remains of my burned-down house, I know I'm between a rock, another rock, and a hard place. Only way out is down in the grave or up and out, cuz I sure as shit ain't about to go sideways. I got to be cool as ice water now. But just to be truthful, I'm sweating *hard*. This riot shit's got the worst timing ever.

Rock #1: The motherfucker named Trouble and twenty of his angry homeboys are stacked up behind me at the curb, every one of them packing, every one of them looking for an excuse to do something to anybody, especially me. They don't like what I find here, if it don't make me innocent in their eyes, they kill me.

Rock #2: Sheriffs rolled me up on drugs charges when I was transporting through Hawaiian Gardens seven weeks ago, but a homicide detective sergeant from the L.A. Sheriff's Department swooped in and offered up a life raft when he told me he didn't give a fuck about the drugs if I knew about murders and could name names, so that's how I became a confidential reliable informant for the LASD. If Trouble knew *that*, shit, if *any* homeboys knew that, even my own crew, I'd already have a new hole in the back of my head. So far though, so good. I'm still breathing . . .

And kicking ash. That's the hard place, where I'm at right now, dirtying my good boots all up, my snakeskin ones, as I try to find what's left of my bedroom on the lot where my one respectable house used to fucking be cuz what this means more than anything is I have to come back on somebody right when I've been planning on getting out, taking the sergeant up on his offer of relocation.

I can't do that now though. Now I got to get myself out of the first spot: prove to Trouble I had nothing to do with the gun, which means find the safe. At this point, it's guesswork on the floorplan cuz there's some piping and I can see what's left of some tile where the bathroom used to be, but even the walls aren't there anymore and that's some cheap-ass construction work. I entered about where the front door used to be but now it's just the melted-up grate of the security door. In my head, I figure it's about ten steps to the bedroom, so I do that, and then veer right when I see the door of my home-run safe open on the floor. Man, I relax a little then. I breathe, cuz that just saved my ass right there.

In my head, I thank the thieves for that much, cuz those motherfuckers proved my argument by not shutting it back up. This way, an open safe is a ripped-off safe. My gun safe is closed up tight though, so I feel like I know what happened now.

The ones that did this came by Wednesday, Cecilia let them in, they got her fucked up or out of the way or she was in on it, and they hit the gun safe. They took that to Fate and got paid, and then maybe they kept an eye on the house and when they saw I didn't come running, they figured they got away with it, so they came back, and Cecilia let them in again, and part two happened. My home-run safe got jacked and they burned the place to the fucking ground, comprehensive-like.

But right now, the important detail for Trouble is that the gun safe might be closed, but the other one is open. Since it is, Trouble's convinced someone gaffled my shit and burned the house down to cover it, cuz he thinks he's all Sherlock Homeboy now. He don't know that title already belongs to Fate's boy, Clever. And that motherfucker *is*, too. Clever as anything.

"So they really did burn you," Trouble says as he looks around, like he's examining evidence. Really though, this stringy motherfucker with lettered tattoos instead of eyebrows is trying to play me *macho*, telling me what to think. Don't get me wrong, this motherfucker's hard, but he ain't Big Fate hard. He gets his bitch to shave his head every day and starch out his shirt and pants. He'll tell everyone, even people that don't ask. That's the kind of guy Trouble is. Tough, but he likes playing the role almost as much as he likes being it.

"Guess you told the truth after all," he says. "Good for you."

His homeboys in earshot kinda smirk at that but try to hide it by turning away. I might be between rocks, but I'm still not to be fucked with. If any of this was like normal, Trouble comes at me all respectful. He asks for help right and gets blessed with it. Not now though. His brother's dead. The city's on fire. Right now, he couldn't give a fuck about asking right for anything. He's just taking what he wants. He knows it's a numbers game now.

I got a crew of eight to run my business and protection from above, but it's the kind of protection that isn't immediate, doesn't stand in my doorway and scare people off, and right now Trouble's got a click of almost a hundred behind him. I don't play this right, he wipes me out. He's crazy enough to do it. But he needs me too. Needs what I can get him. And he's playing the one card he's got: he says Fate was trying to put me in a frame when he had my gun swiped and used on Joker and that whole party. By his logic, Fate had my gun stolen on purpose so Trouble would think I was helping them and then come at me and kill me in a rage.

The funny thing is, if that's how it went down, it almost worked. That Payasa chick dropped my gun in the backyard of that party. One of Trouble's junkie homies recognized it as mine on account of the white tape around the handle, so when they got everything taken care of with getting people to hospitals and rallying up, they started looking for me. Turns out I wasn't reachable on my pager, which they thought was suspicious, but my thought was: How did I know they weren't trying to rob me or frame me up?

Took them a while to find me at my main stash house cuz I don't exactly advertise that address, but once they did, they came in hard and told me I had to take a ride. It wasn't a kidnapping cuz I had to drive myself, but it was. Took a lot of talking to even get this far, standing in front of the first house I ever bought. The one I eventually wanted to move aunts up to from El Salvador. Now though, my chimney's the only thing still standing. Ain't *that* a bitch.

Now, I can't lie. I got a call. I heard about this soon as it happened, but I figured, why bother coming here? If it's burnt, it's burnt. No point in getting my ass in a car and driving over just to see it ashed up. Besides, how do I know someone wasn't trying to lure me off my main stash to hit that next? I didn't. So I stayed put. I fucking stewed though.

My first thought when I heard was: Cecilia better be a skeleton in there or I'm gonna cut her. Cuz if she's not dead, and that front door didn't get ripped off with a crowbar or a shotgun or some shit, then this was on her. And when it's you, you pay.

"They did you dirty, *esé*," Trouble says. "That don't make you mad?"

I already had one foot out of this life, so to be straight with you, it didn't really. For one, anger is worthless, but for two, I admired it. It was a stone-cold smart play. Whether or not they knew it was my gun, it was a smart play. I figure the likeliest thing they did was put the word out they needed a gun and one of my strung-out hypes knew I was elsewhere and hit hard.

"I don't get mad," I say, "I get even."

Trouble likes hearing it. "That's what I'm fucking talking about, homes!"

What Trouble doesn't know is I'll tell him and his click anything they want to hear at this point. The key is them not knowing I'm doing it. The key is them thinking I'm with them, even though there's no way I'd throw in. Only way I've lived this long is by not siding with one click over another unless it was to my advantage. Those days might be ending though. The way Trouble's going, I might have to pick sooner than later.

You know what did make me mad though? How this shit went down. Trouble's been out of line since he found out it was my gun killed Joker, two other homies, and some girl. And then when two more of his homies went on the chase, they got shotgunned. One lived. One didn't. So the total price for Joker going after somebody not involved? Five bodies. If you ask me, they got what was coming, but nobody's asking me. What's more, if they keep coming, it could be worse next time, but that doesn't even occur to them.

Trouble's already running his mouth about how they're all recouped now, how they looted a pawnshop and got a couple guns, but they need more before they hit back. That's what they need me for, he's telling his homies. Connections. They're all smiling and nodding.

They're thinking stupid about it though. What they're not doing is thinking about how Joker got it. It was as slick a 'hood killing as there ever was, only done by somebody that knew how to do it, somebody that completely knew how people would react under the circumstances. It was almost some military shit. When I heard about it, my first thought was it could only have been Fate and I wasn't wrong about either.

But here's the real problem though, here's why Trouble isn't thinking for shit right now: when he was breathing, Joker was Trouble's little bro. He was blood. And both of them were blood to the girl Lil Mosco shot up in that club parking lot too. The way it is now, Trouble's an only child and the way he sees it, it's all on Fate's crew, and he's gonna take it out on them. This personal shit's the worst kind. It clouds your judgment. But it makes you dangerous too. Trouble don't care about tomorrow, only right now, and he'll do whatever it takes to get back on them for what they did.

Don't get me wrong. Trouble's crazy and committed, but that shit only goes so far. That motherfucker plays tic-tac-toe, but Fate plays *Risk*. He been stacking motherfuckers up to defend, ready for whatever's about to come, I'm sure of that, and I'm not about to get in a shooting match with him, but I sure as hell need Trouble to think I'm down, and right now this idiot is still playing me *macho*.

He's with a girl that's got big teeth and her hair picked up. She's acting a fool too, cuz that shit is always like a cold, it catches, and some people are more prone to getting it than others. I don't know why he brung her. This is man's business.

She says to me like she's even allowed to talk, "How'd he get in your safe, huh?"

How does anyone get in a safe? It's fucking obvious. They know the combination, they figure it out, or they break in. That's it. It's not like it's some rocket science. I don't say that though. I want to, but I don't. Instead, I just don't fucking answer. I don't even look at her.

"I got to make some calls," I say and start back to my car. "Run some errands. Get some shit picked up."

Trouble grabs my arm. When he does, I rip it out of his grip and square up on him. Down on the curb, my man Jeffersón steps to and I fantasize, just for a second, about cutting Trouble's head clean off his neck with a machete, one-chop-like, just how the death squads used to do it back home, how they orphaned my ass and got me sent up here at three to live with Tio George before he got sick and passed. I been running these streets since before Trouble was rocking diapers. Cudahy, Huntington Park, South Gate, Lynwood. Sooner or later, he needs to show an O.G. some respect before I make him respect.

"It's cool," Trouble says, in a way I know it's not. "But I'm coming with you. We're in this together now, you know? Us against them."

"Obviously," I say, and I smile like I was hoping he'd say that, but my stomach feels like somebody just kicked it into my throat cuz I'm right back where I started, stuck between a rock and a rock and a hard place, except now the hard place is Fate's click. And it's bigger, badder, and smarter than Trouble can even wrap his fool head around. The squeeze's getting tighter. I feel it. But I smile, cuz the worst always brings out the best in me.

2

That open safe bought me some time. Enough to cruise down the street and see if I can see anybody who knows how my house took fire. There's really only one dude I'm looking for, this O.G. named Miguel, cuz he knows this neighborhood, and he'd understand this whole situation without me even needing to explain it. I head for his house. It's still on the block.

Trouble's sitting in the back with his bucktoothed girl like I'm *Driving Miss Daisy*. Yeah. It's cool though. It's cool. I'll remember this shit. Jeffersón sits up front with me. He wants to shoot Trouble. I can feel it, but I just nod at him, you know? Like, it's cool, Jeffersón. He'll get his in good time and now isn't it.

And it's a good thing too, cuz it's right then that I notice two more cars of Trouble's homeboys following me. Trouble notices me noticing that and nods at me in the rearview mirror and puts on a big-ass grin back there too. He lounges back like my Caddy is his fucking couch, and he puts his hand between his girl's legs. I smile, cuz that's cool, motherfucker, you know? I'll *remember* that shit. I'm keeping score on him in my head, and right now he's just adding up the bullshit.

There used to be a time when this would work my every last nerve, this shit Trouble's doing. It's all ego trip. It's all about being the big man. And me? I got three kids and two women. They know each other, so it's cool. I seen enough to know I'm not the big man and I don't wanna be. I sure am ready to be out, though. All the way out. Living in the San Diego 'burbs or some shit. Learning how to surf, cuz why not?

"Hey," Trouble says from the back, "it's hot up in here. You got any conditioning in this bitch?"

I drive a '57 Cadillac. They hadn't invented it yet. I got a swamp cooler in the trunk I bring out sometimes, but I don't tell him that. Fuck him. He can sweat.

"Nope," I say.

"Well, you should!" When Trouble sees I don't response to that, he changes the subject. "I been wondering, how the fuck you get the name Momo anyways?"

This motherfucker, he don't know how I came up in the motels, moving from one to the other, dealing, whoring, whatever brought money in. Blow one motel when the owners or the cops come by, roll to another. Set up all over again. It was the momo life for me, and people always knew where to find me: posted up in a fucking momo. Ask anybody and they'll tell you which. Wasn't long before that got to be my name. And Momo was always easier than saying Abejundio, so that's just what it got to be. A name people knew. A name people were scared of. I tell you though, you live that life long enough, that set-up-and-teardown life, it gets to be starting over don't seem so hard. Tio George always said never leave anything behind you ain't willing to lose. Shit sounds better in Spanish, though.

"I don't know," I say. "One of the O.G.'s named me."

"Bullshit," Trouble says.

I shrug. I don't feel like playing this game. The young ones, they want to be known. They'll do anything for it. It's like some shit straight out of Medieval Times. I took my daughters there once in Buena Park. You got the red knight and the blue knight and the green knight and the yellow knight and they all stand up and say where they're from and, like, what their valor is, what they done, and my kids ate that shit up, but I'm sitting there thinking, like, how different is that to what the streets do? You got a place you're from. And you got a name, and maybe a title. And you got some shit you did. It's the same thing, almost exactly.

Before I get to Miguel's house, I see a bum walking the neighborhood with a hood up on his sweatshirt, so I roll up on him. Bums know all kinds of shit and will usually talk if they're not too crazy. You'd be surprised what they have to tell if you take time to ask. So I get close to him and stop, and before Trouble can open his big mouth to question what I'm doing, I say, "Hey, man, you know about the house that caught fire on this block? You seen anything?"

The guy turns and he's a black dude, but he's got blue eyes, glassy-ass eyes, and he says, "I've seen this city taking itself to heaven in pieces."

Oh, man, *whatever* to that shit. I step on the gas. Motherfucker is too crazy to make sense, and everybody in my car knows it, so I cruise down to Miguel's, which is only one more block. His kid Mikey's little European scooter is in the driveway when I pull up and get out. I don't have to ring the bell though, cuz Mikey's walking out and meeting me halfway with his red suspenders and big black boots and some kind of polo shirt buttoned all the way to the top. I got no idea where he gets the idea that dressing like that is okay, especially with an old man like Miguel. Normally, I'd call him out for it, but I don't got time for that.

I say, "Is your pops around?"

His old man used to bang hard-core back in the day, but he's legit now. Word is he did a lot of work up in East Los. I got nothing but respect for Miguel cuz he did his time and got out. He cut a tattoo straight out of his hand after that, one between his thumb and first finger, just so most people wouldn't know he was ever in. But I called him out on that scar once and he said he used a hot knife to do it. It's a lumpy scar like a caterpillar now, an inch long and no joke. Like I said, hard-core.

"No," Mikey says. "My dad's out."

That throws me off, but not too much, cuz I know Mikey sees everything on this block, riding his scooter going up and down like he does. He's smart too.

So I say, "You seen what happened to my place?"

"Yeah," he says.

I smile and give him a look, like, *Okay, spill that shit then.*

"I saw a scrawny guy throw a Molotov cocktail in through the front door."

I say, "Scrawny like what? What was he wearing?"

Mikey goes on to describe Lil Creeper to a fucking tee: how he dresses, how he moves, the way he always looks like he's talking to himself. I make a simple promise to myself to kill that motherfucker or have someone else do it as soon as possible.

But I'm trying to build the scene in my head, so I backtrack a little and say, "The front door was *open*?"

Cuz that means Cecilia was probably in on it, or she was fucking stupid, which is also a possibility I had yet to think over.

"Yeah," he says.

"He with a girl?"

"No. She was inside when he threw it."

That shit throws me for a little loop so I say, "How you know that?"

"After he left, I poked my head in and saw her lying on the carpet."

"Dead," I say, "or passed out or something?"

"I didn't know, so I grabbed her. Burned the hair off my arm doing it too."

He holds his arms up and sure enough, his right's smooth and his left's all hairy.

I only want to know one more thing, so I say, "Where is she now?"

"I don't know," he says, "she left last night. Took thirty-one bucks from me too."

That sounds like Cecilia. Never can leave a wallet around that girl without her going through it.

"Give my respects to your old man," I say to Mikey as I turn.

I get back in the car and thump it into gear.

3

We pass Ham Park on the way to Imperial and I see there's a big black spot where the handball wall used to be, and in my head I'm, like, *Why in the hell would anyone burn that down?* But Trouble answers my question before I even make it out loud.

Trouble says, "Man, *good*! The splinters from that shit were the worst, homes. Maybe they'll actually build a good one now."

I see a bunch of knuckleheads up on the end of the park, so I pull over. It's mostly little homies and wannabes. One of the little homies with a scar over his left eye recognizes me and comes over with his head kinda bowed, how he should. I go through the list real quick: just so they know, I tell them how there's a green light on looters and if they don't believe me, that's cool, cuz they'll find out for real once they get locked up. I also tell them how firemen are off-limits. I tell them we don't do it how the black gangs do it and we sure as hell don't set fires as traps cuz we got business we don't intend to disrupt. If I find out anyone's setting fires and bringing cops and fire down here, I'll find them and do them Jamaican style like they do down in Harbor City: you know, pour lye down their throats all slow through a funnel and leave them to die on the rail-road tracks, burning from the inside out.

"That was kinda tough," Trouble says as I drive away. "I got to remember that."

I don't response to that, either, but I smile so he knows I heard him cuz he's the kind of person that can't handle it if he's being ignored.

We stop off at the Cork'n Bottle cuz I need to hit that pay phone out front. Technically, it's on the wall of the tire store, but it's close enough.

Of course Trouble wants to know why, so I tell him for me to make arrangements, I got to make some calls. The kind of people we need to get at don't take well to people just showing up. This is a lie. But Trouble believes it. Their business is professional. I've shown up plenty of times out of nowhere needing something and they always make it happen.

I park in the back and give Jeffersón a nod so he knows he needs to stay in the car and keep watch on the lovebirds so they don't fuck on my upholstery.

As I'm getting out, the bucktoothed girl says, "Hey, get me one of them iced teas with the lemons."

Trouble and his girl bust up laughing at that as the two carloads of homies pull up behind and block the alley. I figure I've got two minutes before they get itchy to roll out.

I dial a number I memorized, but it rings and rings and nobody picks up. It's been like that for two days. It's driving me crazy.

So I hang up and call Gloria. It's ringing.

I'm planning in my head how to leave a message, been planning for like three months. But that's tough shit. Like, how do you tell a girl she's the only girl you ever loved, the only one that kept you in line and she's done so good since she dumped you, going into nursing and all that, and you just need to hear her voice one more time, and you need to tell her that you're ready to see your son again, cuz he's yours too and—

"Hello?" It's Gloria. She sounds exhausted.

My head's still spinning that she picked up, so all I come up with, "Is, uh, hello, is that Gloria?"

Real smooth. Already I can tell I fucked it up when her breath catches and she knows it's me, and she told me never to call again, ever.

"Thirty seconds, Abejundio. I'm timing you. Go."

She's the only person who ever called me that besides my family.

"I'm calling," I say, and I pause to look behind me and to the side, back where the parking lot is, to make sure no one's in earshot, "I'm calling cuz I'm getting out."

She scoffs at that shit. I don't blame her.

"Twenty," she says.

I go all panicky and light-headed when she says that, so I push. "I got rolled up by sheriffs. I can't really talk about it. But I been helping them and they're gonna help me get out. Gonna help *us* get out."

All she says is "Ten."

"See, uh, we can go together. Me and you and our little man. Someplace far from here. I know it's been so long since I seen my little boy but I talked to the sheriffs and they say they can take all three of us. They call it, uh, they call it reloc—"

The phone clicks as the connection goes. I stare at the receiver for a second. I know she hung up but my heart don't know it yet, it's still running, still thumping up happy cuz of her voice, still trying to explain, but my brain tells it to shut the fuck up cuz I burned that bridge, and my heart runs smack into a brick wall as I hang up and feed the phone another quarter.

I got to make one more call.

4

Before I dial, I check around the corner again, and I check to my other side to make sure no one walked around the Cork'n Bottle neither, but I'm good. I dial the first number I dialed but I got this feeling there's no one there at Detective Sergeant Erickson's desk in Sheriff's Homocide. He's got an office in Commerce, off Eastern, that I only been to once to fill out paperwork, but I had to switch cars twice to do it so I knew I wasn't followed. Once I was in the system, I was in.

I don't drop dimes often. Yeah, that means snitching, but it also means calling in, even though it don't cost a dime to call local anymore. Mostly, I'm getting interviewed in a car as we drive around. Like, I'll walk out of my neighborhood, make sure I'm not followed, and get in a tinted-up unmarked cop car, and they'll run the tape and ask me questions and I'll spill what I know. I won't testify until they got all the cases lined up but that takes forever.

The answering machine kicks in and tells me what I already know: this is Erickson's desk and I should leave a message.

As soon as I say, "It's CRI," I have to say my ID number so they know I'm in the database. After that, I start whispering as fast as I fucking can, "I been calling for two days and you know I don't leave messages. If this shit were normal, I wouldn't do this, but I got serious shit about to go down here and I need you to scoop me up and get me the fuck out cuz when this hits, it's gonna have a lot of bodies on it. I think it's gonna be Duncan. Duncan Avenue.

Sometime this afternoon or tonight. When I know, I'll call, but I'll be back at mine in two hours. You *gotta* come get me."

I check my back again, and my sides. No one's watching, so I breathe.

At first, Erickson pressed me hard for gang cases, so I told them little things to get them hooked. Gave them scraps, you know, but true scraps. I told them word was Lil Mosco shot up that nightclub and put a bullet in Joker's sister and that sooner or later there'd be some comeback on that, but they didn't much care about the comeback as much as solving the murder. So I heard they been trying to pick up Lil Mosco ever since, but he's up and vanished cuz Fate's too smart with moving him around.

Of course, I never told Erickson that I was there, getting head in the parking lot from Cecilia when Lil Mosco walked up on them two and shot. I heard the beginning of the argument too, what with Joker's sister's boyfriend yelling at Lil Mosco walking away that he was gonna rape Mosco's sister, Payasa, with a knife and all that. Now, I like a knife as much as the next dude, nothing better to make someone talk, but that was a line right there and he stomped all the way across it and thought it was cool. Was he really that shocked that Lil Mosco came back on him?

After they know that information from me is good and I'm listed reliable, Erickson tells me they're liaising, that's his word, *liaising* with the FBI about trying to get some big homies. I about laughed in his face when he told me that. Of course I don't know no big homies, I said to him, but I know who holds the keys. Then I told him he wanted big homies, he better put me in the fucking witness protection program cuz I'd never say shit without changing my name to Theodore Hernandez and living in Argentina. What I do after that to prove I'm real, though, is I give up some Jamaicans in Harbor City. They listened to that good.

What I hear, those cases are just about ready for arrest and indictment and that's why it's almost time to jump. Last week, they told me to pack my goodies up and I did. I got a bag in my trunk. I'm fit to split, but now I can't reach nobody. And that's like a sinking feeling if you want to know the truth.

"Hey," Trouble says as he walks out the front of the store holding what must be the last iced tea in a looted-out store, "you done or what? Let's go."

He turns away, but then he turns back and goes for his pocket as he says, "What's up with my manners? You want some blueberry gum?"

For the first time since I seen him today, Trouble gets real quiet after that.

"My brother used to love this shit," he says, "like, *love-it*-love-it."

5

On the ride down to Harbor City I think about what a shame it is that the Gun Store burned, cuz that would've been a prime jacking target, and I wouldn't have to be paying emergency prices for some fucking guns to prop up Trouble and his homies. I'm going in the hole about $8,000 to be out of this.

We go and see a guy I know called Rohan in Harbor City. He's the guy that taught me about the lye. In a redbrick office park north of the PCH, where Frampton elbows into 240th Street, he's got a small warehouse that's good and tucked back from the street and there's even some trees around, which is nice. It's got a garage door built into the side—you can roll it up and take deliveries—and that's where he's waiting for us.

He's tall, taller than me by a few inches, and he's a mixed Jamaican, part white, part black, and part Asian, I think. You can tell that last part from the shape of his eyes. He operates a plumbing parts supply out of here, completely legit. The inside's full of all different kinds of piping and accessories. He's been working on his Spanish too.

To me, Rohan says, "*¿Qué onda, vos?*"

I hear Trouble whispering to one of his homies behind me. He says, "That's a fucking trip, homes! This island motherfucker speaks Salvi!"

If he hears it, Rohan doesn't say shit. Instead, he asks if I've got money. He says, "*¿Tienes pisto?*"

I nod and he leads us back to the office where there's music on.

You learn way too much about reggae hanging out with Jamaicans. Like now I can tell that for once Shabba Ranks isn't on. Instead, Toots and the Maytals is playing one of their live albums in the background, and it's the song about a prison number, "54-46," and it's odd how appropriate that is. This track's live from London way back in the 1980s, Hammersmith Palais. I know those bits cuz it's important to Rohan that I know them, that I respect his culture like he says. Now I never been to England, but the thing that's so crazy about it is how the crowd sings so loud on the record when me, Jeffersón, and Trouble sit down in Rohan's office.

Rohan knows Jeffersón, so I introduce Trouble to him, and somehow Trouble manages not to do anything else stupid, which is helpful. It goes quick and painless, except it's only painless if I don't mind paying an extra $2,000 cuz Rohan raises the price for six shotguns and fifteen semiautomatic handguns of various makes, all unregistered, to an even $10,000 because, well, couldn't I see that the city was just one big ass for the taking?

"And if we got the right type of dicks," Trouble says, all expectant to get his hands on them guns, "we can fuck anything."

There's no use arguing. I've got $9,000 in cash on me, which Jeffersón goes and gets from the compartment in the passenger-side door, and when Rohan has it run through the counters, he says he knows I'm good for the rest and he's pleased we could do business and did I know what was playing on the speakers? When I tell him it's Toots, he laughs and smiles, proud of me. Right then I wonder if he'll ever know it was me that threw him to the sheriffs when they come busting in someday soon. He'll deserve it too for jacking up his price like this, bloodsucking motherfucker. I smile back across the table at him. I do it all warm and then I thank him before going outside.

I'm standing in the lot with only our cars around, watching the guns get loaded inside some basic-looking piping boxes into the trunks of Trouble's homies' cars and I'm thinking, *Thank God I can wipe my hands of this shit.* I went above and beyond the call for Trouble's crew by backing them this hard, but for me, it was just a play to get rid of them cuz I got a stone-cold feeling the big homies won't be happy to hear about Fate's and Trouble's clicks going at it, much less knowing I put in for it, but it's got to go down now. It's unavoidable and I have no idea how it's gonna play. I almost don't want to know, but from the mood right now, it's feeling like some O.K. Corral shit, some last man standing shit cuz these fuckers are gonna go in *hard*.

I watch them finish loading and close the trunks of their cars. I'm ready to give them a homeboy send-off, but Trouble looks at me sideways and says, "There's no such things as sidelines anymore, homes. You're fucking coming with us and doing work. You backed us, so you're with us now."

I smile cuz it feels like the bottom parts of my lungs crinkle up when he says that. I try to take a normal breath and can't, but fuck it, I know how to act when I got to act.

I grin when I show him the nine I got in my waistband, also with the handle taped up in white athletic tape cuz I hate my hand sweating when I'm holding one, and I say, "*Símon*, man, I was hoping you'd say that. We'll draw up a plan, and—"

"A plan?" Trouble laughs. "We going now. Surprise attack. Guerrilla shit, *vato*."

I been going along until now, but this shit is straight-up suicide and that's when it hits me. A suicide run is exactly what Trouble has in mind. My stomach turns itself into a pretzel just thinking about it, and there's no way I can be in on that.

"I don't think so," I say. "Fate's got the keys to Lynwood."

If they do something stupid like shoot up a house or something while dragging me with them, we're all through. Even if we survive, we're through. Green light and all. My stomach isn't a pretzel anymore. It's a black hole, trying to eat my whole body from the inside out.

"Damn, Momo," Trouble says, "I thought you read books and shit. Keys are just things, and they're there to be *taken*, homes. Anybody can hold them. When the king's dead, there's got to be a new one, right? *El rey ha muerto. ¡Viva el rey!*"

His homeboys get their heads nodding at that shit.

"And besides," he says, "I don't recall giving you no kinda choice."

I feel my smile hardening on my face as I nod at that and my sweat's starting up cuz I can't really believe how stupid he is, and I know there's no way of getting out of this, so I nod at Jeffersón to get in the car, and I get in the car, and I pray Erickson got my message as we fucking ride back the way we came, but now the cars behind us are riding heavier on their axles cuz they're loaded down with enough guns to wipe out a whole neighborhood.

DAY 4
SATURDAY

IT WAS THE WILD WEST WITH PAVED STREETS.

—RONALD ROEMER,
FORMER LOS ANGELES FIRE DEPARTMENT BATTALION CHIEF
ON HIS TENURE IN SOUTH CENTRAL

BENNETT GALVEZ,
A.K.A. TROUBLE,
A.K.A. TROUBLE G.

MAY 2, 1992

1:09 A.M.

1

When I'm about to do bad shit, I don't shake but I sweat. I get real hot on the back of my neck, feels like sunburn or something, and I get real slick back there. I can't help it. Can't stop it. It's just how I'm wired up. Is what it is. And right now I'm hunching into my collar to catch it, soak it up with cotton, cuz three cars of us are going in for this mission, and all's I'm living for is to lay that bitch Payasa up in her own blood puddle for what she did, cuz where I come from you can't hit my family like that and not pay. I want her feeling what I been feeling for these past couple days. I *need* that. Cuz you can't take away the only sister and brother I ever had and expect different.

I never told nobody this, but I been on fire since I seen Ramiro die right in front of me. My body don't feel right. Sometimes it's like a low heat in my feet, the bottoms of them, and also in the backs of my knees, and other times it's my whole body and it feels like I'm gonna burn up and I can't stop it. The heat changes with my thoughts sometimes, like what I'm thinking about. It gets hotter with what I been replaying in my head. Can't help it.

I was in the living room, waiting for the beer my girl was supposed to be getting me from the kitchen, and I just remember thinking how good I felt that we got one of theirs, that Ernesto. It was like, finally! It felt good, you know? We had to wait over a month for payback for my lil sis. My parents had to go on the news and everything. We had to have a service in the house with the coffin next to the turned-off TV, and the funeral home didn't like that much but they did it cuz I paid them, and I paid them cuz my mother would've killed herself if her little girl didn't come home at least one last time. After, we had to caravan out to the graveyard to bury her. I had to watch my lil sis go in the earth through this fat border of green Astroturf set up around the hole in the ground. I had to stand close and hear the lil gears of the lifting machine grind as it sunk her down there. Sounded like a dog chewing metal chain. I don't think I can ever forget that sound, even though I want to. I had to be the first to shovel dirt cuz my dad couldn't do it. Not wouldn't, *couldn't*. He was sitting in his wheelchair, holding his hat in his hands, so me and Joker had to step up to put the dirt on our lil sis's coffin. On our Yesenia. And when that dirt thumped wood, my mother started wailing. Real high-pitched. That's a sound you don't forget. It stays in your ears. Sometimes, it wakes you up at night.

So, yeah, when I heard that the dude working the Tacos El Unico truck was *related* to the Lil Mosco that killed our Yesenia, was actually his blood big brother, which I never knew cuz he wasn't involved or nothing, well, it was *on* then. He didn't have a name before then. After I found out, he was Lil Mosco's corpse of a brother to me. I called him that in front of all my homies, and they laughed at first cuz maybe they didn't know how serious I was.

I got to be honest, I didn't give a fuck if he was involved or not. Far as I could see, Lil Mosco put him in the conversation. If Lil Mosco kills my sister and disappears, well, then, it is what it is. Lil Mosco basically killed his own big brother when he did that cowardly shit instead of taking what he had coming like a man. So when this city decides to go to war on some Rodney King shit, I figure it's time to tell Joker to follow that motherfucker and see if we can't get back just a little bit of what they took from us when our Yesenia got killed. We didn't get who we wanted, not Lil Mosco, but we took one of theirs and it was even. My lil sister, your big brother. Fair, I thought. That's it, I thought.

And I was standing in that same living room that same night, looking at the top of the TV with the little cloth with canary birds on it my mom folded three ways so it wouldn't hang down too much, and on top of that, all them tall and glowing prayer candles with saints on them and Jesus with a big red heart floating outside his chest. In front of those, a picture of my lil sis smiling in her braces from three years ago even though those things used to cut her mouth up bad and Ramiro and me needed them too but my dad was on disability by then and he only had enough savings at the time for hers, and to the left of all that was the empty space where my sister's coffin was sat during the service and I remember looking at the patch of carpet that night Ernesto died and thinking the space where her body used to be wasn't as empty somehow, you know? It wasn't full, but it was something. It was avenged. It was paid.

What happens next, it fucks with me to this day. I see, like, instant replays of it in my mind that never stop. It just keeps going, over and over. It starts with my girl coming up with the beer in one of them shiny red plastic cups, all smiling like she's proud of me, pushing her hair behind her ear with her other hand, and then, just, *bang*. Outside. A gun shot. And my girl jumps then cuz she's surprised, and that beer flies out of that cup and through the air at me, and when it hits me, it soaks the bottom of my shirt and the top of my khakis good.

I know that bang was a gun. Even as I'm turning toward the big glass patio doors, I know. And over the tops of people's heads, I see Joker falling and blood coming out his ear or his neck or I don't know what, and seeing that, the last good thing in me, the only good thing I had left breaks into a million pieces, but I don't know it then cuz I'm too busy looking at the girl with the lace gloves and the Glock up high, how she aims on Fox then, and blasts his chest all out the back of him, and there's so much blood from that, it looks like somebody threw a ketchup bottle onto the cinder-block wall behind, and exploded it, and—

From the backseat then, Momo says to me, "You doing okay or what?"

It's not like a genuine question though. It's, like, *superior* the way he says it, like he's better than me. But if he says nothing, I don't find out I'm holding my collar and pulling it back and forth over my slick neck like a towel or something. I must've been doing it without realizing.

"Don't worry about me," I say. "You worry about *you*."

I let go of my collar though. I put my hands in my lap. We're almost there. Almost to the Boardwalk those motherfuckers love so much. It's almost time to end it.

I been getting like this lately, kinda lost inside, losing track of things, losing track of time. Is what it is. I was like this when my sister got it but not as bad cuz it didn't happen right in front of me. I didn't see her blood. But Joker's? Yeah. *Too* much.

I remember running for the doors as other people run away from them, and there's more shots, and I can't really see cuz there's too many people in front of me, and I'm screaming at them to fucking move as the patio door slides open, and that's when I hear a big *boom*, like a .357 boom, or a .44 boom, a big one. But I don't care where it's coming from, cuz I'm scrambling to that door and kicking fools out of the way, punching, I don't give a fuck, cuz I'm trying to get to Ramiro and when I'm out the door, I forget there's two little concrete steps and I miss both, and I fall forward hard and scrape the fuck out of my left knee and both palms, but I don't feel nothing, I'm up and I'm next to him and he's still breathing and he looks at me as he's, like, shaking all over, trying to do . . . what? Talk? And the only word I know right then is *no*, and I'm saying that shit over and over, so much and so fast, it loses its meaning. It's just sounds coming out of me when Ramiro stops breathing, this little fucking kid I taught to ride a bike cuz Dad couldn't, cuz of his chair. I got this little fucker propped up in my arms, this little fucker that always wanted to be just like me, and I'm thinking, like, he's messing with me. He'll breathe again. He's just playing a joke. And so I laugh, like, maybe that's what he was waiting for, for me to laugh so he would breathe again . . . but he don't. His lungs don't rise, they sink. And this gurgle sound comes out of his neck, so I try to cover it up with my hands. Can't help it. I try to cover up the bullet hole there, one that's dime size. I push with two hands. Hard. I press and press, but I can feel his heart's not beating no more. And I keep saying no. All quiet. Not like big and loud dramatic, just no. No. No. No. And right then is when the biggest boom of all comes. The shotgun.

Prolly this is why I haven't slept since it happened, not *slept*-slept. I drink to stop seeing my brother's face like that. I drug up to stop seeing his neck all open. It's all I can do. The only thing that works for sleep is for me to black out, but then when I open my eyes and it's hours later, it don't matter. Everything's still there, right back in my head, and I got an ache all over and I'm still on fire. Is what it is.

I'm all kinds of serious when I snort a fat line of coke off my thumb after we meet up and park on Virginia, all three cars. That burns too. After, I kinda pack up what memories I have of Joker inside me right then, cuz it's time to do work. Like I could open my ribs up and put it away and close them on it and fasten it down. That's how I keep him inside me. Keep him close. It's not long before I feel like I got lightning inside me, pumping me up. And that's good, cuz right now, I can't be me anymore. Can't be Bennett with all his fucking problems. I got to be Trouble. Got to be the one everybody knows is down no matter what.

There's nobody out on the street but us and some homeless-looking black motherfucker rooting through open trash cans up the block. There hasn't been trash pickup in days, but people still put them out anyways. Dumb-asses. I don't need to stare to know this is the same weirdo that Momo asked if he knew anything about his little house fire and got some crazy-ass gibberish back instead, something about shit going to heaven in pieces or something.

Apart from crazy dude's slow shuffle, it's a ghost town. Lights out all over this block, curtains closed up tight, only streetlamps. Nice thing is, it smells like flowers over here, I don't know what kinds, and only a little bit of smoke. We're over the line all right, right off what they call the Boardwalk. My lil bro told me about this. I know Fate and his click treat it like an escape route, from sheriffs, from whatever, but right now, it's a path straight into the heart of their turf.

2

The coke's fucking hitting me and I feel better now. Strong. I feel like it's time to get ours back, pull some fucking cards. We got nine homies, just the hard-core *veteranos*, cuz we can't afford bitch shit on this one from a lil homie trying to earn stripes. They know this is a suicide run, and they're all down cuz I'm down. I been doing this for a long time and I'm untouchable at it. Nobody expects you to run up in a house and blast fools on their couch, pure *vato loco* style. But I been doing it and I stay living. And right now, my wild card is that I don't care. I don't care about nothing. Before with runs like this, it was just me. I never had to work an operation this big. Just getting everybody over Atlantic was a hassle. There's more National Guards out patrolling around or sitting on intersections, so we couldn't've done a car train. We had to be smart, so we avoided them by splitting up into two different cars, four into one and five into another, before going different ways to meet up and park.

Cuz we weren't about to bother them Guards. We got three in there, called up and deployed out of Inglewood. What, you think National Guard don't got gangsters in there? Shit. Time to wake up. We got three. Ain't gonna tell you their names though. I'm sure other gangs got homies in there too. Turns out it's a real good way to learn about guns and tactics and shit. Bring it home, you know?

I told Momo we were gonna hit Fate and them in the after-noon, like right after that trip to see that Chinkmaican where we picked up all that heavy L.A. Gear but we didn't, and we never were gonna. I lied. Fuck Momo. We would never have rolled through in broad day. Besides, we had shit to do first. Had to bust up a parole office and make a pretty fire with some records so some people could stay free.

That shit was so fun we had to get high to celebrate. Let me say that again, but fix it right this time. Momo got us high courtesy of the goodness of his heart cuz he's so generous and obviously not trying to save himself like some *vibora*. That's a viper right there, one that'll bite you if you let it.

Momo's been acting off for weeks. I'm not the only one to see it. He's not been answering pages or questions when you get in front of him. He's been disappearing, you know? If I didn't know no better, I'd say he was fixing to snitch, cuz when I first met him, like *met-him*-met-him, he wasn't this way. He didn't say much, but he was real, and since I know he ain't been straight with dodging my pages when we *knew* it was his gun that got Ramiro, then I got cause to worry, and I don't got to be straight with him either.

My girl said something smart too, about not letting Momo near no more phones on the chance he might try to call someone about how we're treating him all disrespectful, so I did that and I did one better, I sent his boy Jeffersón home on the end of my new shotgun. Now he didn't like looking down that barrel, but what was he gonna do but stop looking tough and get the fuck out, all backing up cuz he wasn't about to take his eyes off me? Nothing, that's what.

While he was walking out, I told him the only one Momo needs watching his back is me. Which's exactly why this bitch is on my hip right now, looking all kinds of scared, gripping his busted-looking gun with its tape cuz his hand sweats, cuz he never pops, that's why.

I look at him and say, "Don't got any smart questions for me now, do you?"

"There's a time to talk," he says, "and a time to act."

He sounds tough, but you can just tell he don't even want to do this, but he's doing cuz he knows I'll take his head off his shoulders from a foot away if he don't. That's the beauty of getting one of the shotties all to myself. I could've taken him out earlier but it's way more fun this way, making him march.

I tell both drivers to stay at the cars and keep them warm cuz we're coming out hot and right when we're all ready to roll up, I make Momo go first, right in front of me. A shield if I need it, you know? The six of us and Momo roll up army style, pure stealth passing through that Boardwalk where the only sounds are our footsteps and leaves and branches getting pushed back. I smile knowing they won't even see us coming. We're Viet-Conging this shit. For Ramiro, for Fox, for Lil Blanco that got it by the fence, and all them others at the party that got caught up.

We go through an alley with garages on either side and then back into the Boardwalk and out onto Pope in one long fast line like ants, looking both ways but nobody's there either, and then we go through one more alley to Duncan Avenue. Momo's first out and I'm second. Right away I spot the house Fate and that *manflora* Payasa and them been living in and jog my ass up the block.

Turns out Momo was good for something after all, with the way he came up with that info on where they stay. I asked him how he knows for sure, and he says his hypes say all kinds of shit when they're high, and when this motherfucker Lil Creeper gets high he talks and talks and so Momo would ask him questions sometimes about Fate's click so he could keep track of what was up, you know? When he said that, I just kinda nodded, cuz that was smart but it was still some viper shit.

Right now the house's set up behind a chain-link fence hip-high that leads my eye to three mailboxes out front of a shared driveway that goes way back. To the right of that concrete strip is the house. It's a boxy, sand-colored piece of stucco shit, one with a roof that slopes toward the street, like a baseball hat down low, and it's held up by six spaced posts. It's got a front door between the middle two and windows on either side that look out on the saddest lawn you ever seen.

The shades are drawn up tight, but there's a cut of light in the left one showing from the inside, a lamp or something. There's a TV throwing out colors too. *Good.*

I put my hand up right then and I go up the driveway first, around the boxes and onto the lawn, coming straight at the door. No hesitation. For Ramiro. For our Yesenia. When I'm in a good spot, I set my feet and we all do. When I open up, we all open up. We go Al Capone right then, just a line of gangsters unloading.

The window bars don't stop us, but they must be doing something cuz I keep hearing *ping, ping, ping,* and I think that's weird but don't think much of it cuz we blast that glass all the way out. It goes everywhere, scattering over the walkway, the lawn.

I laugh when I blast the security door, like *boo-yaa,* cuz I feel invincible, and you know it ain't iron the way it bends and curls after I put the shotgun on it, and reload, and go again, and when it's kinda hanging there, I'm right up on top of it cuz I rushed up and I'm kicking it off its hinges and ripping at the doorknob and the handle's all dented with buckshot and it comes off in my hand, and I'm like, "Hell, yeah!"

I lean back as far as I can and kick the door, putting all my weight into it, and that shit is wood with no knob or deadbolt so it should just bust under my boot.

It don't. I fucking bounce off!

And my heel *hurts.* My knee too.

So I kick it again. But it's the same thing. Nothing moves.

Behind me, somebody's like, "What the fuck?"

And real quick I scope the hole where the knob used to be, but there's not really a hole there. I mean, it's a hole, but there's something behind it. Iron.

I shove into it with the lip of my gun but it don't go nowhere. Must be thick as manhole covers. It's got dents in it from buckshot and I run my fingers over it and it's still so hot it burns my fingers and as I rip them away, I'm like, *What the fuck?*

That's when it hits me like a rush of hot water down my back. That's when my whole body gets hot again. And I'm embarrassed and I'm sad and I'm mad all at once. No. No, no.

This shit is a *setup*. The most fucked-up setup there ever was. No. I walked us right into this shit. Me. *Fuck!*

My mouth's dry when I'm about to yell out for homies to save themselves but then lights come on. No, no . . .

Blinding yellow-white lights behind me and from the side, making me blink as I turn, making me close my eyes and raise my shotgun up to my eyebrows to block the light and duck down and that's when I hear the first shot from far away and hear fools scramble.

And I'm thinking *What?* as I scrunch down low as I can and get my back to the house and slide across the stucco and it digs into my back, cutting me as I move fast sideways, toward the corner of the house so I can break out behind.

I scream when I say, "Get the fuck out!" But it comes out strangled.

I hear more blams, faster this time, closer. Like, *blam-blam-blam* . . .

No.

Bullets whiz and one hits the house over me and stucco explodes above my head with a *crack-thump*, chucking dust and pebbles down into my face, and then it's the worst noise I ever heard, a *brrrat, brrrat* . . .

And that right there's the fat lady singing cuz that's what sound an AK makes when it spits. I don't know how far away it is or where it's aiming, but I feel that noise in my chest, moving my heart around, and I know we're getting done, right here, right now. No, no.

I hear screams everywhere, all around me. My heart's beating hard and fast in my ears, making my head hot and hurting.

No. Everything's too loud now. Too fast.

"No," I say, and that's all I can think to say.

This shit is my fault. But this's no time to mess with guilt. We gotta do the only thing we can and shoot our way out.

I got almost a roll call of all the homies I let down running in my head. Best I can do for Ramiro right now, and our Yesenia, and Lil Blanco, and, and . . .

For Fox, and Looney, and . . .

"Shoot them lights out," I yell, and I pump my shot and raise up blasting at black outlines moving in front of the brightness.

I pump and blast and kill one of the lights with sparks and a *kssssss*, so I pump and blast again, and that's when I'm out and I know I'm out, but I pump and hit the trigger anyway. But nothing happens.

Is what it is.

I say, "Motherfuckers, you better fucking kill me! You better—"

Whatever else I'm gonna say, the words don't come. I'm flat on my side and I don't even remember falling down.

My ears ring like I got sirens in them. And I'm coughing. That's when I hear four quick pops, like *pop-pop-pop-pop*.

And then somebody falls on me, right on my shoulder too. Hard.

And I wanna see what's going on but I can't really keep my eyes open right then, they're just so heavy.

ROBERT ALÀN RIVERA,
A.K.A. CLEVER,
A.K.A. SHERLOCK HOMEBOY

MAY 2, 1992

12:58 A.M.

1

With the way we shot up Joker and them, we knew their homies were coming, we just didn't know when, so Fate had us do everything we could to bunker up. Lu wasn't happy about the plan at first, because it was her house that had to be the decoy, but she came around to it. She liked living better than she liked the other option.

So two nights ago we went door-to-door to clear the block three houses in every direction. It was me, Fate, and Apache mostly, unless homies lived there, and if they did, they talked to their own families. We explained to people that it'd be really a good time to see relatives or friends. We even helped a few load up their cars to get ready. Apache even carried someone's *abuelo* to the car because he couldn't walk himself. Everybody might not have liked it at first, but they did what we asked and left, which was good because Fate didn't want it on his conscience if bullets started flying like he thought they would.

Lu didn't go with us. She'd had a fight with her girl, Lorraine, right as we were gearing up to go. It started in her room first and got louder and louder till the door flew open and they ended up in the living room. There was some screaming and crying from Lorraine and through the doorway, I saw Lu packing a bag with all her girl's clothes and everything in it, and Lu told her not to be such a dumb, dramatic bitch. Right after that, Lorraine threw a bottle of nail polish at her, hard too. It caught Lu in the left eye as she flinched away, and it gave her a shiner almost instantly. I was surprised Lorraine didn't get her ass beat after that, but Lu held off, and that's when I knew Lu was doing right by her, getting her out, because it just wasn't safe to be here. Her pushing her away meant she cared, but some people you never can explain that to, and Lorraine didn't get it. She drove off crying.

In a way, it worked out for Lu, though, because Elena Sanchez came by to say thanks for killing Joker not too long after that, and they went into Lu's room and shut the door. At first I thought it was just to hear how it went down, even though I know Lu wasn't one for talking about that kind of thing. I didn't know if Lu was trying to flip her to the other team, but I wouldn't be shocked. She's a player. If she could, she would. I guess it depends on if Elena was up for that, but I can't speak to whether or not that went down for sure. They were in there awhile though.

I left before Elena did because Fate needed me across the street. A couple of O.G.'s caught the score of a lifetime by stealing an official city truck that first night of the riots, the tall white kind with a city seal on the doors and a big, tall bed almost four feet high in the back. Ever since they took it they've been able to go wherever they want, wearing the orange vests, and cops and National Guard just wave them through, wherever they want to go, so they've just been driving around looting, hitting construction sites mostly. They got a bunch of tools and materials that got abandoned when everything popped off. They sold them to people in the neighborhood.

Also, they picked up a grip of steel plates, just recruited a small crew of guys to pull them up off the streets and load them in the back. It was the kind the city uses as a base for asphalt or to cover potholes they weren't ready to fix yet, or might never. That steel was half an inch thick and some of the slabs can weigh over three hundred pounds depending on dimensions. We took that right off their hands and used it to secure the house.

We had homies haul it in through the front door and line it up all along the front wall. Each plate took six of our biggest homies too. The metal was so heavy the drywall groaned when it had to take the weight to the left and right of the front window. We blocked that off to protect the inside of the house, so that if somebody wanted to shoot in, they'd have to aim for the top two inches to get anything through. At first, it was plated up completely, but I took a look and knew it wouldn't work, so I had them moved till a sliver of light could show through and then I set the curtain so you couldn't see the iron from the outside. To me, that was the key to the whole setup. It wouldn't work unless they thought people were inside, so I turned the TV on too and made sure it could be seen from the lawn and from the street.

"If you don't put a flame up," I said when Apache asked me why I did that, "you can't draw any moths."

2

We've been taking shifts across the street since we finished, waiting up in the house of our *compadre* Wizard. It's a little casino house he runs, but he's not here. He's back with his wife in an apartment they kept from when they lived in Lil TJ over on Louise, because he's kind of *paisa*, but the good kind, reliable, even if he's a bit country.

This whole place is empty now, except for us. It doesn't have much of a living room, not one with couches and chairs arranged around a TV or anything. Instead, it's got gambling machines along every wall and little brown chairs in front of them, like the cheap kind you'd find in a bar, the ones where if they break, it's not a big deal.

Gambling is a nice side. You'd be surprised how much money we make on it in a month. The whole block can't get enough of it. People even come from other neighborhoods to check it out because they hear about it. There's twelve machines in here altogether. Ten are slots and two are card games. We call it Mini Vegas. There's a moneychanger machine in the back corner, right next to an iron and an ironing board with a box of wax paper on it because the change machine is picky. Sometimes, people need to iron bills out flat by sandwiching them between two sheets of wax paper. That was Lu's idea, and it works. After the cash is crisp enough, you put them in and it spits out quarters so you can play Gold Rush with its little miners on it holding up full pans, or Star-Spangled Winner, or any of the other ones.

Nobody's playing the bandits because we cleared the place over a day ago, but still the machines sit there and flash. We're all just sitting in this room, me, Lu, Fate, Apache, Oso, and a couple soldiers here and there. Everybody's strapped up good. Sherms aren't allowed tonight because Fate said so. He wants us sharp, so no drugs. A Cypress Hill tape is playing so low in the background that I only hear guitar squeal samples or snares coming from the boom box.

So this is how we wait, how we've been waiting. Lu's quiet, staring out the window, a little sawed-off across her lap. She's got a good purple shiner on her eye now. On the other end of the room Fate's reading a book called *The Concrete River* by Luis J. Rodriguez, only really stopping to turn the page or take a swig from a beer he sets down between his chair and an AK-47 he's got propped against the wall. Oso's pacing back and forth, but he's careful to avoid Apache, who's flat on his back in the middle of the room, catching some zees. That's how calm he is. The other two are just posted up on chairs, looking at their guns. We've all got sunglasses hanging off the front of our collars, even sleeping Apache, because they'll be important later.

Normally we're not this quiet, but there's a lot weighing on this room. Not only are we wondering when Trouble is going to get it into his head to do something stupid, but by now we're all pretty sure Lil Mosco is never coming back, and that's not something that will ever get talked about. The aftermath of a disappearance like that is always quiet. It's not like you have a heart-to-heart and find out exactly what went down, before the right party apologizes and everybody cries and understands like on TV. Around here, sometimes things have to go unsaid if you want to stay alive.

Nobody's asking me, but I'm okay with Lil Mosco going. I'm not saying I'm good with it, but I'm okay. He was too out of control, to the point where you couldn't always count on him, but even though that's true, I know the only reason it would ever happen was if it was an us-or-him-type situation, a trade, almost, like in baseball. You send one guy and get another in return. Fate gives the big homies Lil Mosco, and we get to keep Fate, or the other scenario is we trade Lil Mosco and the whole click gets to stay alive. I'm fairly certain it's one of those two options, so I convince myself that's how it went down, because right now, there's bigger stuff to deal with.

"Trouble ain't coming," Oso says. "They didn't come last night neither and that's cuz nobody's that stupid to come in here and try to shoot us up. I mean—"

He shuts up quick when Fate looks at him and gestures toward Apache, in a reminder to Oso to be a little more considerate. It's too late though, Apache's blinking awake. He's yawning.

"Sorry, Patch," Oso says. The only person on earth who can get away with calling Apache that is Oso. That's family, I guess.

Apache shrugs. He doesn't take it personally. Oso, the big dumb bear, is his cousin and really only here to lift heavy stuff if this goes right. We all know he's jumpy. We all are in our own ways. He's never been through a stakeout like this before, and waiting to kill or die can wear you out. It's exhausting being eyes-up on the block for hours. Which reminds me, have you ever noticed how the loudest sounds seem to be when people are trying hard not to make noise? I think that's because you're tuned in. You're listening hard. You're aware. That's how it is in Mini Vegas right now. And I guess that's what's making Oso so nervous, because he starts talking just to talk, just to hear something other than silence.

"Hey, Patch," Oso says, "tell us again how you scalped that fool."

Apache shakes his head. No way is he telling that now. I don't blame him.

"Okay, so"—Oso keeps trying to avoid the quiet by running his mouth—"you guys heard that one about the O.G. homie that cut his Pachuco cross straight out of his hand with a knife? Was just like"—Oso makes his right two fingers straight and digs at the thumb web in his left—"ahhhh."

I swear, Oso likes stories too much. I look at Fate and he looks at me. We know this story has gone around forever. It follows me, and maybe it should, because it's about my dad. Nobody really knows that but Fate, though. Most just think it's about some faceless homie, but my mom told me when he left his click in East Los, and when he left us, he cut his cross out of his hand so no one would know he used to be in. He left his click on good terms because he'd put in work and kept his mouth shut. All that bullshit you hear about people having to die to get out is just that. Somehow, though, the way my dad cut his tattoo out grew into this story of a dude who wanted out of the gang so bad he cut it out in front of everybody at a party just to show he was serious. That didn't happen though. My mom says he did it in the garage with a kitchen knife he heated up on the stovetop first.

Fate knows all this. He also knows just by looking at me that I don't want to hear it all over again, the Oso version, so he says, "Hey, Oso, how about you tell us about that one time you shot up all them Crips by yourself when your car stalled?"

Oso smiles and starts telling about how this one time, he was out driving and how, at this red light on Imperial, a car came up beside him with five blacks in it and they looked at him and he looked at them and the big motherfucker driving starts licking his chops like a cartoon wolf and Oso tries to floor it, his car stalls, and right at this big point in his story, right when he's being all quiet for dramatic effect, I sniffle. Not on purpose. Because I can't help it. The smoke has really been bothering my sinuses lately.

Oso jumps on that. "Damn, you still sniffling? You better not get me sick."

"He ain't sick and he won't get you sick," Lu says, coming to my defense without turning around in her chair. "He's got allergies and the smoke's been fucking his nose up ever since the city was on fire."

"Oh" is all Oso says before he wraps his story with a sad little "so, you know, I just took care of business."

Lu's already shaking her head at that. She never did like Oso.

"New booty motherfucker," she says under her breath.

I've known the Veras, and Lu in particular, since before they were involved, which is almost twelve years now, ever since we were next-door neighbors on Louise Avenue, across from Lugo Park. Well, it will be twelve years in August, because my mom moved us from East L.A. in 1980. Out of everybody, Lu is the person who has known me longest in the world. We got along right away and stayed tight all these years. When I joined up, she did too.

I'm pretty sure I'm not like most people. When homies are gone, I don't miss them, even if we spent a lot of time together. For me, when they're not there, they're just not there. I don't even think about it. I don't know if that means there's something wrong with me, but probably there is. As it stands, I know Lu's going through something and I can't imagine it. Ernesto was like my older brother too, but he wasn't, not blood-wise. I've always been an only child, but she has gone from being the youngest to the only kid in the span of a couple days. That's got to be rough.

I've been thinking about it, and my conclusion is Lu knows Lil Mosco's gone for good. She knew on the street a few days ago when she shot up that car. She was sitting right next to me in the backseat and I was watching her as she was breathing in, holding it, and biting her lower lip. I've seen her make that face a few times before: when her dad passed, when Fate told her the house was too hot and she had to move her mom out, and after she got robbed walking home once on Wright Street. She only ever does that face if she's accepting something she doesn't like, something she can't change, and when she's holding in breath like that, biting her lip, and before she needs to breathe out, that's when the Lil Mosco thing must have clicked, because she said, "Shit." She whispered it, really, like she was finally accepting it. I don't think anyone else heard her say that.

Right at that moment, Lu sits straight up at the window like she sees something. She leans forward, almost pressing her nose to the glass, and her spine freezes like a predator's when prey wanders into its zone.

"They're here," she says, but says it like the scary little blond girl in *Poltergeist*, *hee*-ere, and my heart spikes up in my chest. I grip my .32 Beretta, ready for whatever, because I know we prepared for every possible thing we could, but I've also been around long enough to know anything can happen.

Things you plan, they don't always work out how you think.

3

Fate's up and moving, tossing his book across the carpet like a Frisbee, putting on gloves, tucking his sleeves into them, and grabbing the AK. Apache's right behind him, killing all the power in the place. The music from the boom box, "Hand on the Pump," dies just as it's starting. The gambling machines snap off at the same time and we're in darkness. I hear Oso cock his borrowed Glock like he's in the movies or something, pulling the slide all the way back, but he's already got one in the chamber, and a bullet flies out, hits the carpet, and rolls to the baseboard with a tap.

"Fuck," he says and gets down on the ground, looking for it.

"Good one, stupid," Lu says.

I'm up at the window, on Lu's shoulder. My heart's going pretty steady as we see a line of seven fools drift in through the dark with serious gear. The best part is, they're on the other sidewalk and they're so focused, they don't notice the extension cords we've strung out from this house to the curb and up into the bed of the city truck, which, right now, is parked directly across from Lu's house and has two stolen trees of multiarmed construction lights in its bed, the megabright ones, hooked up. So far, things are going right, which is good, because I count four shotguns. Lu does too.

She leans back and stubs her finger on the glass right about the time Oso gives up looking for his lost bullet.

"Hold up," she says, "isn't that Momo right there? What the fuck's he doing with them on a mission?"

I don't like hearing that. Killing him might not go over well with the big homies because you know a guy like Momo pays his taxes, but it's not like he's giving us a choice if he's here. If things went down with the big homies like I think over Lil Mosco, I'm sure Fate has some leverage to set it right after we do what we have to though.

"One way to find out," Fate says as he undoes the deadbolt and opens the door real slow, steps out of the house, and looks up. He gives a little wave to the homie we got on the roof with a sniper rifle. Ranger, his name is, because he used to be in the army until he was dishonorably discharged for brawling with some other gang members in his unit. They were from Detroit. He put one of them in a coma and got stockaded for a year in Colorado first, but he's out now. He's the best shot we got, and he knows not to open up until the lights come on.

I've never seen Trouble close up before—I've had no reason to—but I've heard of him. Everybody has. His name rings out from all the suicide missions he did when he was coming up. He got known for running up in houses and shooting snitches on their couches, in their kitchens, whatever. One time, he even shot a homeboy when he was doing his business in the bathroom, on the toilet and every-thing. Word is, he got his name before people really knew who was doing those missions. People would say, *Did you hear about such-and-such?* And the response would be, *Yeah, the fool that did them is nothing but trouble*. Pretty soon, that just became his name, with a capital *T*.

They're in the yard now, the seven of them, raising their weapons like they think someone's in there, and that's when a ripple of pride shoots through me because I know the trap worked. Fate knows too, because he hits me light on the shoulder. It's our last calm moment before the night blows up.

It sounds like the Fourth of July when they start blasting on the house, except heavier. Here, there isn't the sound of explosions sputtering out in the air. Instead, it goes boom and then ends in fast, hard thumps as bullets and scattershot bury themselves in walls and window trim. It ends in pings and pops when those same things hit the security door or the iron behind the windows, which smash out and go everywhere in a hurry.

We duck down in a line and head for the truck together. A little homie in there pops his head up when he sees us. Muzzle flashes light his eyes up and I can see he's as scared as anything, but that's okay, all he's got to do is turn the lights on when Fate signals. He doesn't, not yet.

The little homie keeps his eyes on Fate as one shooter with a shotgun stops firing and runs to the door. That has to be Trouble because of the way everybody follows him.

When he gets to the front door, he says, "Hell, yeah!"

He kicks the door hard and stumbles back, and all I can think is how much that must hurt, trying to kick a door with two hundred pounds behind it. It must be worse than kicking a boulder. Still, he kicks again, because he obviously didn't figure it out the first time. And this is when Fate pulls his sunglasses off his front collar and puts them on, so we all do.

Somebody else on the lawn says, "What the fuck?"

Which must be when Trouble sees the iron, because he shoves the barrel of the shotgun against the door, and then puts his fingers on it and tears them away fast like it's hot. He stands up straight right then.

And that's when Fate signals the little homie inside the truck bed, and the six-foot-tall construction lights go on with a pop behind us. Almost immediately, the lights of both houses next door go on too. After that, Ranger's fastest. He puts a perfect bullet through the left eyebrow of the one closest to us and I see the blood mist out the back of his head and into the air like someone spraying Windex. He goes down like a puppet with every one of its strings cut.

Trouble gets low right after, trying to shield his eyes. He tries to yell for his little crew to get the fuck out, but it doesn't come out too loud, and besides, it's already too late. Me and Lu, we're down on one knee at the fence and sticking our guns through, steadying our barrels on the bottoms of the chain-link holes.

We open up at hip height on the runners. Lu shreds some knee-caps and pumps, and then she does it again. I aim for Trouble and miss high, but Fate's behind me, walking up, unleashing the AK. Even from feet away, it shakes my whole body when he lets off a burst and sprays all the way across the front of the house, cutting people the hell down. That's when the ones who can still do it start screaming and that sets something off in Trouble because he's up and walking straight toward us.

"Shoot them lights out," he yells, pumps his shotgun, and raises up blasting.

4

Buckshot piles into the truck behind me and I feel something hot bite the back of my neck, but I run my hand over it and there's no blood, so right away I know it's nothing. I'm more concerned with Trouble pumping again, firing high, and taking out one of the construction lights on the truck. He pumps again, but nothing happens. Trouble's out of ammo and he knows it.

He says, "Come on, motherfuckers! You better fucking kill me! You better—"

Right then the guy behind him steps up and puts a gun under Trouble's ear, on the black smudge of one of his neck tattoos, and fires. The bullet exits Trouble's neck on the other side and for a big second, there's a pause, because no one saw that one coming, not even Fate, as Trouble hits the deck.

Lu says, "Fucking Momo just blasted him!"

One of Trouble's homies I shot in the side sees this and puts four bullets in Momo's chest right after. The last thing Momo ever does is sneer at Trouble's body on the ground like he'd wanted to do that since forever, and he smiles as his legs give out and he goes down hard on top of Trouble. That's when Ranger snipes one through the neck of the guy who shot him.

Neck wounds are the ugliest way to go. With them, there's nothing but coughing and sputtering and bleeding out. He trips over and hits dirt as Ranger's next bullet smashes into the house where his head used to be.

"Jesus," Apache says, steps up, and taps his gun to the guy's skull and sends one through the dude's brain with a crack.

His skull kicks up with a jolt and he stops breathing, but for a moment it's so quiet you can hear the blood still coming out of his neck with little splashes as Oso and the two other soldiers go real carefully from body to body, taking guns away. There's still a few breathing, enough for the little homies to step up and earn stripes by finishing them off with one to the head, but I'm already moving because we don't have much time.

Sheriffs will be coming soon. Probably Vikings. Maybe National Guard too. Even with three houses cleared in every direction, somebody will be calling this in. To counteract that, we had homies with orders to speed to Montgomery Wards when this started and try to put an old Chrysler through one of the security gates there. We also called in six fake 911 calls in six different locations miles from here.

It's safe to assume we have ten minutes at most to clean up, three at the least.

5

One of the O.G.'s who stole the city truck jumps in it and backs it up to us at the curb in front of Lu's chewed-up house, and when it finishes beeping, I toss my gun in the bed, a little sad to see it go, but not sad enough to ever get caught with it. Everybody else who shot does the same. Those are my rules. Lu's goes in next, then Oso's, Apache's, the soldiers', and even Ranger's rifle and the AK. After a few more pops when the survivors get what's coming, those pistols go in too, along with all of Trouble's crew's gear.

We leave the lights in the truck, along with the body of the little homie who flipped them on. Trouble took half his face with his last shot that put some lights out. I didn't even know his name. Lu didn't like seeing him where he was, half sitting up, propped against the back wall of the truck bed like he was playing hide-and-seek and still waiting to be found.

She spits before she says, "Dumb lil one wanted to watch. Should've put his fucking head down, huh? Might've kept it that way."

But something else in the truck is bothering her, and it's been bothering me too. The gun Momo used, the one with the tape on it, looks identical to the one Fate bought from Lil Creeper for her to use.

"Do you think," Lu says, "the one I used on Joker came from the same place? That it was Momo's too?"

"Wouldn't put it past Lil Creeper to rob Momo," I say and then sniffle. "But that doesn't mean Trouble knew that. Might explain why Momo was with them anyway, and maybe even why he popped Trouble when he had the chance. They could have thought he helped us before, so they forced him to come."

"Don't matter so much now though," she says. "He's *done*."

She's right, so I shrug and we step to the side to make way for the other dead bodies of Momo, and Trouble, and Trouble's crew to go into the bed of the truck. Oso, Fate, and the soldiers move all seven of them no problem, chucking bodies in the back like they're just big bloody sacks of rice. Now Lu's house is just a shooting scene. There are no bodies and no weapons.

Apache, Lu, and I drag trash cans off the curb from where they were behind the city truck and open them. The smell overpowers us at first, but between us three, we pull out three sets of bedsheets that have been marinating in gasoline for days and get them into the bed for a little homie to spread out over the bodies. He holds his breath the whole time. It doesn't help. When he jumps down all wobbly, Oso and Fate and the soldiers are there to throw firewood on top from the back of a pickup we got parked right next to the truck last night and then, on top of all that, Lu chucks in one more bedsheet set.

Everybody strips down after that, chucking their clothes and shoes into a big black trash bag that Apache holds open. The only things they're allowed to keep are boxers or *chonies* if they don't have blood on them. If they do, those go in too. When they get down to skin, they get a blanket from the floor of the firewood pickup and fade away in all directions before sheriffs come. If caught, they're to lie and say they got jumped for everything they had. If asked why they have blankets, though, they're to say a neighbor lady took pity on them. It wouldn't be the first time either one has happened around here. Nobody's going too far, though, three blocks at most.

For Fate, me, Lu, and Apache, though, it's new clothes. Lu's first, then Apache. When he's done, he takes the black bag of used clothes with him and hops into the city truck. It takes off toward MLK, followed by the Cutlass. Lu's driving that. I don't hear sirens yet. We might have two minutes left.

As I jump into a new pair of khakis, I'm glad to see four little homies I prepped earlier finishing up on the lawn with shoebox tops strapped to their feet and plastic hospital gloves on their hands. Without leaving fingerprints, they sweep up as many shell casings as they can in a minute before scattering old ones from all kinds of different weapons, weapons inconsistent with bullets the sheriffs'll pull out of the house.

Walking over the crime scene, the lil homies leave rectangular marks but nothing identifiable, no shoeprints. It's 'hood, but this way, sheriffs get nothing. The footprints are gone and so are the shoes that made them. After that, the little boxtop homies turn on the hose from the side of the house and soak the lawn down good to destroy blood patterns, and I almost feel sorry for the guy who draws the straw on this scene.

I got a professor, Sturm, he used to be in the military, and he says the word *FUBAR* all the time. I had to ask him what he meant, and he said it's *Fucked Up Beyond All Recognition*. When I first heard it, I thought it would make a good name for a homie, but Sturm uses it to describe how natural events can ruin scene evidence, like rain or wind in some unforeseen way. I don't think it ever occurred to him that I paid real close attention during those talks so that I could be one of those events someday.

6

It was Fate's idea to wait for the sheriffs on the curb, so it's up to me to make sure he's got nothing on him when they show up. He's doing it because he doesn't want them knocking on doors. He knows they'll try to find him, knows they'll want to talk to him, because they'll probably be able to tell from the address that he was a target and he doesn't feel like being on the run when he can just get it over with. It's not like it'll be the first time he's ever been questioned.

Truth is, we're hoping the National Guard shows up first. We'd feel safer with them than Vikings. With Vikings, you never know how they'll try to do you. They're sneaky. And the worst part is you never know who actually is one. Sure, they got tattoos on them, but I've never seen one. It's not like we can see those through socks, through a uniform. Basically, you only know them from their actions, and once you do, it's too late.

Which is why we want Fate waiting out in the open, with plenty of people watching. There's still no guarantee he won't be hurt, but you have to admire the courage of it. Before I send him out to do it though, I have to be extra sure he's got no gunshot residue on his hands.

It's just me and Fate in the casino house now. There's nobody else around because I can't have them contaminating him when I test his hands. It's unlikely there's any present, but if there is, I'll find it.

When a gun kicks out a bullet, it sprays two potassiums in its tiny particles of gunpowder: nitrates and nitrites. But that's the simplistic way of saying it. The chemical elements potentially present in GSR depend on the ammunition type. The major primers are lead (Pb), barium (Ba), and antimony (Sb), which are pretty much in everything, most of the time. To memorize those, I told myself that *Peanut butter Barbers Steal besos.* Does it make sense, haircutting dudes made out of peanut butter stealing kisses? No, but it helps me remember, so there must be something to it.

Combinations of less common elements depend on bullet size (caliber) and manufacturer (and sometimes *region* of manufacturer because certain things are more available or cheaper in different parts of the world), so there can be any of these: aluminum (Al), calcium (Ca), chlorine (Cl), copper (Cu), potassium (K)—*Al Called Clarita Cucumber Killer*—and sulfur (S), silicon (Si), tin (Sn), and strontium (Sr), titanium (Ti), zinc (Zn)—*Simon Silently Snitched,* and *Sheriffs Turn Zombies nightly.*

In the empty kitchen, I heat up some wax over one of the low gas burners on the stove and apply it to his hands. Fate grunts but doesn't say anything. He knows the drill. When the wax cools enough, I peel it off, taking away whatever residue is left with it. This's called an adhesive collection device, but really it's just paraffin. If there's anything left on his hands, anything that got through the gloves, I should be capturing all the substances they'd love to use for evidence to prove he was at the scene and shooting.

In the old days, cops would collect it this way, and then they'd squirt a little diphenylamine and sulfuric acid on the wax. I do that now. If it turns blue, it means it has nitrates on it and Fate would be busted. Nowadays, most law enforcement agencies swab with a 5 percent solution of nitric acid and submit tabs to the crime lab, but even Sturm says it's at capacity or overrun at the best of times. I can't imagine how it is now with all the chaos going on.

"Hey," I say, turning around and showing Fate my back, "do I have a cut or something on my neck? Felt like I got hit with a little something back there."

"You got a red mark, a little burn. The skin's not broken," he says.

I nod and hold the wax under the kitchen light above the sink and check for the kind of blueness that would indicate nitrates of an amount to suggest the recent firing of a deadly weapon, but it is extremely faint. In my determination, it is not consistent, and if it's not consistent for me, it will be the same for anyone else too.

"Clean," I say.

Fate nods at me before heading out to the curb, to wait for whatever's coming.

7

The timing couldn't be better. In less than a minute, our street is flooded with National Guards, two Humvees' worth, about six of them. We have no beef with them. I watch as they lock down the street. I'm sitting at the window of the casino house with the lights off still, but I've opened it a touch so I can hear what's going on.

"Holy shit," one of the soldiers says when he sees how torn up Lu's house is. "That was one hell of a firefight."

When they spot Fate and zero in on him, they ask him to step up with his hands out all the way to his sides so they can pat him down. When they determine he does not have a weapon, they ask him what he is doing there, sitting across the street from a crime scene.

"Waiting," Fate says.

One of the guardsmen, a short black guy with a mustache says, "For what?"

"Sheriffs," Fate says.

"Oh, you're tough, huh? You know the drill?" The guard guy squares up to Fate. "How long you been in a gang?"

"I don't know what you're talking about, sir. I just live here."

"*Right.*" The guardsman looks like he's about to do something, but he backs off. "Well, you just sit yourself back down there till the law comes. I'm sure they'll want to talk your ear off."

Since Fate isn't acting unruly and does not have a weapon, they can find no reason to detain him, but they still hover close to him as neighbors from down the block filter out into the street and thank the National Guardsmen for coming so fast. We told them to do that, but they seem pretty sincere about it, which is a good sell.

Within about a minute, sheriffs arrive. They come screaming up with sirens and lights, pop their doors, and pile out into the street. When there's three or four black-and-white sheriff's cruisers, the National Guards catch another call and caravan off into the night. By then, there's at least twenty people out on the street. Sheriffs are establishing a perimeter around the house and keeping people back when an unmarked black car pulls up and a blond guy gets out.

I recognize him because we've seen him around. His name's Erickson and he's a murder sheriff. Fate's gotten hauled in a bunch to answer questions before. He's known to them. One time, they even arrested him. The furthest they ever got was getting the D.A. to agree to file on charges saying that Fate was an accessory to murder, only to have a judge drop the charges for lack of evidence. They want him bad. They've wanted him for years. Erickson walks up to the fence of the house to look at what Trouble did, and I see Fate see him and stand up.

It's really weird Erickson's here right now because it's against protocol. Normally, he would only show if there was a body confirmed down. They'd have gotten reports of shooting, but without a known death determined by officers at the scene, there's no reason to send murder detectives. They've got enough to deal with, especially in South Central. But seeing Erickson here, now, makes me think he knows something. He got here way too quick otherwise, and I can tell by the tilt of Fate's head that he's thinking it too.

We don't know for certain if Erickson's a Viking, but he sure does have a Viking-sounding name. He looks torn up though, like he's been pulling shifts since this whole thing kicked off and hasn't had one moment of sleep. He's tired looking, squinty, and licking his lips a lot, like he's dehydrated from drinking coffee 24/7. He's got messed-up hair and a messed-up blazer and messed-up jeans like he's been wearing the same ones for a day or two and hasn't taken a shower.

Vikings will lie to you about what they have, whether witnesses or evidence or what. This isn't unusual. Law enforcement is allowed to mislead in order to obtain confessions or further evidence, but these neo-Nazi motherfuckers go above and beyond. A lot of them still remember when Lynwood used to be a mostly white neighborhood, and they'd kill us all if they could get away with it. Some of them already have. We've lost six homies to Vikings so far. We're putting some families forward for a class-action lawsuit against the Sheriff's Department for racially motivated hostility, among other things. They'll get theirs someday. I don't know when, but someday.

But I can tell you this right now: nobody's doing that to Fate with so many witnesses out there, and even better, nobody's framing him either. I drilled him good. He knows to tell his lawyer to ask for a particle count if they want to test him for firing a weapon. If they try to lie to him and tell him there's a positive test, which I can tell you right now there won't be, he knows to tell his lawyer he's been working on his car, on the brake linings, because some of the particles for GSR can come from that too. He knows if they don't bag his hands, we have grounds to argue cross-contamination. In that case, particles can come from the cops at the scene, or even the environment.

Erickson spots Fate out of the corner of his eye, whips around, and walks at him fast. He's pretty much foaming at the mouth the way he marches over, and Fate's taller by about a couple inches, but Erickson works his belt on his hips and points his fucking finger in Fate's face, all disrespectful.

"You're going to tell me what the high holy hell happened here, José, and you're going to do it right the fuck now."

It's not so smart to do that to a guy in his own neighborhood, showing him up like that. Still, Fate doesn't blink.

"Lawyer," he says, and that's all he says, one word that's guaranteed to piss off all law enforcement everywhere, especially in South

Central. Because around here, most fools will talk to law enforcement. They might even waive their rights. Not us though. We know there's a system in place to protect us.

"Oh, listen to this one," some redneck sheriff on the perimeter says. "He already wants a lawyer! He's guilty as sin."

Erickson puts a look on that guy that makes him shut his mouth and turn away.

"Listen, I know who was here and why they were here," Erickson says to Fate. "Odds are, this was probably self-defense for you and your homeboys, but you're going to make me pick you up on proximity? On suspicion of involvement? Look, I just want to know what happened."

Fate just says, "Lawyer." It's the last time he's going to say it.

Erickson turns away, disgusted.

"Somebody cuff this evil genius," he says.

And they do cuff him, but that's when they screw up because they don't bag his hands. If they ever wanted a GSR test to stand in court, they'd have to ensure contamination could not occur. The only way to do that is to bag him, but they don't, the amateurs. They just put him in the back of Erickson's unmarked and bounce.

It takes twenty-three minutes for another detective to arrive and go over the house. I timed it. After he's here, I watch him study the lawn, then the house, and then shake his head. You can tell he doesn't even want to bother, and it makes me feel good. He knows all he can do is pull slugs from the house, whatever got stuck in there, but he knows he doesn't have shit.

They don't know how many people were there, how many guns were fired, how many people were hit, much less who was hit, or where they stood, or if it was fatal. This is a blown scene and without the bodies, if there even are any bodies, they have nothing. There's nothing even close to prosecutable here and it's a waste of his time, but he still walks over the muddy lawn, laying his numbers for shell casings that likely won't even match the ammunition in the house, photographing the bullet holes in stucco, all that. On this lack of evidence, they won't even be able to hold Fate. Only way they could is if they had a witness statement, which they don't, and never will.

He'll be out in a matter of hours.

8

I wait over an hour for the sheriffs to leave before I take Wizard's little .22 pistol from its shelf in the closet and slip out the back into the alley. I need it just in case. I'm certain there's at least a couple getaway drivers of Trouble's out here somewhere. With any luck, they took off when they heard the AK and then none of their boys came back. But you never know, so I'm not taking chances.

The alley behind Mini Vegas is empty except for a stray dog nosing around the base of a telephone pole at the end of the block. Black silhouettes of palm trees sway slow above garages. There's not much wind, but there's some. I'm aiming to go to my girlfriend Irene's house to wait this out until Fate comes and gets me. I sniffle and spit on the asphalt as I go. For a second before I hit the Board-walk, I smell magnolias, sweet and clean, a little lemony, but then my nose stuffs back up and it's gone. That good thing, only with me for a second, is gone.

I decide on a detour. I need to go by the alley where Ernesto got it to check and make sure they picked him up. I've been too busy since we started planning for Trouble, and I haven't even asked if a little homie would run over and check, and ever since I lied to Lu's face about Ernesto not being there anymore, it's been picking at me. When we dragged a gas station manager out of his girlfriend's bed to unlock a Unocal on MLK so we could steal a mess of gas to soak the sheets in, I thought of Ernesto lying out on the asphalt. That happened a bunch of times during our preparations. I'd be rum-maging through the city truck looking for a twist-lock-to-three-prong adapter to make sure we could plug the construction lights into the house because they work on a different type of socket, and I'd remember, and I'd get a stitch in my stomach and I'd want to know if he was still out there, but then there'd be six other things to do to get ready and I'd forget. All this is odd for me. Like I said, I'm not accustomed to missing people or even thinking about them after they're gone, but this is different. I need to know what happened. As I turn into the alley, my lungs get tight and I'm expecting him still to be there, lying flat, with his head wrapped up in Lu's black-and-white flannel like a cowl.

But he's not there.

I sniffle at that. I nod, relieved, and my lungs let go. I walk to the spot where Joker and his homeboys must have caught up to him, where they first stabbed him, and I stand near it. Someday, when she's ready, Lu is going to want to know everything. She'll want to know how many times he was stabbed. Fifteen or seventeen, by my count. The ragged shape of two wounds made it difficult to tell in the light I had, if the knife went in and just ripped out at a different angle, or if he had been stabbed twice in the same two spots. She'll want to know how else they hurt him and I'll have to tell her about the blunt object, likely a baseball bat.

Twenty yards away, just inside an open garage three down on the right with its overhead light off, a dot of orange flares up and fades. I freeze. Someone's leaning on the trunk of a car while smoking a cigarette. I put my hand in my pocket and onto Wizard's gun and I walk a few steps closer until I can see I don't have anything to worry about, so I take my hand out and put it by my side.

She doesn't notice me at first, but I recognize her as the nurse who tried to help Ernesto, the one who talked to Lu about what she saw. Her name's Gloria. I know because my girlfriend's dream is to be a nurse just like her. Irene is homegirls with Gloria's younger sister, Lydia, and they both go to school for it now, nights. Irene's got about a year to go.

From what I can tell about Gloria's posture, the way she's perched, she's still seeing him, even now, because her eyes are on the alley floor too. She's thinking about Wednesday night, I know it. She's been looking at the space where Ernesto finally came to rest, at the place we found him after he'd been dragged and the wire had been removed from his ankles. This nurse, she's been looking at what I've been looking at. A space where a person used to be. A place where a person no longer is. But she still sees Ernesto too, the memory of him.

I make a little noise, kick a couple pebbles, as I shuffle closer on the side of the alley across from her, but not too much. I don't want to startle her but she still starts a little when she sees me, and the car beneath her bounces up on its axles before settling back down with her weight. If Gloria recognizes me as someone who was here before, she doesn't show it. We share a look, though, a look I'm not sure goes both ways, but maybe it does. It's a look of understanding, a look of, *I know, I saw it too*, and I'm not sure what that is exactly, or what it means if it means anything, but maybe it's something for people to know they aren't alone in feeling a bad thing.

I nod at her. She doesn't return it. Instead, the lit cigarette returns to her mouth and that orange dot gets bright as she inhales. To show her I'm not a threat, I break eye contact and look away. I look up.

The sky is more dark purple tonight, not as black from smoke as it has been the past couple nights, which means fewer and fewer fires are happening. *It's almost over*, I think, *the riots, these days of freedom*. Above us, I see the blinking red lights of a plane. It's descending, going to LAX. I get thinking it's the first airplane I've seen in a while and I start walking again. I don't look to the nurse as I go. We've shared whatever it is we needed to.

9

I need to get to Irene's so I pick up the pace. I can't be out like this much longer. I sniffle and look back up at the airplane again, right before it passes out of sight. I wonder who's on it anyway, and why they would fly into L.A. at a time like this. Maybe people who already had their vacations scheduled and couldn't miss them. I didn't even know people like that actually existed until I went to L.A. Southwest College for the crime scene stuff. I'd only ever seen those people on TV before that. Really, school is a whole other world.

And seeing it, navigating in it enough to get some new people skills I didn't even know I needed, has me feeling like I'm two different people now. There's me the homeboy, Clever, down for whatever, and there's me the student, Robert Rivera. Mr. Rivera, as Sturm calls me. I've got a wall between those sides of me now. It's kind of like I've got a double life.

In a way, I grew into it. Coming up as a little homie, eager to prove myself and be somebody, anybody. I dropped out of school at thirteen because Lu did. School for me was boring and slow. I picked stuff up quick and then had to sit around and wait for everybody else to get it. At home, my mom was never around but that's not really an excuse, just a fact. I hung out with Lu instead of being alone and we did all kinds of dumb shit.

I might've kept doing that if Fate hadn't seen something in both of us, if he hadn't told me I was too smart to be banging how other homies were banging. I had to use my mind instead because it was a more dangerous weapon. He set it up so I could get my GED, and I didn't even know there was such a thing for high school equivalency before he said so.

He got me a tutor and everything to help catch me up. That tutor was Irene. Four days a week she worked with me until I was reading better, writing papers, finding out there was a difference between spoken and written English, that I couldn't just write however I wanted and make sense, that there were rules. She even had me doing algebra in no time. If it wasn't for her and Fate, I'd still be running the streets and nothing else. They changed my life. I owe them both for that. I owe them everything.

I started at Southwest last year, because that's what Fate wanted and he fronts the cash for it. I was scared of it at first, because I'd never even been out of the neighborhood before, but I found out I really like it. I found out I'm good at it. Maybe that's dangerous, though, because it's had me wondering every so often what a life outside the neighborhood would look like, or what I would even do to get it, but I've never told Fate that, Lu neither.

The other day I caught myself thinking about maybe getting a place with Irene, maybe even starting a family. Eighteen might be too young to be thinking that, but I know fools who had kids at fifteen, some even younger. I don't know if Irene would go for it though. She's not the government assistance type. Also, I'm pretty sure we'd have to get married. Her family's pretty traditional. They came here to Lynwood in 1973 from Thailand when she was two. She doesn't speak much Thai because her parents wanted her to be American and only that. They didn't want any language barrier holding her back. She's older than me by three years and the smartest girl I've ever met. She graduated Lynwood High a year early and got into Cal State L.A., but she couldn't afford it when she didn't qualify for a scholarship.

When I'm getting real close to her house, I go the back way, cutting past the garage on the end, hopping a fence, and stepping up onto the ledge of the brick foundation outside Irene's room. I tap soft on the glass until she wakes up and blinks her big eyes at me from the bed. She's five five, with light brown eyes and long black hair she sometimes likes to put up in a bun with a pencil through it. She Jazzercises every day in her room with a videotape, so she's lean and muscular all over and she shows it when she opens the window wide enough to let me in.

She says, "You okay? I heard shooting."

I'd never admit this, but she's pretty like art is pretty. Every time I look at her, I feel pulled in, but a little terrified too, afraid I won't ever be able to understand all of her.

"I heard shooting too," I say. In that moment, I decide not to tell her about seeing Gloria tonight. It'd be too much to explain.

Irene sighs because she knows I've been up to no good and steps back to let me into her room. I straddle the window ledge and duck in. I slip my shoes off right away. Inside, it smells like jasmine, what I can smell of it anyway. She's still got posters of Janet Jackson and Boyz II Men up on one wall and on another, and she's got one for Ice Cube's record *AmeriKKKa's Most Wanted*, even though I've told her a hundred times it's weird she likes black music, but then she hits me with how I love Motown and asks why I have a double standard. I don't have an answer for that, so she won't take them down, but I don't think she'd take them down even if I did. That's Irene. She's loyal.

She had a little place of her own with Lydia until last year, but when her dad got deported for working at a body shop he didn't know was chopping cars, she moved back with her mom and her older sister. Now the two daughters work checkstands at Ralphs on the days, and at nights they do Thai massage at a place in Carson when they can pick up hours. Irene's not big on it, but she never complains. Her mom has lung cancer and can't work, so the daughters support her and try to save up for school and to get their dad back somehow.

I say, "How's your mom? Any better?"

Irene shakes her head, but she smiles. "She's on something called Taxol now. It's new, comes from tree bark. She says it makes her joints hurt."

"Does she know I'm coming by tonight?"

Mrs. Nantakarn used to hate me being here late at night, much less staying over, but she doesn't mind as much since she got cancer and I started my degree program. A couple months ago, I even heard her ask Irene when our wedding is. She said she wanted to see one of her daughters marry before she dies, but Irene just told her to cut it out, that she'd do it when she was good and ready.

"I told her you might come tonight, so she had me make green curry just in case," Irene says. "Speaking of moms, yours called looking for you. I think she's worried."

Irene still thinks the best of my mom. She doesn't know the woman like I do. Truth is, my mom worries more about getting a fix than she worries about me, and if she called over, she needed money or a hookup, even though she knows I'd give her neither.

My mom's O.G. She grew up in East L.A. She was in a gang from way back and so was my dad. They got married young and divorced young, too. So me being in a gang, even if it's not the same one, it's still like a legacy. My mom, she wishes I wasn't involved. *You play, you pay.* She's said that since I was a little kid. She knows from experience. *It might not always be how you think it's going to be*, she's said, *but you pay one way or the other.*

"Are you hungry? If you don't want green curry, I can cook something else." Irene yawns then, and after, she looks at me with one of those caring looks I know I'll never get sick of. "Do you need anything?"

I've been sleeping on the floor in Mini Vegas for two days and I ache all over, so I say, "Can I get a massage out of you?"

10

Irene doesn't say anything. She just steps up to me, so close that the crown of her head is under my nose. This is the type of woman she is. Tired, just woke up, but still taking care of me. I wonder how I got so lucky. I sniffle as she helps me out of my sweatshirt and I set it on the little chair with a stuffed puppy dog on it by her window. She hands me a tissue, and I blow my nose before telling her not to go anywhere near the left pocket and I leave it at that, because Wizard's popgun is there and I know she wouldn't like me having it. I chuck the tissue in the trash. She smells like cinnamon and clean bedsheets as she works me out of my shirt, lays a towel down on the carpet, and me on top of it.

"*Mi corazón,*" she says, and she knows it makes me weak when she talks Spanish at me, "is it time for you to get out yet, like out-out?"

Her voice still sounds a little husky from sleep. For a moment, I feel guilty waking her up and asking her to work on me, but when she starts, it all melts away.

Since I was fifteen I haven't been able to raise my left arm above ninety degrees because we got into it with a bunch of Bloods at Ham Park after they came by with spray paint to cross out our *plaqueasos* right in front of us like they were tough. It was stupid. In the brawl that came next, a guy with a little round afro and a face like a pineapple got me down and stabbed me six times with a broken bottle. He cut up my left shoulder and left lat muscle real good. It was Lu who got him off me. She had a broken bottle of her own and she brought it down on his scalp again and again. Every time she cut his head and blood came out, his hair soaked it up. No kidding. It made a little sound when it did it too, every time, like *fwoop*.

I'll never forget that. You can't. He lived, from what I hear, but I wouldn't want to see his head if he ever had to shave it bald is all I'll say about that. By the time I was fixed up though, my left lat was an inch shorter than my right and I'm weaker on that side. It's why Fate never asks me to lift anything too heavy, like bodies. You should see my scars. They look like little brown constellations, raised on my skin. *Galaxies*, that's what Pint said when he did this little black-and-gray owl tattoo on my chest a while back. I always liked his description of them. It made my scars seem less like healed wounds and more like something bigger, something better.

Irene orders me onto my stomach and sets to working my feet. She bends my left leg at the knee and leans her weight into me, stretching my whole leg, my calf, my thigh, my hamstring. Thai massage is different from regular massage. It took me a while to get used to it, but now that I have, I can't have any other kind. It's more like stretching and pushing, which is one of the truths of our relationship, I guess. She's always stretching and pushing me in different ways. She's even doing it now.

"We could go anywhere," she says. "You know, I don't have to go to nursing school here. I can maybe transfer."

"It takes money for that," I say, "and what about your mom and your sister?"

"They can come with us, and we can always figure out some-thing for money."

"We could go all Bonnie and Clyde," I say and laugh. "I'll be Clyde."

"I'd be a good Bonnie, but I can do without the guns," she says.

"Flip over," she also says, so I do.

I'm on my back, looking straight up at the ceiling, and she's got the sole of her right foot in my left armpit. She's slowly pulling my bad shoulder toward her. I feel the stretch go all the way down my spine and into my right hip. It burns a little.

"I can't leave Fate," I say. "Not ever. He needs me."

"But what if something goes wrong? Not everybody's as smart as you, baby. What if somebody did something that pointed back at you, or even snitched? What if you got locked up?"

I think of Apache. He may not be the smartest, but he does what he's told and he always comes through. I think of how his only job is to drive the truck to an underpass and burn it. For a second though, Irene's words get to me, and I'm scared he might fail, and if he does, what will happen to us.

"All I'm saying is, you've put your time in," Irene says. "You know you can't be banging forever, right? You're going to have a degree soon. You could get a job. You can *maybe* even have a family someday."

I say, "I could never do law enforcement. Hell no."

"It doesn't have to be that. Just *think* about it," she says. "It's like tutoring, right? I'm not telling you what to do, just asking you to think and work it out for yourself."

"Are you saying get out like how my father got out?" I don't real-ize how mad I sound about it until I've said it. "Leave his wife and kid and move away? Start a new family someplace else?"

Irene's quiet for a second, but her hands don't stop. I can tell she's thinking about conversations we've had, the details of them. How I don't like talking about my mom going crazy into drugs after my dad left when I wasn't even two years old. How I don't remember what his face looks like because Mom burned all the damn photos in a rage, but the second she found out he was living in Lynwood or Compton somewhere, she borrowed money from her parents and moved us here, making me the new kid in a place where that wasn't an easy thing to carry, and how that meant I got beat the fuck up most days until Ernesto took big brother pity on me and started making sure I walked to school with the Veras, and how my mom was so deep into the hole she dug with her drugs that she never even bothered to search for my father, just tried to numb the pain every day. *All* that. And still, Irene's hands never stop.

"You are not your father." She says it like the conversation is over now. Over for good. Her words come out tough, like she'd fight me if I disagreed.

I groan then, but not about what she's saying. I'm actually groaning because Irene's pulling harder than she ever pulled before, and the stretch feels like it might pull my tailbone out. She knows I've been all involved for a long time, but she doesn't know any specifics and I'll never tell her. It doesn't do to be pillow talking. In fact, the only time she ever sees Fate and anybody else is if it's for food, if we're barbecuing or something, and nobody talks business then, we just eat.

It goes on like this. She pushes. She pulls. She puts her hundred-and-twenty-some pounds of weight into stretching me. It hurts, if you want to know the truth. She says that I'm in charge of my life. It's my choice. Her dad never got one, and my dad went too far, but I can do whatever *I* want. It's tough sometimes how she talks like this. She doesn't know everything I've done. She has no idea about the big picture. She comes from a good family. I don't.

I was just an angry little latchkey kid getting in fights to prove how tough I was, how much I didn't care I was alone. The only reason I'm something else now all started with Fate, and what Irene doesn't understand is that this game started a long time ago for me. There's no standing up now, no walking away from the table. I got dealt my hand when I got my name, got Clever. And sure, guys have gotten out before. They've moved out of the neighborhood and had kids, but that was before Joker, Trouble, and Momo got wiped out. There's no other game in Lynwood now, just us and some Crips, but we're good with them. We have an understanding. And I don't know much about cards, but I know you've got to play what you're dealt.

Sometimes, though, it's like Irene's hands won't take no for an answer. She has the strongest grip of anyone I've ever met. The more they work, the more she's telling me that I'm still Robert, too, that I'm him and Clever both. And maybe that's the problem now, because I'm starting to open up to the idea that maybe life can be different for me. I blame school for that. I blame her, too. Still, she stretches and she pulls, she makes me see the good, and somewhere along the way, I grow. It's always been this way for us. It's how I got my GED. It's how I got into Southwest. It might even be how I do something else someday. If I did, I think it'd be the only way. And after all the bad things I've done, I'm not so sure my life deserves a happy ending, but Irene always wants to give me one, by push or by pull.

GABRIEL MORENO,
A.K.A. APACHE

MAY 2, 1992

1:22 A.M.

1

A good thing about reputation is you only have to do something once, and have someone see it, for word to spread. I did scalp somebody, but it's not as bad as people think. I mean, that fool was already dead first, cuz I only did it after I put a .22 up his nose and pulled the trigger.

It was good except for it burned all the hairs out of his left nostril, the blast did. The rest of it, like where the bullet went from there and how it fixed him up, was almost instant, really, cuz it was a low enough caliber to stay in his skull and not exit out. It just scrambled his brains like some eggs, so he didn't suffer or nothing. It was quick.

It was the third thing I ever did for Fate, yeah, maybe four years ago, in the summer. This Blaxican, that's half-black, half-Mexican, guy from the neighborhood, went by Millionaire, had been stealing from the click, fucking up the Mini Vegas money, and thinking nobody was noticing. See, Wizard didn't always run the casino house. First it was Millionaire. It was his original idea. But it later turned out he was doing what he was doing cuz he had these two girls he liked to buy presents for a lot. He liked to take them to the mall in Baldwin Hills and go shopping. So if you couldn't tell from the name, he wanted everyone to think he was big, but he wasn't anybody. We used to call him Hundredaire to his face. I remember he was always worried about his appearance too. When word got around from one of his exes that Millionaire was one of them Hair Club for Men guys cuz even though he was young he was losing his hair and trying to do something about it, I knew what I had to do. So one day he comes back to his apartment and I'm already in there with my cousin, Cricket (RIP), and I'm there with Clever, cuz we did up the lock, and they're there watching when I pull back the shower curtain and ask Millionaire all polite to get in the tub so I can do what I got to, and he does, and I do, so that's good. I didn't tell anybody I was gonna scalp him though. I just told Cricket and Clever that I had my knife on me and it was one of them spur-of-the-moment-type things, but really that wasn't true. I'd premeditated it. It ended up working out though cuz it made me known. It made me feared, too, cuz no one but Cricket and Clever knew I scalped him after, not before. Nobody else knows that, though. People been making up all kinds of stories about that day. It was Clever that came up with the name Apache for me though. I've been known that way ever since.

I tell you that story just so you know I'm not under any delusions. I know I'm the brave, not the chief. I do what I'm told. I have a role and I do it. Like now.

The O.G. turning this city truck right onto Wright Road from MLK is named Sinatra. I don't know why he goes by that. He's old as hell, maybe forty, forty-five, and he's smoking a cigar with the label still on it like a little yellow ring. It's one of them thin ones, a *cigarillo*, which is cool cuz it suits him, you know?

He's thin all over, not like Clever's toothpick ass, different. This Sinatra, he's skinny sick. Yeah. He's got big eyes. One of them's green and one of them's brown, and they're out of proportion to his nose. He's got a little stubble-beard made up of sharp lines, too, almost like calligraphy. It's thin on his face, patchy, and right before it gets to the tops of his ears, it dies out completely. It doesn't even connect up to his hairline.

In my head, I'm memorizing him to draw later. A number 2 pencil for the sketch and then maybe I'd layer black ballpoint on top before I erase the pencil out and it's just ink that's left, except for little marks where I pressed with the pencil. Sometimes I like how you can still see those if you look close.

The bag of clothes Clever wants me to burn with everything else sits cherry between Sinatra and me. I've got my arm up on it, mushing the top down so I can keep an eye on my driver.

"I got something on my face?" Sinatra doesn't turn to look at me. He stares straight ahead.

"No," I say, "I'm just glad it's not me driving. I've never driven nothing this big. I mean, how do you even see everything with these mirrors all weird like this?"

The side mirrors are like double-deckers, one on top of the other. The top one's rounded and sticks out and I can see more out of it but it's all warped. The bottom one is flat and it just lets me see straight back but I can't see as much. In both of them, Payasa's driving my car behind us at a good little distance.

"You get used to it," Sinatra says.

Him and a guy called Bluebird jacked this truck on Wednesday from a city worker in Florence about a half hour after the riot started. I guess the worker was out on a job and listening to a Hall & Oates tape instead of the radio so he didn't know about what was happening in the streets. He was still out trying to do his job when Sinatra and Bluebird stuck him up at gunpoint and hauled him out of the truck. They snatched his vest, kicked him in the teeth, and took off. Sinatra came through before my time, before Fate's too, I think. He don't really do much anymore, but with things being crazy how they are, opportunity brings people together.

There's hardly any cars on Wright Road besides us, just one going the other way and then nothing but a bum walking the wrong way on the other side of the road. There's nothing on Wright worth protecting, not malls or anything, so Clever figured there wouldn't be any Vikings, or Guards, or anyone else around.

When we come up on Cortland, I go in my pockets and bring out the matches Clever gave me. Six different packs just in case.

This area always makes me think of Millionaire. I left his scalp in the sink for one of his ladies to find, but I dumped his body not far from here, in a place everybody calls Lil Texas that's just off Cortland in the abandoned warehouses. But right now, for this, not even Lil Texas is big enough. Clever says we need to burn everything, and the only way to make sure a burn has time to do what it needs to do is park it under an underpass so no one can see the smoke until it's too late, he says. And from where we are, I can see the 105 right now.

I think about Lil Creeper for a second, cuz we always used to smoke out and talk about driving up on top of it before it was done, just to be the first, you know? Just to take its virginity and see what it looked like when it was only us up there, only our view. Yeah. Don't get me wrong, that fool is crazy, but he's funny sometimes, just the kind of person you should go on top of an unfinished freeway with.

We're almost to where Clever wants us, and Sinatra's easing the truck under the bridge and onto this little strip of shoulder left under the scaffolding that looks like the skeleton of an animal made out of wood, kind of, like we're going into its mouth.

I had a cat once. I called her Teeny cuz she was so small when I got her. I drew her a lot over the years as she grew up too. I have a whole book of sketches in it with just her. Orange tabby, good muscles. She could jump real high. Green eyes like wet stones too. Chirpy little voice. Sweetest cat you ever seen. I called her cat-dog sometimes cuz she'd even play fetch with me. She liked to chase squished-up balls of aluminum foil cuz of the sound they made, and when I'd throw them, she'd bring them back to me. She used to like biting them too. Well, one day, halfway through one of these fetch sessions, she starts coughing up blood and all meowing like she's dying. Took me over an hour to get her in to see the vet and get her looked at, only to be told nothing could be done cuz she'd chewed up a bunch of tinfoil and it'd cut her up inside, and the whole way to the animal hospital she had cried and fitted and spat up blood before the vet put a shot in her. That was nice of the vet, you know? Teeny didn't have to suffer. Nothing deserves that. She died quiet in my arms, eyes closed, like she was sleeping. How it should've been.

I hate seeing things suffer. Not anything. If a thing needs to get done, okay, that's business, but it don't need to be long and drawn out or nothing. Take that guy in Payasa's front yard. Ranger plugs him in the neck, okay, that needs to get done and he got shot from far away so I'm not mad, but now this guy's there on the ground and he's suffering. Nobody needs to see him die like a fish out of water in front of us, all flapping around with his gills open. It just needed to be over, so I stepped up. Swift is mercy. I don't know where I heard that, maybe from Clever, but I like it. For me, it fits. Bad things happen, they do, but when they do, they can be quick every time and it's better for everybody.

See, that's why when Sinatra turns the keys and the truck shudders off and he leans over to eject that tape from the stereo halfways through some song about crime paying, I put the barrel of my gun to his temple and pull the trigger.

There's a bang so loud in the cab that it makes my ears ring and behind his head the door goes red and gets a hole in it. Sinatra flops a little after that but it's just nerve reactions. He's all gone.

I open my door and step out of the truck and trade Payasa two packs of matches for a big bottle of the cheapest vodka on earth. I uncap it and pour it over the whole inside of the truck, just throwing it everywhere, mostly over the dash and wheel and carpet where the *cigarillo* rolled and it kicks up, but definitely I throw it on Sinatra too, on his thin beard and now I know for sure how I'm going to draw it. A black felt-tip, with no undersketch. Short, quick strokes.

It needed to be done, Fate said. Sinatra's face has been getting seen all over the city. These trucks have numbers. They're registered, and at some point, this truck's getting reported stolen if it hasn't been already, and at some point they're going to come looking for it when everything gets cool enough to actually care about things like trucks instead of riots, and the guy Sinatra jacked it from will know him cuz he didn't wear a mask and that's not good for us cuz Sinatra knows us and what we did tonight. There's something else too though, and it's that word has gotten around about Sinatra, how he got careless in some roughhousing with his ex-wife on Thursday night. He shot her in the back but she lived. She's over at St. Francis now. He might not have known we knew, but we did. We hear everything and we act when we need to. The law would've been coming for him eventually, and we just needed to make sure he had nothing to trade when they got him. Sinatra needed to go, so he went.

Since the floorboards are already going pretty good, I light a match and toss it quick to the seat. The black plastic of the clothes bag flames up and shrinks back in the heat. I roll the window down a few inches so the fire can get good air, close the door, and hike myself up so I can see over the lip of the truck bed where Payasa's got a fire going. I toss my gun in, my gloves, and another lit match just in case before I hop down with my hands in fists, careful not to touch anything with my fingers. Then we get in my Cutlass, me behind the wheel this time, and I flip a U-turn and point us back toward MLK and I park by the side of the road and we watch the truck burn in my rearview.

When I was coming up, one of my jobs was to be lookout for the *veteranos* when they burned stolen cars. They'd make me stay till the engine blocks dropped out mostly, but if we could get away with it, if nobody was coming, we'd stay till they blew. Cars never blow up how they do in movies. I mean, maybe that would happen if you threw something down in the gas tank, but if you're just lighting the interior, you're going to be waiting awhile. I think it was pretty much about fifteen minutes every time for the fire to touch the fuel and pop off, and the size of the explosion always depends on how much gas is left in there. I didn't see how much was left in the city truck.

Even with things as they are, it's not smart for me and Payasa to stay that long. I mean, Clever's got people hitting Wards, and he's got emergency calls all over, but he only told us to wait until the fireworks go off.

I study the shapes of the flames until then. Flickers, I guess you could call them. Yeah. I watch the orange climb up the metal construction lights like living vines or something. The cab windows pop first, spraying glass everywhere. Right after, the horn starts going nonstop, and then, when it gets hot enough, the glass and bulbs of the construction lights smash out. By then, the fire's kicking up black smoke on the underside of the bridge, and the concrete stays black, like it's being painted with soot almost.

Payasa says, "So when do we—?"

Bang! We hear another one right after that, all loud too, and that's when I put us in gear and push the gas pedal down nice and easy and as we pull out of there, it sounds like a couple more fireworks go off in the truck behind us, two more blasts and two faint dings in the truck bed cuz the fire's so hot now it's setting off the extra bullets in the guns, the ones left over from before.

2

My car smells like raw meat still, and we haven't even cooked it all yet. The little homies Fate had clean the trunk out didn't do such a good job. Three hours they worked on it for, and there's no stains on the spare or anything, but the carpet's all discolored back there and I'm starting to think like it'll never be clean, like I might always smell rotten hamburger meat. That's when I decide I need a new car. It's time to sell this to some fool who don't know no better. That don't fix anything now, though, so I roll my window down halfway to bring some of the night air in.

Payasa turns to me and says, "Got any sherm?"

Sherm's the same shit Fate said to lay off tonight. I do have some though. I just haven't used it.

"Fate said no more," I say.

"Yeah, but he said before, not *after*."

"It's not good after," I say, "only before."

She gets to staring off into the distance for a minute. I never really fucked with watercolors before, but seeing how the night sky looks kind of wet even when it's not, I want to try, cuz the way that black is all soft around Payasa's face and the way yellows from streetlamps hit her nose in profile, it's real nice. She's pretty, you know? And I don't say that in like a sex way, but in like a she's-my-little-sister way, and seeing as how she don't have any more big brothers left, we're just gonna have to be that for her now. Me, and Fate, and Clever, and everybody.

She breaks the quiet in the car when she says, "Fate's making me move back with my mom just to cool me out for a bit. I don't get why he's gotta punish me like that. I mean, didn't I do good with Joker?"

At first, I don't say nothing, I just kind of let it sit as we ride. Payasa does too. We're going to my cousin Oso's to wait till we hear back from Fate or Clever.

Eventually though, I have to say, "Maybe that's not such a bad play."

She hits back quick, saying, "What do you mean?"

And then she eyes me up hard after that.

"You did better than good," I say. "Best shooting I seen pretty much ever. You know most people can't hit for shit when their adrenaline's up. I mean, you saw how many missed shots there were back at your house, right? A ton. But you're not your brother, you know?"

"Which *one*?" She says it heavy, like she's feeling sorry for herself. Shit. It's not like she don't got a right to, but still.

"You know which," I say, "Lil Mosco. You're more Ernesto than him."

If I'm honest, I'm not real comfortable with her doing what I do. It's not for women, you know? Call me sexist, call me whatever, but I think most people would agree with me.

"You stepped up big," I say. "Did what you had to. You did justice."

"You think?"

"Yeah, I think. But, see, I also think you're not me."

She looks mad, like I'm disrespecting or something, when she says, "What's that supposed to mean?"

"It means what it says. You're not me. But I mean it, like, you don't got to go on from this and keep doing it. You don't got to do what I do, Payasita."

She kind of puffs her chest up to argue before saying, "You telling me not to?"

I look out the windshield at the sky for a minute, in all its charcoal-type blackness. I'm shaking my head, gripping up on the wheel a little bit, like I might choke up on a bat if I were in the batter's box and I needed a hit.

"Let me tell you something, Lil Clown Girl," I say.

I call her Lil Clown Girl sometimes cuz that's what Payasita means on the literal *en Español*. I only use it when talk is just between us. It's like a pet name. Yeah. Nobody else calls her that, and if they did, I wouldn't let them. It's ours. But right now I need her stupid sixteen-year-old ass to *listen*, so I use it.

I say, "This one time, I was over on Josephine, right? On the park side. I couldn't've been more than a year younger than you are now. I'd been packing for a while though. I'd done some work, and I thought I was rough cuz the older homies were telling me I was rough and that I was growing up right. So they'd be giving me little contracts here and there, things to keep an eye up for, you know? This one time, a snitch named Booger came out of the house he was staying at, one across the street from the park, and I'd actually been waiting for him cuz I was supposed to take care of him. So when I saw him, I got so hyped up that I just ran, right? I ran to the curb, all hard, and I pulled up cuz I didn't want to run in the street and I yelled out, 'Booger, hey, Booger!' and he looked at me, and I saw his eyes seeing me, and I aimed. I had this piece Fate gave me, I loved that thing, I think it was a nine-millimeter, a Smith and Wesson six-five-nine, which was actually kind of a big gun for a lil homie, but that didn't matter to me back then. I had that thing out of my sweatshirt in a damn rush when I saw Booger and I went *bang, bang, bang* at him, but, the thing of it was, right as I was opening up, a car came between me and him." I hear Payasa let out a little moan, like *oh fuck*, but I keep going. "See, I was so hyped, I didn't even pay attention, didn't even see it coming, and it happened so quick. All's I remember is the back windows of this station wagon blowing out at the same time, like *ksssh, ksssh*, cuz my bullet went in one and out the other. It had went all the way through."

I kind of pause after that, not for effect or nothing, but cuz I have to.

I must take too long too, cuz Payasa says, "What happened?"

"There was this car seat in the back," I say, "you know, for babies?"

"Shit," Payasa says. "What *happened*?"

"What happened is, I didn't get Booger. That fool ran off."

"Fuck Booger! What happened to the baby?"

"I don't know," I say.

"What do you mean you don't know?"

"I mean, all's I heard was crying, like, really loud crying and screaming from the backseat and the car's swerving back and forth and speeding away, and all I can think about is all that glass in the backseat, you know?" I shake my head remembering it. "All that glass."

Payasa's kind of angry now. "Did you ever find out? Like, was everything okay?"

"No," I say, "I never did find out. I tried, but nobody heard nothing about a hurt baby, and I never saw that car again, not by the park or anywhere else."

"Come on," she says, "really? *Never?*"

"Babies come to me in my dreams sometimes," I say, "all cut up."

"That's messed up," she says.

"Yeah, it is," I say, "but what I did was messed up too. And I only told you that story to say that doing this shit sticks to you. Cuz I don't ever want you looking at me and thinking it all just slides off. That's all's I'm saying, Lil Clown Girl. That's it."

She gets quiet then, and I don't know what to say, or if I even made my point, so I wait a little before saying, "If Fate's for real making you move out, maybe it's not such a bad thing, you know? Being out of the neighborhood for a little? I mean, if you were out, what would you do? Have you even thought about that?"

She pushes her head back into the headrest and stares at the ceiling. After a little while she gets a smile, a small one, but it's there, so I call her out.

"What?"

"Nothing," she says. "It's stupid."

It's not stupid, I want to say, *cuz that's the first smile I seen on you since before Ernesto was lying up in that alley.* But I just wait. I give her time. I try to memorize what it looks like on her face. Bigger than Mona Lisa's. It crinkles her nose a little at the top when she does it, between her eyebrows.

"I'm kind of into the idea of seeing Elena," she says.

"Wait," I say, just to get it straight in my head, "the one that wanted us to cap Joker and tell her she sent it? *That* one?"

"Exactly the one," she says and licks her lips a little like she's thinking of doing something else with them, something good.

"There you go," I say, "crazy love."

She kisses her teeth with one of them loud, sharp *tsk* sounds. "Hold up, I did *not* say it was love."

"Have it your way. She's *loca* but fine as hell. The ass on her," I'm saying but I kind of fade out there cuz I'm thinking how good Elena looked in jeans and how nice it would be to take two big handfuls of her, and I get lost in that fantasy for a second and can't really finish what I was saying, so I'm just like, "*Man.*"

I just say it for effect, you know? But Payasa knows exactly what I'm saying and she laughs at me. Whyever she's doing it, it don't matter. It's good to hear her laugh. One of the best things about Payasa is you never got to worry about talking to her like she's a girl.

You can say whatever the fuck you want usually and it's cool. She's a homie like that.

"Yeah," Payasa says. "*Man* is fucking right. I'm working on her."

That gives me a mental image real quick and I trip on it for a few blocks.

"Damn" is all I can think to say, but I figure I should maybe keep Payasa talking about Elena cuz it seems like it's keeping her mind off everything else heavy. "You thinking she'll actually switch up off of guys? Why?"

"There's always a chance," she says, "especially if I can get her seeing me like her protector now."

"Like, a knight in shining armor?" I look at Payasa and she nods her head up a little and smiles that secret smile again, only this time it seems to say she knows things about women I never even knew existed, and she does it so confident that I don't even doubt it's true. "So defending her honor and that?"

"Women care about that shit," she says. "They need to feel safe."

"You say it like you aren't one," I say.

I pull us up to the curb on Louise, right in front of Oso's. There's a light on inside, and I see my aunt moving back and forth in front of the kitchen window, hovering over the sink like she's washing vegetables or something. Just from seeing her like that, with her hair all pinned back like she's been sleeping, I know Oso got her up. She spoils him more ever since Cricket died, lets him eat all hours of the day or night when he's hungry. It don't matter when he asks, she'll get up and make him something.

"I'm not a woman like how Elena's a woman," Payasa says when I shut the car off. "A girl like that, she needs somebody to take care of her. Someone like me, I need to take care of somebody. That's just how it goes. That's nature. The roles don't change much just cuz we're both *chicas*. That shit's ingrained. That shit's human."

I shrug cuz I'm gonna have to take her word for it, and I open my door, but when the cabin light goes on above our heads, Payasa catches my arm and I can tell she's not done talking, so I pull my door closed and the light snaps off.

She says, "Is this over, like over-over? Is it gonna cool down with Joker and Trouble and Momo out?"

"I don't know," I say, and I really don't.

She tucks her chin down kind of and frowns at that, and that's how I know I called it right before. She actually wants it to be over. Lil Mosco never would've been like that. He would've wanted war for a long time, any and every opportunity to get wild. He would've loved it. Payasa, though? She doesn't. She just stepped up and did what she had to, when she had to do it.

"Somebody's always related to somebody, huh?" She sounds exhausted how she says it, like she's a granny. "Or homies with somebody?"

"You're not wrong," I say, "but if you don't like how you pay, don't play."

That might seem cold to say to somebody who just lost her only two brothers and the whole front side of her house, but she knows it's just true, and somebody's got to say it to her. Might as well be me. I watch her rock in her seat a little, and I open my door just so I can see the white cabin light on her face again and I think I might try a portrait of her black-and-gray style. You know, use a tiny little model brush and model paints, the kind that even when after they dry, they still shine.

To my Lil Clown Girl, I say, "You hungry? Looks like my aunt's cooking in there, and trust me on this, if she's fixing up *enchiladas*, you don't want to be missing them."

"I could do that," she says. "But after, could you maybe take me to *mi mamá*'s?"

I'm not the chief, I'm the brave, but I figure I could make an exception, just for her. Just this once.

DAY 5
SUNDAY

THE POLICE WERE ALSO TELLING GANG MEMBERS THAT THE NATIONAL
GUARD WAS, IN EFFECT, A MUCH, MUCH BIGGER GANG. THEY FELT
THOSE WERE TERMS THE GANG MEMBERS COULD RELATE TO.

—MAJOR GENERAL JAMES D. DELK,
COMMANDING OFFICER OF NATIONAL GUARD FORCES

1

Let me get one thing straight: I am the Big, Bad Wolf and as far as anyone who needs biting is concerned, I do not exist. Tonight I am tasked with assaulting a number of gang-involved residences, and I can tell you that I am personally going to enjoy it. Due to the extra-legal nature of this operation, however, I cannot tell you who I am or where I work. Technically, I cannot tell you what I do, either, not as a day job, but this is a matter of extraordinary circumstance, so I can walk you through what I do when I do it, and you can fill in the rest in your head. First, however, some background is needed.

Currently, I am in command of two transport vehicles carrying sixteen men south on the bone-dry concrete bed of the Los Angeles River. We entered the culvert via a tunnel entrance beneath the Sixth Street Bridge. Channelized with concrete by the Army Corps of Engineers over a period of years beginning in 1935, the basin is more road than river, and today it will serve as both our bridge and back-door entrance into South Central. We are en route to a residence wherein multiple known gang members reside and conduct illicit business. Prior to this mission, my team was stuck in a hurry-up-and-wait scenario because, in my opinion, no one at the top had the stomach to sanction our deployment until one hour ago. Up to that point, we had been on standby, sitting on a forward command post for the LAPD and all emergency services.

This was particularly frustrating to my team and me because police and National Guard forces all over Los Angeles have been engaged in standoffs and skirmishes with domestic enemies more skilled in urban guerrilla combat than most foreign combatants. This is not a view you are likely to hear espoused in public, but it is the correct one. Such situations occur because this city is effectively Balkanized. What you have in Los Angeles is a particularly toxic mixture of citizens with disparate cultural backgrounds and belief systems, but what you have above all is a highly fragmented gang population numbering roughly 102,000. (When I was first briefed on this number, I said, "That is not a statistic, sir; that is an army.") In 1991 alone, this group was responsible for 771 murders in the city—over two per day.

It gets worse: LAPD had a directive to protect gun stores city-wide when the riot began. They failed. Over three thousand guns (nearly all semiautomatic, although some fully automatic rifles) were looted in the first two days. Though verified, this number has not been made public, and neither has this: nearly all remain unaccounted for. As such, it is operationally necessary to know that black and Latin gangs in this area are heavily armed.

So you know where I am coming from: when I use the term *black*, it means something. As my southern-raised father frequently said to me, "You was born black, and you'll die that way." I grew up in Watts, pre- and post-1965 riots, and Los Angeles today is very different from Los Angeles then. I was born in Lynwood, at St. Francis, April 1956, because there was no hospital in Watts at the time. When I was nine, my own neighborhood rioted in response to the arrest and beating of "that Frye boy," as my mother referred to him since she knew his mother, Rena, from church. Lynwood was still considered a nice place for whites then, and my mother herself took the bus there to clean houses. I find it unnecessary to further detail my early life, so I will simply say I shipped to Vietnam in 1974 and did two tours. Afterward, I went career army before taking early retirement to accept a certain job, with a certain U.S. governmental agency that I cannot currently name. That is all I can tell you about me, but I felt it vital to be clear that I have a personal stake in this mission. It is on my patch, so to speak.

It is, however, not as if this situation were created overnight. I can tell you from personal experience that nothing got solved after Watts, economically or otherwise, and yet, I do not exaggerate when I say the powder keg is significantly bigger than it once was. Only 7,900 officers and sheriffs police this city of almost 3.6 million, and county of 9.15 million. (Consider the nearly 102,000 active gang members against this number of officers.) As it stands, this is the worst ratio of all the major urban areas in the country, and yet, it is even worse when one considers the size of the policing area. Los Angeles County is a beach blanket. It is flat and it is spread out north-south from the port encompassing San Pedro and Long Beach up to the Pasadena foothills and the San Fernando Valley, and west-east from the Santa Monica beaches to the desert of the San Gabriel Valley.

For the sake of comparison: the Watts riots took place in six square blocks of my old neighborhood. It was contained accordingly. However, on the first night of our present civil unrest, fires extended over 105 square *miles* of city and county area in South Central. As a result, curfew was about as well enforced as Prohibition, because policing an area of that size, with that large a gang population, even during the best of times, is extremely arduous. But during a civil disturbance the likes of which this nation has never seen before? Well, it simply is not possible. That is the bad news up to now, but here is the good: it changes tonight.

At the FCP, I spoke to a number of fellow Vietnam vets, National Guardsmen mostly, but some CHP, and some police. Nearly all of them spoke about how similar their emotions are now to when they were "in country" over two decades ago. They mentioned the unknown. They confessed to having difficulty recognizing the enemy. I understand both, but my team is not tasked with defending shopping malls. We are targeted, guided by an L.A. Sheriff's Department Homicide liaison with exceptional knowledge and reliable informants within the South Central gang world. He selects our targets, and we do our job. In short, we are the payback.

"Don't worry," I told the old-timers in the chow line organized by the good folks at the U.S. Forestry Service. "I know who the enemy is, and not only am I going to break his ribs for you, I am going to look him in the fucking eye when I do it."

The sentiment, I must say, was much appreciated. Every day and every night since this began, gang-involved thugs have been threatening guardsmen and cops all over this city. I have yet to meet a guardsman who does not have a variant on this story: gangbangers drive by slowly, showing off their guns while pointing fingers at the men in uniform and saying, "We'll come back and kill you after dark."

In my line, that is considered a terrorist threat and deserves swift retribution. That is the angle from which we must approach this situation, because desperate times call for desperate measures. Within the EOC, there are already rumbles that the situation citywide is now contained on a level that would allow the curfew to be lifted tomorrow, so our mission is for tonight and tonight only. We have less than twenty-four hours to send a very loud message.

The silver lining to the chaos of the last five days is this: there is no possibility of what we are about to do blowing back on us. We go out, we teach the bullies a lesson so they know who is bigger and badder, and then we go. It is caveman stuff, but it also happens to be the only language every gang understands.

Our engagement parameters are twofold: one, we are to spend no more than six minutes at any given property, and two, we may act in any way we deem appropriate, so long as we do not fire unless fired upon. I agreed to both in the EOC, but I remain a realist. The one thing you can count on when on the ground is circumstances changing. All the same, I could not help myself in our mission briefing when some desk-riding, newly flown-in marine commander with more stripes on his sleeve than sense told me that not firing unless fired upon was the only thing separating us from the gangs.

"Separating us, sir?" I said to his overly serious face. "We *are* a gang."

You should have seen his jaw loosen. He is not my CO, and I do not report to him. He was only informed of the mission as a matter of professional courtesy. The gang parallel always seemed perfectly obvious to me, but I suppose it is not.

In this vehicle, I have a handpicked crew of highly trained men. We are all wearing identical tactical uniforms of green suits and helmets. We have a common goal of "rolling up" (as the parlance goes) on another gang and reminding them as forcefully as possible where the line is. This is something gangs also must do from time to time. Whether in turf or conduct, there is a line, even among criminals, and in a civil disturbance situation, again, the likes of which this country has never seen before, humans tend to forget where that line is.

Until now, that is. Now, the line gets redrawn. Now, we are more dangerous than we have ever been because there is no oversight and, best of all, we do not have to do paperwork on it in the morning. No forms. No narrative. No reports in triplicate. It is about as perfect as a government-run operation ever gets because it is dead simple, and technically, it will never be recorded as happening.

We have no names sewn on our uniforms now. We are as anonymous as the wind. What we do will exist only in whispered stories. Only the bad guys will ever know we did this, and they do not count.

I have issued one directive, and one directive only: aim to maim, and when you do, maim for life. I tell my men this, and I also amend our first mission parameter.

"Do not, I repeat, do not wait to be fired upon," I say as our vehicle hits a bump and keeps going. "If anyone so much as aims a gun at you, you cancel his fucking Cinco de Mayo."

2

So with what I have revealed so far firmly in mind, I would ask you to do one thing. I need you to steel yourself. Take a breath if needed. When we do what we must, I would advise you not to get soft. This begins with viewing our prospective targets neither as victims nor as people, but as unpunished criminals getting a dose of the only medicine they understand. I would recommend heartily that you not pity them. The criminals we are targeting, they have it coming and they have had it coming for a long time. Most important, they will know that they have brought this upon themselves.

Past the Rio Hondo confluence of the Los Angeles River, there is a drive-out that leads onto Imperial Highway. We leave the riverbed there, utilize the access road, undo the fencing, and enter the street. I double-check the Duncan Avenue address obtained from our LASD Homicide liaison with our tactical drivers. Although I specifically requested that our liaison be detailed to my unit, I was rebuffed. He would love to be, he said, particularly to see the looks on the faces of these "little Mexican fuckers" when they get some justice, but he cannot risk someone recognizing him. He was at this same address last night, and he questioned one of these gangbangers as well. He still polices here he said, whereas we are "just visiting." I told him I understood.

As we have the element of surprise, standard procedure is to assault the residence frontally. However, we have eyes-on in this case and have been informed that there is a gathering currently occurring in the back patio area. In addition, we know that a driveway borders the north of the property. As such, I have ordered one squad of four to disembark the tailing vehicle halfway down the block and flank the residence with weapons high in order to bottle up the gathering and funnel any runners back into the patio while the other squad from our tailing vehicle assaults frontally, and the two squads aboard my vehicle will cut off a lateral escape route.

As the flanking squad departs, they pass a possible gangbanger traversing the sidewalk away from the target residence. It is reasonable to assume he may be leaving the gathering so we confront him. He immediately puts his hands up and does not attempt to warn anyone of our presence. When he is told to get down in the grass and spread-eagle, he complies and is searched for weapons. He is clean. He is told to stay where he is, he nods that he understands, and my squad proceeds to the flank.

I have a newly adopted issue, German-style helmet that I am still getting used to, and I am wearing kneepads, thigh pads, and a Kevlar vest—basically, about as much padding as a football player. In my right hand, I am carrying a retractable tactical baton made of solid steel, also German in design and issue. At full extension, it is twenty-six inches long. It weighs one pound and seven ounces and it is a startlingly effective piece of equipment when in the proper hands. For a moment before the vehicle comes to a full stop and we jump, I feel invincible.

On my call, we exit the vehicle and spread out in formation as one of our targets yells, "Goon Squad's here. Get the fuck out!"

I smile at that description. Goon Squad is not far wrong.

When we enter the patio, equal portions of food and drink splatter the concrete. Plates and cups get dropped as various gangbangers attempt to escape. This patio hosts a propane grill and two small picnic tables with benches built in. The area is concrete and roughly twenty feet square. The back edge abuts a metal fence three feet high. Beyond it is the front yard of the next house, dotted with close trees. Those targets attempting to jump the back fence freeze on the very top of it when they see the barrels of multiple M-16s poking through foliage. Upon seeing them, they scramble right back over the fence to the patio, and now they are mine.

There are nineteen gangbangers present. Most have the look of scared rabbits ready to bolt at any opportunity, but there are a few cool customers in this bunch, and that is good. It means they are likely operating under the notion that we are here to arrest them and that it will happen in an orderly fashion. We are not, and it will not.

Of my sixteen men, all have sidearms, but eight carry the same metal baton I have, and the rest are equipped with M-16s. Much has been made in the news about lockplates installed in National Guard weapons, rendering them incapable of automatic firing. I assure you that is not an issue for my unit. Should it become necessary, we can and will go fully automatic. As previously instructed, one of my men removes an empty box from the vehicle in the driveway and opens it.

"Let's make this easy," I say. "Those of you who are packing, put your weapons in that box right fucking now. Safeties on if they're not already on."

They do as they are told. It takes less than a minute for two of my men to pack the box up and secure it in one of the vehicles. This is where the fun starts. We have five minutes to truly ruin this party.

I make my way to the chef, the one standing over the grill. Our liaison marks him as the leader.

When I go toe-to-toe with him and show him I'm the bigger man by a few inches and twenty pounds, two gangbangers rise from the nearest table. One is wafer thin, but the other has an Indian look to him and is thick in the neck like a wrestler. My second in command steps between them and me while locking and loading his weapon. The racking of a bullet into the chamber of an automatic weapon is an extremely effective sound. It demands obedience.

They back up then, these two tough guys, but they certainly do not want to. A pretty little Asian hides herself behind the skinny one then. I have no idea what she is doing in a place like this. However, intel did indicate that this gang was not averse to using female members, so I note her presence accordingly.

I turn my attention back to the chef, and he looks at me with a stare that gives absolutely nothing away. He holds a metal spatula in his right hand, but it is frozen above the grill, the surface of which is brown with meat scrapings. When little runnels of clear fat fall from the spatula, they sputter and hiss on the hot charcoal below.

"You," I say, "Mister Big Fate, have got to fucking stop killing people."

He does not respond to that, but he does not need to. I nod to my SIC, who steps forward and holds his weapon in the ready position. At six foot four and two hundred and thirty pounds of muscle, he is a machine built for one thing and one thing only, and that is to hurt. When Big Fate (honestly, I cannot understand these names for the life of me) turns to look at my SIC, my SIC butt-strokes his skull. At that point, it is safe to say that Mr. Big Fate hits the concrete faster than a paratrooper without a 'chute.

I lean down to his bleeding face and say, "You need to stop killing people!"

Repetition is the only thing that gets through to these animals. I know this because I am an animal myself. The only things I have learned over the years, I have learned because I have done them ten thousand times. Ask my current wife, and while you are at it, ask my two ex-wives.

Now that Mr. Big Fate is down, my SIC works on his upper right arm. It is ringed with a Mexican-style tattoo. After one particularly thumping strike, the spatula drops from his hand and clangs to the concrete. As it settles, my SIC hits the very same spot on the arm again, bringing the butt of his weapon down on the same inky swirl. This is his new target, and he keeps hitting the same spot every time I say a word.

"You," I say to Mr. Big Fate.

Butt-stroke is a nice way of saying something awful.

"Need."

It is when you disable an assailant with the butt of your rifle.

"To."

Fully loaded, a service-ready M-16 weighs 8.8 pounds. When wielded properly, it is capable of generating more than enough force to break bones.

"Stop."

My SIC hammers the biggest bone in the upper body, the humerus, in the exact same place, again and again.

"Killing."

Under normal circumstances, it takes tremendous force to break the humerus, and that usually only happens in car wrecks or high falls.

"People."

In this case, however, my SIC has hammered the same spot until it fractured, and then he hit that fracture until the whole bone snaps with a crack so loud that it sounds like somebody hit a home run with a wooden bat, that is how clean the crack is, and at that moment Mister Big Fate's arm bends the wrong way, and he roars, but that is not the end of it, because my SIC decides to step on the part of the arm that now hangs limply. This, he grinds with the sole of his combat boot. He puts all his weight on it, my SIC does, all two hundred and thirty pounds. I do not care how tough you think you are. No one can withstand that kind of pain. Mr. Big Fate is no different. He passes out right beneath my SIC and falls backward, smacking his head on the concrete.

When that happens, all hell breaks loose.

3

The stocky one goes for my SIC while the skinny one jumps at me, full of rage. It is almost comical the way they both go down. The stocky one walks into a judo hold that my SIC takes to completion, popping his shoulder right out of its socket with a thumping crack. The skinny one, I hit him in the ribs with my baton and finish him off with a rap to the top of his skull. All his breath leaves him in a rush before he hits the concrete knees-first and tumbles over in a heap. Behind him, one of my men has the Asian girl down and raps her wrist with a standard-issue metal baton. I hear her bones break from where I am standing. She screams in pain, and the skinny one, with blood streaming down his face, yells her name.

"Irene!"

I believe that is what he says anyway. It is hard to keep track precisely, because whoever was not running before that happened is running now. They jerk like antelope for the fence and go over it, or they run for the house. It is chaos, but for us, it is effective chaos, because at this point, it is simply time to work.

I strike three to the ground before they can pass me and get to the back door of the house. I hit throats. I hit ears. I hit whatever presents itself as the most advantageous soft target.

My SIC stands over his two examples, bellowing so loudly that he does not need a bullhorn to be heard by everybody on the block.

"We know you've been looting," he says. "We know where you got the shit hid!"

Our game plan is simple. We aim for joints and small bones mostly. We break hands. We break ankles. We break knees and elbows too. We are not especially particular. It is mainly an issue of strategic opportunity, of what presents itself as someone with little to no martial arts training attempts to defend him- or herself. In such an instance, there are multiple options: he or she might turn and run—in which case, trip with baton and go for an ankle; he or she might try to kick out at you—in which case, dodge and strike the knee or ankle of the standing leg; he or she might face up to you, and you might feint a strike to the head, which might cause your target to reflexively put up his or her hands—in which case, strike fingers, wrists, or elbows.

I have told my men it is remarkably like fast food. Just grab and go. Bend something back against itself and wait for the scream, then pull until it pops. Then do it again. Once you have done it once, it is easier to reexecute. Two in ten actually fight through a pain reflex that strong. The rest give up. Once he or she succumbs to horizontality, that is when you strike ribs to be absolutely certain he or she will not take another deep breath again without thinking of you and how hard you hit. For the rest of their short lives, they will think of you. Change lives tonight, I told my men before we rolled. Sometimes the best learning experiences on earth are the bad ones, and today we must deliver them.

It smells of burning meat now as I seek one more example to make. The stocky one is at my feet, crawling toward Mr. Big Fate as the girl cradling her limp wrist curls herself around the skinny one.

It's the stocky one I grab by the ankle before whipping off his laceless shoe. He rolls to look at me, his eyes widening as I bring my club down on his toes, turning every single one on his left foot into bloody, hanging bits at the end of his sock. You have never heard anyone scream like he screams. When I am done, what is left of his toes looks like nothing more than smashed maraschino cherries seeping through his white sock. Tears of shock stream down his face when I break his ribs. I stop at six. God willing, this little monster will never run or breathe right again. Good. Slower criminals are better for everybody.

He whimpers as he wheezes though, this one.

"Shut the fuck up." I'm breathing heavily when I say this to the crybaby. "You play, you pay. Nobody has to tell you that. Count yourself lucky I didn't shoot your whole fucking foot off. Imagine that! Imagine having to be a criminal with a stump. Why, you wouldn't even be able to run from me next time."

He bites his lip after that. He suffers in the loudest silence I have ever heard. At this point, I check my watch. We are at five minutes. Time is almost up.

The patio area has thinned out. By my count, two got away and that's two too many. The meat on the grill has gone black, and it releases its own little towers of smoke. What a fitting microcosm that is, I think, Los Angeles as an untended grill, burning the meat unlucky enough to be stuck on top of it.

I count seventeen gangbangers down on the concrete patio. In their own ways, they are moaning, writhing, and/or gasping. It is not enough by half, but our orders are to get in and get out, so I order the withdrawal.

"We're coming back whenever we want," my SIC says to the stocky one trying for all the world not to look at what's left of his foot. "We'll confiscate all the shit you stole, but we won't round you up, won't stand you for trial, oh no! Next time, we're just going to fucking *shoot* you."

He waves good-bye in the creepiest way possible, my SIC. He

brings his hand close to his face and just flexes the tips of his fingers down, like the way my son first learned how to wave at me.

For the record, I wish everything my SIC just said was true. It is not.

That is the biggest lie of our little operation tonight: we will not be coming back, no matter how much we might threaten it. Already we are back in the vehicles and moving on to a new location to deal with the next little batch of cancers. They are all getting done today before order is officially restored and curfew is lifted. All we are meant to do at this juncture is to keep them in line. We know they have been killing, but crime scenes citywide are cold, nonexistent, or wrecked. Arrest and prosecution is simply not going to happen at this stage. This is why the best-case scenario for law and order is a heavy-handed slap on the wrist—the kind that takes a great deal of time to heal, or might never heal, if we did it right.

Tonight, we will hit every notorious gang hangout or residence even remotely worth hitting, because the brutal truth is that there are too many criminals clogging the lockups in this city as it is. Department of Corrections was overburdened to begin with, but when over eight thousand people get arrested in four days, it doesn't even begin to define the term *strain*. Systems have capacities and that one was reached on Day 3.

As I understand it, we are now only saving space for the special kind of dirt, the killers dumb enough to get caught in the act mostly. The arsonists, if we ever catch them. The ones we can actually build cases on and convict. Everybody else that is in our books as a known offender and we may or may not have information on, whether from tips or informants, we will visit tonight. We will throw some excellent surprise parties. It will not be enough, it will not be what they deserve, but it will be something, and with any luck, they will remember it the rest of their natural-born lives.

JEREMY RUBIO,
A.K.A. TERMITE,
A.K.A. FREER

MAY 3, 1992

4:09 P.M.

1

One, spiders sinking their fangs into my eyeballs. Two, getting pitched off the 710 overpass and belly-flopping onto the bed of the L.A. River so hard that all my bones break simultaneously. Three, finding a virgin city bus that no one ever graffed or scribed on before parked in a layup and I don't have any paint to write my name with, and also I don't have my mean streak, or my scriber, or anything. My cousin Gloria says I got a whatdoyoucallit? An overactive imagination. She's right. I do.

But what I just said? *Those* are the three things that scare me *less* than going to the house Big Fate lives in to pay my respects to Ray and Lupe for Ernie, and I have nightmares about one through three all the time.

And I might still be a little high from this morning. But I've already waited too many days as it is. I never wanted to come, to be real honest with you. If I didn't though, it would get noticed. Also, I need to find out when services are, cuz no one has heard anything, and my aunt has already asked me twice if it's going to be Catholic.

So I'm here, standing in the front yard of where Ernie used to live, a front yard that kinda smells like burnt paste for some reason, staring at a house with more bullet holes in it than I can count. I feel sick looking at it, a little dizzy. I don't even know how he lived in this house.

I know Ernie didn't get hurt here, but it still makes my legs feel like rubber cuz this is some for real shit and it definitely doesn't help when my Walkman grinds like *ka-ka*, and it sounds like a train on tracks as it switches directions from side 2 to side 1 of my "Bombing Mix Tape, Vol. 6."

Side 2's all rap. Side 1's sound-track songs. I got it turned down real low cuz this is *not* the neighborhood to be caught slipping in. I submit as evidence this spectacular bullet-hole collection before me. I'm actually trying to count how many holes there are when the first song on side 1 pops into my ears and it kinda crushes me cuz I knew what it was but I forgot.

It's the song from *Star Wars* about Luke's burnt-up house. Uncle Owen's dead. Aunt Beru's dead. And now I got *that* scene associated with Ernie too cuz the song's got like a, whatdoyoucallit, a weepy trumpet sound before the strings come in and jump up and down on the track like they own it. I just got to sidenote right here, and say that John Williams is the *shit*. Fact.

For a sec, and I mean for just a second, my brain switches gears then, and I think about how hard it would be to write my name in bullets on something. Prolly impossible.

I snap my music off with the stop button and I hear people in the back so I go up the driveway until I see people out on the patio. *I got to be careful*, I tell myself. *I got to be observant, respectful, and I got to get away with whatever I can get away with.*

When Clever sees me, he says, "Look at who it is, the tagger."

We went to continuation school at Vista together, me and Clever. Well, until I dropped out anyways.

"Hey," I say, to him and to everybody, and swipe off my headphones even though they're not on anymore cuz it's rude, and I can't be looking rude around here. Never.

When Clever calls me tagger, he says it like talking down to me, like taggers ain't about shit, like I'm a little kid playing grown-up.

But I write FREER now. I used to write DOPE. But then I heard someone around Hollywood was writing it too, so I said *fuck that* and quit. After that I went for ZOOM, which I used for like two weeks and gave up, but not cuz someone else was writing it, cuz I hated how my *Z*'s looked and a double *O* was boring to write. They always just looked like giant cartoon eyes to me. *Garfield* eyes.

I like FREER way better than either of them anyways, cuz there's tons of kicks and loops possible with double *R*'s and double *E*'s but also cuz it *means* something. When I first thought of it, I got obsessed with it, cuz I meant it, like, *look at me, motherfucker, I can do this crazy shit because I'm way freer than you ever thought you could be.* It's like a statement. If I wasn't freer than you, then how could I get up and write my name wherever I wanted?

On the streets people know FREER cuz he gives the least amount of fucks out of anybody. Except for maybe CHAKA or SLEEZ. Those guys put in work on another level. But to be honest though, I do give a fuck, especially in this neighborhood.

"I just wanted to pay my respects for Ernie," I say, and just in case people might know him as something different, I also say, "for Ernesto."

A big guy, I think it's the one called Apache, says, "Oh, you just wanted to pay respects, huh?"

The FREER inside me wants to tell him that I just said that, but I only nod.

Big Fate's on the grill, sticking thermometers in stuff, moving sausages around, slapping burgers into buns on plates and looking to hand them off. There's a loose line of people kinda hovering around him, waiting to scoop some . . .

For a sec I stop and think, *They're like his solar system, these people. He's the sun and they revolve.* I should prolly grab my notebook out and write that down cuz I like it, but my hands are still shaking a little and it feels like I got a badger rummaging around in my stomach like it's cabinets, like he's hungry and looking for stuff to eat and coming up disappointed.

FREER never has badgers in his stomach. FREER writes his thoughts down whenever the hell he feels like it, dammit. And you know, FREER's even the kinda guy to tell people to wait so he can write shit down. That's who FREER is. But me, I keep my hands in my pockets when I say, "Is Lupe here?"

Fate weighs me up for a sec and then says, "Nope."

"Um," I say, "do you mind if I ask where she's at? Maybe I could wait if she's coming back."

"She's at her mother's place," Apache says.

"Where's that at?" I'm not trying to pry, just trying to pay respects, you know?

"Can't say," Apache says.

I nod and say, "Okay, um, is Ray here then? I just wanted to, uh, give my condolences to the family, for Ernesto."

I might still be fuzzy. But, man, some weird vibes pass between people in their looks when I say Ray's name. Heavy stuff. Apache looks at Clever and Clever looks at his hamburger like it needs to be studied, and Big Fate mashes a patty down on the grill where it spits and sizzles.

Eventually, Fate says, "So you know this merger's going down, right?"

Of course, he has to change the subject on me and bring up the one thing I've been dreading more than anything. More than needles under fingernails. More than eating grasshoppers dipped in rat guts. I'm not trying to be a gangster just cuz my tagbanging crew's getting absorbed into Big Fate's click. I'm *really* not trying to do that.

"Yeah," I say, "I heard."

"So you made your choice or what?"

When he says choice, he means quit tagging and disappear or keep tagging and join up. But the way he says it, it's not a choice to him. He wants me to join up is what he wants. I'm trying not to panic here, trying not to sweat this more than I already am, so I think I have to talk up school again. It's bought me time with Big Fate before.

"You know, I been going to continuation school again—"

Clever cuts me off. "No, you haven't," he says.

Man. He burnt me good on that one. I look at him, and he looks at me and shrugs. This fine Chinese chick he has behind him kinda looks at me cold too, like she thinks it was a dumb play for me to say that and for a sec, I don't even care, cuz I would totally bone her.

Big Fate doesn't look up from the grill. He says to me, "You haven't?"

That sharpens me up. Brings my attention right back.

"I'm enrolled for next semester," I say, "just starting back up. I had a little problem I had to take care of. But I'm trying to do the right thing. Get my GED."

Big Fate doesn't care. He says, "Everybody knows shit's changing, and you've had a pass up till now cuz of your dad, but that expires next time I see you."

My dad's been in San Quentin since I was like eleven, so six years ago. My mom says he was a big man, had the juice card around here and everything. He put Big Fate on, kinda trained him up for what he's doing. People used to say he was real smart. But I guess Big Fate's smarter, huh? Cuz *he's* not doing life in prison.

But I'm not my dad and I'm not trying to be him, or Big Fate, or anything to do with this click. I don't care if my name came from my dad saying I could eat through anything when I was a kid, that I was just a little Termite. That name's not really me now. I grew out of it. I'm FREER.

And anybody that's actually got some art to them, that cares about their letters and inventing new styles, not just some hard-core vandal for the absolute punk rock fuck-off-itude of it, they're all nerds and rejects. All of them. Me too, man. I love me some fucking Bode *Cheech Wizards*. I love *Star Wars* and I still got them faded x-wing fighter sheets. I'm a thrift-shop-raiding, four-for-a-dollar LP junkie. Don't matter if the vinyl's scratched up, fucked up, whatever. At that price, they're worth it for the covers. I put those up in my room with tacks. Herb Alpert & the Tijuana Brass, man. Martin Denny. Henry Mancini. All the sound tracks I got came from there.

I record them from my dad's old turntable to cassette cuz he sure isn't using it. And that's just me. Every other writer is weird in his own special ways. All of us are just some fucked-up little smart kids born in the wrong places.

Well, that's not entirely true. I mean, we're not all smart. Some of us are just fucked up or drugged out, but we do get fixated on shit. That's tough news too when there's no outlets for us but to write on the world. No avenues except *actual* avenues to getting your name out in the one city where all that matters is if you're fucking famous, where all that matters is if you're white and on a billboard twenty feet tall, or in the movies, or on TV. But I don't got those routes. I'm Mexican, *raza*, the hidden race.

Well, hidden unless you're Cheech Marin, or fucking *L.A. Law* Jimmy Smits. And I'm not. Nobody cares about me that way. I'll never have a face that's known. But I got letters. I got those. Five little letters that when people see them, they see my soul somehow, and they know that the guy that did that doesn't fuck around. That guy puts in work. My letters say something more too. They say I'm here, you know? They say I did that. They say I exist.

Somebody opens a back screen door from the kitchen and yells out to Big Fate that he has a phone call and he tells whoever picked up to take a message, but then the person says it's from up the street and he stops.

"String that out here then," he says to the guy and then to me he's like, "You can go. Next time I see you, though, it's time to fucking choose. It don't matter who your dad is. Sure would be good to have you in though. Keep it family business."

"Thanks," I say, and I'm not really sure what I'm thanking him for but he's got the phone in his hand now so I'm backing out, nodding at Clever, avoiding Apache's look and skirting around the house to the driveway and then to the sidewalk as fast as I can.

Cuz if I didn't know it before I walked into the middle of Gangsterland today, I need to get out, like, all the way out. Out of L.A. even. Go to Arizona or something. My mom's sister out there owns part of a dry cleaners in Phoenix. She's always writing me to come out, to leave this life behind, and that sounds pretty damn good right now.

I need money to do that though.

I make a quick little list in my head of who owes me. It starts and ends with Listo. I can sell some stuff to Fat John and Tortuga too, and I can maybe hit up Gloria. That should be something.

First comes the legit stuff. I worked three days last week on the Tacos El Unico truck before this whole thing started and it got shut down. But the stand has been open all the way through the riots, 24/7, and my boss hasn't been putting me on. I know something about him though, and he's about to know I know.

It's what FREER would do.

2

I press play and I'm back to the mix tape and it's back to John Williams, the end of it anyways. I'm just starting to calm down as I walk, taking deep breaths and everything, when I notice how much of a ghost town this is right now. There's nobody out. None. Windows closed up. No lawns getting watered or mowed. And I guess it's not for me to wonder, but why were Fate and them having a BBQ anyway?

Couldn't be because they're strategizing how to absorb tagbangers. That'd be too scary. I walk in silence for a bit, feeling heavy. It's tripping me out what graffiti evolved into in L.A. It started in the riverbed back when it was being built in the 1930s, straight-up hobo carvings and tar pieces and shit. There's *placas* from zoot suiters back then too. And all respect to the East Coast, but they didn't invent *shit*. CHAZ was doing *Señor Suerte* back when New York fools were just learning how to write their names on walls like some little fucking babies. In L.A., we've always been more advanced. But then things got crazy. When my generation came up, it wasn't just about tagging no more. It was about tagbanging.

It used to be you put your name up and that was it. There were beefs if somebody was crossing your name out or going over it, but it grew up into something else, a whole new beast. Right now this graff scene is basically the Wild West cuz now my generation's running the streets. It's not just pioneers and piecers anymore, guys who want to do big, filled-in letter pieces that don't bother nobody. Kids my age, most of us come from bad places and we don't like being disrespected. That's how graffiti got violent. And when it got dangerous to tag, people started going together to paint in groups, and eventually those groups got bigger and got tighter and formed crews, and if the crew got big enough, it became a click with multiple crews all over the place.

That's how tagbanging became like a new spike on the fork of L.A. graffiti. It mutated into something completely new cuz it's this weird mix between graffiti and the gangster life, where the line between the two just gets fuzzier and fuzzier now. Tagbangers carrying guns to protect themselves or shoot somebody that's disrespecting by crossing them out? Shit, that's real as hell. I got one, a little .22 throwaway that's easy to hide. I just didn't bring it with me cuz the last thing I needed was Big Fate deciding I needed to be searched and then what? Have to explain that? No thanks.

I got a feeling in the pit of my stomach like my life's never gonna be the same. It feels like I swallowed up a bunch of nails and they're just rolling around in me. I mean, you know it's bad, you know it's gotten way out of hand if a fucking nerd like me is packing. And I'm not the only one. It's so far out of control that everybody took notice. There's green lights out on taggers now. Pressure from big dogs way above Big Fate to get these renegade tagbanging crews in line cuz some of them are basically doing gangster shit anyways, shooting people over tagging territory and whatnot.

It's really not so crazy to think about legislating them cuz some tagbanging crews are so big they're gangs in their own rights. I'm talking like four hundred people big. You just can't have that many people running around unchecked. It fucks up business. I'm sure that's Big Fate's take. Anyways, it's prolly safer for everyone for it to be a little more regulated in the gangster system, and if you're down with that, and some are, okay, but I'm not. Hell no. I'm not about to lose freedom that way. I'm not about to be forced into doing gangster shit just cuz I want to paint.

There's this pause on my headphones as I hear the heads turning with a soft little *whisk-whisk* sound before the theme from *A Fistful of Dollars* rolls in. That's my strolling music right there, man. I can't lie. It's on there cuz it's more trumpet. I'm down with trumpets lately. I don't know why. They just speak to me, just spark something in me. Like puppies nuzzling on my ribs. Warm-good. That's what it feels like when a really clean trumpet hits me.

But that feeling drains right down my body and out of my toes when I look up and see some sort of tank-truck-things coming up the street. Big, armored trucks they look like. Two of them. And, man, are they ever coming fast! I pretty much freeze right then, cuz what the fuck else am I supposed to do? I'm praying they just go right by me, just right on by without even looking at me. But they *don't*.

They fucking stop in the street alongside me!

I swipe my headphones off my head as brakes squeal and some sort of back hatch must open cuz I hear metal bang and then there's four guys out and . . .

Holy shit! Dudes in helmets and serious gear point their guns at me. I never been so scared in my life. I just kinda fall forward onto my knees and put my hands up, you know? All the way up, because you can't expect to run and get away from that. The badger's back and he's going to town on my stomach with his claws so good that my heart freaks out and runs into my throat to get away from him, and it just sits there, right on my Adam's apple, pounding.

"On the ground," one of them says from behind a whatdoyou-callit? A giant gun I know the name of, but I forget what it is when it's inches from my face. A military gun though. A long gun with a handle on top of it.

And it's so calm and quiet the way he says what he says that it freaks me out more. I get on the ground, right flat on somebody's lawn. There's a dandelion clump near my face with white fuzzy tops and next to it is an old piece of dog shit so I turn my head the other way so I don't have to see it or smell it.

"Spread-eagle," the same voice says, and I must not do it fast enough, cuz real quick there's hard cold metal forcing my legs open wider and my arms further apart and that's when it hits me that they're using the barrels of the guns to do it, to move my arms and legs and I want to throw up on the grass right then, cuz what if one of their fingers slips and I get shot?

My throat's dry, but I manage to say, "Please don't shoot me."

"You got a weapon on you?" the voice wants to know.

I shake my head no. They pat me down anyways.

I say *they* cuz it feels like four hands.

When they don't find anything, the same voice says, "I'm going to need you to stay down until you count two hundred. Begin."

I nod before I say, "One, two, three, four . . ."

On my neck I hear the song "Everybody Wants to Rule the World" from the *Real Genius* sound track starting up. I can tell from the guitar and synthesizers. And that's all I can hear. This low little rhythm in the grass. For just a sec, I'm blown away by the fucking crazy strange timing of it, but then I'm focused on something else.

I don't even look up, but I hear boots run away from me, and then I hear the two truck-things in the street rolling again. They pass into my vision as I see them head up the street. The first one, oh fuck, the first one turns up into the driveway I just walked out of. They're hitting Big Fate! Oh, Jesus fuck. That's bad. That's really, really bad.

"Nineteen, twenty, twenty-one . . ."

The other truck-thing stops in the street, and four more guys with machine guns roll out and rush the house. Two put their shoulders into the front door and it gives with this awful groan and a loud-ass crash before they go in with their guns raised.

"Thirty, thirty-one, thirty-two."

I stop counting there. I look around and see nobody near me. No army dudes, nothing. My cuff's in the dog shit though. *Ugh*. I get up slow and easy, and nobody says anything, so I run cuz nobody's stopping me.

Fuck, man. My headphones are up and bouncing around my neck as I get hold of them and jam them down on my ears as I book it down the block cuz I'm in the shit now. I'm *actually* in the shit.

I'm getting it on all sides, man! Everybody's fucking with me. I got my aunt telling me every two minutes how I'm gonna end up dead like Ernie if I don't stop tagging and she won't listen when I say Ernie wasn't painting, he never did tagging or nothing. But that's not something she gets or will ever get.

And on the other hand, I got Big Fate hassling me about joining up and time ticking down on that. And now, on the other-other hand, there's this? Soldiers jumping out on me, throwing me on the ground? Soldiers rolling up on Big Fate and giving a perfect advertisement for why the fuck not to be a gangster, cuz there's always somebody bigger and badder around the corner, somebody who can fuck you up quicker than you ever thought?

Shit. I feel more than *ever* like I got to get the fuck outta L.A.

3

You don't really think what a nice day it is until you think you're gonna die. But now I look up after several smoky days and find that I can see the sky again through partial clouds and it's blue. Well, it's like a gray blue. But it's warm. Over 70 degrees prolly. And under that sky on Atlantic and Rosecrans, on the roof of the building where the Tacos El Unico stand is in a little strip mall, is a guy with sunglasses on, an automatic rifle, and a bulletproof vest.

That's Rudy. He's Guatemalan. But he's cool. He does security for us. I never seen him with that kinda gear before though, and I don't know where he got it. It's a little unnerving if you want to know the truth. I wave at him and he doesn't wave back. He nods. I wonder how long he's been up there. I mean, El Unico's always

open, even through curfew it's been like that. He must be sw.
with somebody, I think.

Before I get to the door, I say hey to James-the-Homeless-Dı
cuz he's standing in the parking lot, leaning on his cane. James is
crazy, but he's mellow. He comes by a lot. Ernesto always used to
feed him, no questions asked. You know that shit came out of his
check too, and I always told Ernie, I said, you know that makes
it harder to save up when you're trying to scrape money together,
right? He always told me not to worry about it. A taco here or there
wasn't going to stop his dream, and it helped people, so that was
always worth it. Just remembering him saying that, I shake my head.

"Hey," James says to me, "do you know where Ernesto's at?"

He tunes out when I say I don't know. I feel bad not telling him
what happened to Ernesto and all, but I don't want to make this little
homeless dude feel bad. He liked Ernesto plenty and I can tell his
life's been rough and I don't want to add to that or take on the responsibility of feeding him the way Ernesto did when I'm already planning on being out. I say bye to James and he says bye as I head for the
front door.

Inside, there's some National Guards sitting and eating. They
say what's up to me, and at first I think what'd I do? But they're
saying hey to everybody who comes in. I keep talking to them
though. Not everybody does. They say they got hooked up with
free food and it's *so good*. Best tacos and burritos they've had, they
say, and that makes sense cuz they're mostly white and black and
I-don't-know-what, but I can tell they don't have anyone cooking
Mexican food for them at home.

They're from Company C, they say, stationed in Inglewood.
Third Battalion, 160th Infantry, they say. They've been here almost
the whole time and gesture across the street. I look to the 7-Eleven
convenience store there and see some sandbags and stuff on the corner where there are four more of them, and I can't tell from this distance but, even in uniforms, they look like *cholos* to me. It's just the
way they stand. At that point, guards in the restaurant can't really

keep quiet about it any longer and they tell me I smell pretty ripe and at first I don't know what that means, but then I remember the dog shit and I apologize and duck behind the counter.

I nod at the chef working and start washing the cuff of my flannel good with soap and water so hot it burns me a little. I get my hands good too cuz being here reminds me so much of Ernie, of how he used to call me out and everything.

We didn't work much here, we mostly worked the truck, but every so often we'd be in the stand together and he'd give me endless shit about not washing my hands. Turns out spray paint gets on your hands pretty bad. I'd always wash them after, and the color would come off the skin, but it'd stay stuck to my nails. I'd try and try to get it off, but eventually, I'd give up and come in and chop for him. Tomatoes. Meat. Lettuce. Whatever. But the first thing he'd do was always look at my hands and bust me fast.

Ernie'd say, "What the hell are you doing? Why didn't you wash your hands?"

"I *did* wash my hands," I'd say. "They're clean."

"How come your nails are still blue then? How about that?"

"They're *clean*," I'd say.

"Listen, someone hands you a plate and they got paint on their hands, would you want to eat that? It's gross, man. Don't do that. It's not professional."

And then I'd be like, "What do you know about professional?"

"Listen," he'd say, and his tone would be different, calmer, "I'm not your dad. I'm not telling you what to do with your life. You wanna paint on your off-time, okay. Go crazy. Have your fun. But once you're eighteen or nineteen, maybe you need to think about knocking that graffiti shit off, because that's the kind of thing you do county time for, and they don't like that stuff in there."

Ernie was always my voice of reason, always hitting me with constant reality checks. I didn't really want to hear it, you know? With him gone, I guess I need to take that on myself from now on, which is tough, cuz I kinda don't want to. It's hard.

I get to drying my hands with the paper towels before rolling one up in my cuff so it looks like one sleeve is white on the end. I stare at the sink for a few seconds before going to the back and asking to sit down with my boss.

He's got a tiny desk in a little supply closet. He's pretty much *paisa*, so he loves sitting down behind the desk and holding court. I don't know where that word comes from. Maybe we stole it from the Italian *paisano* and turned it into a Spanish word or something. To us, though, it means something like *fresh off the boat* means to Orientals, I think. Somebody from the old country that still acts like it, somebody not American yet, or maybe they never will be.

My boss, he's a good dude. Sometimes you just have to remind him to be one is all. Behind his back we call him Listo-Listo cuz he always asks if we're ready before shift in a real annoying way every day, like, "*¿Listo, listo?*"

He repeats himself like that all the time. So much that you get to feeling he doesn't actually think you're ready, so he's always reminding you to be. I dunno. Sitting across from him, I smile. He likes when you call him *jefe*, so I start that way.

"*Jefe*," I say, "I worked the week before last and then Monday and Tuesday last week, and on Wednesday you sent me and Ernesto home from the truck, so—"

In Spanish, he tells me he was real sorry to hear about Ernesto but that's not really his business, and speaking of, things are tight right now with the banks not being open. Maybe tomorrow he can pay me, he says.

I can see he's lying to me though. I've worked here long enough to know we do most of our business in cash and that's how it goes when you sling a lot of food to people who may or may not be documented, so flow's definitely not our problem. If anything, we got too much sitting around in the safe cuz the banks have been closed and he's nervous about it. That would help explain Rudy with the gun on the roof anyways.

As cool as I can, I ask about his wife and he says she's good, so when he says that, I make sure to ask about his girlfriend and he freezes up cuz he knows who I'm talking about. One night two months ago, I was out dropping trash in the Dumpster and I saw something going on in his car and I thought for sure someone was trying to steal it, so I crept up and ended up seeing something I didn't need to see, but I'm glad I did. I mean, how was I to know that he'd be fucking some girl from behind in his backseat?

Even better, I knew who she was. Cecilia something. I don't know her last name, but I'd seen her around, mostly with that curly-haired dude with pits in his face called Momo. That one is legit bad news, man. He always orders *lengua* tacos. He loves him some beef tongue drenched in *salsa verde*, like, so much that the taco basically falls apart in his hand and when it does, he finishes it off with chips. Don't ask me why.

I drop a hint to Listo that maybe Momo was responsible for what happened to Ernesto and what would he do if he knew my boss was with his girlfriend? I let that kinda fly around in the air and he gulps as he thinks about it.

I don't feel good doing it, but I think Ernesto wouldn't be mad at me cuz Listo used to try to fuck him out of money too.

"I don't know what you're talking about," Listo says, and his eyes look kinda panicked.

"Whatever you say, *jefe*," I say. "I believe you, man."

Listo doesn't like anything about doing it, but he leaves the room and comes back with $291 in cash and says he has to withhold for tax and whatnot. I don't fight him. I say thanks and leave. He doesn't tell me not to come back. But that's the message.

I'm okay about it. The bridge is burnt to a crisp, but it's a start. I got a nest egg. Now all I need to do is grow it up and hatch it.

4

Tortuga, Fat John, and me are all standing in my cousin Gloria's garage, which is sometimes where we meet up before missions. I let us in with the key I know Gloria keeps around the side in a little stucco hole she plugs up with a rock. I tell her not to do that, that it's not safe and somebody's gonna steal her car someday, but she keeps doing it. You think she'd learn, but sometimes people don't learn unless bad things happen.

Fat John says, "Why are we here again? I know it's not to say what's up to your cousin and her sweet tits."

"Just wait," I say, too focused to get mad about the sweet tits comment, but before I can say what I want to say, Tortuga slaps me on the shoulder and nods at me.

"Well, I thought we were here cuz shit's going crazy out there," he says. "I heard your cousin's homeboy Puppet set some fucking homeless bum on fire! Just, like, chucked gas on him, lit a match, and *whoosh*!"

Shit. Sleepy does have a crazy-ass junkie homeboy named Puppet and I've met him. He's bad news, man. I stare at Tortuga for a second and the only mental picture I got in my mind is James going up in flames. Shit is gross, man. It turns my stomach. This whole city is officially off-the-rails insane. Once again, I know I got to get the fuck out of here. Right now. Today.

"That's bullshit," I say. "Besides, we're not here to tell stories and gossip like a bunch of bitches. We're here to do some business."

I didn't expect Gloria to be home from work yet, but her little Geo Metro is right there in the middle of the garage, red as can be, kinda blocking where I need to get to, so I climb over the trunk and it dents a little under my weight but pops back up when I get off, and I go under the tool bench that's built in the wall that she never even goes near and I pull out my grandpa's old army bag that's olive green and taller than me. It clinks and clunks as I drag it over the concrete.

Tortuga says, "Is that what I think it is?"

When I've dragged the bag back over the car, I plunk it down on the oil-stained garage floor, unzip it, and say, "Check this shit out!"

"Holy . . ." Fat John makes a face like he can't believe what he's seeing. "What the hell, man?!"

"You're a legend for this, homes," Tortuga says.

"Yeah," Fat John says, "*yeah*."

We just stand there for a minute, counting the cans. There's forty-seven cans of spray paint in that bag, and the only time most people have ever seen that many before is in the store. I got Krylons mostly, in silver and black, to keep it Raiders style. Got thirty of those. The rest are all mini Testor cans in red, blue, and white.

I been stocking up to go out with a bang. It's obvious.

"Well, shit," Tortuga says, "now I know what you been doing while everybody else was keeping his head down. Straight up racking cans."

Stealing cans is exactly what I was doing. I hit up Ace Hardware and put everything I could get my hands on in a backpack and ran. Up until now, Fat John and Tortuga didn't even know I had any.

I'm not stupid enough to ever show these paint fiends this much paint at one time. Sure, we're friends, but they'd fuck me over. They'd get drunk and break a window if either one was thin enough to squeeze through the opening and gaffle the whole bag. This is also why I won't be telling them that I need to be getting the hell out of Dodge too, cuz the less people that know, the better.

"I got tips, too," I say and pull a little baggie out, one full of yellow and blue and purple glass cleaner tips that you can switch onto spray paint canisters to make the paint spray out with different techniques and styles.

One's a Windex tip I stuffed a bunch of needles in, and when you use it, paint flares out real good. I pick that one out and put it in my pocket. They can't have that one. It's special. Took me forever to figure out how to fuck with it just right.

Fat John sells weed sometimes. I know he's got cash on him.

"A buck a can," I say. "I'll throw in a few tips for free."

They both look at me like I'm crazy, but then Tortuga asks if I got mean streaks and I say no, just spray paint. He nods at that, like, okay, and then he starts doing mental math so I let him.

I pick out the cans I want first. Ten of them in Ernesto's favorite colors: black and silver. After that, we cut up the rest real quick. Fat John takes twenty and Tortuga snags the rest. Fat John has to spot Tortuga, but only when Tortuga promises to hit him off with the money next week, along with some cakes and things from his mom's *panadería* when she opens it up this next week, which sounds like a fair deal.

I pocket the $37 and add it to my stake from El Unico, which takes me up to $328, all told. Now the business is settled, Fat John asks what's gonna happen to our crew with the merger into Big Fate's click happening. He's worried too.

The three of us are part of a click that's part of a bigger crew. A crew that started up way far away from here and feels even farther than that now. Tagbangers or not, they can't protect us from getting absorbed into a gang. To be honest, I don't know how the soldiers rolling up on Big Fate changes this situation. It might, but then again it might not, and I don't think I want to hang around to find out.

"Do it or don't do it," I say. "That's really all the choice there is now."

"Like," Tortuga says, "can't we call the main heads though?"

I say, "They're not answering pages cuz they're putting in work up in Northeast, but I don't even think that matters now. We live in Lynwood. They don't."

"True," Fat John says, "that's true."

Tortuga says, "So shit's on hold until we drop crew and go in with their neighborhood?"

"Pretty much," I say.

"And you're sure," Fat John says, "that you don't wanna join up? Even with that being your dad's old neighborhood and everything?"

"Hey," I say, "I'm not gonna do this forever, but right now this is what I'm about. And why do you think I do graffiti anyways? I don't like people telling me what to do. What, I'm gonna join Big Fate's click and have a bunch of new motherfuckers telling me what to do and how to live?"

"What's a matter," Tortuga says, "you don't want to end up like your old man, locked up twenty-three hours a day and fucking a fifi?"

I don't hit back verbally. I give Tortuga a real good glare, like, *all right, motherfucker, that's your free one.* As far as a fifi goes, I really don't think you want to know. When I found out, I wished I didn't.

So I change the subject. I tell them that everybody knows me as a bomber. But I want to do pieces too, like illegal though.

They nod at that like I'm preaching, but then Tortuga says, "How're you going to do that with the green lights on?"

"I got a plan," I say.

"What plan?"

"I'll tell you later," I say. "For now, I gotta go see my cousin."

"Sure you do," Fat John says and grabs his dick.

I punch him in his stomach, playfully but hard, you know? So he knows he can't insinuate shit around me anymore without some kinda payback. Tortuga laughs and we all say good-bye. When they're gone, I wait for a good five minutes and check the garage door windows to make sure they're not hanging around or nothing, snooping to see if I got more paint and I'm just hiding it.

I don't, by the way. But they'd think it.

After that, I throw the ten cans for Ernesto in my backpack and I pull something else out of the bag, something they didn't see.

It's my throwaway gun, a black .22 pistol cuz you can never be too careful. When I got it down good and firm in the back of my waistband, I pull my shirt out over it, do my belt up, and go inside to surprise Gloria.

5

Gloria's on the phone when I get in, twisting the cord all around her finger like it's a ribbon or something. She jumps when I shut the back door and gives me a look like I just stepped on the back of her dress or something.

The phone's mounted on the wall in the living room and she

takes a step forward and tries to shoo me out of the kitchen, but the cord's not long enough so she gets jerked back and comes up looking really mad, especially when I smile wide at her and go in the fridge for whatever's in there.

I see cheese pizza wrapped up in plastic cuz Cousin Gloria is boring and doesn't like toppings on her pizza, and I see some Chinese food in its little white containers and then I see something worth seeing. There's some *tamales* left over from what her mom made for Christmas.

Gloria must've unthawed them from the freezer the other night but couldn't finish them cuz they're sitting where the eggs usually are. I pick one out and pray it's a sweet corn, *queso*, and *jalapeño* one, but when I sink my teeth in, I find it's the boring pork.

Gloria waves her hand at me kinda frantically to get out and looks disappointed when I don't. Instead, I finish the whole *tamale* in two bites without using a plate. She glares at me then, and after that, her voice gets real quiet on the phone and she whispers to the person on the other end that she's really sorry but she has to go, and she'll see them soon, and then she hangs up and comes at me with a hand in the air.

She swings and misses and I make the mistake of laughing cuz that's when she gets me square on the cheek. She gets me good too. Like, *bam*. I see a couple quick stars, and as I'm rubbing my jaw where it's still stinging, I say, "Hey, that's not nice. That's not lady-like behavior, you know?"

She picks up a mug, sips, and says, "I don't care. You weren't invited."

"I'm family," I say and shrug. "Like, what would your mom even say if I told her you hit me?"

"She'd say you deserved it probably."

"My aunt would never say that."

"Yes," Gloria says, "she *would*."

We glare at each other a little before I ask her if she's got any money I can have.

"I don't have any cash," she says.

"Sure you do," I say, "you were saving up for the TV and everything."

She puts her head down and says, "That money's gone, Jermy."

She calls me Jermy when she's serious, so I back off a little. She wets a cloth and dabs at the floor where I was eating the *tamale* and must've spilled. After she tosses it in the sink, she tells me she had to spend all that money on something, but she won't tell me what. She tells me I'll understand someday.

After that, she gives me $10, but she says that's all she has cuz she and her coworkers won a scratchers pool at work. I seen her go in her purse and everything, so I can tell she's not lying. Ten bucks really was all she had. That's me at $338 then, which should just about be enough to get me to Phoenix and started up, I think. I hope so anyways.

After she hands me the ten, she says, "All right, have you seen Aurelio or what?"

Her little brother's older than me by two years, but I haven't called him Aurelio since we were kids. Sleepy, sure. Sleeps. Sleep Machine. Sleepertón, I call him sometimes. But not Aurelio. Never that.

"Haven't seen Sleepy and haven't heard about him. Why? You think he's out fucking up or something?"

She shrugs, which means yeah, not only does she think that, but she worries about it. *Constantly.*

I decide to change the subject so I don't got to hear about it for twenty minutes.

"Where's Lydia at? Where's the little man?"

"Together," Gloria says. "She took Mateo to the Chuck-e-Cheese to give me a break."

"Hey," I say, changing the subject again, "can I borrow your car?"

She gives me a good long look over her white tea mug that she must've been sipping on while she was on the phone. It says GILROY: GARLIC CAPITAL OF THE WORLD on it. It has a little drawing of a garlic head on it too. It's done all up in a green outline.

"For what?"

"A thing," I say.

"So, to do that graffiti nonsense you do."

"No," I say, and I think I play it pretty cool, pretty genuine, but yes, to do graffiti.

Obviously, yes.

"Sorry, *primo*," she says. "I can't. I got a date."

She hasn't had a date in as long as I can remember, so I say, "With who? Is it that Cookie Monster dude?"

I'm playing, obviously, cuz Cookie Monster's from the neighborhood and he's three hundred pounds give or take a couple burgers, but she throws a banana at me from the fruit bowl on the counter, and when I duck it, it hits the door to the garage and then falls to the floor.

As I pick it up and put it back, I bug her to tell me who she's got a date with, and I keep that up for like three whole minutes, but she's real serious all of a sudden and won't tell me. She just kinda smiles to herself and twists her hair like she was twisting that phone cord.

Finally, she cuts me off with "I got to take a shower. You better not be here when I get out."

I nod, cuz I can do that, and when she leaves the room, I go in her purse and fish them car keys out, the ones with a little Mother Teresa charm on the ring. I feel bad taking her ride, but not that bad. She'll understand when I'm safe in Phoenix and I tell her all about how I did it cuz I didn't want to be a gangster. She'll be glad. Maybe not today. But someday. I know she will. She loves me. She wants me to be safe.

6

I'm not a total asshole. I am a little, but not all the way. I do take Mateo's car seat out of the back first and I set it on the floor, not even in an oil stain or anything. After that, I roll the garage door up as quiet as I can, put the car in neutral, push it out, shut the garage door, lock it, put the key back in its hole with the rock, then start the car up and get rolling. I need to get to my aunt's place and pack up quick before Gloria finds out I took the car and calls her mom and they both freak out on me. It's a little complicated.

I live with Gloria's mom and dad and her bro, Sleepy, but her dad's only home about eight days a month cuz he's a truck driver and Sleepy's never around, so it's usually just me and my aunt Izel. She and Gloria don't really get along too good cuz Gloria's not married and had a drug dealer's kid in sin and right now she and my little kindergartner second cousin are living with Lydia in the house their grandmom left to them. I'm with Aunt Izel now cuz my mom is back in Mexico. She left me in California cuz she thought I had a better shot at being something here than there. My aunt in Phoenix, the one I told you about? That's my mom's sister. So, anyways, like I said, *complicated*.

Soon as I turn the ignition on, some musical jumps out of the speakers, and even worse, I know what it is cuz Gloria made me listen to it before, that song "America" from *West Side Story*. She says it's all smart and well written and I should learn to appreciate it, especially coming from where I come from, but I think it's fucking gay.

I eject the tape and throw that shit in the back where Mateo's car seat used to be. I'm trying not to get it lost somewhere in the pile of clothes she's got back there. This thing is a closet on wheels. She's got like three different coats piled up on each other, a few pairs of shoes, all of them white and clunky, arch-support specials.

I shove my mix in the deck. Tex Ritter's "High Noon" from the Gary Cooper movie gets near its end and stops abruptly cuz I fucked up the mix and cut the tape before the song faded out, but it had to be done.

I only get thirty minutes a side on these cassettes I got at the swap meet, and besides, I wanted "Hurry Sundown" in there, a song that makes a lot more sense to me on today of all days. It's about having a bad fucking day and wanting it to end quick, so you want nighttime to hurry up and come. That's some Hugo Montenegro music, totally underrated. It starts out eerie with a guitar and humming and then turns into a duet, and that rolls up like a wave and breaks at the end with a full-on chorale. It's almost like a spiritual. Well, I think it is, anyways.

I decide to take Wright Road to the 105 so I can scout if there's any way I can paint the underpass if it hasn't been totally done over by now.

The first time I ever fell in love with tagbanging was standing on Rosecrans facing the 710 Freeway when everything in my field of vision was bombed with black spray paint. I'm talking the curb in front of me, the sidewalk, almost every inch of the wall thirty feet high, the fucking palm tree next to it. Man, it looked like a ninja army did it. That day changed how I see the world. It made it so I don't see concrete so much anymore. I don't really see walls, or even buildings. I see opportunities, you know? A place to put my mark. I see big, permanent canvases just waiting to be hit . . .

Hang on, there's some sheriffs and fire trucks up ahead of me and it looks like they're detouring people onto Fernwood. At first, I can't see why cuz there's a big, tall Jeep the color of brown puke up in front of me with a flat spare tire still stuck to its back gate, but as it turns onto Fernwood, I see why we can't go through.

There's what looks like a big city truck under the freeway and it's completely burnt out, and so is the concrete under there too. Right as I'm about to turn, two firemen release the back gate and it falls. Ash goes everywhere in this big black cloud as the singing on "Hurry Sundown" fades out and something new starts up, one of the real weird songs on this mix.

It's an old *Sesame Street* track, "Be Kind to Your Neighborhood Monster," from a totally genius and totally ignored album called *We Are All Earthlings*, and I'm always kinda stuck between shivering and laughing when I hear this song cuz I guess that stuff means something a lot different to me living where I live. I mean, I don't picture hairy purple monsters when I hear it, put it that way. I picture *cholo* dudes with tattoos, shaved heads, pulled-up socks, and a long perfect crease in their khaki shorts.

It's my turn to turn right and I can almost see into the truck as this sheriff in his brown uniform and hat is trying to wave me through, and he looks back at what I'm looking at and freezes for a sec like he can't believe it either, and then when he turns back to me, he waves me on faster. I blink, cuz I can't believe what I'm seeing.

Behind me, somebody honks.

"Holy shit," I say to nobody at all, trying to make out the black shapes on top of each other. "Are those fucking burnt-up *bodies* in there?"

The *tamale* in my stomach tells me it's in danger of pressing the eject button, so I gulp, look away, and speed the hell up.

I might be completely wrong, but if Fate's click did this, it makes a ton more sense now about the Goon Squad rolling up and kicking doors in. A ton more.

I'm in a haze, more focused on what I saw than what I'm seeing now. I mean, I think I saw an AK-47 sticking out of there. And so much ash . . .

Fernwood becomes Atlantic, becomes Olanda, and I'm passing Wright again on Olanda, when I kinda click back in and stop in front of my aunt Izel's place.

I go in the back door, real grateful it's not a restaurant day. Sometimes, my aunt runs a little restaurant out of here and I help out. She's from Tlaxiaco in Oaxaca, where they do some real traditional Aztec dishes. A couple days a week, we put tables on the back lawn and she cooks for people that come up. She bakes chicken thighs in yellow *molé* that she cooks in a clay pot for like two days first. She does tortillas from scratch. Around here, she's famous for her *lentejas oaxaqueñas* though. It's two bucks for a bowl of little lentils and pineapple and plantains and tomatoes and spices.

Anyways, today is her normal prep day, and some neighborhood markets finally opened back up this morning, so she's out buying ingredients, which is good for me cuz I'm in and out like a thief.

I'm snagging my toothbrush and paste, my aerosol Right Guard, my Santa Fe cologne, before grabbing my vandal kit, a little *G.I.*

Joe logo pencil bag I've had forever. I stay maybe two minutes after that, throwing my T-shirts and jeans and sweatshirts and socks and underwear and my favorite Reeboks in a little round-ended duffel. I take both black books with my sketches and that's it. They got my other aunt's letters and her address in Phoenix for bookmarks. From the kitchen, I take peanut butter and all that's left of a loaf of bread, maybe five pieces. I'm back to the car and pulling it out before anyone even knows I'm there.

My only thought is to cruise by a few layup spots and hope I get lucky.

7

Did you know that San Francisco is only seven square miles? I didn't. When Fat John told me that last month, it kinda blew my mind. Cuz L.A., she's endless. There's beaches, hills, tar pits, mountains, Downtown, desert, and a big old concrete river. We go on and on. We're our own fucking country. I feel that now more than ever.

I'm cruising Lynwood, looking for layup spots. I check one I know of on Atlantic on the other side of the 105. There's nothing though.

I keep my eyes peeled for parked buses. They're almost always a small street off a main one, like, a few layers back from a boulevard, maybe in an industrial area or a cul-de-sac, with a shoulder big enough to park a bus cuz sometimes RTD just sets buses aside for whatever reason, like, they might be having mechanical problems, or some dude got sick or was late for a shift and wasn't able to come in and take over so they just got to park it till somebody can pick it up and drive it back to the yard, or maybe there was a big fucking riot that lasted days and service was disrupted and shit went unaccounted for. Buses are like the holy grail of graffiti right now cuz it's a prime way to send your name all over the city and show everybody what you're about.

All my life people have said graffiti is a menace. They say it's completely useless. I get the menace part, cuz it is. But it's not useless. For me, it's like a video game. It's taught me how to use maps, how to navigate. It's taught me about politics. What gang is where, who owns what. Places you can go. Places you better not. It's taught me to watch my back. It's taught me how to be bold. When I started, I was just a toy that didn't know shit, I was gun-shy, but over time you get good if you keep going, and you learn, and you adapt fast. It made me FREER. Well, that and Ernesto did.

I got that shot-up house of his in my head again. I kinda can't believe he lived with those people, with Big Fate, in the same house, under the same roof, without being involved. It hits me now how bad he must have wanted to get out and that shit makes me sad. Ever since we hit up that sushi spot with the railroad tracks all out in front of it, he wouldn't shut up about it. He had plans, that guy. *All* kinds of plans. It was inspiring, you know? Made me dream too. Made me want to be more than I was. Made me want to be FREER. So I put in work. And now I am.

Every insane vandal needs a kit. In my passenger seat, I got my backpack with my pencil case in it that's got six mean streaks, some sandpaper squares, and two scribers, and also there's the spray paint I grabbed, Krylons and Testors. Sandpaper is only for big scribes, and spray paint is self-explanatory, but mean streaks are *the* L.A. marker. You can write on anything with them, cars, glass, metal, *anything.* It's solid paint. You twist at the bottom when it runs down at the top. In fact, you can even twist them all the way out, cut them vertically, and blend colors together. Lately, I been getting psyche-delic, so I cut my streaks three ways to combine yellow, white, and blue. Scribers are drill bits that look like arrowheads with their sides filed off, perfect for carving over anything, especially glass.

I check another layup, and again there's nothing and I'm start-ing to get discouraged, like I won't have anything to pay tribute to Ernesto with and I got to start making a list of walls in my head if I come up empty one more time.

Dammit, I want to hit a bus so bad though. That's status. They're the daredevil shit right now cuz there's a million ways to get caught. It's nonstop cat and mouse, all adrenaline. Drivers are always looking out for you. Undercovers have always got their running shoes on and their little fanny packs for their badges and cop shit.

Sometimes whole crews take buses over and try to tag the entire interior, even the ceiling, and I heard once about how an undercover tried to lock a bus down so, like, the hundred dudes inside it had to bust out the emergency exits and run not to get caught. Like I said, it's the Wild West out here. I'm telling you.

I hit the third layup spot, right behind Tom's Burgers on Norton, by Imperial and MLK, and I'm driving by thinking, *fuck, another wasted layup,* when the sun bounces off a windshield and almost blinds me. I turn Gloria's car real fast, completely by instinct, and pull faceup to a perfect bus, and I mean *perfect.*

Maybe it got left here only minutes ago, maybe yesterday. Who knows and who cares? It's in front of me and it's pure. Unbelievably, not a single motherfucker has tagged on it. I'm the first. *I* get to take its virginity.

It's hard to explain, but I feel so lucky that I'm actually paranoid, like, is this a setup or what? Are cops staking this shit out? Trying to catch writers? I guess they got bigger things to worry about.

But then I figure if it is a setup, fuck it. I have to at least try. This bus can be my legacy. If I hit this right, heads will talk about it for years. *Years.*

I don't even really remember parking in the closed-up bank's parking lot across the street, but I did cuz I'm here and the car is off. I unzip my backpack and go digging in my pencil case as I step out of the car. I'm so excited right now that my mouth's drying up and I'm babbling to myself when I pull my headphones up and on.

8

Feeling like I'm buzzing down to my toes, I go straight for the front of the bus. I hit play on my Walkman. That's when Wagner and his

Valkyries ride straight into my ears. Just hearing them strings starts me getting hyper. Getting all into it.

I'm so excited I'm shaking, so I take a quick deep breath and try to calm down enough so my hand doesn't twitch. When I let it out, I'm good.

Still though, a virgin bus all to myself? A virgin GMC bus with the tinted side windows I'm about to hit with a streak I just cut last night?

My God, dude.

I feel like I died, went to heaven, strolled through them pearly gates and Marilyn Monroe just begged me to sex her.

My heart's still going crazy wild fast in my chest, smacking on my ribs, as I hit a destination on the front windshield. Fucking brand-new streak, dude. I uncap it and it smells like Windex, perfectly like Windex.

Tagging the windshield's called a destination cuz that's where the name of the destination is on the bus, at the top, above the driver's head. But that's blacked out right now cuz the bus isn't on. But right then I decide to scribe first instead.

I pull out my scriber and catch a big one right where the driver's face would be, going F.R.E.E.R! with all kinds of punctuation and everything as I dig the glass out, but here's the crazy shit: I do it *backward*. That way, everybody in the bus will see it as they're going, and people in front of the bus looking in their rearviews will see it too!

I wait for a sec when I'm done hitting it. If there's gonna be sirens, if cops are gonna swoop up, it's gonna be right now. I wait ten seconds, and I wait ten more, and then it's shopping spree time. Time to go crazy.

I take my mean streak I did up with white, yellow, and blue, then stand on the front bumper and go as fucking big as I can. I go top to bottom, taking the whole glass, going F R E on the left side, and then skipping the little black bar that splits the windshield in two, and then I go E-R.

I spend an extra few seconds making sure every one of my angles is tight. I fix up the last *R* and make it so sharp the legs could cut somebody. After that, I put *x*'s on the right legs of my *R*'s, like in a pharmacy, cuz my style is like medicine.

Under all that, I tag my crew name.

I never had this much time before. *Ever.*

Anytime before this when I hit a destination, it was just a little one on the left outside, and I hit those when Fat John's running interference, arguing with the driver about transfers and I'm leaning and scribbling it all unperfect. But this? This is a masterpiece, dammit! This is what FREER's all about.

I hit two big outsides on the left side of the bus, one letter per tinted-out window. I do some throw-up letters with crisp, right-angle outlines like some high school letterman jacket shit, and on the entrance-and-exit side doors I do some vertical handwriting styles where I loop like fucking crazy and I might as well be twirling spaghetti with my streak. I'm so into it that it's not until I'm done with the front entrance door that I notice the driver left his fucking RTD jacket, which, trust me, is a huge fucking score in the graffiti community. He must've left so quick he forgot it.

I don't know how long it takes me to kick the bottom glass out of the door, but when it's all the way broken, I wriggle in and grab the jacket. I shrug it on and it's one size too small but I don't even care. I keep it on cuz it's like wearing the pelt of a bear I killed. That's how much rep it's worth. As I'm tripping on that, I realize doing a scribe on the inside would be insane, so I knock *another* one out on the windshield right next to where the ticket machine is, so everybody will have to see it every time they ride, and then I duck back out.

The right side of the bus I hit fast in a big one-liner, which means I just hit the tip of my spray paint and spray in one long line, not picking up as I transition from letter to letter with my silver Krylon. I kinda cheat though cuz I never done it before, and the whole thing ends a bit before the last wheel well, so I go back and put a few loops and arrows to make it look like it's flying and everything.

If I had more time, I'd make it a whole piece, but it's not safe just sitting out here. Every second that's passing is about to give me a heart attack. I feel like cops could roll up at any time cuz this still stinks like a setup. But I can't help myself. I saved the best for last.

On the back of the bus, the part that's facing the street, I get up on the bumper and I lay down a sketch of my letters in silver and fill in like a motherfucker. I keep it real blocky, like it's a big silver mirror on the black back of the bus that looks like blinds, and you've got to shoot up underneath them to make it look solid all around.

On top of my silver fills, I do thick black outlines on the letters, writing E-R-N-I-E. It pops so hard that you can prolly see the black outlined letters with shining silver middles from two football fields away if you've got an angle on it. I even spray little cracks and crevices over the top of the letters so it looks like they're rocks kinda. In the bottom leg of the last *E* in Ernie's name, I do an R.I.P. in black. After that, I stash everything back in my bag and grab my disposable camera out.

I start snapping pictures from all angles. Front. Side. Back. Other side. Low. From far away. Up close. And it's when I'm up close that I feel eyes on me and turn around.

About thirty feet back, there's a little kid watching me from a bank parking lot.

I take my headphones off and turn his way.

9

He's twelve, maybe thirteen. He's got dark eyebrows though, and big, dull-looking eyes. His hair's all slicked back and he's dressed like a little gee, but he's breathing with his mouth open. He's a mouth breather.

I give him a look that he doesn't respond to, so I say, "You want to hit this up?"

I mean the bus. But he doesn't move. He just keeps staring at me so I tell him to come over and he does. The kid's right next to me when he looks at my ERNIE piece and says, "What is it?"

"It's a tribute piece," I say.

"Who for?"

I look at it, and then I look at the kid, and I'm thinking, *Is he this stupid?* But he's squinting so I just figure, fuck it, might as well state the obvious.

"A guy I knew named Ernie," I say. "He passed away a couple days ago."

The kid nods at that and doesn't follow up with anything, so I say, "You not interested in graffing at all?"

"Naw, not really," the kid says. "I seen the gun in your belt while you worked though. I'm interested in that. How much?"

"I dunno," I say as I measure the kid up and pull a number out that I figure he can't afford, "a hundred bucks?"

"I got fifty," he says, and I watch him pull a fifty-dollar bill off a wad that has a few more on it.

"That's cool," I say, like, *no thanks.* "What, are you slanging for somebody or something? Where'd you get that wad anyways?"

He doesn't say yes and he doesn't say no. He just holds his hand out with a hundred in it this time.

"Take it before I change my mind," he says.

I give him a look, like, *Who you trying to mess with, little man?*

But I figure, you know what? Fuck it. I trade him the gun for the cash and pocket it. The kid looks at the pistol. He turns it over in his hands before taking it with his left, pointing at me, and cocking the hammer back.

My smile drops off my face, not cuz I'm scared, but mainly cuz I can't believe this little banger just tried to pull that on me.

"Give me the hundred back and everything else you got," he says. "Now."

I'm up to $438. If this little dude thinks he's getting his hundred back, he's stupider than he looks, and that's pretty damn stupid.

I say, "You know that shit isn't loaded, right?"

He eyes me like he thinks I'm trying to trick him.

"Check it," I say. "I'll wait."

I take a step back so he can feel safe to check without me taking it away from him. He pulls the cylinder out, and I see him put it right up to his face. I see his brown eye in all its dullness through one of the empty holes. He blinks.

"Make sure you buy twenty-two-caliber bullets for it," I say. "That's the only size it takes. I'd say hit up the Gun Store and go in the quarter bin for the littler ones, but I heard that place burned down."

"Yeah, it did," he says. "So twenty-two caliber?"

"Yup," I say.

"Okay," he says.

Out in the distance, I hear a helicopter humming.

I say to the kid, "You got named yet or what?"

He looks around. "Maybe," he says.

I'm guessing that means no, and I'm about to hit him with one to think about when this woman comes stomping around the corner of the little medical center across the street. Wearing a short-ass skirt and heels that have been worn down from too much walking, she's got black hair and she's older than me, looking midtwenties and torn up. Even from a distance I can see sores on her mouth and a black eye.

"Hey," she says to the back of his head and he doesn't even turn, "we going or what?"

I'm not trying to be rude, but I say the first thing that comes to mind, "That your mom?"

"Fool, you better shut the fuck up," he says with a snarl. "That's my *fresa*, homes. That bitch sucks my dick."

Jesus, I fucking hope not, not with all them sores. But I got nothing to lose, so I say, "Man, shut the fuck up. You're so young, you can't even get a fucking hard-on."

He grabs his belt and says, "*Whatever*, homes."

His *fresa* says something too. "Yeah, he can. And it's *good* too."

Fresa means strawberry, slang for the type of woman who trades sex for drugs, usually crack or coke. Man, I'm so grossed out by all this I can't do anything but half smile at this kid, mainly just for the size of his bravado. This little motherfucker *is* a dealer, and maybe a pimp too. That's where that money came from, the money in my pocket right now. She earned it the hard way.

"I'm gonna call you Watcher," I say to him, "cuz you been watching. Keep it if you want. Throw it out if you don't."

He looks like he's about to talk shit, but he just licks his lips, nods his head back, and points his chin at me instead.

"Watcher," he says, like he's trying the name on for size.

"Yeah," I say, "it's a good one. You take care."

I turn and head out.

As I'm going I hear his *fresa* asking his permission to go get a peanut butter shake at Tom's Burgers. He's starting a sentence with "Bitch, shut the fuck up . . ." when I'm getting in the car and peeling the fuck out.

The kid watches me go like he's trying to memorize my face, like he thought I just got over on him with the gun sale and with what I said, and he's never gonna forget it. I kinda laugh then, cuz, man, I really don't need this shit.

L.A. has gone fucking crazy. All the way crazy.

When I'm back on the street and going, far enough away that no cop can connect me up to the bus, I breathe and think about my day, how my plan didn't really go like I thought, how I should prolly just take this here money and run. It has sense to it.

I think every guy that ever did anything on the street, even if he did a lot, there's always a gap between how much he wanted to do and how much he actually *did*, and I'm feeling that right now, feeling like a failure, even though I just made a whole bus my own personal graffiti playground. That shit is going to be legend when people see it. And people will ask about Ernie. They'll wonder who he was. And for a moment, he'll be alive in their minds. But I'll be gone.

People will talk about me for a while after this. I'm sure Fat John and Tortuga will see it, but I still decide to make prints and copies of the photographs and mail them back to them. I think about the bus a bit then, how crazy that luck was.

Maybe it's a good good-bye, but maybe it's not a big enough ending, not over-the-top enough. People will prolly say I ranked out, but whatever. I never signed up for that other thing, that gangster thing. I always just wanted to be free. I just wanted to go all-city, hitting Hollywood and Downtown and Venice and writing ©'s under my name everywhere I go, like OILER and DCLINE, cuz it's my golden time with just turning seventeen.

I figured I had a year of hitting it hard, and if I got caught, how much time could I ever do on a graffiti charge? I mean, prolly I'd get a couple hundred hours community service and a few weekends of JAWS, that's Juvenile Alternative Work Services, and at worst I'd do a little bit of juvie, but no county time, nothing serious, nothing on my permanent record. This was my time to take it all the way and be famous and now it's gone, just like Ernesto.

Something people don't understand about graffiti is it's a way to be somebody, it's a way to piss people off, and it's a way to claim your territory, but it's *also* a way to remember. And I did that last one for Ernesto and the city that killed him. ERNIE R.I.P. the back of that bus says. It's letters, sure, but it means something more.

It's a middle finger and a headstone all rolled into one.

10

After I get my one-way ticket to Phoenix for $49 on special at the Long Beach Greyhound bus station, I call Gloria and tell her where she can pick her car up. Surprise, surprise, she's not happy *at all*. She tells me she's gonna kill me, and I'm cool with that cuz it's definitely not the killing the monsters in my neighborhood would do if they saw me again and I said I didn't want to join up.

Gloria says, "You made me call my *mother* looking for you, Jermy. I swear—"

I got to cut her off.

"I had to, Gloria," I say. "I'm sorry. Really, I am. I didn't mean to ruin anything for your date, but someday I'll tell you why and you'll totally get it."

She's legit mad. I can hear it in her voice when she says, "You better tell me why right now."

"I'll call you," I say, "when I'm safe where I'm going."

She says, "Where's that?"

"It's better you don't know," I say, "cuz at some point, someone will ask you if you know, and I don't want to lie to you, and I don't want you to have to lie to them."

I hear a long breath hit the microphone on the other end, sounds like *krrrgh*.

"Okay," she finally says.

In the background, I hear tapping and then Gloria gets real quiet as I hear her walk to the door in her slippers and then it gets even quieter so she must be looking out the peephole. Her breath catches up in her throat then and I know something's wrong.

I say, "What?"

"Uh," she says, "I gotta go."

"What is it?"

"It's not what, it's *who*," she says. "Ernesto's little sister's outside my door."

I hear the knocking again, much closer this time. At first I'm wondering if she's there for me, but that doesn't make any kind of sense.

"Hang on, Jermy," Gloria says, and I hear clothes getting pressed to the microphone like she put the receiver on her stomach or something.

Real faint, I hear door latches undo and then the door opening with a little creak.

"Hey," Lupe says, "you said you were a nurse, right?"

My cousin must nod, cuz a second later Lupe says, "You know how to make splints for broken bones?"

Again, my cousin must nod, cuz Lupe says, "What stuff do you need for it?"

My mind's kinda racing and I'm wondering what went down, but my first clear thought is *The Goon Squad must've been up to some shit.*

I don't get a chance to say anything else though, cuz Gloria says, "I gotta go," real quick and then it's a dial tone in my ear.

I say, "Bye," to it anyways.

I'm a little sad when I put it back up on the cradle. I have to get out of the way though cuz a black dude behind me needs the phone. He looks like how Martin Luther King Junior would look if he got old and fat.

It's depressing me that there's nothing in Phoenix. No fun, no people, no nothing. Just my aunt and another restaurant job prolly but then it hits me.

There's freedom in Arizona, more than I ever dreamed of.

Out there, I bet nobody gets checked just walking down the street, like, *Hey, this fool looks like he writes and I don't see any tattoos, so hit him up.* I don't have to worry about the gangs out there or the turf, or that people think I'm ranking out, that I'm not living up. And I feel that badger in my stomach calm down a little.

Over the loudspeaker, they call my bus and I go out in the parking lot and give the driver my duffel and he puts it underneath in the compartment that folds up like a DeLorean door in all them *Back to the Future* movies. It even makes that noise when it opens too. Like, *shimp.* I keep my backpack with me when I get up in the bus and sit in the middle. It smells like stale bread in here and dog hair. I start flipping through my latest black book.

I never been, but as far as graffiti is concerned, Phoenix must be like some little kid shit . . .

Hold up, though.

Maybe that's not a bad thing. *Maybe* that means I got possibilities now, and FREER isn't so much dying as evolving into something entirely new and strong.

I mean, I could bring a whole new advanced style out there. I could be the *first*. I'm starting to like that. I mean, like it a lot. I could open up a whole franchise of L.A. style out there. I could be that thing from science class, whatdoyoucallit? A catalyst. Yes. I could be that for the Phoenix scene, pump it up a few notches. And besides, what's FREER than leaving whenever the fuck I want to?

Nothing, that's what.

On the bus, it looks like I'm not the only one getting out. There's lots of Mexicans and Central *Americanos* on here. They've got their kids with them, too. I don't blame them. Shit, if I had kids, I'd have them on the bus out too. It's pretty easy not to want to be in L.A. right about now with all the looting and the shooting.

Fuck, I know I won't miss twelve-year-old little dealer-pimps buying my throwaway from me and then trying to rob me for the money right back.

I won't miss Big Fate giving me ultimatums.

I won't miss getting rolled up on the block by the fucking Goon Squad, getting machine guns stuck in my face.

L.A.'s fucking crazy, man. But I will miss her.

Who knows though? Maybe I'm getting out at the right time. Like, before it all goes boom and slides into the ocean.

I push play on my Walkman, but it doesn't want to go in. It's fussy sometimes. The button's black and as big as my thumb tip. I press it and hold it in a bit before the heads eventually get turning and the music starts up.

Some strings come in as the driver pulls us out, and out the windshield, the sun is setting and it's magical how we pull onto Pacific Coast Highway from Long Beach Boulevard as Nancy Sinatra's voice comes in with the orange light of dusk and sings at me, telling me I only live twice. That cools me out pretty good, so I just sit and watch the buildings passing by out the window as we pull through the city, over what there is of the L.A. River, and down onto the 710 North.

After a little bit, we pass Lynwood and I watch it go and I don't feel bad. I feel like it's a box for everything bothering me, everything heavy, and it all stays there, stays behind, and leaves me light as a feather, free to float somewhere new.

Free to go wherever.

Free to be whatever I want.

JOSESITO SERRATO,
A.K.A. WATCHER

MAY 3, 1992

8:17 P.M.

1

I got this gun and it makes me real now. Makes me ready to do work. I feel good. Everybody knows how dead Momo is. Everybody heard he was laying up in that truck the pigs found on Wright Road. What was left of him anyways. I say serves that motherfucker right for going at Big Fate. Be big or be dead. I want to go to Big Fate and be down with him and his click. So I walk over to that Mini Vegas nobody ever shuts up about and knock on the door and wait to be let in. They let me in and search me and find the gun and hang on to it. That nurse lady is there. She looks at me funny cuz she recognizes me from that night when the brother of Miss Payasa died up in the alley. Miss Payasa is there too. Next to the nurse lady. Miss Payasa tells her she better go and she thanks her for everything. Miss Payasa puts money in the hands of the nurse lady. Some folded hundreds. I eyeball it for a grand. That nurse lady gives me a look like she wants to take me with her. Like maybe she was fixing to save me or something. But Miss Payasa pushes her outside and the door closes in the face of the nurse lady just as she says that everybody she helped out needs the hospital soon. Big Fate has his arm up in one of them giant sling things across the room. Same with a grip of other fools. That Sherlock Homeboy has a bump on his head like a baseball and he has an ice pack on it. Next to him is some fine Chink bitch with her wrist all wrapped up mummy style. One look and I could tell she was the kind some hypes would pay good money to fuck. I keep that to myself though. Especially cuz I see that Apache motherfucker that scalps people looks fucked up too. He plays a gambling machine with his good hand and it spins and makes noise while he sits in the corner drinking something gold in a big glass bottle. Big Fate sees me looking everywhere at wounds and casts and shit. He calls me over so he can shrug his shoulders and say the beat and release program is still going strong in the city of Los Angeles. He calls me lil homie and says they can knock us down but we always come back and come back stronger. He says *la neta*. So I say *la neta*. Cuz it *is* the truth. Nothing but. They are still here. Every one of them. They took a beating and they keep going. Not like Momo. Not like Trouble. Not like none of them fools. This click is nothing but straight-up killers. Survivors. Tough as fuck. Not even fucking sheriffs can win against them. Out of nowhere Big Fate asks me what I go by cuz he wants to know. I used to have a name I hated that everybody called me. Baby. But I got a new one now. I puff up and tell him I got the name Watcher but I make sure not to tell him where from. He nods at me like I did something good. He says he likes that name. So I say the name of the click then. I say it all proud. Also I say Lynwood *controla*. Cuz obviously they control Lynwood and nobody else. He looks at me funny after that and says he been asking around about me since I helped out. He heard I was slanging for Momo. And I answer that right away. Like yeah. I *was*. And he laughs at that. He asks if maybe I might be ready for something new. I tell him hells yeah cuz I got nothing but respect for how he did what he had to do. *So you ready to be down or something?* Big Fate is asking me. Fuck yes. I say that twice and nod the whole time through it. *¡La clica es mi vida!* Till I fucking die. I say that too. He waits for a little bit. The room gets real quiet. So I remind him how I came straight up and told him about the brother of Miss Payasa. He says I did good on that. And right after that he says to jump this little motherfucker in then. Fuck yeah. That shit makes me so happy that I just close my eyes before the first punch comes. Or the first kick. Whatever. I could give a fuck what it is or where from. It will hurt. It will hurt bad. But it will be worth it. All of it is worth it to be down.

DAY 6
MONDAY

THERE WERE FIFTY-TWO DEATHS.

WE WERE LOOKING SERIOUSLY AT SIXTY AND AGAIN THERE WASN'T A *WHOLE* LOT OF INFORMATION.

JUST BECAUSE SOMEBODY DIED DURING THE TIME FRAME DOESN'T MEAN IT WAS DIRECTLY RELATED *TO* THE RIOT . . .

WHICH BROUGHT UP AN INTERESTING POINT.

ARE ALL GANG SHOOTINGS AT THIS TIME RIOT-RELATED?

WE HAVE GANG SHOOTINGS EVERY DAY OF THE YEAR.

WHAT WOULD SET THESE APART FROM BEING RIOT-RELATED? . . .

WHAT WAS INTERESTING WAS ONE OF THE CASES I WAS LOOKING AT WAS IN

HOLLINGBACK [*SIC*] DIVISION. HOLLINGBACK IS EAST L.A.

THEY DIDN'T HAVE *ANY* RIOT-RELATED DEATHS IN EAST LOS ANGELES.

SO, UM, ONE GUY WAS FOUND, UM, I CAN'T REMEMBER IF HE WAS STABBED OR SHOT

INSIDE OF A DRAINAGE PIPE, AND THEY SAID NO, IT WAS DEFINITELY NOT RIOT-RELATED.

I DON'T KNOW WHETHER IT WAS A LOVERS' QUARREL OR . . .

OR A BAD DOPE DEAL OR WHAT, BUT THEY SAID IT DEFINITELY DIDN'T HAVE ANYTHING

TO DO WITH THE RIOTS, IT WAS JUST ANOTHER HOMICIDE.

—LIEUTENANT DEAN GILMOUR, L.A. COUNTY CORONER

JAMES

1

Everything's been burning in Our Lady, the Queen of the Angels. Even people. This camper, somebody lit his ass on fire while he was sleeping and you don't live through that. Sonofabitch, you sure don't. You give up your ghost is what you do. You go to your heavenly rest.

I saw that smoke going up yesterday. A bridge north of me on my same riverbank. Only I didn't know it was *his* smoke yet. It went up after two black trucks drove the riverbed like they owned it. Went right past my pipe. Big and fast but too quiet for their size. When I saw that, I did my sign for heavenly protection and turned around twice.

Normally when I'm all set up in my pipe I pull my curtain. I got a rod for it and everything. I got a chair too. Anyhow, I pull that curtain and the world can't see me, not even trains going by on the far bank. It makes me disappear. But that day I didn't pull it because I saw smoke. I didn't know what it was at first.

Our Lady says to me then: *You knew what it was.*

I scream right back at her. I tell her I didn't know what it was till I walked up and saw him a black little skeleton on his bedroll. I smelt gas-soaked dirt too, and what hurt was watching campers divvy up his things. His name was Terry. I don't know no last name. Just Terry. I stared on his bones while these other campers took his last good belongings. They didn't even pay his spirit respects first. Goldarn sons of bitches. They picked him clean.

His dog he tended to, gone. His good pants hung up on his fence, gone. Every last person on earth is trying to steal from you or wanting to beat on you and take and take.

I asked around how Terry died and got it told simple. Puppet did it. I asked how we knew and got told we knew because we knew. Campers know faces. Campers talk. We find out things we want to. And campers know somebody calling himself Puppet walked down into the camp with a gas can and emptied it on old Terry where he slept and then he lit him. Nobody knows why.

When I heard this, I let Our Lady have it. I said to her: *You're a goldarn black city! You're a black city with a black heart and black ash blowing around your black asphalt streets. That's what you've been. What you are today. What you're always going to be. And your river's the only good thing about you.*

And she said back: *That's not true.*

I yelled at her more after that. I told her she couldn't tell me how to feel when I stood next to the ashes of a dead man that somebody burnt up for no good reason while campers picked his stuff clean and walked away without one good word for the man.

Campers are meant to be better than bums. I don't like the word *bums*, or *homeless* neither. They don't hardly describe the life. None of them say what we do, except *camper* does, because we camp. We like sky so much we need to see it every night. We don't lock ourselves in anywhere. We're free. And this is the Land of the Free! And we need to feel where we are, the most elemental city on earth.

It's true too. Our Lady gets forest fires. She gets Santa Ana winds. She has ocean too, and her earth's always a step away from quaking. With a makeup like that, you're gonna need to shake the bad out sometimes. You have to, because it builds up.

She interrupts me how she does then, she says: *I do?*

And I say back to her: *Yes, you do. It's nature.*

She's quiet after that, but just because she's not saying anything doesn't mean she's not with me. She follows me everywhere I go, always coming into my head with the questions. Like now, when I'm hungry, when I'm walking the street called Imperial that don't have anything magnificent about it.

But there's no better way to know her than with your own two feet. You need Our Lady at your eye level. You need her beneath your soles, feeling her heat. You need to be breathing her in, smelling her. Taking her goldarn atoms in and making them you. No better place to do that than at the river. You can walk for miles in the bed and find everything you need. And I know too.

I've been around rivers my whole life. The Mississippi. The Colorado. The Mekong. Rivers protect me. Keep me safe. I don't feel right if I'm not near one. I lose focus. I lose my center and do bad things like the drink. But not at her river I don't. Her river's ancient. Back when Our Lady was a tiny pueblo on a mound of dirt, the Messican-Indians knew the Arroyo Seco was a sacred well of power with spirit-juice so powerful that one day a goldarn great city with too many people would rise up of it. That's how powerful her river is. It gave birth.

And this thing is teenage now and alive and angry and it's tearing itself apart. I've seen fires just about everywhere and red flashing fire trucks going up and down her black streets. I haven't just seen Terry. I've seen a body with almost no face on it in the street, no ear even. I've seen trucks on fire, buildings, and a house too, one that might've taken the whole neighborhood if neighbors hadn't put hoses on their own roofs to wet them down. Sure shows what they thought of that one house though.

I say to the city people when I see what I see, I say: *I've seen this city taking itself to heaven in pieces.*

Because that's what fire does. It takes. It's the prettiest and ugliest mathematical division there ever was. City fire is the worst of its kind though, because it takes more than it should. City fire don't know how to care. It punishes everybody. It gets at the innocent, like at Terry. City fire's greedy that way. But it's just fire being fire. It has to reset everything as close to zero as it can, so it burns things down into the smallest bits. Bits the winds can carry. Those are the remainders. But we can't hardly see them unless they're stuck together in a stack of smoke. That's how the littlest pieces add up together, you know? It's a big black fact.

MIGUEL "MIGUELITO" RIVERA JUNIOR,
A.K.A. MIKEY RIVERA

MAY 4, 1992

9:00 A.M.

1

When my alarm goes off, I wake up with the beat of a Specials song in my head, so I kick my sheets off, go find the tape of it, and put it in the deck. I'm pressing play on "A Message to You Rudy" as my dad knocks next to the space where my door would be if I had one. We're redoing the house. Actually, *he's* redoing the house—again.

Where my wall used to be is a wooden skeleton of support studs that I stuffed with books because it looked like an empty bookcase sitting there on its own, but also because it makes it more private, at least a little. Still, I can see him looking at me past the spines of my Richard Allen pulp novels.

My dad is a contractor. He got his degree in drafting from Santa Monica City College, but he doesn't do much with it. Mostly, he sells tile and does installations—bathrooms, kitchens, that kind of thing. His claim to fame is that he did both bathrooms in Raquel Welch's guesthouse in Italian marble. There's a framed, autographed picture of her on the wall of his store, Tile Planet. It's on Western, in this little strip of Palos Verdes that cuts into San Pedro. You can see all of L.A. from up there. You can look down on it. I think that's one of the reasons why my dad likes it. He likes looking down on things, especially people.

"You don't need to knock," I tell my dad, but I don't press the stop button on my music. "The wall's open."

He doesn't get the sarcasm. He steps into my room a little and says, "You want breakfast or what?"

I eye him for a moment as the ska bops along between us. My dad hates this music. It gets on his nerves, which obviously makes me love it that much more.

"No?" My dad crosses his arms at me. "I made some, and you don't want any?"

"I'm thinking," I say.

"Well," he says, irritation in his voice, "think *faster*."

When my dad uncrosses his arms, it means I'm taking too long to answer him. Six years ago, this would've meant something bad was about to happen because he didn't get his way, but he just balls his hands into fists. The scar on his left hand tightens and goes purple when he does this. Just seeing it turns my stomach. For the longest time, it meant the worst was coming. Purple meant I'd be bruised soon. He sees me looking at it and unclenches both fists before saying, "I asked you a simple question."

"Fine," I say so he'll stop bothering me. "I'll have some."

I watch him go through the spaces in the beams, over the tops of books and around them. I only see the black wave of his hair slide past Lee's *To Kill a Mockingbird* and Terkel's *Hard Times* from my Great American Books class. When my dad enters the kitchen on the other side of the house, I lose track of him, but I hear him clinking, moving around, shaking plates and cutlery.

Things have been bad between us for a long time. He's been different the past few days though. He's actually been paying attention. Still, why is he making me breakfast? I figure he wants something.

My dad has always taken being a member of the Beat Generation literally. When I was younger I thought for sure that I was in that generation too, because I got beat all the time. Put it this way, on the days I was lucky, it was a belt strap. On the days I wasn't, it was the buckle. My back is pretty scarred now. A white ex-girlfriend once asked me if I'd ever gotten hit with a grenade. She wasn't entirely kidding. My dad has always been short-tempered, and I'm the only child, so that was how it went until I turned thirteen and pulled a knife on him when he tried to hit me. That was the day it stopped for good. The weirdest thing was though, instead of yelling at me, he smiled and told me he was proud to see me stand up for myself like that, and then he walked away like maybe I'd finally stopped disappointing him.

That messed with me for a long time because it made me think back to every time he ever hit me and I wondered how much of it was on purpose and not out of anger. It was worse to think of it that way, so now I just try not to. It wasn't the end of him being disappointed though. Since then he's just found other things about me not to be proud of, like how, on the first night of the riots, Kerwin and I did acid and went out and rode our choppers.

He wasn't happy to hear we'd been looking for fires to stare at. There was no way to explain to him that it was worth it, that I saw birds and dragons rising from the flames and flying up into the air, thousands and thousands of them turning black and becoming the night sky. He almost took my bike away after I told him that and I don't blame him. You can't bring an unconscious girl home without explaining every single step about how she got there, not to my dad.

2

I've got a Vespa bike, P-125 model. We call them choppers because we chop them down. If I ever wreck one, it's easier to chop it than get a new one. I kitted the engine on mine. I chopped down the cowlings, extended the forks. That took it from a 45-mile-per-hour max to over 90. You can hear its whine for miles. It's practically a *Road Warrior* bike.

That's what I was riding when coming home from Kerwin's the next morning and right as I was going up our street, I saw this twitchy guy chuck a flaming Molotov cocktail right through Momo's front doorway. I couldn't believe it. There's this kid, younger than me probably, dressed all in black, but he's got this white square of napkin on his hairline, held there by dried blood. Next to him was this van parked on the lawn. I cut my engine and coasted in when I saw him because I didn't know what he was going to do. For the longest time he just stood there, with the bottle burning in his hand.

I thought for sure it was going to explode on him. It looked like he was talking to himself, whispering, all the while not noticing how serious the situation was, and it must have gotten to the point where it burned his hand because he screamed and threw it as hard as he could through the front door. Right after, he turned to the van, and looked at me like he wanted to do something about me sitting there on my chopper, but he took off instead.

I went to the door after that because I wanted to see if there was anything of Momo's that could be salvaged quickly, but the second I looked in, I saw a girl lying facedown on the living room floor and any thought I had before that just evaporated.

Next to her, a giant rippling triangle of orange fire climbed the wall, like in the movies, except louder, and so hot. Just getting a few feet from it made all the hair on my right arm shrink down to little black nubs and all I could think to do was grab the girl's ankles and drag her out the door. Doing that, I scraped her chin and cheek pretty bad on the porch concrete before I got her onto the lawn and flipped over. She was bleeding and unconscious as I panicked and searched for a heartbeat.

In my room, I hit stop on the Specials. It's a good thing I think showers are overrated, because our water is off again—something to do with the plumbing being worked on. I don't even question it anymore. I swipe some deodorant on, grab a blue Fred Perry, do the collar up, and put on some red bracers. After that, it's just bleach-stained jeans with a rollup high enough that you can see every inch of my black Docs. My dad sees me this way every morning and rolls his eyes. He's had it explained to him so many times, but he still doesn't know what a mod is, or why his Mexican American son would ever want to be one.

He doesn't get that culture is different for my generation, that we get to choose. It's not about whatever it was when he was my age. It's about *cholo* stuff now. Gang stuff. It's selfish. He doesn't get that music saved me. The ska, Two-Tone stuff, Trojan records, it keeps me out of that world. Sometimes I think my old man would be happier if I was out banging, though, because maybe that's closer to how he grew up, even though he never talks about it—even though he's got other scars that can't be from learning construction work even though he says they are.

My mom gets me though. She's happy I'm not involved. In fact, she's the reason I'm still living at home, even though I've been graduated from high school for a year. She's already at work by now. She got a call last night that the accounting office she works at would be opening back up today after being closed last week for the riots, so she left early, before I woke up because she was afraid of the reports she'd been seeing about snipers on the news. When she's gone, it's tougher for my dad and me to talk to each other without it sounding like we're fighting.

3

My dad's sitting at the kitchen table when I get there, dousing his omelet in ketchup because he's the only Mexican on earth who doesn't eat it with salsa. He says he can eat it however he wants because he pays for it.

As soon as I sit down across from him, I say, "What do you need, Dad?"

"What do you mean, 'what do I need?'" He waves his fork at me. "I need to eat."

"Yeah, but why'd you make some for me, too? What's your motive?"

He scoffs and forks a bite into his mouth. "'Motive'? You watch too much TV, *mijo*, using words like that."

He's only being defensive because he knows I caught him. He

does need something from me. All I have to do is wait it out. I look out the kitchen window at the half-tiled fountain in the backyard that my dad hasn't finished yet.

It's shaped like a circular, three-tiered wedding cake with a moat around the base, and it looks like a place where broken rainbows go to die because the tile on it is green and red, blue and yellow, purple and white, all mixed together. My dad does his work-order jobs with the good stuff, but at home, he's cheap, so he tiles with the mashed ends of things from the shop. Orphans, my dad calls them, and then says he has to find a home for them, it's his penance. Even though I've asked, he never has explained that.

My dad stares at me like I'm an asshole for a good thirty seconds before he finally says, "I need you to come with me to Compton and check on the Victorian. Bring one of your friends. There's no telling how safe it is out there."

I think I can call Kerwin, and that he's probably awake by now, but I also think if I do this, my dad can do something for me too.

"Okay," I say, "but I want to go by the hospital and check on Cecilia, too."

My dad sighs. "She's bad news, that girl. You need to stay away from her."

"I just want to make sure she's okay," I say.

I never planned on lying to Momo about Cecilia. It just happened.

One moment I was in the house watching television about all that's been going on, and the next, Momo was on my lawn with a car full of *cholos* behind him. I didn't expect that, so I panicked and went outside. Next thing I know I'm lying when he asks about her. I lied because it sounded like he meant to kill her if I told him where she was.

The truth is, she never ran away. She'd inhaled smoke, but there was something else too. She was seriously glazed over. It wasn't pretty how coughing fits would break her moments of almost deathly stillness. I put her in the back of my mom's Honda and drove us to St. Francis Medical Center on MLK and Imperial. I filled the forms out as best I could for her, but all I really had was a first name from when I met her months ago and Momo's address. When she went beyond the admittance doors, I told her I'd check up on her, and I meant it.

Right now, though, my dad is looking at me like I'm stupid enough to make a move on a drug dealer's girl. A girl I wouldn't make a move on even if I was attracted to her—which I'm not— because I told Momo she was okay and gone, not still here in Lynwood and hooked up to a respirator. I'm in enough trouble as it is.

"Fine," my dad finally says.

We're definitely related. He says it the exact same way I agreed to eating breakfast with him, like it isn't fine, but he'll do it. He'll drive me to the hospital.

We have a deal.

4

At noon, we head to the hospital, but while we're on MLK, my dad asks if I want lunch, and when I tell him I'm not that hungry, he ignores me and pulls into Tom's Burgers and parks anyway. This is more like my dad, I think, not much of a listener, always doing what he wants regardless. Tom's is right across from the hospital. I think he's doing it to prove a point. He didn't really want to come, so he's going to string it out.

Inside is busy. We pass by the little arcade and up to the front to order. A little black kid is playing an old Centipede machine as two friends cheer him on. The other two video games stand unplayed. Tom's is a neighborhood place, known to be 'hood good—which means cheap, filling, and occasionally tasty—and seeing it full of families sitting down to a meal, or couples sharing fries, makes it seem like life is returning to normal, at least a little bit. There aren't any smiles passing back and forth between strangers, but I get the sense others feel the same way. Eyes aren't darting. People aren't hunched over food. They're all just trying to get on with their lives.

We wait through a line that's eight deep, and it's smoky as hell from everybody and their cigarettes. The whole time we're standing there I'm just wishing we were at Tam's on Long Beach instead. They have the best chili cheese fries. I know, Tam's and Tom's, it can get confusing, but not if you're from Lynwood. Everybody I've ever met prefers Tam's, but it's not close to the hospital, and this one is.

"Make sure you know what you want," my dad says. "When we get up there, I'm ordering."

"Fine," I say, and another of the Rivera fines makes an appearance.

My dad always knows what he wants, and when I don't, on anything, it drives him crazy. Sometimes, I use this to my advantage, but on a day like today, when I'm not all that hungry and don't really want to be here anyway, I'm willing to oblige him as I scan the menu on the wall behind the register. I figure just a cheeseburger. That's safe. No thousand island, no onions. *Jalapeños* though. I can put the ketchup on myself. They always sit that out at the condiment station.

When it's our turn to order, I tell the counter girl what I want and she writes it down. She says, "That it for you?"

"That's it," I tell her.

"That's not enough for you," my dad says, "and I really don't need you telling me you're hungry later. Get him some fries too."

It's embarrassing. Of course, it'd be less embarrassing if the counter girl wasn't so damn cute, which she is. Her name tag says Jeanette, and I'm about to apologize to her for my dad when a guy behind me taps my dad's shoulder. My dad shrugs him off, but he's already got a story going.

"Sir, I'd never be a problematic on purpose, but I'm hungry. I'm diabetic. I haven't eaten right since this whole thing started." It sounds like he's reading a list. "A guy named Terry upriver from me got lit on fire . . ."

He goes on like that. It might be true or it might be a rap he pulls all the time, but I doubt it somehow. I watch my dad size him up as a black dude who has had a bad couple days. He looks like a bum. He looks exhausted, this light-skinned black man. He couldn't be more than five foot four with his long black T-shirt and dirty shorts to cover his chopstick legs. He's leaning on a cane that has feathers tied to it. His hair's pulled back in a little braided ponytail that's fraying and limp on the end, but he does have a big scar down his nose in the shape of the letter *C*, like someone tried to cut a nostril off and missed. His cheeks are dotted with faint freckles, and he looks stoned out of his gourd—pupils so wide that they only show thin circles of blue irises on either side.

My dad tells him to tell the counter girl what he wants, which is odd, because my dad *never* does that. The guy orders a bacon cheeseburger and fries with extra seasoning salt. This guy then tells me I got a real good man for a father and asks what my name is, so I say Mikey. He asks my dad's and learns it's Miguel. He says his name is James. He says he's glad to meet us, and of course he is because my dad just bought him food. In fact, I can already see my dad tuning out as James thanks him again for the kindness. To my dad, he did his deed and he wants to be left alone.

While this is going on, I watch Jeanette take the order down, and make a handwritten note on the receipt for James's stuff as "to go," which is good, because James is going on about Vietnam now, about being a vet, and how unappreciated that is in this country, before switching to talking about the river.

People are watching us as my dad pays. Until the change comes back, I stare at the mashed-up tile on the floor, one with a million different pebbles in it, all squashed flat. My dad would know what it's called.

My dad finally cuts James off. "Listen, I got you food and they'll bring it out, so go sit by yourself. We got our own problems. We don't need to hear yours, too."

It might sound cold, maybe, but that's the truth. Everybody's got problems. That's just how it is. Best to just shoot straight with people and let them know what you can or can't do.

"Goldarn," James says, "there's no call to get rude on it."

I don't know what goldarn means, but he sounds southern from all I can tell, not from around here. His speech has a lilt to it, a softness that doesn't fit with how messed up he looks. As I'm trying to figure him out, my dad takes my elbow, which I wriggle out of and glare at him. He looks at me, sighs, and makes his way to a corner table. I go to the condiment station and grab ketchup, a bottle of Tapatío, and some napkins. James follows me there.

"Telling me to sit by myself," James says, "that's mixing messages right there. Our Lady would never do that. She'd never say that."

"Payasa," a male voice at a nearby table says behind me, "handle this shit."

5

A muscular girl a few inches taller than me gets up from where she's sitting with three guys and steps in between James and me. She's a real *chola*. I can tell by the way she angles a look at me. She's got light brown eyes, the color of brown beer bottle glass with light shining through.

"Excuse me," she says, "is this dude bothering you?"

"No," I say. "It's fine."

"Okay then," she says to me, but she turns back around and gets in James's face. "You better step out if you want to eat that food these nice people provided you with. They didn't have to do that. I wouldn't've."

I edge away to the table where my dad is sitting, and I see James has a look in his eye now, a glint of crazy.

"Land of the Free," James says to the girl. "I'm a vet, goldarnit."

"Yeah, we heard that the first time," she says. "Thank you for your service. Now do everybody a favor and shut the fuck up."

James's jaw drops at that, and he starts huffing as he pulls up the sleeve of his tracksuit jacket to reveal a forearm with two long scars down the length of it.

"A machete." James draws a finger down his forearm. "I'm a vet, goldarn son of a bitch! Land of the Free!"

I'm no expert, but I guess it could be a machete wound. I look to my dad to see if he thinks the same, but he's looking down, reading a chunk of the newspaper he brought with him from breakfast. BRADLEY LIFTS CURFEW TONIGHT, the front page headline says, and beneath it: HE WON'T SPECULATE ON DEPARTURE OF TROOPS.

"Shit," Payasa says. "That ain't nothing."

I slide into the wooden booth, still staring at Payasa as she pulls up her shirt to show a cluster of scars along her side.

"That's not a scar," she says, pointing at James's arm. "*These* are scars."

It looks like a blind person tried to write Roman numerals on her, mostly *I*'s, an *X*, and a *V*. It takes me a moment before I realize they must be old stab wounds. I count ten of them and I'm not done before she puts her shirt down.

"Land of the free," she says, "but only if you pay your fucking share."

She's about to clock him, I think.

James must think that same thing too because he takes a step back.

"I *already* paid," he says, but he's whining now. He lost this contest somehow, in a way I don't quite understand, but I know it happened, because he's different now, more hunched. "I paid a blood share, that's what I paid. This is a black city!"

People were uncomfortable with the display before race got brought into it, but that comment just snaps the room in half. The dining room looks about fifty-fifty, black and Hispanic, with a Samoan family thrown in. I see people taking sides in their heads, getting ready to react if something is about to go down. I watch my dad take the Tapatío bottle off the table and turn it around in his fist like he'll use it if he has to. It's so calm, so quiet, that I almost missed it. He does it without taking his eyes off the front page of the sports section that says, LAKERS REFUSE TO BE SWEPT ASIDE.

Payasa laughs. This doesn't diffuse the tension in the room. It makes it worse.

"No," she says, "this ain't a black town, but maybe you should stick around. In ten years, there won't even be rib shops anymore, just taco stands."

James's eyes almost bug out of his head. He looks like he might explode.

"You know why though? Cuz we fuck more than you," she says. "We have more babies than you, and we stick around too. We already won. It's just a matter of *when*."

James opens his mouth, but the counter girl saves the whole situation by handing him his food in a bag. He stares at the girl, at Jeanette. She mouths the words *just go* to him, and he must decide that isn't a bad idea, because when he does go, he backs out the door looking at Payasa.

"Yeah," this *chola* says with a look of self-satisfaction on her face, "that's what I thought. Go back to eating your meals, everybody. You're safe now. Show's over."

As she sits back down, my dad puts the Tapatío bottle back on the table and slides the thin tin ashtray to him before going in his chest pocket and pulling out a pack of cloves. I give him a look to show him I don't appreciate having to eat next to someone smoking, but he bats it right back at me with a look of his own.

"What? I'll put it out when we eat," he says.

Across the street from our table is St. Francis's glass tower stuck to a rectangular building topped with a little cross. Next to that is a strip mall done up with white siding that I know my dad would pronounce as terrible. At the end of the mall is a payday loan place with armed guards standing out front with rifles. Two doors down from that is a nail place, but it's closed. None of this is as interesting as Payasa.

I turn my eyes to the girl, to the table she's at. She's faced away from me, rolling her muscular shoulders. Her hair is done in two tight braids on either side of her head. They look like pigtails, except fiercer. I've never really seen a female gangbanger before. Here and there, but not standing up like this, not as an enforcer.

I watch her table for a moment, and it makes sense now why she was the one standing up. The three guys there are all hurt. It doesn't take much logic to figure out that they've just been to the hospital. One of them is in a wheelchair with a leg elevated. He has a sling around his arm too. The skinny one next to him has a wrap around his head, and I notice he's staring hard at my dad's hand—at the scar, I guess. He's got dead eyes like my dad sometimes gets when he doesn't want anyone to know what he's thinking, but something's going on in there, because this guy pushes his food away from himself and turns his whole body toward the window. I wonder why he'd do that.

Lately I've been trying to keep my eyes open for stories, and I decide there has to be a good one in how those four ended up at their table looking like *that*. I also decide I wouldn't want to meet who did that to them because they look about as tough as it comes. I'm going to El Centro Community College for small business management because my dad wants me to, so I can help him with everything, but I really want to be a writer instead, so I sneak English classes whenever I can get them.

"My burger's overdone," the one in the wheelchair says. "We should've done Tam's."

"Don't worry about it," the biggest one says. His partially tattooed arm is in a fresh cast that doesn't have any signatures on it. "If I could cook, you wouldn't have to eat it, but I can't, and Tom's is close, so Tom's it is. You're welcome."

He sounds like my dad, a provider—more than a little put-upon.

"My bad," the other one says.

They don't say much after that, and it occurs to me they're pretty exhausted themselves. My dad and I finish up, but only after I make my stand by not eating the fries he ordered. He eats them, staring at me the whole time.

When we leave, I feel eyes on us again, but I don't turn. As we're walking out into the parking lot, I see a bus parked on Norton. The side of it is covered in graffiti, but I can't read it. Maybe an *F* and something. A *P* or a *K*, maybe? It looks like a *K*. I walk toward the bus and step over a little wall, into the nearby bank's parking lot. From there, I see the back of the bus, and I can read what's there, clear as day—it says ERNIE. In the bottom leg of the last *E*, it says R.I.P.

To my dad I say, "You see that?"

"Sure," he says as he fumbles with his keys.

I ask him what he thinks about it.

"I think he died," my dad says and shrugs.

He gets in the car then, but I keep looking because it's there to be seen. Next to me, the truck starts up. I step back down. It occurs to me that you don't get something like that unless somebody cares and unless something really sad happened to you. It's a tribute, and it's meant to be noticed. Not everybody who sees it will care, but at least when they put eyes on it, they'll know he existed. I wonder what Ernie's story was, what he went through for his name to end up on the back of a bus like that.

My dad honks the horn at me.

"Okay, fine! I'm coming," I say. "You don't have to honk at me!"

My dad yells from inside the cab with his window up. "You're the one who demanded to go to the hospital!"

He's right. Of course he's right, but if anything has changed in me since the riots began, it's that I'm noticing things now. I'm seeing, *actually* paying attention to my city again. Before, I'd stopped seeing it. Moving around L.A. was just something that happened in between the important stuff of eating or hanging out with friends, but now, after five days of it, with the National Guard coming in, and the U.S. Marines coming in and making things safe again, moving around actually *is* the important stuff.

I take one last look at ERNIE, and I hope he had a good life, the best life he could have had, all things considered, and then that seems stupid to me, because I never knew him, so I just get in the truck and we go.

6

On the way to Cecilia's room in Acute Care, in the elevator that smells of ammonia and doughnuts, I eavesdrop on two nurses talking about something that happened in the lobby outside St. Francis's Emergency Room on Friday night.

"These two gangsters walked in waving guns around," the shorter of the two nurses says. "Nobody knows why they did, but they did. And they both walked right up to a family of three that got burned in a house fire, minor burns, you know, but still, and they were waiting for help, this family, holding wet washcloths to their arms and necks when these gangsters went and put guns in their faces, even a little girl's."

A concerned sound escapes the tall nurse then, and she says, "How old was the little girl?"

"She couldn't have been more than eleven or twelve," the shorter nurse says. "The odd thing was that these two gangbangers didn't seem to *want* anything. They weren't there to rob anybody. They didn't ask for wallets. Mainly, they were just there to terrorize people, you know? To strut around like they were tough or something."

"I never known homeboys to just show up and do something like that for no reason. I bet they were looking for somebody and maybe they couldn't find him." The tall nurse sniffs. "How long did it go on for?"

"Twenty minutes," the shorter nurse says, "and then four National Guardsmen showed up, aimed their rifles at them, and told them to get the hell out or there would be serious consequences. They said it like that too. *Serious* consequences."

At this point, one of the nurse's pagers goes off behind me with three shrill beeps. I don't know which one it belongs to, because my dad and I got into the elevator last and are politely facing the doors, but I hear them both check.

"Duty calls," the taller one says and exits on floor four when we get there.

We're headed for floor six, and to my relief, the shorter one stays on.

"Excuse me for listening in," I say, "but what happened after that, after the National Guardsmen got there?"

She eyes me for a moment, as if she's trying to decide if I'm worthy of hearing the rest. She has black hair, blue eyes, and an upturned little nose like a ski jump.

"The gang members actually backed off, saying something like, 'okay, man, whatever, it's no problem, we were just having some fun.'"

I blurt, "Wow, *that's* 'having some fun'?"

She gives me half a shrug and tilts her head at me like she's try-ing to figure out if I'm sheltered or just naive, because around here gangbangers do all kinds of things all the time, and why wouldn't they do something even crazier when there was nobody there to stop them? I'm neither. Sheltered or naive, that is—but she wouldn't know that. She's just making me nervous with how pretty she is. I wonder if she knows that now. My dad does. I feel him smirking beside me.

The silence is almost awkward now, but I wonder if there's more to the story than that. "So that's it? They just left?"

"Yup," she says, "they left, but when they did, the whole room broke out clapping."

"Cool," I say. It's not the best response, but at least I said some-thing.

As we get off on floor six, I thank her for telling me how it ended and she blinks her blue eyes at me and says, "No problem," as the doors close.

7

Visiting hours started at 10:30 A.M. but we're here now, a little after one. All hallways in hospitals look and feel the same to me: white walls, white floor tiles, fluorescent lights, and impersonal, clean, echoey. At the desk a nurse who has a weird, layered haircut that looks like gray cabbage tells us that Cecilia should be just finishing her lunch and they're prepping to discharge her to—

She stops herself right there.

"I'm sorry," she says, "are you family? I can only tell you if you're family."

I say no before my dad does, because I know he would.

"It's good you're not," the nurse says. "If you were, I'd have to put the full-court press on for personal and insurance information. We've done a lot of free work lately."

She hands us the guest sign-in clipboard and while I'm writing my name and my dad's, the nurse tells us the whole medical center has too many patients. Right now they're just trying to treat and release. After that, she tells us Cecilia's room number. When we get there, the door's open.

The room she's staying in was built for two but in addition to the two normal beds, there's a gurney parked in the space along the wall below the television. Both it and the other bed are unoccupied. Out the window, I see Lynwood Park and its greenness, six floors down. It has a baseball diamond and a playground with yellow tape around its perimeter.

I knock on the door frame. Cecilia is up and cramming herself into jeans. Her hair is flat and limp from the shower, heavy on her shoulders as it drips a growing wet patch onto a T-shirt that reads: THE CITY OF LOS ANGELES MARATHON, YOUR LIFE, 1989. These aren't the clothes she was wearing when I brought her in.

"Hand-me-downs." She says it like she's reading my thoughts. "Can you believe this shit? Hospital people all telling me my clothes were too smoky to keep. Said they were a hazard and they had to get rid of them. They're lying, that's what I think."

She fusses with the top button of the jeans. She's paler than when I last saw her, if that's even possible, like she lost ten pounds from sweating in the time between. The scrapes on her chin and cheek have scabbed over though. She looks better, all things considered.

She says, "They wanna send me to treatment, but I'm not going to that shit."

The way she talks is odd. It's like we're there, she registers us, but we're not. Her words don't seem for us, but more just because she wants to say them to whoever happens to be standing in front of her.

She keeps going. "These hospital people thinking they're so smart, saying I'm lucky they don't report me to the cops for illegal drug use, but how they going to report me when they don't even know my full name?"

She laughs at that, like she's smart, and I can feel my dad's eyes on me then, burning an I-told-you-this-girl-was-fucked-up look into my cheek, but I don't acknowledge him.

She says, "I got to get back to Momo."

Wow. This is definitely the last thing I want to hear. I don't even know how to respond to that, but I manage to say, "I don't think that's such a good idea. This could be, you know, a fresh start for you."

Her eyes look wild after I say that, like I just suggested something crazy.

"It is so a good idea," she says. "I want Momo. *He* can be my fresh start."

Already I feel like I'm drowning here, so I do something risky. I've got no choice.

"It's better for both of us if you don't remember how you got to the hospital. Momo thinks I rescued you and that you were okay and you robbed me of thirty-one dollars and took off. Can you remember that number if he ever asks you? Thirty-one?"

She looks appalled that I'd even suggest it. "Why would I lie to him? I wouldn't lie. Not to Momo. I *love* him."

It goes on like this, me trying to convince her to go along with what I told Momo and she doesn't want to, so we never get anywhere, and I walk out frustrated and scared for what might be coming when Momo finds out I lied, because when he knows that, he'll want to know why, and the last thing a scary dude wants to hear in that situation is that you were just trying to do the right thing and protect her from him.

My dad doesn't say anything to me in the hallway, or in the elevator—no, he holds it until we're in the lobby before he says, "Do you think your life would be a lot easier if you'd just let her burn in there? If you never even got involved?"

I don't respond. I just aim myself at the exit and walk.

"Listen," my dad says to my back, "you shouldn't worry about it. I'm telling you, if she goes back to him, okay. Fine. Won't be the first time a woman ever went back to a bad man. And who cares what she says to him?"

My dad, for all his faults, has never hit my mother.

I stop where I am. I turn to him and say, "What do you mean?"

"I mean she's a druggie, *hijo*. Wake up! Nobody knows that better than Momo because probably he made her like that. He already knows he can't trust her because his house burned down on her watch. Anything that comes out of her mouth now is going to be seen as an excuse, or like she's covering her ass. So it doesn't matter *what* she tells him. Even if he comes back to ask questions of you, you're more reliable than she is. He'll believe you instead."

My dad raises his eyebrows at me and I say, "How do you even know all this?"

My dad sighs again, and he examines the linoleum beneath our feet. It's plastic, fabricated to look like white rock. He kicks the toe of his work boots at it because he thinks it's cheap shit, but he understands, because it's easy to clean.

He brings his eyes back up and looks at me like he's not sure what to tell me before he shrugs and says, "Your old man knows more than you think."

It's just like him to say he knows something without saying anything specific. There's no fighting it. My dad, he's an expert on everything.

"I'm worried he'll kill her if she goes back," I say.

"This girl is not yours to worry about," he says to me. "You're too sensitive, *mijo*. Didn't I raise you tough enough? What happens from now is not your business."

There it is. Sooner or later, every conversation where we butt heads comes down to me being too sensitive.

I say, "You really don't think it's worth it trying to save someone's life?"

My dad's forehead wrinkles up and he looks sad as he pats his front shirt pocket for his clove cigarettes before taking them out and slowly removing one from the pack.

It's this brown stick that he points at me when he says, "But you already saved her life when you dragged her out, *hijo*. What you can't do now is save people from *themselves*. The rest is on her, and trust me, druggies will only disappoint you and make you sorry you ever tried."

It sounds so heavy when he says it, like maybe he's tried to save a druggie before and failed, which is weird, and I don't even know what to say to that, because I've never even heard my dad use that word before today, so I break eye contact with him and look at my watch. It's past the time I told Kerwin we'd pick him up, but I don't need to call. He'll be out in front of his house when we come by, just sitting there, waiting.

My dad leaves me and walks out into a late afternoon that looks hot and white beyond the sliding doors. He expects me to follow, but he's giving me a moment. Out those doors, cars are moving but they're slow, cautious. It's like the world is starting to get going again, but it wants to look both ways first before it really tries.

8

When we pick up Kerwin, who was waiting outside just like I thought, he gets a choice: sit in the back of the pickup truck or cram in the cab with my dad and me. He picks the bed, which is good because he's big and black: six foot two, wide shoulders, and a bit of a belly on him. My dad and I are both glad not to be sharing the front seat. Kerwin sits with his back to the cab and his legs extended out in front of him. He props an elbow up on a cardboard box my dad has in the back. I open the window between us and we yell at each other.

Kerwin starts. "Remember how those black dudes threw tires at us the other night when we were out tripping on fires?"

I look at my dad, but his mind is elsewhere, so I answer how I want to. "That actually happened? I thought I hallucinated it."

"One hundred percent real," Kerwin says and laughs.

Kerwin and I are in a band together, Forty Ounce Threat. I play bass guitar and sing. Kerwin's lead guitar. It's Oi! music mostly, street rock and roll.

I'm in charge of the radio as my dad drives us south into Compton. I find KRLA, hoping for some soul, but there's a doo-wop group on that I don't recognize. In the rearview mirror, I see Kerwin bobbing his head as we go left on North Alameda from Imperial and I roll my window down to watch the city passing.

We're only going six blocks or so. This whole area is pretty much just industrial and manufacturing, and none of it seems affected by the riots. There's auto glass places, granite places, lumber places. When we pass Del Steel, I notice their warehouse looks fine. They do ornamental stuff. My dad works with them every so often. L&M Steel, in their curved-roof warehouses, seems fine too. My dad says this area used to be hopping in the '60s, plenty of business to go around, but now it's lying down to die. There's cheaper steel from China and it comes pregrinded or heat treated. On top of that, American workers cost too much money. Manufacturing has been going elsewhere for some time. Even before the recession, it was going somewhere else.

When the song is over, a DJ comes on and says Mayor Bradley has lifted the curfew, so that's it. The riots are over.

"Welcome back to sanity." There's sarcasm in how the DJ says that.

My dad snorts.

The streets feel normal to me right now. At least, it feels like whatever normal was before the riots. It's South Central as I've always known it: mostly quiet, with people going about their business and working hard. Still, people all over the world think Los Angeles is a city of angry black folks now, a city of arsonists and gangbangers. Those people must think that what happened to Rodney King was isolated, but they don't know that everybody's got a Rodney King in his neighborhood, somebody the cops beat like a drum for good or bad reasons. He might not be black, either. He might have brown skin instead.

After we pass Banning, we get our first glimpse of destroyed property. We smell it before we get there though. I don't know if I ever knew what company was in this warehouse. It's completely gutted now, but the charred skeletons of two walls are still standing. Against the white walls of another warehouse behind, they look more like charcoal sketches than anything that ever used to be solid. In front of them, an old man in a Raiders cap hacks at the roof with a hand ax—the roof that caved in and is now flush with the ground. I roll my window up and ask my dad what this place used to be.

"Machine tools," my dad says.

"Do you know who owns it?"

My dad doesn't. We turn onto El Segundo from North Alameda and I see Willard Elementary School on the corner. It hasn't been burned, but someone cut the fence with wire cutters for some reason, which makes me think that maybe somebody tried to rob the school, but I lose track of that thought because I'm expecting to see our two-story apartment complex, white with a black roof and thirteen apartments, right next to the school—but there's nothing there.

Instead, there's an empty space where our building used to be.

"*¡Hijo de su chingada madre!*" My dad sits up in his seat, on the very edge of it. "All this shit I built up to lose."

My dad smashes his hand against the steering wheel a good few times. I wince, but I'm glad somehow. A few years ago that would've been me getting thumped.

As we get closer, we see the husk of what's left, a black shell sucking up the last of the setting sun. Here and there, little bits of unburned white wall show through. The rest is black. My eyes skirt past it then, over to the Victorian—which appears untouched—but beyond it, in the next lot, isn't another apartment building like I'm expecting, one that used to be the mirror of the first, same plans and everything: white walls, black roof, and thirteen apartments. But there's nothing there either. It's still a mirror, just a black one, because now the Victorian sits unharmed between two blackened lots, because two of our buildings got torched to the ground.

It's getting hard for me to breathe as my dad pulls past the Victorian and into the little alley that runs alongside it. From there, we get a good view of what's left of the second apartment building as two blackened support studs stick out of the lot like charred goalposts. We park there, on the dirt, next to the untouched Queen Anne Victorian he owns, the one he's been fixing up since I was nine. My dad built the white picket fence out front himself. Behind that is a symmetrical one-level with two peaked towers that push out either side of the front door, making it look like a face with two rectangular windows for eyes, a door for a nose, and a flat porch for a mouth.

I'm relieved it survived, sure, but I'm still taking in how the two apartment buildings are completely gone when something finally occurs to me, something going to school for small business management should have made me think of days ago.

"Dad," I say, "are we ruined?"

9

It's a stupid question. The answer is right in front of me. Since I've been taking accounting, my dad has been showing me loan statements for the past few months. He's trying to teach me how to run the business when he's gone. Between these three properties, he has sunk in over a million dollars. He mortgaged himself up to his eyelashes to get that kind of money.

That's because my dad never skimps on materials when he fixes anything, but he has to cut costs somehow, so he declines all insurance except earthquake protection. He figures if he fixes something up fast enough, it'll be fine. The Victorian is the only exception to that rule. It was built in 1906, back when the Sunset Strip was one big poinsettia field. *This* he has insurance on. It's his baby.

My dad has got his eyes closed when he takes a breath in and it comes out in a cough. I can't watch him like this, so I pull Kerwin down the alley to where an ancient gas pump used to be, next to an avocado tree so big that it could've been in the movies.

Kerwin breaks the quiet with a whisper. "All your dad's stuff is burnt?"

"All except this," I say, pointing at the house with my chin. My dad bought it from the Kellys, one of the last white families to leave Compton.

"There used to be a gas pump here," I say and point at a long line of dirt on the back lawn where the grass can't grow anymore.

Kerwin wants to know why, so I tell him this house is older than gas stations. My dad has been buying and selling property for about a decade. My mom says he always wanted to improve South Central, wanted to make it better, so he bought one building and sold it, then he did two. That got to be a pattern. After four sales, he got the tile business on Western, and now he has five buildings: three in Compton, one in Watts, and one in Lynwood, but the Victorian house with vaulted ceilings, two bedrooms, a library, and a den in Compton, it was always the pinnacle.

"This was my dad's dream," I say. "Proof he could build something not just good but beautiful. That's what my mom thinks anyway. For a long time, my dad only seemed happy here. I'd go with him on weekends when he came to fix it up."

I remember how the saw was always in the kitchen. For years, the house smelled of freshly cut wood and had sawdust everywhere. I'd bring him whatever he needed, a hammer, a wrench. He taught me how to wire lighting at fourteen. To this day I know the work I did then was one of the only things that ever made him proud of me. It helped that I never fell off anything, never stepped on a nail. I was careful. I got that way quick though when the belt might be the penalty for any misstep.

"The neighborhood changed quick though," I say. "All kinds of these old houses got knocked down. Warehouses got built, but you saw it when we drove in. Pretty soon, no one wanted to live on this street anymore."

Kerwin shrugs. "Who'd want to live next door to a warehouse?"

It's not the kind of question that needs an answer, but I do it anyway. "No one."

Despite the neighborhood changing, my dad still kept working on restoring this house. We got by renting out four apartments in one complex and five in the other, but we couldn't rent out the Victorian, and we couldn't sell it.

"It's just a relic in the wrong place now, but it has been for a long time. The worst part is, people around here know it. They know nobody lives in it and when people know that, bad things happen."

"What type of bad things?" Kerwin is from South Central. He knows what type of bad things go on around here, but he can't keep himself from asking. Maybe none of us can. Maybe that's just human.

"A dead body got dumped on our property, in our alley. We

found out when two sheriffs showed up at our place in Lynwood and wanted to take my dad in for questioning. Maybe two months after that, a gang rape took place in the backyard under that avocado tree."

I point at the tree. We're not standing too far from it now, the old scene of the crime, and I'm looking at it because something is off about it. It's not just that it's heavy, with branches weighed down from fruit that we didn't pick this year because we never got around to it, it's that there's something at the base, on the other side of that great big trunk. It being the back end of dusk, I can't make out what the shape is for the life of me. It's too big to be a dog, but that's what it looks like. A dog lying down, stretched out under the tree.

"Hold on." I drop my voice to a whisper. "You see that?"

Kerwin's right next to me, crouching in the dirt.

"Yeah," he says, whispering right back.

"Are those?" I'm squinting now, trying to make out the long shapes on the ground, extending away from the trunk. It's not a dog after all. "Are those legs?"

"Yeah," Kerwin says. "They fucking are."

10

These legs are bare from what I can tell, hairy too. At the end of the right leg, on the right foot, is one white sock. We move forward together, Kerwin and me. As we get closer, we circle to the side and I see how dirty the bottom of the sock is, almost black. We see the whole body it's connected to next, propped up against the trunk, sitting up with its legs stretched straight out.

I hear Kerwin breathing behind me. He's got a Dodgers minibat with him, must've brought it from home. It's wood, maybe a foot long, the kind they give away in limited quantities as a promotion item for going to a certain game.

"Is he shot?" Kerwin wants to know. "Is he stabbed or what?"

"I don't see blood," I say.

It's clear now this person has no pants on at all, just red-brown boxer shorts. On his top half, he's wearing three flannel shirts and they're all open at the cuff and pulled up at the elbows to dangle. It's hard to tell if the chest is rising and falling with all that cloth there.

"You touch him," I say to Kerwin. "Poke him or something. See if he moves."

"No, you."

I tell him, "You're the one with the bat!"

Kerwin looks at his hand just to confirm he's holding the damn thing and then shrugs like maybe he will poke him with it, and maybe he won't.

That's when I notice there's something on this guy's arm.

I say, "Hey, do you see that?"

I point. Kerwin squints. We both do.

"Yeah," Kerwin says. "Ugh."

There's a needle sticking out of this guy's arm crease, but not like a syringe. Just a needle. It almost looks like somebody wanted the syringe and the needle was stuck in his arm, so they just unscrewed the damn thing, leaving this metal needle sticking out of him like a half a safety pin that got jabbed in. There's dried blood around it, some dabs and dots, and down the forearm is a tattoo in long, *L.A. Times*–style cursive letters.

I point at the tattoo. "What's that say?"

Kerwin has to tilt his head sideways to read it. I do the same, but it's hard to tell from all the dirt and dried blood on him. I want to brush it off but don't.

"Sleepy," I say. "I think it says Sleepy."

"Is he dead or what?" Kerwin has his hand over his mouth. "He looks dead."

"I don't know," I say, but I'm thinking he is. The skin on this guy's face is half bearded and matted with dirt. He's the color of my dad's used ashtrays. Ants roam his leg hair, and there are even a few bumps from bites that are so raised and red I can make them out without much light.

"Do it then," I say, and when Kerwin hesitates, I nudge his shoulder with my own. "Do it already."

Kerwin pokes the body with the bat. He puts the fat end of it on the guy's chest, right over the heart, and pushes. A little air comes out, like a sigh or something, and we both jump back, but the guy's eyelids don't even flicker. They don't even move.

I'm thinking out loud. "That could've been, like, trapped air or something, right?"

"How would I even know that? It's your turn. Tell you what, though," Kerwin says as he hands me the bat, "damn, am I glad we aren't on acid for *this*."

"Me too," I say.

Now, I don't know what I'm about to do with a bat that he didn't just do, so I hold it at my side and take a step forward and reach toward the face with my free hand.

This freaks Kerwin out. "Mikey, what are you *doing*?"

My heart's pounding up in my throat, and I don't know what I'm thinking beyond that I just need to see if he's breathing shallow and if I feel his breath on my finger I'll know for sure, but I can't reach far enough standing back, so I step closer. As I'm putting my foot down though, my sole crunches down on something. I look down to confirm what it is and I step back quick, only to find it's the guy's right hand. I didn't even see it in the near dark. As I'm realizing this, I hear Kerwin draw in a fast breath and the first thing I do is look up into the guy's dirty face to find that his eyes are *open*.

I jump back right into Kerwin, bounce off his shoulder, and somehow manage to keep my feet. The guy scrunches his face up at us. He smacks his lips a few times before he opens his mouth.

"What're you doing, fool?" His words come out slow and dusty. It's not even like he's mad, just confused and dehydrated. "Why'd you step on me?"

I don't hang around to answer and neither does Kerwin. We're already retreating, walking fast backward, not taking our eyes off this guy we thought was a corpse, and we're not about to have a conversation with him either. This guy keeps talking though, keeps saying hey, as we go, like he's trying to get our attention, but we're moving too fast toward the front of the house, toward my dad.

"Oh fuck," Kerwin says. "I about had a heart attack. Oh shit!"

I'm right there with him too. I don't know what freaks me out more now, the fact that I thought we found a dead body or that the dead body ended up being alive.

When we get to my dad on the porch, he's looking in the window on the right side of the door. My boots crunch glass before I realize that the front window he's looking through isn't even there. It's been broken out and my father is staring in through the hole. When I look over his shoulder, what I see makes my stomach drop, but it definitely explains the man at the tree.

11

Druggies have been flopping here, more than just the guy under the tree. A pack of them. Maybe they even spent the whole riot here. Inside, it smells like a monkey cage. The floor of the library, with its built-in bookcases, is littered with broken vials, a broken glass pipe, and a few more syringes without needles. In the corner where I used to build forts out of two sawhorses and a tarp so I could drag a hanging light underneath and read *Treasure Island* is a pile of wadded newspapers that our unwelcome houseguests have been wiping their asses with and then keeping nearby. I have no idea why anyone would do that, but it makes me not want to see the bathrooms.

I say, "One of them is still under the avocado tree."

My dad nods up at me. I watch him weigh this information before saying, "Some Goldilocks shit, huh? Did he look dangerous?"

"No," I say. "He didn't even move."

My dad looks back the way we came, to the outline of the avocado tree against the purple-black dimness, but there's no way he can see the body from that distance, and it doesn't look like he cares, either.

He spits off the porch and says, "Leave him then."

My dad pulls out his pack of cloves, takes one out, and lights it. He takes a pull and breathes out smoke as he says, "This house is plagued."

Kerwin looks at me with concern. I've seen my dad's crazy faces before, I know them better than anybody, and seeing how the vein in his forehead is working, I know he's on the tightrope of rage right now. When he turns to me, I see a spark in his eyes.

He says, "How did that kid burn down Momo's house?"

I'm still thinking about the guy under the tree when I snap out of it and say, "He threw a Molotov cocktail through the front door."

My dad says, "That it?"

"Yeah."

"Good," my dad says and heads for the truck.

When he gets to the bed, I watch my dad pull the cardboard box to him and open it. From inside, he takes out a glass bottle of whiskey three-quarters full, uncaps it, and stuffs a rag as far down the neck as it will go.

"Whoa," Kerwin says and takes a step back. "Is he gonna—?"

I look behind us, into the street, to see if anyone's watching, but no one is. We're all alone.

I say, "Dad?"

But he's not listening as he walks past me—I hear liquor sloshing back and forth in the bottle as he goes—and when he gets to the porch that we reslatted by hand, he takes his clove cigarette out of his mouth and touches it to the rag.

"It's mine," my dad says. "I can kill it if I want to."

12

How I feel right now is confusing. I don't want him to do it, but I understand why. All the work he put in—*we* put in—and all that time we spent. Every bit of it goes up in flames the second the bottle hits that back corner of the library and catches on the newspapers and the bottom of an inset bookcase, still empty after all these years.

I blink and my dad is back in the truck and starting it. The radio jumps to life as he guns the engine before sliding over in the seat and popping the passenger-side door. Halfway through a chorus, a Shirelles' tune pours out into the night, "Dedicated to the One I Love," and my dad is yelling at me over the top of it.

"*Mijo*, get in the truck! Let's go!"

But I can't. I'm too busy watching the Victorian die.

"Kerwin, goddamnit," my dad says, "get *in*."

When Kerwin does, and shuts the door, my dad yells at me again. "Don't make me *put* you in here!"

I don't feel my legs moving, but I must be walking because I'm up in the truck and into the bed, and then I'm sitting down with my back flush to the cab, just like Kerwin was before, and I hear him say to my dad, "He's in!"

The truck peels out in reverse and I watch El Segundo Boulevard race up to meet me as my dad takes the turn too quick and the right-side tires go off the curb. I'd bounce right out of the truck if Kerwin didn't have a hand on my shoulder.

I'm about to thank him when he says, "I got you!"

I'm looking back behind us, too busy wondering if this is the last fire of the riots, or if somewhere, for other reasons, people are doing the same things. I get my dad's logic. It's the one property he has fire insurance on, so he might as well, but burning the house won't break us even—the payout would never be enough to get us back to zero on all three properties—but right now it's the only way to lose by less.

It occurs to me then that maybe that's how these riots are for everybody around here. You know you're gonna lose, but you kick and fight to lose as little as possible. It could be property, or health, or a loved one like ERNIE, but it's something and when it's gone, it's gone for good. No one feels peace tonight, and we haven't for days. The curfew may be lifted, but it doesn't mean things are normal, or that they're fixed, or that they will be anytime soon.

In L.A., it only means that things are different from the last time you could go out at night, and from now on, when we talk about these days, we'll talk about what they did to us, we'll talk about what we lost, and a wedge will get driven into the history of the city. On either side of it, there will be everything before and everything after, because when you've seen enough bad things, it either breaks you for the world, or it makes you into something else—maybe something you can't know or understand right away, but it might just be a new you, like when a seed gets planted, yet to be grown.

Kerwin turns up the music, and the chorus hits as the boulevard spools out beneath me with its yellow dotted line racing alongside before falling away into asphalt blackness. I think about how the guy with a needle in his arm has a front-row seat to this as wind whips my face.

A warehouse next to the nearest burned apartment complex quickly blocks most of the Victorian from my view, and all I can see is the library window flickering orange like a winking jack-o'-lantern eye before we get too far down the road and that light is gone too. All that's left to see of the house then is where it's going, skyward, as a black tower forms above it. I'm hoping to see it better the farther away we get, to understand more, because maybe if I see the rest of the neighborhood and how it burned, if I see how other people were targeted and suffered too, I can understand, but right now all I can focus on is our house, and how much it hurts to see it go, and how the distance doesn't give me any perspective.

So I close my eyes.

I put both my hands palm down on either wall of the truck's bed and hold tight to metal and chipped paint as the rhythm of the street bumps me forward and back. Through the window behind me, I hear the song winding down. I hear it running into the wind, tangling with the whooshing sound of it, and I picture how things used to be. I see how the Victorian looked when I was fourteen, faintly blue in early morning light. I see underripe avocados in the grass, hard and green, the kind I used to pick and play soccer with, and beyond the tree that dropped them, I see one of the apartment blocks stands tall like a sentry, its roof only just going orange in the dawn. Something turns heavy in my chest when I imagine my own neighborhood, the one I grew up in, intact again. I see Ham Park's wooden handball wall still up, kids playing on it and grown men too, and the thumping sounds of their Saturday games echoed for blocks, and as far away as Momo's house, it just sounded like a heart beating—and maybe it was even the city's heart, beating too fast. In my head right now, Momo's house is whole again, his car's parked out front and he's walking to it with keys in his hand, nodding a hello at me as I go by on my chopper, and that's when it hits me: my memories are the only places I'll ever see any of it again, and I wonder if this is what writers are supposed to do, rebuild places in their minds—places long gone, places that disappear, and I wonder if that's true, is it true of people who disappear too?

The song's fading out now. I hear the girls' voices melt into the bass line as what's left of their harmony gives itself up to the wind and the grumble of the truck's engine. For two good breaths, I don't hear anything but sirens far away. I don't hear anything but the truck worrying its axles. When a new song begins, a different kind, one with a loud drumbeat, I don't recognize it, and it's a small thought that hits me then, but I feel it rumble and grow with each building whipping past. With each block, I feel myself agreeing with it. L.A. has an engine too, and it won't stop. It can't. It's a survivor. It will keep going, no matter what, and it will push right through these flames and come out the other side of them as something broken and pretty and new.

GLOSSARY

Abuela/abuelo: grandmother/grandfather

Adónde: literally, "where at?"

AK: assault rifle originally manufactured in the Soviet Union, and abbreviation of AK-47, itself an acronym of Avtomat Kalashnikova 1947—which is a combination of the weapon's automatic capability, its inventor's surname (Mikhail Kalashnikov), and the year it was invented

All involved: slang for someone participating in gang activity

AO: Apparatus Operator, a driver and operator of the ladder truck during firefighting missions

Bala: literally, "bullet"

Banda: a traditional form of Mexican music that incorporates brass, woodwind, and percussion instruments

Bomber: graffiti term for someone who takes part in graffiti, often on clandestine missions; a bomber typically tags one pen name (e.g., FREER or JUKER) repeatedly, as opposed to executing more complex pieces

Bombing: graffiti term for the act of putting aerosol on walls for public display, typically painting many surfaces in an area

Bonjuk: a Korean stew, typically rice based, resembling porridge

C-Spine: abbreviation of cervical spine, typically referring to a collar needed to immobilize the cervical vertebrae of the neck after an injury

Cabrón: all-purpose vulgarity that can mean "swine," "bastard," or "fucker," depending on context and tone

Carnicería: a meat market or butcher shop that may sell groceries as well

Cerote: a piece of excrement; in slang, typically used by Mexicans or Chicanos to denigrate Salvadorians

Chavala: someone who acts or dresses like a gangster; a female child or young person, the diminutive form (*chavalita*) means "little girl"

Chichis: female breasts

Chilaquiles: a traditional Mexican breakfast dish made by quartering and lightly frying a corn tortilla before pouring salsa or molé over it; this dish can also include eggs or meat

Chola/cholo: a Chicano gangster, typically favoring a style of fashion unique to Southern California: flannel shirt, wifebeater, and khakis

Chorizo: a spicy pork sausage

CHP: California Highway Patrol

Clica (or click): a gang, or a neighborhood portion of a larger gang; in graffiti, the terms *click* and *crew* are most frequently reversed, with *click* meaning a smaller group and *crew* connoting a larger grouping

CO: Commanding Officer

Compadre: literally, "buddy" or "friend"

Controla: literally, "control," typically used in conjunction with a click and city name, signifying that said click controls the stated area

Crew: in gang terms, a smaller grouping within a gang or click; in graffiti, the terms *click* and *crew* are most frequently reversed, with *click* meaning a smaller group and *crew* connoting a larger grouping

Cucaracha: literally, "cockroach"

Culero: literally, "an asshole"; used by Mexicans in reference to a "coward" or an "asshole"

Culo: literally, "ass"

Dušo: a term of endearment, literally "my soul" in Croatian

El rey ha muerto; viva el rey: literally, "the king is dead; long live the king"

EMS: Emergency Medical Services

EMT: Emergency Medical Technician, someone trained to administer first aid and lifesaving procedures during emergency situations

Enchilada: a Latin American dish of a corn tortilla rolled around a filling and covered with a chili pepper sauce; can be filled with a variety of ingredients, including meat, cheese, beans, potatoes, vegetables, seafood, or a combination of these

EOC: Emergency Operations Center

Ese (or esé): Chicano slang, typically used between men to express "dude" or "man"; can be used derogatorily (typically with the accent on the second *e*, as in *esé*) or in a familiar, nonthreatening manner

FCP: Field Command Post

Fe: literally, "faith," but can also mean "intention" or "will"; although in the immediate aftermath of being shot and in shock, Big Fate mishears the word first as "Fate" and ends up taking his name from it

Felicidades: literally, "congratulations," typically used on special occasions such as a birthday, a wedding, or Christmas

Gabachos: a derogatory term for English-speaking people of non-Latino descent

G/Gee: gangster, or gangbanger

Gee'd up: someone who recognizably dresses the part of a gangster

Goldarn: euphemism for "goddamn," most typical in the southern United States

Grip: slang for "many" or "a lot"

Grito (or Grito Mexicano): a high-pitched, often musical cry

Hijo de su chingada madre: literally, "son of your fucking mother" or "son of a fucking bitch"; typically considered the worst insult in the Latino communities, particularly among Mexicans, due to its historical meaning ("son of a raped woman"); the verb *chingar* comes from a Nahuatl (Aztec) word meaning "to rape"; when Spaniards arrived in the Americas, their raping of the indigenous women was so widespread that *chingar* became a curse, similar to the word *fuck* in English

Hina: a desirable girl or possibly a girlfriend

'Hood: abbreviation of "neighborhood," typically an area with distinctive characteristics relating to the residents' ethnicity or socioeconomic status; often used interchangeably with "ghetto" or "the projects"

Huevos: literally, "eggs," or in slang, "testicles"

ICU: Intensive Care Unit

ILWU: International Longshoreman and Warehouse Union

Jefe: literally, "boss"

Juice card: slang for the most powerful or influential person in a given area; though it is not physically real, it is considered something that is held, similar to the way a boxer holds a title belt

Keys: another slang term for power; similar to a juice card—though they are not a physical set of keys, they are considered something that is held, similar to the way a boxer holds a title belt

Kruškovac: a Croatian liqueur distilled from fermented pears

La clica es mi vida: literally, "the click is my life"

LAFD: Los Angeles Fire Department

LAPD: Los Angeles Police Department, the city's policing body

LASD: Los Angeles Sheriff's Department, the county's policing body

Layup (or layup spot): a consistently used temporary parking area, usually off a main bus route, where drivers park a bus in order to change shifts or leave a bus if it is in immediate need of maintenance and is not capable of returning to the nearest bus depot

Lengua: literally, "tongue," most frequently beef tongue cooked and served as food

Lentejas oaxaqueñas: a lentil-based Mexican dish, typically spicy-sweet and meatless

Leva: a traitor or sellout

Loca/loco: literally, "crazy"

Machismo: strong masculine pride, possibly chauvinistic in nature

Manflora: Mexican Spanish slang for "lesbian," or "gay"

Mayate(s): literally a "black, dung-eating beetle," it is slang most frequently used by Mexicans and Chicanos to denigrate dark-skinned people

Mi corazón: a tear of endearment, literally, "my heart"

Mi vida loca: literally, "my crazy life," frequently used to describe gang life

Molé: a traditional Mexican chili-based sauce that can be made with a variety of ingredients

Neo-Geo: a popular 24-bit video gaming console developed by SNK; released in 1990, the system was discontinued in 1997

Neta (or la neta): the absolutely true, or literally, "the truth"; also used interchangeably with "really?" or "seriously?"

O.G.: Original Gangster, typically describing someone who has been in the gang life for an extended period of time

Ojos: eyes

Pachuco cross: often associated with gang involvement and tattooed in the webbing of the left hand between thumb and index finger, it is a cross symbol with lines radiating from its top

Packing: slang for carrying a concealed weapon, most frequently a gun

Paisa (short for paisano): literally, "countryman" or someone of rural origin

Palillo: toothpick

Panadería: a bakery that may also sell groceries

Panocha: pejorative slang, literally means "cunt"

Papas: potatoes, or sometimes potato fries

Pinche: a Mexican Spanish curse and intensifier, similar to *fucking*, though not indicative of sexual intercourse

Plaqueasos: lettered graffiti, most frequently done in aerosol on outdoor walls, often signifying a gang, a gang member, or gang territory

Por favor: please

Pozole: a Mexican stew, most frequently made with maize and chicken or pork

Prima/primo: cousin, its masculine or feminine form depends on gender of relation

Prométeme: literally, "promise me"

Puchica: Salvadorian slang for "shit" or "damn," derived from the indigenous dialect, Caliche

Pueblo: an American Indian settlement, typically consisting of adobe buildings of one or two stories

Puta/puto: an all-purpose vulgarity that can mean "bastard," "asshole," "whore," or "son of a bitch," and the insult can be intensified by changing the gender of the noun to the opposite of the person being targeted

Qué onda vos: literally, "what's up, dude?"; Central American (especially Salvadorian) Spanish differs from Mexican Spanish in its utilization of the "vos" form, which is a second person singular pronoun and is used beside, or in place of, *tu*

Qué pasa: literally, "what's up?" or "what's going on?"

Queso: cheese

Quincé (short for quinceañera): literally, "fifteen," or an abbreviation for the celebration in Latino communities where a girl becomes a woman, or reaches maturity, at fifteen years of age; it is similar to a cotillion or coming-out ball

Raza (or La Raza): literally, "race" or "the Race"/"the People," this term can also express unity and/or racial pride among Latinos

RN: Registered Nurse

RTD: Rapid Transit District, this government body overseeing public transportation in Los Angeles merged with the Los Angeles County Transportation Commission on April 1, 1993, forming the current mass transit body in the city—Los Angeles County Metropolitan Transit Authority, or LACMTA (also known as MTA)

Salsa: literally, "sauce," typically one tomato based, though it can also be green (*verde*), black (*negra*), or even made with an onion base

Salvi: Chicano slang for someone from El Salvador, often derogatory; or a familiar, nonthreatening expression of identity between Salvadorians

Señor Suerte: literally, "Mr. Lucky," an iconic character composed of a stylized, mustachioed skull wearing sunglasses, a fedora, a fur collar, and crossing its bony fingers; created by artist Chaz Bojorquez in 1969, he later ceased painting it altogether as it had been adopted as the primary symbol of the Avenues, an L.A. street gang

Sherm: PCP (phencyclidine), also known as angel dust, a hallucinogenic drug; in reference to a joint or cigarette dipped in liquid PCP

Shotty (or shotties): slang for shotgun(s)

Símon: Mexican Spanish phrase meaning "of course" or "absolutely"

Slanging: the act of selling or dealing drugs

STL: Strike Team Leader

Tagger: term used for graffiti artists who most frequently write their pen names on public walls to promote the individual graffiti writer, not a gang

Tamales: a pastry made of cornmeal dough, typically filled with meat or cheese and baked in a corn husk

Tia/tio: aunt or uncle, its masculine or feminine form depends on gender of relation

Tienes pisto: literally, "do you have money?"; pisto is a Central American Spanish (especially Salvadorian) term for money

Toy: term used by graffiti artists to either refer to novices, or graffiti done by novices

TRW: abbreviation of Thompson Ramo Woolridge; an American aerospace and engineering corporation, it became the victim of a hostile takeover by Northrop Grumman in 2002

UCLA: abbreviation of University of California, Los Angeles

Varrios (or barrios): literally, "neighborhood"

Vato: Mexican slang for "man," there is a certain seriousness implied in the word

Veterano: literally, "veteran"; an amount of experience is conveyed with the word, and when used in Latino gang culture suggests that such a person has frequently participated in criminal activities

Viejo: literally, "old," typically meant to refer to an "old man"

Wet (or getting wet): slang for PCP use, or to add a dose of PCP to a cigarette or joint by dipping it in a vial of the substance

Whitecoats: slang for hospital emergency personnel who wear white coats, typically doctors or, occasionally, nurses

Wifebeater: a cotton undershirt, typically a white tank top

For further information on Chicano culture, please see: *Chicano Folklore: A Guide to the Folktales, Traditions, Rituals, and Religious Practices of Mexican-Americans* by Rafaela G. Castro

CITATIONS

The quote from Joe McMahan that begins Day 2 was transcribed from a live television report made during the riots for *7 Live Eyewitness News*.

The quote from LAPD Chief Daryl Gates that appears in "The Facts" and the quote from Rodney King that begins Day 3 can be found in *Official Negligence: How Rodney King and the Riot Changed Los Angeles and the LAPD* by Lou Cannon.

The quote from Major General James D. Delk that begins Day 5 can be found in his book, *Fires & Furies: The L.A. Riots*.

The quote from Lieutenant Dean Gilmour that begins Day 6 can be found in *Twilight: Los Angeles, 1992* by Anna Deavere Smith. The [*sic*] added was my own, as there is no "Hollingback Division" in Los Angeles. There is, however, a Hollenbeck.

I am greatly indebted to all three books and their authors for broadening my understanding of the events that took place from April 29 to May 4, 1992.

Except for Anthony's speculation on the amount of bullets fired after two days of rioting, or the 9.15 million L.A. County population (*L.A. Almanac*), every statistic used in this book was found in either Cannon's or Delk's work.

Throughout this process, the *Los Angeles Times* was an absolutely invaluable resource for my research. The headlines used in this book are real.

ACKNOWLEDGMENTS

Álvaro, who was the absolute guiding force for this book; thank you for helping me to plan every crime in the novel as if it were real. I could not have written this without your input and great generosity.

Evan Skrederstu, who never hesitated to listen or tell me what worked and what didn't.

Everyone else in UGLAR (Unified Group of L.A. Residents): Chris Horishiki Brand, Espi, and Steve Martinez—without you all, this book would not exist.

Stanley Corona, who shared with me how deeply the riots impacted his family.

LAFD Battalion Chief (Ret.) Ron Roemer and Engineer (Ret.) John Cvitanich, as well as Captain Skelly, Engineer Zabala, and Firefighters Meza and Bennett of 112s.

California Highway Patrol Captain (Ret.) Chuck Campbell.

Marisa Roemer, who listened to every chapter the moment it was written and always knew what rang true and what plot needed to go where.

William J. Peace, M.D., who oversaw all medical references in this book.

My entire family—most especially Grandmother Annazell, Mom, Dad, Brandon, Karishma, Big Sister Char, and Alexa—who motivate me by loving me more every time I fail.

Kevin Staniec, Corrie Greathouse, and my incredibly supportive artistic family at Black Hill Press, who are always there for me.

Chapman University Independent Study (Editing) students Jennifer Eneriz and Zoe Zhang, who copyedited the text, fact-checked for historical accuracy, and provided vital language assistance during the glossary creation process.

Gustavo Arellano and P. S. Serrato, who are tremendous teachers of Southern California culture in their own inimitable ways.

Bryce Carlson, who never grew tired of talking L.A. or schooling me on sound effects—*shimp*, indeed, sir.

Lizzy Kremer, Harriet Moore, Laura West, Emma Jamison, Alice Howe, and Nicky Lund at David Higham, who believed in this work from day one.

Simon Lipskar at Writers House, who made an exception for me, and Kassie Evashevski at UTA, who helped make a dream come true.

Last, but never least, there are a number of people who participated in the research and background that led to this book who wish to remain anonymous. I will always keep your trust. Please know this novel would not have been possible without your insight and I cannot thank you enough for sharing with me.